"Goblins on one side, kobolds on the other," Halmarain said. "What do we do now?"

"For a line of deserted hills, this place certainly is busy," Trap said to himself half an hour later. He had rounded a curve in a gully and saw the retreating back of a goblin. Forgetting the wizard's warning, he stepped out, shouting to catch the last goblin's attention.

"Hello!" he called as the last in the line of humanoids stopped and turned to stare at him. "I'm lost. Can you tell me how to get out of this maze?"

The goblins stopped to confer, and Trap decided they were working out the best directions for him. Then, from an intersecting passage just beyond the goblins, came another shout and the kobolds rushed into sight again. They charged in Trap's direction.

The kender waved and smiled. . . .

DragonLance® Saga

DragonLance® Saga

TALES OF UNCLE
TRAPSPRINGER

Dixie Lee McKeone

Tales of Uncle Trapspringer

Distributed to the book trade in the United States by Random House, Inc. and in Canada by Random House of Canada Ltd.

Distributed to the hobby, toy, and comic trade in the United States and Canada by regional distributors.

Distributed worldwide by Wizards of the Coast, Inc. and regional distributors.

Cover art by Don Clavette.

Interior art by Jeff Easley.

DRAGONLANCE and the TSR logo are registered trademarks owned by TSR, Inc. All TSR characters, character names, and the distinctive likenesses thereof are trademarks owned by TSR, Inc.

TSR, Inc. is a subsidiary of Wizards of the Coast, Inc.

First printing: November 1997
Printed in the United States of America
Library of Congress Catalog Card Number: 96-60826

9 8 7 6 5 4 3 2 1

ISBN: 0-7869-0775-4
8387XXX1501

U.S., CANADA,
ASIA, PACIFIC, & LATIN AMERICA
Wizards of the Coast, Inc.
P.O. Box 707
Renton, WA 98057-0707
+1-206-624-0933

EUROPEAN HEADQUARTERS
Wizards of the Coast, Belgium
P.B. 34
2300 Turnhout
Belgium
+32-14-44-30-44

Visit our web site at http://www.tsrinc.com

This is a story about my Uncle Trapspringer. It seems that a long, long time ago . . .

Chapter 1

In the great library of Palanthus, Astinus, the chronicler of the history of Krynn, was recording important events on Ansalon. . . .

The lobo wolf peered through the brush, his yellow eyes seeking enemies and prey, his sensitive nose sniffing for danger on the breeze. He crouched beneath the bushes on an unnatural rise of tumbled stones overlaid with earth and undergrowth and gazed at a place nature had no part in building.

Man-place, his senses warned him. A place of two-legs with their flying, wounding shafts. He had no concept of structures, but he knew straight walls were no part of nature; they were man-work. His experience also told him that man-work falling down, walls crumbling, was no longer the den of his mortal enemy. He had seen other places where nature was taking back what the tall two-legs had left when they moved on to new lairs.

Off to the right of where he stood peering through the bushes, he saw the dimness of a narrow entrance, almost obscured by creeping plants. The darkness within suggested it was covered above. It called to him, its shadowy depths promising safety from his enemies, even if he did not find food inside.

He crept through the brush, through the high weeds and across the new spring grass that separated the man-place from the forest, sniffing as he went. He discovered the three-day-old trail of a rabbit. Fresher was the trail of a mouse and the owl that had caught the rodent and made a meal of it, but no man scent. He stopped at the dark entrance and noticed the scent of more mice. He crept into the shadows of the ruin, found a bed of leaves that the wind had blown into the shelter and curled up to sleep.

The wolf felt safe because he knew the tall two-legs were gone.

He was wrong.

The ruin was not abandoned.

Two hundred feet below where the wolf slept, a heavy-boned man walked down the passage of an old, deep dungeon. As he passed down the corridor, torches set in wall sconces burst into flame as he neared them and magically died away after he had passed. The stones in the walls and the arched ceilings still emanated an aura of the pain and suffering that had taken place in the dungeons of Pey. The horror had been mortal and had no power to disturb Draaddis Vulter.

His torture came from a different source. Nothing fearful impeded his path as he walked to his work chamber, but he dreaded making the journey. Once there he could be subjected to horrors only the most twisted of minds could conceive, and his return trip would tax all his mental reserves.

He was paying the price of having offended his god.

The huge domed vault that served him for a laboratory

had long ago been stripped of its tools of misery to make room for a different kind of evil. It was now the laboratory of the black-robed wizard. Draaddis would have preferred a tower, but to show himself openly would put his life in danger.

More than a century after the Cataclysm, wizards and clerics still hid and worked in secret. The people of Krynn had never forgiven the users of magic for the disaster that sundered the world of Ansalon. The knights, the wizards, and most of the clerics had not taken part in the destruction, but, in truth, they might have been able to prevent it.

The responsibility for the disaster belonged to the Kingpriest of Istar and his followers. The clerics of Istar had grown in power until neither the wizards of Krynn nor the priest-knights of Solamnia had been willing to openly oppose them. As time passed the Kingpriest and his followers grew enamored of their own holiness. In their conceit, they demanded an end to the balance of good and evil that held sway over Ansalon.

The Kingpriest of Istar challenged the gods.

The answer had been swift and catastrophic. The great lands of Istar, with its magnificent temples, sank beneath the Sea of Blood. All over Krynn mountains crumbled, new ranges rose, torn out of the earth by the anger of the gods. Seas flowed in and drowned great cities. Then, following the rending of the world, came war, plague, pestilence, and starvation, all riding on the winds of the immortal wrath.

In the minds of the citizens, the wizards and knights shared the blame. They had known the inevitable result of the Kingpriest's arrogance and had done nothing to stop him. The conclave of wizards had debated what details they could surmise of the imminent upheaval. They had decided not to interfere. The white-robed wizards dedicated to lawful practice, the red-robed neutrals, and the black, the followers of the evil Takhisis, were one in their desire to maintain the balance of good and evil.

The Cataclysm came and went, and Draaddis Vulter, the most powerful of his order, hid in secret and trod the passages of an old dungeon and used the torture chamber for his laboratory.

Shelves lined the walls and ancient books in their black bindings were strewn about carelessly on the work tables, as if pulled from the shelves, searched, and thrown down in anger and frustration.

Across the vaulted chamber other shelves held the results of vile experiments, grisly parts of what had once been living beings, denied a natural death. In one, an animal heart continued a slow, even beat. In another a scaled and clawed hand, severed at the wrist, grasped at the air as it pushed against the side of its glass container. Open crocks held working mixtures, their surfaces in slow and constant movement as bubbles broke the viscous surfaces and slowly popped, releasing noxious gases.

Draaddis Vulter ignored his abandoned or ongoing experiments and strode to the center of the room. He approached a stile, four feet high, covered with a black silken drape that was lavishly trimmed with gold. He lifted the drape, exposing an iridescent black globe two feet in diameter. From it emanated an evil that caused the wolf, in the ruins two hundred feet above, to whine in his sleep.

An eye appeared in the globe. Heavily lashed and slightly slanted at the outer corner, it was definitely a female eye. Draaddis gave a low bow.

"Takhisis, Queen of Darkness, Our Lady of the Dragons, Ruler of the Nine Hells," he murmured. "Greetings."

"Why have you called me, Draaddis?"—the voice was low and sultry, filling the wizard with shivers of fear and delight—"Have you found an answer?"

"Not one of my own making, my queen, but I may have discovered a way for you to enter this world. I wanted to lay my findings before you in the hope that your divine wisdom would help me decide if the discovery is what we seek."

The single eye of the evil goddess brightened. More than a millennium had passed since Huma, riding the silver dragon Gwynneth, had used the dragonlances to drive Takhisis and her chromatic dragons from the world of Krynn. From the First Plane of the Infernal Realms, Takhisis could only peer through magically constructed windows like the globe. She lusted for the corruption she could create if she could reach the world of mortals again.

"Tell me," she demanded. "Show me,"

"Ten days ago, while traveling on the shadow plane—"

"Ten days?" Takhisis hissed and the chamber floor suddenly flowed with serpents. They coiled on the tables and slithered down the stools, massing on the floor and crawling over each other to reach the wizard. Draaddis's tongue stuck to the roof of his mouth. He shuddered uncontrollably. They slithered up his legs, wrapped themselves around his arms, their fanged mouths struck at his face and neck. The fangs tore at his flesh and the poison from the fangs burned through his veins like rivers of fire.

He trembled violently and forced himself to remember illusion was the only power the goddess could use against him.

Shut them out. He ordered his mind to shut out what his eyes and nerves told him was true.

He found his voice and continued his explanation. He forced himself to think beyond the crushing, biting pain and the fire in his blood.

"And while on the shadow plane I chanced to meet another wizard, a young red robe, seeking a way to the Core of All Worlds," He gasped out the beginning of his tale. With it went the image of the serpents. With them went the pain. He touched his face to assure himself of what he knew. The torture had been an illusion; his skin was whole. Draaddis took a deep breath and went on with his story.

"The red robe had some garbled tale of stones that could be gathered there. He claimed they would open a portal to any plane—"

"Bring him to the orb, I will question him," Takhisis demanded, but Draaddis shook his head.

"I fear, my queen, to learn even the little I did, I was forced to strip him of his knowledge." Draaddis shrugged.

"He was a fool, with more courage than strength, and as I said he was young, still learning his art. He did not survive my entry into his mind. I have his knowledge, but it was incomplete. For the past ten days I have been searching out the mysterious red robe who has a set of these gate stones."

"Did you find him?"

"I have found him, my queen, and more. I have used a construct to place a viewing disk in his work chamber so we can judge for ourselves the worth of his find in the Core of Worlds."

Draaddis waved a hand in the direction of the largest table, where a red-eyed rat sat scratching his ear. A closer look showed a pair of wings pressed flat to its back. When the eye of the dread queen turned in its direction, the rat backed up to hide behind a stack of books.

"You have done well," Takhisis said, momentarily drawing back from the globe. When he could see her entire face, Draaddis trembled even more violently. In her human form, the Dark Queen's beauty was incomparable. Her perfect features and eyes held more allure than any mortal face. Her sensuous mouth, even in repose, gave promise of delights no mortal woman could offer. Just gazing at her made Draaddis forget the danger inherent in the presence of the ruler of the Abyss.

"Show me!" With the command she put her eye to the globe again and all he saw was the dark pupil that followed his movements around the chamber.

"The seeing disk is mated to this one," Draaddis told his queen, opening his hand. He showed her a small, intricately carved disk of gray-green glass. A tail of carved magic runes, individually too small for the unaided eye to discern, swirled out from a small carving in the center to the edge of the glass. Draaddis placed the disk on a round, unadorned mirror that lay flat on the table.

The stile that held the black globe disappeared, along with the black-robed wizard, the shelves, the grisly experiments, and the dusty murkiness of Draaddis's work room. It seemed as if they had instantly been transported into another underground chamber. By the barely discernible odor of vegetable decay, it had in the past been used as a huge food larder. This, too, was a wizard's laboratory and held all the clutter of alchemy, save the experiments were not of such a grizzly nature. The chamber was cleaner and clean-burning torches purified the air. Old carpets of intricate design covered the floor, and the wall sconces that held the torches were ornate enough to have graced a lord's dining hall.

Two people were in the room. Orander Marlbenit, a master wizard in red robes sat at a table, pouring over a book. Across from him, what Draaddis first thought was a child of four or five years, stood on a bench, pouring tea into a cup. The pot was too large for her tiny hands. The little figure also wore a red robe, and beside her a short staff leaned against the bench. Thick, curling black hair framed her face and tumbled down her back. When she turned to put the pot back on a tray, they saw her face. The diminutive size was at odds with the maturity of a young woman in her twenties.

"At least have a cup of tea before you begin," she said. Her voice was highly pitched and childlike, but the tones were that of an adult. When the wizard continued reading she became exasperated.

"Master Orander!" she spat. "You need strength for your studies, and even more if you try the experiment."

The larger figure raised his head. White hair peeked out from under his hood and bright blue eyes sparkled beneath a pair of heavy white eyebrows. His beard, also white, had been inexpertly cut short, a concession to convenience rather than style. He smiled at his companion.

"You make too much of it, Halmarain. I won't be in any danger, and I won't be gone long. I'll just test the stones on a benign plane." He pointed at a passage in the book he was reading.

"Alchviem says here that the tone is everything. Once the vibration starts if we keep the note soft and steady, there's nothing to fear."

"But there's still a doubt," Halmarain snapped.

Orander frowned. "Halmarain, we are students of the nature of magic, and we will face any danger to further our art. You will either accept that fact or find another teacher."

"I would rather keep the one I have," she retorted. Her eyes were softer than her voice and they showed her concern. "Remember, all you've learned will be gone if you don't come back."

Orander laughed. "All this argument, and we don't even know if the stones *can* open a portal to another plane."

"I almost hope they don't," the tiny woman replied, shaking her head.

Chapter 2

When my Uncle Trapspringer set out on his first great adventure his sister, Ripple, went along to keep him company. They were approaching Lytburg when they saw some soldiers who spied them at the same time. . . .

"Kender!" the soldier shouted, pointing toward Trapspringer and Ripple Fargo who had just rounded a bend in the dusty road. The warning alerted the rest of the troop, who were taking advantage of the forest shade to rest and eat a midday meal. The soldiers tossed food and flasks aside as they jumped to their feet, most dashing for their horses.

"Wow, look, they certainly seem glad to see us," said Trap, as his family called him. He watched the soldiers run into each other as they tried to reach their mounts.

"Lytburg must be a friendly place," his sister, Ripple,

9

replied. She waved at the few soldiers who were still staring in their direction, then brushed at the road dust on her leather leggings and boots and swept a hand from her forehead to her top knot, checking to see if any tendrils had worked loose.

"I told you we should have found a stream and washed away the dust from the road," she said. "It's the least we could have done for people who are glad to see us. I'm so glad they are here, I've been so tired of not seeing anyone on the road, and they're eating, do you think they might share some of their food with us?" She gave a skip as she walked at her brother's side.

The soldiers certainly were excited. The first to reach his horse was obviously the leader of the troop. He wore a shining, ornately trimmed helmet and a glittering coat of chain mail while the others wore metal-trimmed, hardened leather breastplates. He jerked the reins before he had his right foot set in the stirrup. His mount shied and the rider slid sideways in the saddle. The other rushing men, the sidling horses, and an off-balance rider threw the leader's mount into a panic. He bucked and turned, blocking the next two riders as they tried to pass him.

Trap and Ripple watched, fascinated. As the horse sidled back and forth, the leader's armor sparkled in the sun and reflected small sunbeams onto the road and into the deep shade of the forest. The kender were so busy enjoying the show that they missed seeing the archers who had eschewed their mounts and crept nearer using the bushes for cover. Both kender forgot the struggling rider when an arrow whizzed by Trap's shoulder.

"That's not friendly!" Ripple gasped, her eyes wide.

"They've made a mistake!" Trap said. Neither he nor his sister had done anything to incur the wrath of the patrol. Still, the soldiers seemed too intent on shooting them to listen to explanations. He grabbed Ripple's arm and jerked her away as a shower of arrows arose from the underbrush.

He led the way as they raced a few paces up the road. They would never be able to outrun arrows, so he jerked

Ripple to the right and pulled her into the underbrush close to the side of the road. The showers of arrows continued. Trap felt a thud as an arrow struck him. He had not even felt the pain. He released Ripple's hand as he gingerly felt for a wound.

"It hit your bedroll," she told him and led the way into the denser undergrowth.

Behind them they heard pounding hooves and running feet followed by the sound of snapping branches. Another shower of arrows arced through the forest. The sharp metal points pierced soft bark or ricocheted off the tough old trunks.

"Up," Trap said as they reached a huge ancient oak and dashed around to the northern side, opposite their pursuers. At his gesture she cupped her hands and bent her knees. He stepped into the stirrup she provided and she jerked herself upright as he straightened his knees. Their combined force threw Trap high enough to grab the lowest limb. He locked his feet around the limb and dropped, his arms extended as he reached down for Ripple. She swarmed up his body until she stood on the limb. Then she lowered a hand to pull him up.

Working together, they reached the higher limbs and lay flat while the soldiers beat the bushes below. Long, breathless minutes passed before the determined searchers moved out of sight, deeper into the forest.

Trap and Ripple climbed down again, dropped from the last limb and worked their way west through the thick undergrowth that bordered the road. When they were a few hundred yards away from where the soldiers searched, the two kender crossed the beaten track and entered the woods to the south. Safe for the moment, they followed a creek until they reached a beaver's dam. They sat on a log to rest, to the indignation of the beaver who had just cut down the tree.

"I don't understand," Ripple shook her head. "No one could be angry at us."

"They didn't want us. They said 'kender,' " Trap reminded her. "Either they don't like any kender or. . . ."

"That's not possible," Ripple interrupted. The entire race of kender took justifiable pride in being the friendliest people on Krynn.

"Or . . . do you think there might be kender outlaws?"

Neither had ever considered the possibility. They occasionally heard tales, most of which they discounted as soon as the stories accused kender of "stealing."

Trap and Ripple knew that every other civilized race on Krynn considered kender to be thieves. Their racial reputation was totally justified, of course, just as it was patently untrue. Kender were not *thieves*, they were *handlers*. Their curiosity and their insatiable desire to poke and pry and touch led them to handle anything they could pick up. That same curiosity could draw their attention away from what they held. Anxious for some new experience, they often, and quite unintentionally, tucked the articles into their pouches. The oversight usually came from a desire to free their hands for something new, and they often found themselves with items they could not remember acquiring. In a kender city, an oddly shaped rock or piece of glass, knife, scarf, or dish could have a hundred owners in a busy week. Outside their own lands they had learned to make up excuses for unexplained possessions.

"I was keeping it for you."

"It must have fallen in my pouch," or

"You must have put it in my pouch by mistake," were three of the most common used to races who did not understand the kender habit of handling. If the owner of a purloined object wanted it back, the kender cheerfully returned it.

"What should we do?" Ripple asked, her brow wrinkling in disappointment. "I wanted to see the city."

Trap understood his sister's feelings. They had been born and raised in Legup, a village in the mountains of Hylo, and like the rest of the Fargo family, as soon as they had reached adulthood they were stricken with wanderlust and had set out to see the world. They had yet to see a city of humans and dwarves firsthand.

Their great-grandfather had walked east from Legup to

Solamnia and south to Kaolyn and Abanasinia. After the Cataclysm the geography of Krynn had changed, and now an unnamed sea divided Northern Ergoth and Hylo from Solamnia and its political and geographical neighbors to the south and east.

Trap and Ripple had left the port of Hylo by ship, intending to travel across the channel to one of the port towns in Solamnia. A sudden storm had blown the ship south. The wind screamed through the sails and the sea men dangled from the masts and spars in an attempt to trim the sails. The kender found the trip exciting, but as the storm blew itself out they grew bored. At the first opportunity they asked to be put ashore. The captain was glad to do so after he lost his favorite knife, a carved and silver chased inkwell and several maps. He had not even waited until they reached a port.

He dropped them on a deserted beach. Without knowing their starting point, they had three choices. They could go north or south, with no idea how far they were from the ports shown on the map, or they could strike inland. They were on the western shore of the continent, so most of the cities would be to the east. A day later they found a high road that angled in a northeasterly direction. Correctly guessing it led to a city, they followed it until the soldiers attacked.

"I know," Ripple brightened, slipped her pack off her shoulders and rummaged in the depths. "We'll change clothes so the soldiers won't recognize us, and we'll wear these," she pulled out two crumpled hats with tall crowns and floppy brims.

"You're determined to take a bath and change clothes," Trap laughed, though he had no objection. It had taken them five days to amble the sixty miles from the shore to their present location. They had stopped frequently, inspecting the local flora, animals and anything else that interested them. The afternoons had been hot and his skin was sticky with sweat.

An hour and a half later, Trap stood with his feet wide apart and his hands braced on his knees as he leaned

Dixie Lee McKeone

forward. Strands of his long, dark brown hair, freshly
washed and nearly dry, moved in the light breeze. His sister caught it and twisted it into a smooth roll, then she
expertly flipped it into a loop close to his head. Using one
slim finger, she pulled the coil through the loop. With a
gentle jerk, strong enough to set the hair, but not hard
enough to cause Trap any pain, she tightened the top
knot.

Many kender used thongs, cords, metal rings and other
devices to manage their long hair, and in Hylo some cut it
short to be rid of the bother. The Fargo family had always
adhered to the ancient custom of the actual knot at the
exact center of the crown. When Trap stood, the ends fell
just to the nape of his neck.

Ripple leaned forward and he tied her much longer
hair. Then he caught up the blond ponytail and flipped it
around his finger. When he let it go it fell in one shining
curl that reached her waist. But no one would be seeing
that thick, shining tress for a while. She leaned sideways,
caught it in the crown of the hat and seated the headgear
firmly on her head, hiding both the topknot and her
pointed ears.

The hats had been a parting gift from their uncle,
Skipout Fargo, and he had given them cryptic instructions
to go with the headgear. Obeying the advice of Uncle
Skipout, Trapspringer wrapped his bedding around the
forked end of his hoopak and attached his pack to it.
Ripple did the same with her whippik. When they were
finished, Trap surveyed the result and shook his head.

"Gee, we don't look like ourselves," he complained
when they were ready. With their top knots and ears hidden and their weapons camouflaged, they resembled
slender twelve-year-old human children.

"I think it's what Uncle Skipout intended," Ripple said.

"I can't think why." Trapspringer murmured with a
frown, but when an idea struck him his face lit with a
smile. "Maybe humans like kender to look like them."

"I see, we're doing it to be friendly! I like that," Ripple
said, nodding her approval. "Remember what father said."

As she took a step away from the log a low branch nearly dislodged her hat. She leaned her whippik against the tree, readjusted her headgear, and as she reached for her camouflaged weapon, noticed a small, interesting flower: a pink puff on a short stem.

"What did father say?" asked Trapspringer, who had been gazing into the bushes where a rustle had given evidence of a hiding animal. He decided he had been mistaken and had picked up the thread of the conversation.

"It's very pretty."

"Father said your hat was pretty?"

Ripple looked from the flower to her brother and said, "Did he ever see my hat?"

Brother and sister exchanged smiles and shouldered their weapons and packs. The typical kender conversation flowed along a serpentine course with eddies of unrelated but interesting sidelights. To a human, the entire point of the conversation would be quickly lost, but since the kender seldom wanted to make any point they were usually satisfied.

"I hope the soldiers aren't mad at us anymore," Ripple said as she stepped over a log.

"They made a mistake, and when they realize it they'll be sorry," Trapspringer said. "We shouldn't be angry about it, it could happen to anyone. I know they'll apologize, but right now, I think we should keep to the woods as long as we can."

Walking through the forest was more pleasant than traveling the dusty road. Spring was well underway, it being the beginning of the month of Flower-field in the kender language, Fluer-green in Solamnic. The trees had been in full leaf for less than a fortnight. The day was lazily warm so they enjoyed the shade. Busy insects buzzed through the shadows and into the dappled sunlight where their wings glowed in the bright beams.

The forest stretched east another two miles. When they reached the road again they saw no sign of the patrol, so they continued until they stood looking at the walled city. The ship captain's map that had mysteriously appeared among Trapspringer's belongings had listed the name of the city as Lytburg.

"What do you think?" Trap asked his sister.

Above the outer defenses, bristling with battlements and bartizans, they could see the towers of the keep, set far inside the city's fortifications.

"It looks as if they're expecting trouble," Ripple said, undaunted by the prospect of danger. "It looks interesting."

"Interesting" was the rallying cry for the entire race of kender, who would rather face death than boredom, so they continued up the road.

As they drew closer to the bridge at the gates of the city, they noticed a deep trench that ran along the outside of the city's walled defenses. Abatis lined the ditch. The bark of the securely anchored, up-thrust logs and strong tree branches had grayed with age. The pointed ends showed blackened tips, suggesting they had been hardened with fire. Below the black char the pale, freshly cut wood indicated that the points had been recently sharpened to cut away the rot.

A stone bridge with sturdy stone railings limited the access to the gate. Several farmers' carts were drawn up as close to the left railing as possible. The drivers waited for the gate guards to inspect their cargo. The wide sharp tips of the city's military weaponry gleamed as if newly sharpened. The soldiers roughly shoved one of the farmers about. They demanded to know the farmer's business and poked at the baskets of potatoes and cabbages in his simple cart.

"The guards look busy," Ripple said as they approached the end of the bridge.

"They're important to the city," Trap replied. "We shouldn't take up their valuable time."

Ahead, a guard ordered the arriving cart to pull to the left. The vehicle was unwieldy, piled high with hay. The mules objected to the wall and the soldier kept shouting at the driver. When the wagon finally stopped, the guard reached up and grabbed the arm of the farmer, hauling him off the seat.

The two kender had been about to skirt the cart and cross the bridge, but just then a troop of soldiers came through the gate, leaving the city. The leader shouted at the guards and the farmers to make way as he urged his horse forward. Behind him the troop, riding two abreast, were shoving the farmers and the guards up against the carts.

Trap and Ripple ducked back behind the last cart and he climbed up on the left bridge railing to get out from underfoot. The stone facing had once risen to a knife-sharp angle, but age had rounded it. Kender in general had excellent balance, particularly the Fargo family.

"We can just walk along this railing to the gate," Trap said, leading the way. "The guards will be grateful to us for not bothering them, and we won't get in the way of the horses and wagons."

The two kender walked along the railing behind the carts, entered the city unnoticed, and strolled down a busy street. The locals, mostly human and dwarf, hurried in both directions on unknown errands. Occasionally they saw an elf, but they had not seen any of their own people. The height of the humans' shoulders were well above the heads of the kender, so their view was limited to the buildings they passed.

Two and three story half-timbered buildings, most with cantilevered second floors, shaded the pavement and the smell of mustiness mingled with the odor of bodies.

Their diminutive height had kept them from seeing what lay ahead. Then, through a break in the crowd, they saw a sunlit open square and caught a glimpse of awnings over rough stalls.

"Wow, it's Shadow Day," Ripple said with delight.

"Call it Bracha here," Trap reminded his sister. Whether they used the kinder or the Solamnic name, it did seem to be the seventh day of the week, market day.

They increased their pace and in minutes they reached the open square. There they slowed, stopping occasionally to look at the displayed merchandise. Everything in the world seemed to be on sale in the square. They saw pigs and horses, furs and vegetables, hoes and plows, wagons and fowls roasting on spits. Bolts of silks, wool and velvet lay cheek by jowl with cured leather.

Farmers in homespun clothing, with the mud of their fields still on their boots, rubbed shoulders with the city dwellers, some in filthy rags, some in clean, well darned clothing, some in silks and velvets. Hawkers carried trays and baskets supported by leather straps or ropes around their necks or over their shoulders. They shouted over the noise of the crowd as they announced their wares. Calls of "Roasted Nuts!" "Meat rolls!" and "Melon slices!" rang over the arguing, bargaining, shouted greetings and laughter of the shoppers.

Further on they discovered a traveling baker's stall and behind it an oven made of iron sheets cleverly fitted together. It could be taken apart in minutes. Trap stopped to consider the oven, wondering if it was of dwarven design. Ripple continued down the row of stalls.

Trap picked up a still warm loaf, inspecting the crust to see if it was to his liking. Across the way a shouting match broke out between two would-be buyers for the same pig. The kender hurried over to see if there would be a fight, but the seller, a narrow faced little man with a twitching nose, decided he had undervalued the pig. He upped the price and the two bearded, roughly dressed farmers suddenly allied against him.

When the shoppers stomped away, Trap lost interest and wandered on down the stalls. He forgot he was still holding the bread until he caught up with Ripple. She spotted the loaf, too large for Trap to eat alone, and asked if he planned on sharing it with her. He looked down at the bread in surprise and she understood his expression.

"You forgot to pay for it," she observed, knowing her brother was all kender. They had promised their parents they would be careful to pay for whatever they took, and their pouches were bulging with steel pieces.

"I went to see a fight," Trap explained his possession of the bread. He promised himself he would return and pay for it, but at the moment there was so much to see. He would pay the baker when they returned up the row of stalls.

"We really should eat it while it's still warm," he said as he tore the loaf in half and handed Ripple her share. He was just going to take a bite when he saw two human children hungrily eyeing the food. Trap broke off two pieces, giving each a warm, crusty hunk.

Ripple had walked on ahead again and stopped at a jeweler's stall to admire a bracelet of gold set with blue stones. The owner of the stall, a dwarf with a magnificent black beard streaked with gray, was in the middle of a bargaining session with a portly, well dressed human. Three young boys came racing through the crowded stalls, scuffling and pushing each other playfully. Two, wrestling each other as they ran, knocked into the right support of the dwarf's stall. The temporary shelter swayed. The pegged display board, raised to a steep angle to better show the glittering wares, was in danger of toppling. The dwarf caught it and pulled it back into place. He was not in time to keep two necklaces and a wide gold bracelet from falling to the ground.

Ripple knelt and picked up the jewelry. She was rising, reaching to put them back on the display board when a female shopper passed, oblivious to the problems of the jeweler. The woman was carrying a wide basket on her arm, and it brushed against Ripple's hat, knocking it off.

The dwarf had seemed happy enough to have Ripple's assistance, but when he saw the topknot and pointed ears, he roared and ducked under the display.

"Thief! Kender thief!" he roared and pushed past the portly customer as he reached out, grabbing Ripple's arm.

Chapter 3

When the dwarf shouted thief, Ripple was still half crouched. She looked around, trying to spot the criminal as she picked up her hat. She had not realized the dwarf glared accusingly at her, but Trap saw the direction of the stall owner's attention.

"That's not nice! She's picking them up for you," he explained, but the dwarf shook his fist at Trap before racing around the far open end of the stall. The jeweler's attention was all on Ripple as he pushed by Trap and made a dash for the kender girl.

Trap leaped forward. In a flash his hoopak was in his left hand. He thrust the steel pointed end between the jeweler's feet. With his right, he grabbed Ripple's arm and jerked her away just in time to keep the dwarf from falling on her. The dwarf hit the ground with a thud and a curse.

Ripple was stunned by the accusation, and was still holding out the jewelry she had picked up when the portly customer took up the shout.

"Kender thieves, robbing honest folk," he shouted and made a grab for the two necklaces Ripple held. "Thieves! Thieves! Call the watch!" As he turned to alert the crowd, Trap saw him tuck the two necklaces inside his gold-trimmed sleeve.

"I saw what you did!" Trap yelled at the human. *"You're* stealing! *You're* a thief!"

Trap knew little about humans, but he did suspect a rich townsman would be believed before a stranger. They could flee or find themselves in the city dungeons. He gave Ripple a shove toward the narrow space between the jeweler's stall and the one beside it where iron kettles and pans were on display.

Ripple had been shocked by the accusation, but her quick wits rivaled her bother's. When the tinker tried to grab her she struck him on the head with her whippik before dashing through the narrow opening. Trap followed on her heels. He had just passed the staggering tinker's table when the man stepped into one of his own pots and fell on his own display. The table legs collapsed, throwing the kettles under the feet of two burly men who were leading the chase after the kender.

Trap and Ripple dodged out into a space between the back of the stalls, a place the shoppers seldom saw. They dodged around bundles and baskets of merchandise that waited for display room in the crowded stalls. Behind them they heard the call of "Kender thieves!" as it passed throughout the market square. As they ran they pulled their packs from their weapons and slipped their arms through the straps.

They fled down the deserted row and wriggled their way through a narrow space into the next market isle, but the alarm had traveled through the square. They had not taken two steps before a tall, bearded man grabbed Trap's arm. He let go when Ripple poked him in the stomach with the end of her whippik.

They danced down the isle, skipping away from reaching hands. They tripped two more people and swung their weapons toward the others, keeping them at bay.

At the end of the isle a dark, narrow mean street led out of the market and Ripple dashed into its relative protection. At least they could not be grabbed by reaching hands on every side. They still had a large group of irate shopkeepers and townsmen on their trail. They ran down the street, turned onto another at random and then into a narrow alley.

Trap's hope for escape sank as he saw a rickety shelter blocking the alley, but then he noticed a narrow space between it and the building on the right. Ripple, running ahead of him, had seen it too and wriggled into the space with her brother right behind her.

They slipped through to the other side and Trap was slowing his pace when he heard shouting behind him. He looked back and through the narrow crack he could see the first of their pursuers trying to stop. The momentum of the crowd behind the leaders of the chase shoved them forward, against the shabby lean-to. The rickety structure collapsed with a crash. As the kender ran on they heard the sound of humans in pain and others swearing in their anger.

Trap increased his speed again and a few steps further he saw two pair of eyes staring out of the dimness. He had not thought the alley dark enough for anyone to hide in it. As he drew even with them, he recognized two gully dwarves. As if to prove the reputation of their race, these two were so grimy their clothing, hands, and faces had blended with the dark gray stone.

One of them had been rolling a wagon wheel toward the little lean-to, but with a quick move he sent it careening in the other direction, and chased after it.

The Aghar rolling the rickety wheel was in the lead. He was taller and had darker hair. The second, smaller, thinner, and with blond hair, ran in his wake. They had turned so quickly Trap had little time to notice their features, but even in the semi darkness he could tell the smaller gully dwarf was younger than the other. Like kender, the Aghar developed facial wrinkles early in life. The smaller gully had no wrinkles.

The gully dwarves were only two paces in front of Ripple when they reached what Trap thought was a dead end, but they whirled around a corner. The gully dwarf with the wheel gave it a practiced turn to change direction and the kender followed. Behind them they could hear running feet again so they put their trust in the gully dwarves.

After a series of turns, all into alleys that became increasingly narrow, dark, and dirty, they saw what had to be the end of the chase. The dirty little gully dwarves still had one trick left. They whirled around a huge pile of rubbish and disappeared. Still trusting the gully dwarves' sense of survival—it was said that was the only sense they had, including the sense of smell—Ripple followed them.

Trap heard Ripple squeal in surprise. Her brother, following, tripped over a low stone that could have been a door step, and fell into darkness. The darkness hid a smooth, descending ramp and he tumbled down a steep, dark chute.

He rolled to a stop with something moderately soft under his legs and his mouth full of hair—he had at least found Ripple. The soft thing under his legs complained and he discovered by touch and smell that it was a gully dwarf. When he tried to sit up, he found that his left leg was caught up in the spokes of the dwarves' wagon wheel.

Far above they heard voices that echoed off the walls. The humans had followed them.

"Don't worry about them," one voice, louder than the others remarked. "They'll never get out of there, they're done for."

The four at the bottom of the strange shaft remained still until the echoing footsteps faded away. Then, after a few aborted attempts that resulted in feet in faces, elbows in stomachs, and fingers in eyes, the two kender and the two gully dwarves sorted themselves out. They discovered that their landing place had a ceiling high enough so they could stand up.

"What happen?" asked one of the gully dwarves.

"We run away," the other said.

"From what?"

"Don't know."

"You want torch?"

"Why? Got no light."

"I've got a tinderbox," Trap said.

"Who that?" one of the gully dwarves exclaimed.

"Kender, I think," the dwarf's companion offered. "Never seen one before."

"You've got a torch and I've got a light, so you can see one again," Trap suggested.

"You can see two," Ripple added. "Though why you've never seen kender before, I can't imagine."

After a considerable amount of fumbling (during which Ripple had to slap someone) fingers caught the hand Trap was holding tinderbox with and guided it to the torch. More fumbling followed before he lit what turned out to be a musty bundle of already half-burned rags around a broken mop handle. Once the first torch was lit, they were able to find a second, and light it too. The two kender and the two gully dwarves stood quietly, inspecting each other.

Trap decided his first estimate was correct. The tallest, with the beginning of facial wrinkles, was the eldest. The wrinkles were easy to see, being filled with grime. His hair was dark, probably dark brown, but overlaid with dirt that lightened it slightly. The smaller dwarf had no wrinkles, but was no less dirty. Their hair was approximately the same color, but the subtle difference of dark hair lightened by dirt and light hair darkened by dirt, led Trap and Ripple to believe that the younger dwarf was originally blond.

The gully dwarves were dressed in ragged cast-offs that had once been human clothing. Their trouser legs and sleeves had been carelessly rolled into bulky cuffs. During the run the smaller dwarf's right pants leg had unrolled and fallen down over his boot so he was walking on the bottom portion of the trouser leg.

Finished with his inspection of the Aghar, Trap considered their surroundings. They were in a passage, rock lined and arched. A few feet from where Trap stood, an empty sconce showed where one of the dwarves had found the torch.

Ripple blinked against the light and walked to the bottom of the steeply canted chute that had dumped them more than a hundred feet below street level. She tried three times to climb it, but the bottom was slick. It was marginally too wide and high for a kender or a gully dwarf to reach the sides or ceiling. They could not brace themselves to climb.

"Beans!" she said as she slid back a third time. "We'll have to find another way out."

"Could have told them," the first dwarf said.

"Me too," said the second.

"Hello," Trap was already growing tired of the dwarves conversation that excluded the kender. "I'm Trapspringer Fargo. This is my sister Ripple."

"His name Trapspringer," the taller dwarf said.

"She Ripple. She pretty," the other replied.

"Thank you. That's very nice. What's your name?" Ripple asked. The compliment had made her forget her irritation.

The larger of the two seemed to draw himself up. "Me Umpth Aglest. Me leader mighty Aglest clan."

"You have a clan?" Ripple asked. "Can they help us? Maybe they could drop a rope down the chute."

"That's a good idea," Trap nodded.

"No. Clan here," Umpth pointed at his companion. "Grod Aglest, brother. Him clan."

Trap looked around, peering up and down the passage as far as he could see in the light of the sputtering torch.

"Which way?" he asked of no one in particular. Umpth immediately pointed to the right and Grod to the left. They exchanged glances and both pointed in opposite directions. Since Ripple had not expressed an opinion, Trap set off to the left, with his sister close to his side. Behind him came the dwarves. Umpth rolled the wagon wheel.

"Kender smart," Umpth observed. "Me point this way."

"Me too," Grod said.

"What is this place?" Ripple asked.

"This no This Place," Umpth answered. "No live here."

"I know you don't live here, I just thought you might know about this place."

"No *This* Place," Umpth said again. "Not know what place this is."

"Kender don't talk good," Grod said.

"Don't know This Place from any place," came the reply.

"Do they make any sense to you?" Ripple asked Trap. She spoke softly, not wanting to hurt the feelings of the gully dwarves.

"It's hard to tell," Trap replied. "I hear words I think I know, but they're not strung together right."

"Kender have big words, no sense," Umpth observed.

"Keep eye on him," Grod suggested. "Me watch her. She pretty." He reached out to touch the single long golden curl that had fallen over Ripple's left shoulder, but she stepped back, away from his grimy hands.

As they walked along the passage, they occasionally saw old torches in the wall sconces. Ripple inspected them, taking the first three that were at all usable. When she found more she gave Grod three to carry. They had been walking for half an hour when they found a set of steps going up about thirty feet. At the top was a door with a heavy lock.

The dwarves ascended the stairway behind them, but were having a hard time rolling the wagon wheel up the steps.

"Why did you bring that wheel?" Ripple asked, looking back at the struggling dwarves. "It's no good. Half the spokes are gone. The rim is loose too."

"Wheel magic," Umpth said. "Aglest clan magic."

"Wow! Really? Big jiggies!" Trap asked, suddenly interested. "How can a wheel be magic?"

"Belong to ancestor. All left of wagon bring Aglest clan to This Place. Ancestor magic strong."

"I've never heard of a magic wheel," Trap said, not sure

he believed it, but at the first opportunity he wanted to see what the wheel would do.

"See, no sense," Grod said. "Not know This Place, not know magic, no sense."

"Don't be rude!" Trap said with a dark look over his shoulder. In his irritation he forgot his interest in the wheel.

While Ripple held the torch, Trap pulled out the set of lock picks his father had given him as a traveling present. After a few pokes and twists the lock clicked. Trap pushed the door open to the squeal of rusty hinges and a shower of crusted dirt and small stones fell way. Obviously it had not been opened for many years.

They found themselves in another passage. This one was already lit with torches, dry and swept clean, though a few cobwebs decorated the arched ceiling. The air was reasonably fresh, kept so by the burning torches, and from a distance they heard voices. Ripple put out the light she carried by the simple expedient of rolling it on the floor until the flames died. The four wanderers crept down the hall as quietly as the rolling wagon wheel would allow.

The voices became louder as the foursome reached a doorway at the end of the passage. The thick heavy door stood ajar, and Trap looked in to see a huge chamber, one unlike anything in his experience. Shelves of books in red bindings lined the wall on the far side of the chamber. At the end of the room more shelves held hundreds of glass jars containing strange and wonderful objects. Old but still colorful rugs overlapped each other on the stone floor. In the center of the room, a litter of books, scrolls, and strange paraphernalia covered four tables.

A human in red robes stood on one side of the room. He pressed his elbows tight to his sides and bent his arms so his hands, palms up, were close to his shoulders. From each palm came a pale, glowing light. He was humming a soft, even tone. The glow from his hand rose to form an arc of light above the man's head. Behind him stood what Trap thought was a child in a red robe. The girl played a lute, stroking the same note the man hummed. Their tune could get boring very quickly, so Trap thought the two humans might enjoy learning more about music.

"That's very boring," he called across the room. "If you like, I'll show you how to make—" He intended to offer his help, but he had startled the small one, who jumped and struck a sudden loud, discordant note. The man's voice rose in the same discordant note and suddenly the arc of light changed, disappeared, and a blackness deeper than velvet opened around the red-robed human. He stepped back with a cry as a hot wind, strong as a gale, blew through the hole.

The torches blew out and a variety of objects, impossible to see in the sudden darkness, were hurled about by the gale. A piece of cloth hit Trap in the face and as he jerked it away an unknown object struck him sharply on the shoulder.

"Orander!" a voice called out in fear.

"Halmarain," a man's voice called back. "Stay away from the portal!"

"A portal? What is a portal?" Trap asked the room at large. "Is it a magic door, does it lead to some interesting place?"

No one answered him, but he heard what he thought was a cry and a whimper, though he could not positively identify the sound. Suddenly the chamber filled with a roar that had nothing to do with the hot wind. Dimly, over the roar, he heard a thin scream that could have been human or kender, and he wondered if Ripple had entered the chamber.

He heard the sound of splitting wood and the thud of heavy furniture hitting the wall. Suddenly Trap was grabbed by a huge, clawed hand. His feet dragged against an opening as he was pulled through some unseen door. It seemed to be the meeting place of the gale, where the winds were blowing in both directions.

Chapter 4

When the giant clawed hand pulled Trap through the portal to the other plane, the kender found himself in deep twilight. The air was so hot he could hardly breathe. He saw two huge eyes looking at him out of a giant, bestial face.

"Hello," he said softly. "I don't know if you know about kender, but we're really very friendly. We enjoy adventures and seeing new places—Oh! You have a very large mouth!"

A maw opened, wider than Trap was tall, and roared until the rest of the kender's speech was smothered under the noise. The monster thrust the helpless kender back into the darkness. Trap's feet were dragged across the stone floor, then the monster released him and the kender fell on his back. In the darkness, Trap sensed rather than saw the arm reach past him. It swung about as if searching, then gave another roar of frustration and withdrew.

As suddenly as the gale had started, it stopped. Trap breathed the cool, moist air of the stone chamber again. He waited a moment, sat up, and examined himself, gingerly moving his arms and legs. Nothing seemed broken, but he could feel his bruises.

"Trap?" Ripple called.

"I'm here," he answered. "Wherever 'here' is. . . ."

A moment later a light gleamed brightly from the tip of a short staff held by the tiny red-robed figure, and he could see again. He was in the chamber lined with shelves, but they were the only furnishings still in place. Books in red covers littered the floor along with broken glass, jars, and furniture.

In its search, the monster had overturned two of the big work tables and shoved them against a wall. The third lay in splinters. In the center of the room stood the small figure in red robes. She was glaring at Trap.

"A kender!" She spat out the words as if she found them distasteful. "I might have known it would be a kender!"

In spite of its high pitch, her voice proved she was not a child. Trap thought she might be a small dwarf, though from what he had heard about dwarves she certainly was a pretty one.

"Hello, I'm Trapspringer Fargo," he said courteously. "What's your name? Are you Halmarain, the one the wizard was talking to?"

The kender stood and bowed.

"How did you get in here?" she demanded.

"Through a door in the passage," he said, pointing in the direction they had come. "By the condition of the lock and the hinges, you haven't used it in years, probably because you'd lost the key. It's easy to lose keys, people do it all the time—"

"Trust a kender to find a door even a pair of magicians had overlooked," the little wizard muttered. She gazed around the chamber and pushed several books out of the way as she picked up a short stool and sat on it.

"Poor Orander," she said, shaking her head and hunching her shoulders. "I just hope he's still alive."

"Why shouldn't he be?" Trap asked. He didn't understand this at all. "Where did he go? One minute he was here and the next he was gone. What an interesting way to travel. When he comes back, do you think he might take us with him?"

"I wish you had gone instead of him," the little wizard grumbled.

"I don't understand why you're so angry. I don't even know what happened," Trap pressed.

"Just leave me alone and let me think." She made pushing motions as if trying to get rid of him.

"I just want to know why you're so mad at me," he said, following her as she stepped over the fallen books. "I didn't do anything wrong, I just wanted to help. I don't understand what happened."

"And you're not going to stop pestering me until I tell you," she said, glaring at him. "Master Orander, with the use of some magic stones was trying to open a portal into another plane."

"I've heard of planes! A little anyway," Trap said thoughtfully. "I'm trying to remember. . . ."

"What you remember is unimportant. What happened is that while he was holding the stones and we were creating a vibrating tone in a pitch that would take him into one world, you—*you* startled us and we opened a portal to an unknown destination. Now he's some place that could be dangerous—even deadly—and it's your fault."

From the doorway Ripple, Umpth, and Grod stepped into the chamber. Umpth was still rolling the wagon wheel. The three silently stared at the mess. Ripple was the first to overcome her surprise.

"Was that magic?" she asked the little wizard. "I thought magic was pretty. Still, it was different," she added, as if she were considering Halmarain's feelings. "But how can you see what you're doing in the dark? How do you know you're making the right magic? Can you see in the dark?"

"No, I can't see in the dark," Halmarain snapped. "That was magic gone awry, thanks to your friend here."

"That's not fair! He was just trying to help," Ripple defended her brother. "Your song *was* pretty boring."

"I'm sure she didn't intend to be rude," Trap said. "She sounds as if she was frightened by the dark—you remember how it was when we were little. . . ."

Ripple, with ready sympathy, smiled at the little wizard and said, "You don't have to be afraid anymore. We're here and we'll help you light all the torches again." The kender girl looked around dubiously. "Though this place is really a mess. How do you find anything? I hate to mention it, but you don't seem to be a very good house-keeper. Maybe you can cook, which would be very nice since I'm a little hungry. Do you mind if I explore this room? You have such interesting stuff."

Halmarain stared at Ripple as if she could not find words. She shook her head and sat staring at the floor. The others walked about the room, inspecting the havoc wrought on the chamber. Ripple stopped and picked up something from the floor while Umpth pushed at one of the overturned tables that had been knocked against the wall. The gully dwarf jumped back with a cry. From behind the table came a wail.

Trap skittered over a pile of books to take a look; Ripple came right behind him. They stood gazing over the edge of the overturned table at a creature that shivered as it crouched on the floor. It stared at them with eyes enlarged by fright. The little monster was basically humanoid in shape and face, though it's skin was a deep gray-green. Its nose resembled a bird's beak. It's mouth was wider than any humanoid's and as it gave a defensive snarl, it exposed a mouth full of thick, strong teeth.

"What a strange creature. Is it an animal?" Ripple asked, looking back over her shoulder at the wizard. "Is it magic? Did Orander make it?"

"What animal?" Halmarain snapped. "The only living thing in here other than me came with you."

"This didn't," Trap said. "I've seen something like it before—I forget where—but I certainly don't know what it is."

"Don't know," Umpth said.

"Wizard make, maybe," Grod agreed with Ripple.

"Hello," Trap said, extending his hand to the little monster. He introduced himself, Ripple, and the two gully dwarves. The odd little stranger just stared at him and whimpered.

Trap gave the creature a sufficiency of attention and turned away. As he looked about the room, he tried to figure out just where the magic portal had been. Then he realized why the strange creature was so familiar.

"I know!" he announced in triumph. "It looks like the monster! The one that grabbed me and pulled me through the portal."—he hurried back to look at the little stranger again—"Yes, it has the same face."

The little wizard had remained sitting on her stool, her hands up over her face, but now she pulled them down and stared at Trap. In the meantime Trap had spotted an unbroken bottle on the floor and had picked it up. Inside were two dead and dried lizards. He stood, turning the bottle in his hands.

"Well? Tell me about this thing," Halmarain prompted.

"There are two of them, and they're dead," Trap replied as he gazed into the bottle. "How did you get them inside? The neck is awfully small."

"No, about the creature on the other side of the portal," the little human insisted.

"Oh, that one, it was ten . . . maybe even twenty times larger than this one."—he peered over the edge of the overturned table again—"Look, its shivering so it must have come from a hotter place and it was hot on the other side of the magic door . . . do you think you could open the portal and let in some heat? It *is* a little chilly in here."

"You're right!" Ripple announced. "I felt the hot wind in the passage and I bet it was blown through the portal and if the thing that grabbed you was so much larger, then this must be its baby."

When Ripple suggested the origin of the creature, Halmarain rose and used her foot to push books and debris out of her path. She walked over to look behind the overturned table. Lying on its side, the width of the table made a wall too high for her to see over, so Trap obligingly searched out another stool. She climbed up and raised her staff to get a better look at the newcomer.

The strange being that had only whimpered at the sight of the kender and gully dwarves, snarled at the little wizard and lashed out with a clawed hand.

Startled, Halmarain jumped from the bench and backed away.

"Don't do that!" Ripple ordered. "You be nice!"

In answer, the creature whimpered again.

When the newcomer was quiet, the little wizard stared at the blank top of the overturned table that was its shelter, her eyes thoughtful.

"I've seen something like it before," she said thoughtfully, gazing around the room. Her attention focused on the scattered books. She squared her shoulders and glared at the kender.

"Help me pick up these books and get them back on the shelf. I've seen a drawing of it in one of the books of magic. If I can find the reference, I can tell where Orander went. Maybe we can help him."

"I'd love to look at magic books, do they have pictures?" Ripple was more than willing to help.

"You can pick them up, bring them to me and help put them on the shelf," Halmarain said shortly. "If you open one, you'll probably lose a hand. They're protected by spells." She gave Trap a hard look. "You helped to create this mess, so you'll help clean it up."

"I said I was sorry," Trap said. He had already apologized, and her repeated accusations were irritating. Still, he would like to talk to the wizard, which was impossible unless they could open the portal again. He was unfamiliar with books, but he liked handling them. A few had fallen open and he was fascinated by the pictures he could see.

"If there's a spell on these books, why are some open?" Ripple asked. She had always been quick to pick up a fallacy.

"Because they were already open, we were studying them," the little wizard said. "The ones that were on the shelves are still shut. Now get busy and pick them up!"

"I don't mind helping you, but not if you're going to yell at us," Ripple announced. "You haven't been very friendly, you know. You haven't offered to show us any nice magic or anything."

Halmarain's face reddened with rage. "You've come in here, messed up a spell, endangered Orander's life or—" she stopped. "But then, you're kender. Typically kender, I guess. *Please* help me pick up the books and work out my problems, then I'll show you some magic."

"Oh good, we're going to see magic after all," Trap said, hardly able to contain his enthusiasm. They cleared a spot in the middle of the floor and moved a table close to the row of shelves where the books had been. As he helped pick up the red-bound tomes, Trap spotted a small object on the floor and picked it up also. At first he thought it was just a small chip off the walls. On closer inspection, he discovered it was round, some sort of glass, gray-green and carved with a spiral of tiny figures. The surface had been carefully roughened to keep it from shining.

"Are we picking up the books or not?" Halmarain glared at him before turning her attention to Umpth. "And you, you keep an eye on that monster in the corner."

Trap slipped the little glass disk into his pouch so it would not get lost again in the clutter. He wanted to ask the wizard about it when she was in a better mood.

Chapter 5

Astinus the Chronicler dipped his pen and his words flowed on the parchment. . . .

Deep beneath the ruins of Pey, Draaddis Vulter and his god, Takhisis, watched the activity in Orander's laboratory. At least he supposed the Queen of Darkness still watched. By the power of the viewing disk on the mirror, he could not see the globe to know if she was still giving her attention to the activities of the kender, the gully dwarves, and the little wizard.

It was enough to know she had not turned her attention and her frustration back on him. Still, he doubted it would be long before she did. His god was his greatest joy and his greatest terror. For years he had been paying a price for having taken her gifts and misusing them.

Ambition had been his trap. In his youth he worked

and studied until he became proficient enough to take his Test in the Tower of High Sorcery. His examination had been easier than he'd expected. His joy was short lived; he was sneeringly told he had nothing to brag about. All the orders needed minor wizards, those who could serve but would not have the talent to advance to the point where they challenged master wizards and the leadership of the order. For them the Test was not as strenuous.

His triumph had turned to dust. He chafed as he served Grenoten, one of the master wizards in the High Tower. Draaddis was a wizard and he refused to be held back, limited to spells that were good for nothing more than housekeeping chores. He studied, but he found he lacked the memory for the greater spells. He had to face the scorn of Grenoten as well as his own disappointment. Draaddis suffered his servitude and his thwarted ambition for two years before he turned to Takhisis.

He begged to be given the memory and the talent to grow beyond his natural gifts, and promised in return to serve the Dark Queen faithfully. Possessing a good mind and a quick tongue, his arguments and promises were convincing and she gave him the gifts he requested. The next day he found himself able to read and memorize spells with a speed and precision he had not dreamed possible.

For a year he made no show of his new talents. He continued to serve Grenoten, to study diligently, and to put up with the master wizard's sneers. Knowing he was learning faster every day robbed the scorn of its power to sting. Draaddis had a plan of his own and when he was ready, he put it into action.

Using a polymorph spell, he reduced three of the master wizard's minions, and then Grenoten himself, to two inches height. When he finished torturing them, he crushed them with his heel.

His revenge had been sweet, but he had not reckoned on the anger of his goddess. Grenoten and the more learned of his minions had been studying and searching for a portal that would allow the Dark Queen to return to the world of

Ansalon. In her rage she had subjected Draaddis to two years of torture before she put him to work finishing Grenoten's work.

She had even increased his talents, but instead of the glory he craved, he had lived in the ruins of Pey for thirty years, struggling to find a way for his mistress to return to Krynn.

Only when he was studying was he free of her torture. He could walk the underground passages of his quarters unimpeded as long as he was traveling in the direction of the laboratory. When hunger and fatigue drove him to leave his work, vile arms and tentacles reached out of the walls, clutching at him, tearing his flesh.

The arms and the rending of flesh was an illusion, but his mind added pain to the tortures of his queen. She had promised his suffering would end when she returned to Ansalon. She could not want access to the stones any more than Draaddis.

The clutter of Orander's laboratory disappeared. Draaddis was again aware of his own, neater, but far more sinister workroom and his experiments. Around his viewing disk, still lying on the round mirror, a small black cloud hovered, indicating the magic of its mate was blocked on all sides.

"The little thief took the other viewing disk!" Draaddis was outraged. "He put it in his pouch!"

"Shame on them and their evil natures," Takhisis laughed. To the wizard's ears the sound was feminine, alluring, like the tinkling of bells. Still, the influence of her anger at being thwarted shriveled a basket of freshly picked hen's bane until it dried and crumbled to dust. The little winged rat squealed and retreated into a dark corner.

Draaddis was aware she had been mocking him. At least she had not used her powers of illusion to torture him again.

"We saw enough to know the stones worked," Takhisis said, unconcerned about not being able to see more of the action in Orander Marlbenit's laboratory.

"But what good will that do if he took the gate stones to

the Plane of Vasmarg. . . ." He turned to look directly at the orb. "Unless you can travel there."

"I cannot, but the journey is unnecessary. Apparently you did not see the action clearly," the Queen of Darkness replied. "Orander dropped one of the stones before he was pulled through the portal. The male kender picked up the viewing disk, the female kender has the gate stone."

Draaddis took care to keep his expression blank. If he had understood the knowledge of the young wizard who had died giving him the information, both stones would be required to open a portal to another world. Apparently his queen had seen something he had missed. He remained silent, wondering if she would enlighten him.

Takhisis had drawn back slightly, and he could see part of her face as she looked beyond him, deep in thought. Then she turned her head and fastened her gaze on him.

"You don't see the possibilities, do you Draaddis?"

"I confess, my queen, my mind could never match yours."

"The second gate stone will come back to Krynn, my faithful servant. It will come and it will bring an ally. A silly kender has given us the opportunity we seek." Her smile widened when she realized he did not understand. "Death and destruction, war and pestilence, and the opening of the portal."

Draaddis didn't answer at once and Takhisis, correctly divining his problem, gave a soft laugh.

"Don't struggle to understand, Draaddis. I will explain when I am ready. For now, I will tell you how to provide a servant who will not fail to locate the kender. He will bring you the gate stone and the merchesti, as well as the miserable little thieves."

"You want the little fiend as well?" Draaddis asked, puzzled.

"The little fiend, my faithful servant, is crucial to my plan," she smiled. "Through him I will accomplish my every desire, but this too you will wait to learn. I tire of explanations."

"To fulfill your wishes is the purpose of my life, my lady queen," Draaddis bowed.

"True," Takhisis gave him an evil smile. "But we must find the kender quickly, before the young fiend decides he has a taste for kender as well as rocks and wood."

"They are in danger from him?" Draaddis asked. From what he had seen, the young fiend seemed harmless enough.

"Merchesti eat and can digest anything," the Dark Queen said. "Perhaps even the gate stone, so we must get it before the infant merchesti makes a meal of its new friends and crunches up the stone in the process."

Chapter 6

. . . now, Uncle Trapspringer was willing to be helpful. . . .

Trap, Ripple, and Grod picked up the books and carried them to the table while Umpth kept an eye on the little fiend in the corner. Halmarain looked at the titles, put them in separate stacks, and directed Trap as to their placement on the shelves.

The kender stopped several times to explore other objects of interest and the tiny woman had to prod them both to get them back to work. The gully dwarves, who preferred nothing as much as clutter, complained, and she had to threaten to turn them into rats before they could be induced to keep working.

At the wizard's direction they picked up all the books and placed the other unbroken objects back on the shelves. Grod swept the broken glass into one corner of the room.

As he worked he insisted no floor needed to be swept as long as they could step over the debris.

Halmarain set up a ladder that seemed to magically hang in the air in front of the book shelves. She climbed up and down, pulling the books down faster than Trap had put them up. She laid out several in precise locations, and when she ran out of the room, she demanded they set up the remaining table for more books.

"Thing hides back there," Umpth pointed out the difficulty.

"It can hide somewhere else," Halmarain said.

"She's not very nice," Ripple murmured to her brother. "If the thing's a baby, it's probably scared."

"And it's not like it *wanted* to come here," Trap said, nodding in agreement with his sister. "This Halmarain should be more considerate."

"Think what you want," the little wizard glared at them as she tugged at the table, though she was too small to move it.

"I think you're mean," Ripple said as she frowned at the little wizard. "Maybe you're so mean because you're so short."

"Can stretch her," Umpth suggested.

"Then no be mean," Grod added.

"You lay one hand on me and I'll turn you all into beetles," Halmarain warned. "If I seem mean its because I don't have time to be nice. If Master Orander could have returned he would be here by now." Tears formed on her lashes. "He didn't want to go . . . wherever he is. He would have returned right away if he could. Since he hasn't, I have to open the portal and help him if I can."

"Would he show us some magic?" Trap asked hopefully.

The little wizard frowned at the kender, then her gaze turned speculating for a moment. She favored them with a sly smile that was just opposite to her earlier mood.

"He just might show you all sorts of magic."

"Oh, good, if he'll show us magic, we'll be glad to help," Ripple said, her anger fading as quickly as it had appeared.

Trap stepped forward along with Ripple and with a shrug the gully dwarves took a hand. They set up the table and when it was in place Trap went back to the corner where the creature crouched.

"Trapspringer," he said as he put a hand to his chest. He tried three times before the huddled figure blinked, put a hand to its own chest, and said, "Beglug."

"Beglug," Trap repeated, pointing at the creature. He had intended to point to himself again and give his name, working through the process of building communication, but Beglug scampered out of his corner. As he stood upright he proved to be slightly less than three feet tall, just a couple of inches taller than the little wizard. His feet, which Trap had not noticed until the creature was standing on them, were small hooves. He dashed the length of the wall to the pile of broken glass and started eating it.

"No, you'll cut your mouth! You'll cut your insides all to pieces and you won't like that at all!" Trap ran after Beglug and tried to take the glass away. The creature bared its teeth and swatted at him with a hand that suddenly showed extended claws. Trap backed away.

"Waste time clean floor," Grod said with disgust.

Neither the mage nor the gully dwarves seemed to care what the little merchesti ate as long as they weren't on the menu. The two kender watched it anxiously. Beglug consumed the broken glass, apparently without feeling any pain.

Beglug ignored his companions as he happily cleaned the floor of all shards of glass, but when Halmarain climbed down off a stool and tried to pass the little fiend, he roared at her and made a swipe with his clawed hand.

"Keep it away from me or I'll kill it," Halmarain warned.

"He didn't attack you." Trap objected. "He just wants you to leave him alone."

"I wonder why he doesn't like you?" Ripple asked before leading the creature away to the corner where it had hidden behind the table. With a sound akin to a burp, it settled in its corner, closed its eyes, and went to sleep.

"You promised us some magic," Trap reminded the little wizard.

"I don't have time to play games. I need to open that portal."

"You promised," Ripple said, her voice harsh with anger. "You said you'd show us some magic if we picked up the books and we did, but if you're not going to keep your promise we can pull them all off the shelf again."

Halmarain glared at them for a moment, sighed, and pushed away the book she had been studying.

"You'll have to give me time to study something you would like." She sighed. "It can't be much, I need to put my time on more important matters."

"We'll wait," Trap said, making a major concession. Waiting was the hardest chore a kender ever faced. The next hour seemed to last a month.

Ripple, sitting at the other end of the room, near the sleeping merchesti, was playing with a small object. Trap wandered over to see what it was. She held a white rock that gave off a curious little glow when she rubbed it.

"Touch it," she instructed her bother.

"Quiet!" Halmarain shouted.

"Touch it," Ripple whispered. "I found it when we were picking up the books."

Trap fingered the rock. It felt so slick, at first he thought it was covered with a slimy substance, but his fingers were dry when he withdrew his hand.

"Wonder what it is," he asked just loud enough for Ripple to hear. Then he had an idea, one so exciting he forgot to keep his voice down.

"Do you think it's magic?" he asked Ripple. She shook her head indicating her ignorance and continued to play with it, but his question had caused Halmarain to raise her head.

"Is *what* magic?" she asked. "Let me see what you're talking about."

Ripple jumped up and skipped across the room, anxious to have the little wizard explain the stone.

"I found it on the floor, and I was just keeping it until you had time to tell me what it is," she said, holding it out. "It's really interesting, the way it feels wet and slippery, but there's no water on it. Do you know what makes it so slippery? It's like the moss in the creek at home; when you put your foot on it, you slide. Doley Goforth once slipped on the moss and he went—"

"It's one of the gate stones!" Halmarain cried out, staring at the strange little rock in her hand. "That's why Orander hasn't come back! He only has one stone!"

"Then why don't we open the portal and give him the other one," Trap asked. "When he gets back we can—"

"It doesn't work that way," Halmarain interrupted. She lowered her head over her reading, but the kender didn't understand that she was attempting to end the conversation.

"Doors are doors," the sometimes practical Ripple announced. "My brother can open all sorts of doors. He is very good, you're just not giving him a chance." She gazed at Trap. "Remember that door to Longdown Walkalong's house?"

"Sure, I got that open when even Uncle Skipout couldn't."

Halmarain clenched her tiny hands into fists as she forced down her impatience. "Look," she said. "I'll try to explain so even you can see the difficulty."

"To understand portals, you must think in terms of the multiverse. Think of an onion slice, the way the rings circle each other?"

"I like onions in a stew." Trap informed her.

"Planes circle each other like the rings of an onion," Halmarain continued, ignoring Trap's interruption. "There are many worlds on each plane, some are nice, some terrible. To reach them you must go through portals: doors created by magic."

"They're not ordinary doors?" Trap asked, disappointed.

"I've heard kender are good with locks, but you can't open a door that isn't there," the little wizard explained.

"Portals have to be *created*. We can't make one and neither can Orander. At least, I don't think we can. Let me study these books."

"No food," Grod suddenly complained.

"Leave here, find food," Umpth announced, getting to his feet and picking up the wagon wheel.

"You're not leaving here, not any of you." Halmarain glared at the dwarves. "You helped to make this mess and you'll stay and help settle it."

"Done swept," Grod argued, thinking he had done his share.

"That's not the mess I'm talking about," the wizard said. "Now I know what that monster is." She tapped the book in front of her and pointed to the corner of the room where Beglug slept. "It's an infant merchesti. Well, probably not an infant, but so young I doubt it can take care of itself."

"A *merchesti*?" Trap asked. "What is a merchesti? Can it make magic too?"

"It's a creature from the Plane of Vasmarg, and its evil. Apparently they have some innate magic, though this one is probably too young to take advantage of it. That's probably why it snarled at me," she said, her eyebrows rising in surprise. "It's sensitive to the power around it, and afraid."

"It doesn't seem evil," Ripple said.

"It is, but, according to Alchviem, the merchesti are normally not a problem to us, even if we opened a portal. Our world doesn't attract them, it's a bit too cold, he says."

"The wind that came through the portal was hot," Ripple said. "Do you remember the hot wind that blew—"

"And it was hot over there," Trap said, interrupting Ripple's story.

Halmarain ducked her head over the book again and read for a bit.

"Alchviem says here that he traveled on Vasmarg without trouble except for the time when he encountered a merchesti with a young one. Apparently they're vicious when protecting their young. As long as that thing"—she pointed to the corner again—"stays in our world, it's parent will be working to reach Krynn. Merchesti have been known to use portals, or so Alchviem writes."

"So will she open the portal and take her baby back?" Trap asked. He hoped the wizard would return soon. Perhaps he could persuade Orander to take the kender with him on his travels.

"That's what I'm trying to find out. In the meantime we need to keep the creature here, and *you* will look after it. I need to study, to see if there is any way I can protect us from it."

"If Orander can't open the portal with one stone, how can the merchesti do it?" Ripple said, her sharp little mind still alert to fallacy.

"They have been known to enter other planes by their own means," Halmarain said. "Not even Alchviem knew much about the merchesti."

"You said the mother wasn't dangerous, and she didn't hurt Trap," Ripple reminded Halmarain.

"No, I said it wasn't interested in Krynn. If it opened a portal, entered our world, and couldn't find its young, it could kill thousands in its search." She glared at the kender. "It didn't hurt your brother because it was too concerned with finding its offspring to bother with him. Merchesti are evil, they're from an evil world."

Grod, who had been walking around the room, stared at Halmarain with wide blue eyes. The gully dwarf turned to look at the little fiend, then back to gaze at the wizard, and then turned toward Beglug again.

"I don't see how you can be so sure of that," Trap argued. "Beglug doesn't look evil, and he hasn't done anything wrong. He's just little, and if he does things we don't like we can teach him to be good. Remember, Ripple, when little Ham Trotalong wanted to walk off the side of the bridge, his mother taught him not to?"

Ripple agreed with her brother. "And if the merchesti mother loves her baby enough to search for it, she couldn't be evil either."

"Caring for its young doesn't make it good," Halmarain retorted. "Every creature is born with a need to procreate. The need to protect the young usually varies with the number of offspring at one birth. A creature that lays hundreds, maybe thousands of eggs at one time may leave them to their fate, but those have few or single births actively protect their young.

"Protection has nothing to do with good and evil, it's an instinct," the little wizard continued. "That thing is evil. It doesn't seem harmful right now, but if it's in our world very long, you'll soon see for yourselves."

"What can we do?" Trap asked the little wizard.

"I don't know," Halmarain admitted. Her face twisted as if she might cry, but she pulled herself together. "I don't know what I can do, I'm just an apprentice. I don't know enough magic to open the portal, even if we had both stones."

"But you can read Orander's books," Ripple said, encouraging Halmarain.

"Sure, you're a wizard, even if you're just a little one," Trap agreed. "You'll think of something, and we'll help you, if you want us to, particularly if you show us some magic."

The tiny human drew herself up and took a deep breath. She formed her trembling lips into a firm line and narrowed her eyes, blinking away the tears on her lashes.

"I have to try," she said. "If I keep studying the books, I might find an answer. Just keep that beast quiet and let me see what I can learn."

"She's back to giving orders," Ripple said, her sympathy evaporating.

"And you promised us some magic," Trap reminded her.

"Got food?" Umpth asked.

"The kitchen is along the passage, to the right, up five steps," Halmarain told Ripple. "You fix it the meal. Don't let those stinking creatures near the larder or they'll be wearing pig's heads on their shoulders. And don't try to leave. Orander wove protective spells over all the other doors."

"If we try to go through the doors, what will the spells turn us into? It might be nice to be something different," Trap said.

"You'd be burned to a crisp," Halmarain said, then returned to her studies.

Trap decided that a crisp was not the most lively thing to be, since crisps didn't wander. He woke the little merchesti and led him down the passage, following Ripple and the gully dwarves. They walked along the passage beyond the door where they had entered the wizard's lair. At the end, a second narrow hall led into a large scullery.

A huge hearth filled the far wall. To the right, wide shelves held more than twenty large, overturned kettles of various sizes. More than half were too large for the kender to lift. In the center of the room four tables, twenty feet long and six wide, provided a work space for an army of cooks. The tables had been made for the comfort of standing human cooks and their surfaces were at eye level to the kender. Umpth and Grod, short for gully dwarves, were no better off.

Ten tall stools stood around each table as if the workers had just stepped out. Fifty pottery jars bearing the names of spices, sat in a rack across from shelves of pots. Through an arch they could see huge earthen storage vessels standing rank on rank.

A small fire burned in the big grate. The merchesti gave a gurgle of pleasure when he felt the heat and was soon curled up on one end of the hearth.

"What a big place!" Ripple looked around.

"Let's explore," Trap suggested. He followed Ripple into the larder where the torches lit by themselves as the two walked in. Most of the huge jars were empty, but in the smaller ones they found a good supply of staples. Before long Ripple had made a maize pudding while Trap sliced rashers of bacon and had them sizzling in a skillet.

Just as Trap was taking up the bacon, Halmarain entered the chamber. She was still reading one of the red-bound books. She sniffed from time to time as if following her nose.

"Have you found out how to open the portal to the other plane?" Trap asked. He was already bored with the underground caverns.

"I may be coming to the answer," she said. "Let me read this and I'll tell you."

She ordered the gully dwarves back to sit on stools and reached up over her head to put the book on the table. She climbed the rungs of a stool, perched on the seat and continued to read.

The two kender brought the food to the table in bowls and trenchers. They brought spoons for the pudding, but the gully dwarves grabbed the bowls and shoved the pudding into their mouths with their dirty fingers.

Disgusted by the Aghar's lack of table manners, Trap searched for a topic of conversation to help cover the slurping. As he glanced at the wizard, he thought of a question he had wanted to ask.

"You're a dwarf," Trap observed. "What kind? Are you a Neidar or Klar?" His uncle had told him dwarves were suspicious of any magic that wasn't innate to their race. He doubted she could be from one of the Hylar clans, since they usually stayed in their deep caverns in the mountains, though they were sometimes seen on the surface if they were on a mission of some importance.

"I'm not a dwarf," she answered, too absorbed in her reading to sound irritated. "I'm human, believe it or not."

"A full grown human shorter than us?" Ripple was astonished. Halmarain was stouter, but shorter than a twelve-year-old kender.

"Some humans don't grow very much. We're rare, perhaps one in a hundred thousand."

"Big cook place," Umpth spoke up.

"Wizards eat lot maybe," Grod suggested to his brother.

Halmarain ignored the gully dwarves, but Trap was also curious about the huge, well appointed kitchen.

"It's a wonderful place," he said. "Interesting. I liked exploring it. Does it have other rooms?" He was looking forward to exploring some of the large earthenware jars they had not had time to open.

"No, this is it. Before the cataclysm these chambers were the scullery, larder, and storage for the keep," Halmarain said, pointing toward the ceiling. The earthquakes collapsed the upper passages. The people in the keep must have thought all the underground caverns were destroyed. They never tried to dig them out."

Trap wanted to ask more questions, but the gully dwarves had emptied their bowls and were off their stools, heading for the hearth. Halmarain glanced up and threw the kender a hard, warning look. Trap hurried to head them off. He refilled their bowls and his own while he was at it. Ripple's maize pudding was delicious. It was famous in Hylo.

Halmarain continued to study as she finished her meal. She was just closing her book, ready to leave the table, when she noticed the expectant look in the kender's eyes.

"I'll do some magic for you, but afterward I'll expect you to clean the scullery and keep an eye on the merchesti and the dwarves."

Halmarain reached into the salt cellar and carefully counted out twelve grains. She scattered them on the table, waved her hands and spoke an incantation. Twelve grains enlarged, broke apart, and from each stepped a glowing little man. They appeared to be made of small blocks and those at the hips, knees, shoulders, and elbows appeared hinged as the little men began to dance around the top of the table.

The kender clapped their hands, the gully dwarves' grins nearly split their faces as they reached for the tiny cavorting figures, but their fingers passed through them and the little men kept dancing. They cavorted for nearly five minutes before disappearing.

"Now remember your promise in return," Halmarain warned and returned to the wizard's work room. The kender stayed behind to clean up the kitchen. The dwarves emptied the pot of maize pudding and Beglug ate two of the trenchers.

When the kitchen was clean, the dwarves sprawled out on the floor. Since the merchesti was shivering with cold, the kender built up the fire. He slept on the hearth and they wrapped themselves in their blankets and stretched out on the big kitchen tables.

The next day Halmarain studied her books. The kender were bored. They could not induce Halmarain to do any more magic for them, though she promised she would after she found the answers to her questions about the portal. Trap and Ripple explored their own pouches, showing each other their possessions. Somehow, Ripple had regained possession of the single gate stone. An hour later they did the same job again. Trap regained his possessions that had somehow found their way into Ripple's pouches and she took back hers.

Part of the morning passed pleasantly enough when in their third exploration of the underground caverns they found a chest pushed well back under Orander's bed.

It had not occurred to either kender that as well as a lock, a wizard might put a spell on his personal belongings. The lock was child's play for a kender, but the spell blew them across the room and singed Trap's eyebrows and the knees of his leggings. Luckily, he had been slightly to the side of the chest and escaped the worst affects of the fireball. Halmarain had closed the heavy door of the laboratory and had not heard the noise.

They spent another pleasant hour exclaiming over rings and vials and brooches. They examined small, carefully fastened pouches filled with powder, and two strange knives. They were fascinated by three golden rings. When they were finished with their explorations, Trap carefully re-locked the chest so no one could get into it and steal Orander's belongings. Neither noticed the chest was considerably emptier than it had been when they opened it, or that three rings, one of the knives, and several vials had not found their way back into the chest.

Later the same afternoon they rearranged their pouches again, this time trading back and forth, so they both had new items. Trap inspected a knife his sister gave him in return for one he had found in his belongings after they left the ship.

"This looks like one Orander has tucked away in his chest," he said, slipping it into his sheath.

"Yes, it does," she replied. "When he comes back through the portal, you should compare them. If his were magic, maybe yours is too. Gee, that would be interesting, having a magic knife."

The gully dwarves had spent the day making a new "This Place." They found an unused chamber with one collapsed wall and laid claim to it. Their first task had been to take one of the huge stone crocks from the larder and carefully chip down both sides until it fell neatly apart in two halves. Announcing they now had beds, they scavenged for anything useful to put in their new home.

By the end of the day the kender, the gully dwarves, and the little magician had finished most of the food in the larder. Beglug, who seemed to be able to chew and digest anything but had a partiality for wood, had eaten one of the tall stools and part of a table.

That evening, Ripple made another pot of her delicious maize pudding. Halmarain came to the kitchen to join them. She was still reading as she ate, but she sounded as if she were developing a stomach ache. She sighed, moaned, and groaned.

"It couldn't be the pudding," Ripple said, frowning at her brother.

"No, I've found the answer I was looking for," Halmarain said. "Not the answer I wanted—definitely not what I wanted. At least I know what we must do to get that thing back into its own world and rescue Orander . . . if he's still alive."

Chapter 7

"I thought you said the markesi—"

"Merchesti," Halmarain corrected Trap.

"I thought the mer*chesti* could open the portal," he finished.

"If Orander is still alive and had both stones, he could open it. If he's not still alive—and I'm afraid he's not—then it could take the fiend years to learn how to reach our world. This monster would be growing up on Krynn."—she pointed at Beglug who sat on the floor—"The longer it stays here, the larger and more dangerous it will become. If we can't send it home before long we'll have to kill it.".

"No!" Ripple objected. The merchesti was sitting at the foot of her stool. He occasionally leaned his head against her leg as if seeking the touch of another creature for reassurance.

"Stop saying that! He's not evil! You're just mean!" Trap argued. "He hasn't done anything but eat and sleep."

Across the table, Grod's eyes grew wide again.

"It will show its foul nature as it grows," the little wizard passed off the arguments as if they didn't exist. She paused and referred to the book. "But the portal won't open here. According to Alchviem, to open and then close a portal by the use of the gate stones thickens the fabric between planes. The thickening sounds as if it's something like scar tissue over a healed wound."

"I know what that is, I have a scar," Ripple pushed back her sleeve to show a blemish on her arm. "One day when Soso Stepup and I were—"

"I must find a wizard powerful enough to help Orander open the portal," Halmarain said, interrupting Ripple's story. "Maybe we can rescue Orander if he's still alive."

"And Beglug can go home," Trap said. "He doesn't seem to like wandering." The kender shook his head. "I'd think he would like to see new places, but he keeps moaning. Of course maybe he just has a belly ache from all that strange stuff he keeps eating. . . ."

Ripple frowned. "But if you have to go far to find a wizard, how do we know Beglug's mother will find him when we send him back?"

"I don't know," Halmarain snapped. "I don't know what else to do. Alchviem says no one can open the portal from here a second time, so we know staying here won't help."

"Who is Alchviem?" Trap asked. Halmarain had never explained him. "Is he a wizard? Will he do magic for us?"

"He was a wizard who lived a thousand years before the Cataclysm," Halmarain said with a patience they had not yet experienced from her. "He took the red robes, and devoted his life to learning about the portals. He learned more about traveling the planes than anyone has before or since. Orander found his writings and discovered how to obtain the gate stones. When I tell you anything I read in these books,"—she tapped the one she held—"you can be certain there is no better information on Krynn."

"Information? That means learning new things. I like information," Trap said, thinking magic facts might be both interesting and good to know.

Beglug had been wandering around the kitchen, his head down as he inspected the floor, possibly looking for more glass shards. He bumped into Halmarain's stool and jumped back, snarling, claws bristling as he eyed the little wizard.

"Get him away from me," Halmarain cried and made shooing motions at the merchesti.

"I'll get him," Ripple said. She jumped down and took the little fiend by the arm. He was willing enough to sit on the floor by her stool. "He was just scared, he didn't attack you or anything."

"Read us some out of that book," Trap suggested.

"This isn't a story book," the wizard said, slapping it closed with her two small hands.

"And you didn't make much of a story about Alchviem," Ripple observed as she shifted on her stool. "I don't like it here anymore and I want to leave." Her lowered brows were storm warning signs, though the little wizard didn't know it.

"I don't think you understood what I said," Halmarain frowned at the kender.

"Of course we know what you said," Trap was quick to come to the defense of his sister. "Opening the portal made a scar. Remember the scar on Marchon Bolo's hand, Ripple?"

"How did he get that?" Ripple asked. "I forgot."

"Trying to open a chest that belonged to—"

"Forget Marchon Bolo!" Halmarain ordered. "We have a problem. We must take the little fiend to a wizard powerful enough to—"

"—Bagbus Jumpdown!" Trap triumphantly finished his sentence.

"You're not listening to me!" Halmarain shouted in anger.

Her habitual irritation suddenly made Ripple angry.

"Wizard's gizzard, loud and yelling," she snapped.

Trap grinned at his sister. He knew the game.

"Cannot listen, always telling," he added

"Stomps and shouts and gives orders," Ripple continued while Halmarain glared, her flush of anger deepening.

"Makes big noise too," Grod added, inexpertly capping without a rhyme.

Both kender laughed and Grod joined in with clapping hands, then Trap gazed at Halmarain.

"We did hear you," he said.

"You want to take Beglug to another wizard who might open a portal and send him home," Ripple said. "I think sending him back is a good idea if he doesn't like to wander, though I don't understand why he wouldn't like to see new places, but then I remember hearing of a kender who didn't like to wander either, still, I think Trap might be right and he might have a belly ache, but it seems to me that if you can open and read the books, you should be able to take the stone and open the portal and then—"

"Isn't a portal like a door?" Trap asked, interrupting his sister with a new idea. "I can open doors, all sorts of doors, even when they're locked like the one out in the passage—"

"Stop all this chatter!" Halmarain demanded. "I need the help of a master wizard. Salrandin, who lives just south of Palanthus would be the best, I think. But master wizards don't just come when summoned, so I must take the merchesti and the gate stone to him. We either do this or we kill the little fiend before he becomes large enough to be a danger."

"You can't do that!" Ripple bristled. "He hasn't done anything!"

"And I have to take Alchviem's books and open them for the other wizard." The little wizard stared at the kender who still appeared to be unconvinced. She sighed and explained. "As wizard's go, I'm not exactly on the top rung of the ladder. I'm just learning my art. The first spell I learned was one of reading magic, but that only allows me to read it. I can't use the more powerful spells . . . not yet."

"You can make more salt men," Trap suggested hopefully.

Halmarain continued as if he had not spoken. "I know the command to open the books; I can read them, but it would take a wizard with far more power to use what I can read. If and when we find one, even he may not have the knowledge of Alchviem, so we need to take the books with us."

"You've stopped saying 'I' and you've started saying 'we,' " Ripple pointed out. "Are you inviting us to come with you?"

"I've just realized I can't do it alone," Halmarain said with a sigh. "It will even be dangerous to take that monster through the city. There's nothing like the merchesti on Krynn. Some idiot will realize it's an abomination and try to kill it. People often try to destroy what they don't understand."

"You could disguise him," Ripple said.

"That's a good idea," Halmarain said, nodding, thinking out loud. "We'll do that, but the journey will still be too hard and too long. I don't want to try to make it alone. The easiest way to reach Palanthus would be to travel west to Gwyntaar and take a ship from there . . . but the crew would soon see through Beglug's disguise. We'll need to travel overland, by horseback, ponies, I think."

"I love riding," Trap announced.

"I hope so," Halmarain said. "I can't saddle a pony, and even if I could, I could never get that monster onto a saddle. That's why you must go with me."

"We stay," Umpth announced. "New This Place now."

"Plenty good food." Grod added. "All stay This Place." The kender now understood that the gully dwarf was using his race's term for home. "Last This Place knocked flat."

"You're right. This would make a good place to live," Ripple said brightly. "That is, if you want to stay here, but think of all the things you'll miss seeing, and now that I think of it you can't stay here, because you couldn't get out to get more food, and I don't think starving would be interesting at all, but maybe Beglug could teach you how to eat wood and rocks . . . wonder how they taste?"

The gully dwarves traded speculating glances, scratched different parts of their bodies, and appeared to come to some sort of agreement.

"We go with them," Umpth told Grod.

"Find new This Place." Grod agreed

"I won't travel with gully dwarves," Halmarain snapped.

"Gee, I don't see why not," Trap said, staring across at Umpth and Grod. "I think they're nice, and they did help clean up the laboratory, and even if they do eat a lot—"

"You're just being mean. You know you like them, or you wouldn't have asked—did you ask them to help clean up after Orander fell through the portal? I forgot. Anyway, since we promised to help find them a new home after their old one was knocked down, we have to stay with them."

"You must go with me. I need you to take care of the merchesti. Even if I could watch him day and night, that monster doesn't like me. And I need you to look after it while I study my spells." She met Trap's eyes in the manner of a person squarely meeting an unpleasant subject. "I can't make the journey and look after it alone, so if you don't go with me I'll have to kill it before I leave."

"No!" Trap was outraged.

"If its dead, I can travel with a caravan, the way I did when I came south."

"Oh, Trap, we'll have to go or she'll kill Beglug!" Ripple cried.

"We'll go with you, if you promise not to hurt Beglug," Trap said. "Actually, we'd like to see Palanthus. Would we see other interesting places?"

"We'll stay away from cities," the wizard said. "We'll stay away from as many people as we can."

"Thorns and thistles, that sounds boring," Trap announced.

Halmarain took a deep breath, puffing herself up like a frog. Then her look turned cagey. She folded her little hands and stared up at the ceiling.

"Then I suppose you don't want any magic."

"Magic?" Ripple was instantly diverted.

"Aglest clan got magic," Umpth announced, but neither the kender nor the wizard paid any attention to him.

"If you help me get Orander back from the other plane, he will reward you with all sorts of magic," Halmarain replied.

"What kind of magic?" Trap asked. "Will he teach us spells?"

"No, you wouldn't like that," Halmarain said. "You'd have to study magic and you'd find that boring. He might take something . . . like he took my staff and put magic into it."

"Show us! What will it do besides make light?" Ripple asked.

"Well, I don't like to clean the scullery," Halmarain said. "And it takes too much time, so Orander gave the staff some special magic that I haven't learned." She spoke a word of command. In an instant the cups, spoons, trenchers and pots were clean and they lifted off the table, sailing to their appropriate storage areas. With a clatter and clang, the pots hung themselves back on their hooks, the trenchers stacked themselves on the shelves and the spoons dipped, handles down, to stand in a crockery pot.

"Wow! Big jiggies!" Ripple jumped up from her stool and ran over to look at the clean pots. "If I make more pudding will you do that again?"

"Orander will think up something far more interesting for you if you help to return him to Krynn," the little wizard said as Ripple returned to her stool. She sat staring at Halmarain with sparkling eyes.

"Then I'll go," Trap said. "I want a—"

Ripple gave a yelp and threw herself halfway across the table as her stool collapsed. Beneath her swinging feet, Beglug chewed on one leg of her stool.

"Kender want," Grod prompted, reminding Trap he

was about to make a request.

"I forget," Trap said, sliding off the stool to assist his sister. He took the remains of her former seat and used it to coax Beglug to the hearth. Then he pushed another stool under his sister.

"We'll have to disguise the merchesti," Halmarain said. "If we're going to send it home, we don't want it to attract too much interest here on Krynn."

"We won't let anyone kill him," Trap assured her.

"Maybe he'll catch the eye of someone who wouldn't want to kill him," Halmarain suggested slyly. "They might want to steal him, put a chain around his neck and pull him from town to town. Somebody could make a lot of money by exhibiting him to the curious."

"That would be cruel," Trap was shocked at the idea.

"If we're not careful, he will attract attention," the little wizard repeated her warning.

"So will a wizard," Ripple said with a grin.

"If the citizens learn I'm a wizard I'll be in more danger than the fiend," Halmarain said. "And my size—well— some consider me a freak." Her eyes darkened over some memory. "Children like to throw stones at what they don't understand. . . ." Her voice trailed off in sadness.

"But that's not fair," Trap said. "We'd never throw anything at you, we like you, except when you're mad, but I don't think—"

"I know, we can all go as animals," Ripple announced.

"Wow! Great! I want to be a bird," Trap said, falling in with his sister's idea. "Halmarain can put a spell on me so I can fly. That would be fun."

"We could *all* fly," Ripple agreed. She held out her arms and flapped them. The gully dwarves looked doubtful, but they mimicked the female kender.

"No, I can't do flying spells," Halmarain said.

The kenders' hopes were dashed for only a moment before Trap's natural enthusiasm rose again.

"I know! We could be horses!"

"Then we could travel very fast," Ripple urged. "Could you make us horses?"

"No, and I can't make you wolves either, so don't suggest it. We use clothing, I suppose. Dwarves. Beglug and I are a little small, but we might pass as Neidar."

"We could all be dwarves," Trap said. "Umpth and Grod are going with us. We could be gully dwarves."

Halmarain stared at the kender as if they had lost their minds. "I won't do it," she announced. "Nothing would make me pretend to be a gully dwarf!"

Trap glanced uneasily at Umpth and Grod, but they had filled their stomachs and pushed their dishes aside. They sat, elbows on the table, chins propped in the palms of their hands. They were watching the kender and the wizard with an air of impersonal interest as if they had no idea they were the subjects under discussion. They turned their heads to speak to each other and proved they had heard every word.

"Maybe clan grow," Umpth said. "Beglug make good Aghar."

"More good than wizard," Grod agreed. "She too short."

"Got no clan magic," Umpth added. "Not much use."

"Kender got no clan magic," Grod said. "Much trouble. Only Aghar have good magic."

"Thank you very much, but I can handle myself," Halmarain bristled. "And I don't appreciate being talked about as if I wasn't here. It would be bad enough to pretend to be a Neidar, but an Aghar, no." Halmarain shook her head.

"Yes, you can do that," Ripple said. "That would be fun. You pretend to be Neidar . . . you, Beglug, Umpth and Grod. What could we be?" She gazed questioningly at her brother.

"Eagles? Unicorns?" he asked hopefully. He sighed as Halmarain shook her head. "How can the gulleys be Neidar?" he asked. "How will you keep them clean?"

"Not even my magic could handle that," Halmarain scoffed. "I'll need all my art to handle that thing." she pointed at Beglug.

"Wizard like no's," Umpth observed to his brother.

"Have no yes's," Grod agreed.

"I can say yes as quickly as any other if someone suggests a workable solution," Halmarain snapped. "I refuse to look like a fool or a gully dwarf."

"I won't go if you won't stop being mean!" Ripple crossed her arms and pursed her mouth as she stared at the little wizard with tightened lips.

"See a fight," Umpth told Grod, wriggling in anticipation.

"Females fight good," Grod nodded.

"There will be no fight," Halmarain said with a sigh. "You're right, Ripple, I'm letting my concern for Orander override good sense. I'll do whatever it takes to get my master back through the portal. I really don't think I can travel as a gully dwarf, but if we can disguise them as Neidar, I'll try it. They'll need new clothing, and they'll have to bathe."

The decision made, they settled to planning the journey to Palanthus. Once the tiny wizard had decided to cooperate, she started to work. By a water clock in the passage, they knew the evening was well advanced. The shops would be closed, so they set to work doing what they could.

Halmarain decreed the Aghar had to be bathed and scrubbed until years of grime had been removed. Along with the gully dwarves and kender, she struggled with pails of water and armloads of wood as they filled a caldron and heated it. The gully dwarves became increasingly uneasy as the water heated, fearing the wizard would put them in the boiling caldron. They were only a little relieved when the water reached a temperature a bit beyond the best degree for soaking off the dirt and Trap raked away the fire. When the bottom was cool enough not to burn their feet and bottoms, Halmarain gave them a choice: they could climb in and bathe or she would turn them into frogs and throw them in.

"Frogs must wash?" Umpth said, considering the second option.

"Frogs stay in water," Grod said with a shudder and

then turned his attention on the wizard. "Can no make fly, can no make horses. How make frogs?"

Umpth was sitting on the floor. He had removed one boot but he stopped and gazed at his brother as if he doubted such profound logic could come out of Grod. Umpth slowly nodded and put his boot on again.

"I can't make six people into horses but I can turn two gully dwarves into something, and that will be you, and you will be frogs. Now get in that tub!"

Umpth nodded and stripped off his clothing. Ripple and Halmarain turned their backs until the dwarves were in the caldron. Then, to the surprise and delight of the kender, Halmarain touched the dwarves' filthy, ragged clothing with her staff and spoke a word of command. In an instant the garments were clean, the original color restored and all the tears mended. The spell only restored the clothing, it did nothing for the length of the sleeves and the trousers that had been made for humans.

"Oh! Hey! That's good magic!" Ripple clapped her hands.

"I took care of their clothes, you take care of them," the little wizard said. She left Trap to scrub the gully dwarves while she and Ripple returned to Orander's work room.

Trap decided he had the worst of the deal as he tried to keep the gully dwarves sitting in the large caldron of hot water. He argued them into rubbing soap in their hair and beards. He used a brush to scrub at their necks and backs. He insisted they clean the rest of their bodies. They knew nothing about closing their eyes to keep the soap out. Their howls echoed through the scullery and down the passage.

Drawn by the excitement, Beglug came over to watch the splashing. The little fiend thought the bath looked like fun and he hopped into the caldron too. At first he contented himself with trying to bite the bubbles. Then he ate the soap.

"Drink all water too," Umpth encouraged Beglug.

Fortunately, the gully dwarves were as clean as they would get with one soaking. To remove all the embedded grime would take daily soaks for weeks. Still, one cleansing had made a tremendous difference. Umpth did have brown hair that flowed into a brown beard. They matched in a depth of color that was almost black. After a thorough cleaning, his cheeks, nose, and part of his forehead was pink, but the grime in his wrinkles gave the appearance of dark lines drawn on his face.

Grod, without wrinkles, had a reddish complexion that almost blended with a reddish blond beard and hair. His eyes were a startling bright blue.

While the gully dwarves and Beglug slept, Trap, Ripple, and Halmarain talked over their plans again and added details. They had decided the shopping trip to outfit the expedition would be made by Halmarain, who could negate the spells on the doors; with her would go Trap and Grod. One of the gully dwarves had to go to be sure the clothing and dwarf armor fitted. Halmarain fashioned herself a tunic and skirt that would allow her to pass as a dwarf.

"It will work," Ripple said and with a sudden leap, did a back flip.

Early the next morning, the three shoppers walked the long, confusing route through secret underground passages that Orander had cleared for his own use. They came out on a street nearly half a mile west of Market Square. Since Halmarain had spent most of her time far below the city, she knew little about Lytburg. Grod had to be forcibly pushed past trash heaps in the ally before he was convinced to lead them to a narrow, noisy, but clean street that served as the dwarven section of town. Their first purchases were clothing, two sets for Halmarain and Beglug, and an extra for each of the gully dwarves.

To explain their numerous purchases, they told a tale of having been robbed of everything but the clothing they wore and a hidden purse. The story seemed to allay the suspicions of the shop keepers who were glad to make large sales. At the boot makers, Halmarain purchased new boots for the Aghar, a pair for Beglug, and attempted to find something that would fit her small feet. She had to settle for the smallest pair and stuff them with rags.

Dwarves never traveled without weapons and armor so they visited another shop. Trap lost count of the steel pieces they were spending. He was doling out the money because, for some reason he could not explain, he always seemed to have Orander's purse. Halmarain finally told him to keep it. At least she would know where it was.

Under the little wizard's suspicious scrutiny, he had been systematically emptying the bag, but though it was nearly flat when he returned it to his pouch in the second shop, when he took it out to pay for their third bundle of purchases, it was heavy with steel pieces again. He decided it was a magic bag, refilling itself automatically.

When they left the armorer's shop, Grod and Halmarain were dressed in chain mail under dwarven tunics and wore metal helms. Halmarain clumped along in her heavy boots as if she were slogging through thick mud. She could no longer help to carry their purchases since she could barely walk in her armor. All this seemed to add to her bad mood.

Their weapons—axes—would be useless in the hands of the wizard and the Aghar, but they were needed to complete the disguises. Trap struggled under the weight of a heavy canvas bag that held armor and weapons for Beglug and Umpth. Grod was loaded down with bedrolls, clothing, and boots.

They left the purchase of food and other traveling needs for later, since they had so much to carry. Before they returned to the underground caverns, Halmarain wanted to visit an inn, one where adventurers and travelers gathered when they first entered Lytburg.

"And you two, behave," she warned. "You sit with your mouth shut while you're eating, Grod. And Trap, keep your hands to yourself and listen. We want to hear any news about roads, traveling conditions, goblins, ogres, or any other humanoids on the move."

Trap and Grod were agreeable. Grod was hungry and the kender loved to hear any sort of story, no matter if it was only a few words about the travel of goblins. The gully dwarves were familiar with the shops and inns, though they knew them from their trash heaps. Grod led them to an establishment where, he insisted, adventurers and mercenaries often gathered. In addition, judging by the tastiness of what they threw out, Grod said their food was good.

They entered the inn, the Leaping Hart, and took seats at a small table in the corner. A hearth at the rear boasted a roaring fire with a pig roasting over the flames. The day had turned warm, so the inn was stifling. It did not seem to bother the more than twenty rangy, hard-eyed drinkers who were swilling ale and passing stories. Most had weapons and helmets lying beside them. Some had removed pieces of armor and their chain mail.

Halmarain had instructed Trap to order enough food and ale to keep Grod quiet and had told him to watch the gully dwarf's table manners while she listened.

Halmarain suggested they order rib meat, chicken, and rolls for the gully dwarf. Everyone ate bony meat and bread with their fingers, so Grod's lack of manners would not be too noticeable. Trap kept ordering food and ale, cautioning the dwarf to be as quiet as possible while he ate. Halmarain sat a little apart from them, her eyes on her mug as she listened in on the conversations at the other tables. Trap could hear practically nothing over Grod's slurping and smacking.

Bored, the kender fingered the table, his mug and the seat, the only items available for handling. He finally became interested in tracing the raised grain on the well scrubbed table. He forgot to keep his hat on in order to hide his ears and top knot. He took it off to fan himself. He was soon noticed by a tall, rangy human who frowned and pointed at Trap.

"Hey, innkeeper, I didn't think you allowed kender in here!"

Every eye turned toward Trap. The innkeeper had served them twice with food and three times with ale. He knew Trap had paid promptly, but he slammed his tray of empty mugs on a table and glared at the three in the corner.

"Out, you! I'll have no kender stealing from my patrons."

"He is not stealing," Halmarain spoke up, dropping her highly pitched voice in an attempt to sound like a dwarf. "And he paid you in full! He travels with us, and we'll vouch for him."

"And who will vouch for you?" The innkeeper demanded. "If you travel with a kender—"

"Wait," a burly man on the other side of the room interrupted, rising to glare at the three in the corner. "Ask him his name."

"Trapspringer Fargo," Trap said clearly and at once. "I'm very glad to meet—"

"Wasn't that the name of that outlaw kender traveling with Alchar Groomb's band?" someone yelled. "Trapspringer, or something like that?" Several others nodded.

"It's a common name among kender," Halmarain spoke up quickly. "Half the kender in Hylo are named Trapspringer."

Trap turned toward her, already shaking his head. She must have misunderstood the name. As far as he knew he was the only Trapspringer in Hylo. Before he could object, movement among the patrons caught his attention.

They rose from their seats and started forward, their hunger for revenge clear in their eyes.

Chapter 8

Trap gazed at the angry faces of the inn's patrons. Three humans had risen from their seats and seemed ready to charge the kender's table. Trap tried to decide how he was going to save his skin. He had never found hard blows to his person to be entertaining. At Halmarain's insistence, he had left his hoopak in the cavern so carrying it would not make him instantly recognizable as a kender. His only weapons were the small knife in the sheath at his belt, not much use against a number of swords and war axes. His tongue had stuck to the roof of his mouth, leaving him no opportunity to explain.

Grod, who had been sitting as still as a mouse, suddenly stood up and pulled off his new helmet. He bowed his head as he spoke.

"That Trapspringer dead," he announced to the room at large. "A good tale, that."

"Dead?" the first adventurer repeated. He sounded as disappointed as suspicious. So did the others, but they paused, waiting to hear the explanation.

"Yes, he's dead," Halmarain agreed with a sigh. Under her lashes she gazed at the kender and when he didn't instantly agree, she kicked him under the table.

"Dead," Trap said, trying to look sad. He thought of Uncle Goalong, a favorite relative that had recently died. Thinking of Goalong always made Trap sad and in seconds tears ringed his eyelashes; two rolled slowly down his cheeks.

"A friend of yours, was he?" asked a short, heavily muscled man at the closest table when he saw the kender's tears. Along with their reputation for purloining, kender were also known for their loyalty to their companions. They grieved deeply at a friend's death.

Trap gulped back a sob. "My uncle," he said. He had been thinking of his Uncle Goalong.

"If we can't kill him ourselves, at least let's hear how he died," demanded the burly man with the red beard. He glared threateningly at Trap. The kender twisted on his seat, his mind racing to make up a story.

"His full name was Trapspringer Quickhands," Trap said. "He was my mother's brother and the third son of Rogo Quickhands. Did you ever meet Rogo when he was wandering? I think he came by here, though he may not, but he did seem to go everywhere, even down to Solace and south from there to Zeriak where I want to go to see the Icewall Glacier. Have you ever seen a glacier? I hear they're really big and—"

"Get on with the tale of this Trapspringer!" the first adventurer demanded.

"Oh. Sure. It's just hard for me to tell it. The shame, you see." The word shame had brought with it a strong emotion and he gulped a sob. "Our village banished him for his misdeeds and I had not seen him for a long time when I met him on the road a few weeks ago."

The kender hoped the customers of the Leaping Hart were not too familiar with the customs of his race. As far as he knew, no village in Hylo had ever banished anyone. He had picked up the idea from a scrap of conversation he had heard while they were shopping.

"I had not thought he would take *my* purse!" Trap had always been able to throw himself emotionally into his tales and the thought of a kender deliberately stealing from another of his race caused his eyes to flash with anger.

"Robbed his own nephew?" the burly man shook his head. "No honor among thieves today," he added, shaking his head. "Let's hear this tale of how he died."

Kender loved tales, they enjoyed telling them as much, if not more, than listening. They never repeated a story exactly like it happened or as they had heard it. Their agile imagination improved on it, giving it more drama, suspense, or humor. Only a small step separated embellishment from pure invention. Trap decided to base his story on his own recent adventure with the portal.

"Well, now . . . this is hard. We *think* my Uncle Trapspringer is dead, because we don't think he could have lived through his trouble with the wizard. . . ." he began. He paused while the listeners took in the fact that a magic user was involved. Since the cataclysm, wizards were in disrepute throughout Krynn. His listeners would believe anything of them.

Trap wove a tale of the outlaw kender stopping a wizard who was traveling toward Lytburg. Wizards did not use weapons because they were usually too busy studying their craft to practice the art of warfare and this wizard had been caught unaware. For a time he had been at the mercy of the kender's weapons. By the use of guile he had prevented the other Trapspringer from spearing him out of hand.

"And that was my Uncle Trapspringer's mistake," the real Trap said as he looked around the room, allowing the tension to build. That's when he noticed Grod had left his seat and was slipping food off the plate of a fully armed mercenary who was giving his attention to the story. Halmarain had slipped away from her place also, and was bearing down on the gully dwarf. The kender left the tiny human to deal with the Aghar and went on with his tale.

"The wizard threw off his brown traveling cloak, revealing himself in his red robes. This startled my uncle, as you can imagine." He gazed at the burly adventurer. "Have you ever seen a wizard wearing red robes? It's an awful color of red, you know." This last he said with a sly look at the little wizard.

"Just tell us what happened next."

"But wizards are interesting," Trap objected. Halmarain threw him a hard look and he went on with his tale.

"Go on with your story," she hissed.

"Before my uncle could do more than step back," he continued, "the wizard raised his hands and sketched a door, muttering his foul incantations. A black hole appeared in the sunlight of the road, from it sprang a wind, carrying such a stench of rot and decay, that the air turned green and viscous. . . ." As he made up his tale, Trap was suddenly visited with the idea that his aborted journey to another plane had not been nearly as fascinating as his story. He felt a bit cheated as he continued to allow his quick thoughts to add intriguing details.

"And then a black, scaled arm, so large it filled the doorway, reached out and grabbed Uncle Trapspringer."—the kender let the tears trickle down his cheeks—"And if he is still alive, he is in that terrible place.

"We really think he's dead," he added softly.

Most of the adventurers nodded solemnly, but the innkeeper loudly scoffed. A city dweller, he had never believed half the tales of the mercenaries and wanderers who came to Lytburg.

"And how do you know this happened?"

"The—uh—half-goblin in the outlaw band told me of it," Trap added hastily. "He had been with my uncle, but you know his kind," he nodded wisely to the short, burly human who had seen his tears. "They're bullies, but they won't face any real danger."

He allowed the adventurers' dislike of the humanoids to carry the weight of his pronouncement.

"No, they never do," said a red bearded man with a scar. He turned back to his ale, looked in his mug and found it empty. He called to the innkeeper. Neither knew Grod had finished off the contents of several cups while the customers had been listening to the kender's tale.

"When did all this happen?" a shout from across the room left Trap unsure of the speaker.

"I—uh-don't know for sure," he said. He didn't want to ruin his story by saying the outlaw had died two days before he was known to have robbed one of the patrons of the inn. "I heard the story just last night. The half-goblin had the tale so garbled—you know what they're like when you want a straight answer. He was still scared, so I think it must have been recently. Do you know that half-goblin? He has a wart on his nose, just like him." Trap pointed at the innkeeper who, since he didn't like kender anyway, took instant offense.

"You've told your tale, now get out of my inn," the landlord ordered. "I'll have no outlaws or even their relatives in here."

"Let's leave," Halmarain whispered in his ear. "You've made a good tale of it, let's get out before they realize Grod has eaten everything in sight."

They left the inn, sauntered down the street until they were sure they were out of sight of any customers watching them and ducked into an alley. Grod led them, supposedly toward the ruined building that would take them back to the underground passages. Before long, Trap could not recognize a single street.

"I don't remember this street. I would. It's interesting. Where are you taking us?" the kender asked.

"This way. Good trash this way," Grod said without pausing.

"You're not rummaging through any trash dumps," Halmarain told him. "Take us back to the passages. Take us straight there."

Their path took them through the dwarven section of the city, and as they rounded a corner Trap bumped into a dwarf.

"Excuse me," he said politely. He was always ready to admit any small, accidental faux pas.

The dwarf glanced at the kender, looked again and stopped dead, blocking his path. "You were with that other thief!" he shouted at Trap.

Recognizing the jeweler who had accused Ripple of stealing, Trap's anger flared.

"That's a lie, she's no thief!"

Lacking any other weapon, Trap swung his heavy sack full of armor and weapons. The bag caught the dwarf on the chin. Dwarves were doughty fighters and hard to overcome, but being hit with a sack of armor and weapons knocked the jeweler senseless.

"Drag him farther back around the corner," Halmarain ordered Grod, looking anxiously toward the street.

"Here! Stand here and block the alley. We don't want anyone to see Grod dragging him away," the kender said. "Let's put our bags down and lean over them."

"We'll look as if we're redistributing the loads in the sacks." Halmarain agreed with the kender's idea.

They spread themselves as well as they could to shield the gully dwarf's activities.

"That's all I need, kender thieves," Halmarain grumbled.

"Stop that. Ripple didn't steal," Trap snapped. He had already told the tale of the jeweler's tilting display and Ripple's attempt to return the jewelry to the dwarf.

"What's keeping Grod?" Halmarain complained when she tired of poking in the bundles. The gully dwarf had been out of sight for several minutes.

"Here he comes," Trap said as he stood upright and stretched to ease his muscles. He was also tired of bending over the sacks. Before long they reached the underground caverns again. Ripple, Umpth, and Beglug waited in the wizard's work room. The young fiend was curled up in the corner, asleep. Most of the debris in the room had disappeared and Beglug belched between snores.

"By all the gods of Krynn," Halmarain fumed as she glared at the sleeping merchesti. "We forgot the one thing we must have to disguise Beglug."

"Him need beard," Grod said, reaching inside his tunic. He pulled out a mass of black hair, streaked with gray. As the gully dwarf spread it out on the table, Trap recognized it. It was the magnificent beard of the dwarf jeweler.

"You cut it off?" Trap could hardly believe it. "Wow. That was smart." He wished he had thought of it.

"Dwarf grow more," Grod said with a lack of concern that was pure gully dwarf.

"Beglug not grow beard," Umpth said, stroking his own dark facial hair as he nodded approval of his brother's idea.

"I just hope we don't run into that dwarf again," Halmarain said as she sorted their purchases.

"It's from the dwarf that called me a thief?" Ripple was delighted with the beard. "But he won't know us again." She was full of plans for a different kind of hat and had washed their travel clothing so they would not be recognized.

"But on the road, you'll both be kender, for everyone to see," Halmarain said as if she had read Trap's thoughts. "No one will bother us, they'll be too afraid of getting their pockets picked. And speaking of pockets and purses, where's mine?" she held out her hand to Trap.

"You told me to keep it for you," he reminded her as he handed it over. She hefted it and glared at the kender. "It's heavier than when we left," she said. "Did you pay for anything?"

"I paid for everything! You saw me!" Trap objected. "The purse filled up every time I took out a handful of steel pieces. I thought it must be magic."

Halmarain stared at the small leather bag. "Maybe it is," she said slowly. "It's Orander's. I didn't know there was a spell for making steel pieces, but Orander was—*is* one of the best of our order." She handed it back to Trap. "Keep it for now. Before I can blink twice, you'll have it back again."

While Ripple and Halmarain worked on Beglug's beard, the two gully dwarves helped Trap dress the young fiend. He had been born to a hot plane he had spent much of his time shivering when he was away from the hearth so he liked the warmth his clothing provided. He liked his hauberk too, and was attempting to take a bite out of it when Trap slapped his hand.

"No, Beglug."

"No Beglug," the young fiend said, smoothing the intricate steel links. One problem solved, they soon discovered they had another. How were they going to keep the fiend's small, hoofed feet in the dwarf boots?

"Could nail board on hooves," Umpth suggested.

"Could nail boots on hooves." Grod was for cutting out the extra work.

"We won't nail anything," Trap announced, but his eyes lit up. "It might be worth trying just to see his reaction—what do you think he'd do if we—"

"I don't think so," Halmarain replied quickly. "We want it to trust us enough to stay with us . . . ."

"Maybe he'd like you a lot better if you'd stop calling him 'it,' " Ripple snapped.

Halmarain glared and the kender girl, then shrugged and sighed.

"We want it—*him* to trust us until we can get him back to his world again. That's the only hope I have of finding Orander."

They spent a long afternoon seeking a satisfactory method of fitting dwarf boots to Beglug. He seem to enjoy the attention and was fascinated by the footwear. He lost interest when he learned the boots were "No, Beglug" too.

When the gully dwarves and Trap had taught Beglug to walk in his new footwear, Halmarain approached with a jar and handed it to Trap. He seemed to be the most acceptable to the young merchesti.

"Rub this on his face and hands," the wizard said.

Trap covered the merchesti's face with a flesh colored paste and then attached the beard and mustache the females had made. When Beglug was wearing his helmet, they decided he would pass as the ugliest dwarf on Krynn.

As if he knew something interesting was afoot, Beglug became curious about the preparations, so curious he approached Halmarain several times. He had stayed well away from the little wizard, but apparently he was beginning to lose his fear of her.

Since everyone was ready they shouldered their packs, picked up their weapons, and Halmarain extinguished the torches as they left the caverns.

She stopped by the scullery and spoke a word of command as she waved her staff around the room. The pots, trenchers and tabletops were instantly clean, the floor swept itself, and the stools flung themselves back into their places.

On their way through Lytburg they bought food for their journey. When they left the shops, every pack bulged with supplies. They carried bedrolls and ground sheets strapped to the top of their backpacks and reached the city gate in time to mingle with the local farmers and residents of the surrounding countryside who would be leaving the city, trying to reach home before dark.

Trouble developed when they reached the east gate. A group of farmers were arguing with one of the guards and the disagreement digressed into a pushing and shoving match before an officer arrived. He ordered the guards back to their posts and told the farmers to get on their way.

The entire gate was blocked by the fracas, and a queue had developed, waiting to leave the city. The officer watched the exiting flow for a few minutes. Ripple kept a close eye on Umpth and Grod. The Aghar were hard pressed to keep their wagon wheel rolling in the press, but all three passed through the gate while the officer watched the crowd and the guards.

When their superior left, the soldiers chose to take out their bad temper on what they took for two dwarves, one too young for a beard. Trap, just to the side, went unnoticed.

"Who are you and what business did you have in Lytburg?" one of the guards demanded of Beglug.

"Just dwarves seeking to buy precious stones," Halmarain answered for him, but the guard was not satisfied. When the little fiend didn't answer, the guard shoved the point of his spear at Beglug's face.

Beglug leaned forward, bit the steel spearhead off the shaft, and noisily chewed.

Chapter 9

The guard stared at his ruined spear. Trap also goggled at the splintered end of the wooden shaft and at Beglug, who happily chewed the metal point. The kender's sense of survival kicked in quicker than the guard's outrage.

Trap grabbed the little merchesti's arm and pulled him forward into the surge of humans pushing through the gate. Behind him, the kender heard the guard bawling to his companions. Trap, Halmarain, and Beglug melted into the crowd that crossed the bridge.

"I hope we don't have too much of that," Halmarain said between gasping breaths as she trotted after the kender.

"Gosh, did you see? He bit the spear in two." Trap said, skipping along to keep pace with the taller humans that surrounded them. "Traveling with Beglug will be really interesting. I wish we could have stayed to hear the guard explain what happened to his spear."

"I don't," the little mage replied. "Let's get ourselves lost—fast."

They slowed their pace when the crowd thinned out on the other side of the bridge. Trap pushed Halmarain and Beglug into a line of farmer's carts. They walked carefully at the rear of an apple cart, trying hard to stay out from under the hooves of the mules that followed.

"You're going to get us trampled," Halmarain said, ducking her head as the right lead mule nudged the top of her dwarven helmet.

"You said you didn't want the guards at the gate to catch sight of us," Trap said. "Besides, mules are friendly." He reached in his pouch and pulled out an apple that had somehow fallen into it while they were shopping. He fed it to the left leader, which caused it's teammate to nudge more urgently at the little wizard, nearly knocking her off her feet.

The merchesti allowed himself to be bustled along without complaint. He was still happily chewing on the spear point, which had been a large one.

"You know, Beglug's digestive system must be a lava pit," Trap said. "He eats the strangest things. We should try him on rocks."

"He's nightmarish," the small wizard snapped. "And by all the gods, look at his boots. The left had turned sideways, toe out, and the right was completely backward.

"Maybe no one will notice," the kender said hopefully. By skipping and kicking at Beglug's boots as the fiend raised his feet, Trap turned the toes forward again. Half a mile further on, they found Ripple and the gully dwarves. Grod sat on a rock while Ripple attempted to knock mud off the back of Umpth's hauberk with a handful of branches. She looked as if she were beating him, but by his expression, Umpth was unconcerned with the switches.

"He got tired and sat down in a mud puddle," she explained.

"We won't go much further on the road," Halmarain said, using the magic in her staff to clean the gully dwarf's clothing. "If we stay south of those mountains, we'll be able to cross the foothills."

Their destination was Palanthus, one hundred and seventy-five miles to the north, according to one of Trap's maps. A new map had mysteriously appeared among his belongings after their last shopping trip.

The kender had left the decisions on the route to the wizard's apprentice, since they had no preference as to direction. The gully dwarves had no objections to traveling anywhere if there was plenty of food.

Halmarain led the way east along the road for another half mile, where three large barns, each with a big corral, stood just off the road. A faded sign announced: *Glomer's Horses—Bought, Sold, and Boarded.*

"I don't intend to walk all the way to Palanthus, especially since we have Orander's magic purse," the little wizard announced as she led the way into the yard. "And keep those gully dwarves from sitting in the dirt," she hissed at Ripple.

Trap could have spent the rest of the day looking at the animals, but Halmarain chose seven ponies in quick succession. She paid for the animals and six saddles and a pack frame with very little haggling. In a short time they were leading their mounts east along the road.

"You paid too much," Trap told Halmarain. "Not that it matters. We'd better find something else to buy. The purse has already filled up again."

"I know I paid too much," the little wizard said. "I wanted to leave before that . . . before Beglug ate the blacksmith's anvil or the gully dwarves sat down in a pile of manure. Either one would cause more talk than we can afford."

"Who would talk about us?" Trap wanted to know.

"I don't know . . . no one . . . everyone . . . look, humor me. I just have a bad feeling, as if we're not safe."

"Does it come from your magic?" the kender asked, suddenly interested.

Halmarain looked at him with raised eyebrows. "You know, it could," she admitted. "I was trying to learn a magic sensing spell before you . . . before Orander went through the portal. I didn't bring that book. If I had, I'd study that spell. No, I think I'm worried about making this trip."

"Is that why we're going east instead of west, like you said we would?" Ripple asked.

Halmarain stared at the kender for a moment. She nodded, sighed, and shook her head. "I told you I could not make the journey alone. Which way is west?"

They continued east, leading the ponies until they reached a small wooded area and turned off. When they were out of sight of any passing travelers, they tethered the animals to the trees and tied their bundles on the pack pony. As Halmarain had warned them, she could not reach high enough to tie the bundles. She tried several times before she gave up in disgust and left the job to the kender.

"The fun begins when we try to get that . . . get Beglug into the saddle," Halmarain said, staring at the little fiend. The gully dwarves had to lift him into the saddle, but Ripple had the happy thought of taking a stick of firewood from the horse chandler's wood pile. Soothed with a little snack, the merchesti was happy enough.

They soon discovered the gully dwarves presented a more difficult problem, mainly because the Aghar mixed their lefts and rights. Told to stand on the left sides of the ponies and put their left feet in the stirrups, Umpth took a position on the right and used his left foot. Grod, trying to follow his leader's example by mirroring his actions, stood on the left of his mount, but he used his right foot. Both ended up mounted backward.

"Pony going wrong way," Umpth announced, frowning until his grime-filled wrinkles scrunched together.

"Wizard get wrong end ponies," Grod observed as he twisted to look over his shoulder. The pony turned its head to look back at him.

"Get down. Try it again," Trap said. The kender laughed. The tiny wizard shook her head and predicted dire results before they reached their destination.

Grod immediately tried to throw his right leg over the rump of the pony; his boot tangled in the stirrup and he fell from the saddle. His arms and shoulders touched the ground and his blond beard swept the hard packed dirt. His right boot was still caught in the stirrup that was looped over the saddle.

Trap dashed around the frightened pony. He extricated the dwarf by pulling his foot out of his boot, while Ripple calmed Grod's mount.

"We haven't seen much of a city, but we still have some tales to tell," she laughed as she waited for the gully dwarf to mount again. A frustrating ten minutes later they had both gully dwarves properly mounted. Then they discovered the gully dwarves had no concept of the reins or how to use them.

The kender fashioned long lead lines so Trap could lead Beglug's mount and the pack animal while Ripple led the two gully dwarves' ponies.

"Are we ready now?" said Halmarain, who had mumbled and grumbled and tramped restlessly around under the trees. She glared at Ripple.

"How roll wheel?" Umpth demanded, his dark wrinkles twisting again.

"You'll just have to leave it," the wizard said as Trap helped her mount her pony.

"No leave wheel," Grod said, taking both feet out of the stirrups, ready to slide out of the saddle.

"No! Don't do that," Trap objected. He frowned at the large wagon wheel sitting by the tree. "Here's what you do," he said, shortening the lead on Grod's pony so the two gully dwarves rode side by side. He rolled the wheel between them.

"Roll it together; with one of you on each side of it, you ought to keep it going."

"Kender smart," Umpth said as he sat with his left hand on the pommel and his right on the wheel.

"Little wizard no smart as kender," Grod added.

"She fuss all time," Umpth added. "No like Aghar magic."

"You don't have any magic," Halmarain retorted, her eyes blazing.

"She no learn, too," Grod nodded at his brother.

"Little wizard, little smarts," Umpth suggested.

"Little smarts, little magic," Grod added.

"If we don't get moving, I'm going to kill two gully dwarves," the wizard muttered. She whipped up her pony and led the way through the forest.

Trap had expected all sorts of trouble with the wheel, but he was surprised by the outcome. Umpth, riding to the left of his brother, kept his left hand on the pommel of the saddle and used his right to guide the wheel. Grod, his right hand gripping his seat, used his left to move it along.

The afternoon was warm. Trap, like all kender, loved riding. Once he decided the gully dwarves could manage their wheel, he turned his attention to the countryside.

They stayed in the woods as they circled the city to the south and were only five miles west of Lytburg when the sun disappeared behind the mountains. They found a deserted farm with the stone shells of several burned out buildings. Except for the few fire stains that the wind and rain had not erased, the roofless walls could have been built the day before. Not a hundred yards from the house, a spring rose out of the ground and the water meandered away in a small stream.

At Halmarain's insistence, they made camp in the large roofless barn where the ponies would be sheltered. Grass grew within the walls as well as without. They hobbled the ponies and left them to graze at the far end of the walled enclosure.

Ripple looked about. "Why doesn't someone put on new roofs and live here?" she asked.

"After the Cataclysm, and the wars and pestilence that followed, there are more deserted farms than people to claim them," Halmarain replied. "The people who survived those terrible times moved closer to the roads and the rivers."

"Then there won't be other travelers going our way,"

Trap said sadly, but he brightened almost at once. "Still, if there aren't any humans or dwarves, there might be other creatures. We might see bears and mountain cats."

"Hush, don't mention them." Halmarain shivered and looked around apprehensively. Her admonition had been a whisper, entirely at odds with the clumping of her over-size boots.

"Leave alone!" Umpth suddenly shouted, pulling his wagon wheel away from Beglug. The merchesti had slipped it away and was just opening his mouth to take a bite.

"No Beglug!" Trap admonished. "Lava Belly!" Trap shook his head. "He can eat anything."

"Lava Belly no eat wheel," Umpth complained.

Trap looked about, trying to find something to draw the attention of the merchesti from the wheel. In one corner of the barn he found the blade of a rusty plow.

"Do you think rust will hurt Beglug?" Trap asked Halmarain, but Beglug hadn't waited for an answer. He scampered over and pulled the plow out of the kender's hands.

"Beglug?" he said, licking at the rust like a child sucking the sugar off a cake.

"I don't think anything bothers his digestion," the wizard replied.

"How can he eat such strange things?" Trap asked.

Halmarain sighed. "I don't know. Who knows what type of creatures the merchesti really are? I don't trust him. Take care of the little monster while I learn a calming spell to keep him quiet. We're certainly going to need one."

"Ripple and I will make a stew," Halmarain announced when the ponies had been unsaddled and a campfire started. "But there will be no dinner for the gully dwarves or you"—she frowned at Trap—"until they've washed up. How they can get so filthy just riding a pony, I'll never understand."

After their evening meal a pair of disgruntled but reasonably clean gully dwarves sat by the fire, Umpth stroking the wheel and Grod, with uncharacteristic curiosity for an Aghar, looking over the wizards shoulder as if he were trying to read her spellbook.

As the twilight gave way to night, Beglug curled up on the ground close to the fire. Ripple took a flute from her pouch and played a soft tune. Her music was interrupted by her laughter as Trap tried to teach Umpth and Grod the words to the songs. When the gully dwarves tired of learning, Grod sat staring at Halmarain.

"Wizard say do magic," he announced.

"Hey, that's right!" They had not seen any illusions for days, and Trap had spent the evening hoping.

"You're right! She did!" Ripple agreed, glaring at Halmarain.

The little wizard looked up from her book, frowned at Grod and sighed. After sending Grod for a handful of long blades of grass, she spread them out and spoke the words of a spell. The blades of grass rose, glowed with color, and twisted in the air, circling around and through the loops of other blades. The illusion that fascinated the kender and the gully dwarves lasted about five minutes.

"Trap, it's your turn," Ripple said. "I played the flute. Grod and Umpth sang, now you tell a story. I know. Tell one about that Uncle Trapspringer."

"Him dead," Grod said. "Make a good tale, that."

Trap let his mind travel back to his sadness over his Uncle Goalong and tears trickled down his cheeks.

"My poor Uncle Trapspringer," he began. "He never should have ridden that pony backward. . . ."

While Trap wove his tale, Halmarain had pulled a spellbook out of her pack. The large book was nearly half her height and she struggled to spread it out across her short, out-thrust legs. She kept her head lowered as if studying the book, but occasionally she lifted her eyes as Trap wove another tale of a strange and interesting death for his imaginary uncle.

Chapter 10

Astinus of Palanthus bent his head over his work as he described how. . . .

Jaerume Kaldre rubbed his left arm and was surprised again. He was twice surprised. First, that he could feel the huge elbow, forearm, and hand. Second, that with the same arm he could feel the touch of the fingers of his right hand, nearly fleshless.

Both sensations were new. In life he had lost his left arm just above the elbow, but his right hand had been strong and well fleshed. After the loss of his left limb he had managed to maintain his position as the leader of a troop of mercenaries, at times with a knife in the back, though occasionally he openly fought his opponents.

His new left arm came from a dead goblin, the bones attached to his own by Draaddis Vulter, who'd raised him from the dead. Kaldre's appetite for command, never small, had been enlarged when he had been brought back to life in the wizard's laboratory. The skills of the wizard Vulter had allowed him to walk the soil of Krynn again in a sort of half-alive state Kaldre was not too sure he liked. He did like the rewards that were promised him if he completed the task Vulter and his goddess had set for him. Takhisis, the Dark Queen, had personally promised him that he would lead her death knight legions into battle. In life he had not been a general, and the thought of filling that post, even in death, pleased him.

When he left Draaddis Vulter's lair in Pey, Kaldre had been certain he would be able to complete the task set for him. He would have no trouble taking two stones from a pair of miserable kender thieves. An infant fiend from another plane would not be too hard to find, capture, and deliver to the wizard.

Once away from the ruins, though, Kaldre's confidence began to wain. Under orders from Draaddis Vulter, he stood in a large cavern in the Garnet Mountains, staring at his new troops, sure he would be better off without them. In front of him stood a group of fifty trembling kobolds, bunched together at the side of the cavern. Their cowardice and their smell disgusted him, but he was under orders.

Did the wizard and the Queen of Darkness really believe he needed this miserable scum? If so, they had too little faith in his abilities to even consider giving him command of a legion. Or were they testing him? When he was alive, all his followers had been human. He had never worked with other races, and a legion of death knights, spreading terror across the face of Krynn could be made up of many types of warriors.

He shrugged. If they wanted to test his mettle, he would not be found lacking.

"Form up," Kaldre ordered. "We begin our march tonight." His followers could see better in the dark and were weakened by bright sunlight, and Kaldre had discovered one bonus in his new "life," his own night vision was far better now than it was when he was alive.

"We following," replied the kobold leader Malewik. "Muchly quick we following. We doing as wizard says."

The kobold eyed Kaldre with a resentful wariness, subtly informing the death knight that his kobolds were cooperating only because of their instructions from Draaddis Vulter.

The wizard had insisted that Kaldre could depend on the kobolds, but that they had an instinctive fear and hatred of the undead. Beneath Malewik's stolen dwarf helmet his eyes were speculating.

"We hunt two kender," Kaldre told them. "They were in Lytburg when they were last seen, though that was nearly a week ago."

"Humans not liking kender, not liking kender muchly much." Malewik had immediately understood their first and major problem, as his next statement proved: "Is driving kender out of city, doing soon or doing before now. We finding kender not so easy maybe."

"Yes, and if they're gone we'll need to find out when and where." Kaldre agreed. "We will travel west until we near the city. Then I will enter and find out what I can."

Jaerume Kaldre led his motley band from the cavern. The journey began well and continued for almost two miles before the first kobold decided he had traveled far enough and attempted to disappear into the forest.

Takhisis had foreseen trouble with the undisciplined humanoids and had ordered Draaddis to send his messenger—the winged rat—along on the first leg of the journey. The creature raised a racket and Kaldre caught the deserter before he was out of sight of the others. One short swing of his sword decapitated the hapless kobold. Behind him, Kaldre could hear the fearful muttering of the rest of his "army."

"Here, you, the last in line," Kaldre called to the huddled group. He leaned sideways in his saddle and picked up the deserter's head by spearing it through the ear with the tip of his sword.

"You carry this," he said, flinging the head at the group. "You'll all take turns carrying it; it will remind you of what will happen if you desert."

As he rode ahead of the silent kobold column he decided he would use the same tactic on his real legions when he took them into battle. He would make sure he had no deserters. The kobolds obediently followed all night and most of the next day, then he left them in an abandoned barn.

Jaerume Kaldre reached the north gate of Lytburg just after sunset. He dismounted from his blowing, steaming horse on the far side of the bridge and walked across. As he approached the gates he saw four guards on duty and another four appeared, led by an officer.

He slowed his pace and pulled his hood down to keep the light of the torches from showing too much of his pale, skull-like face.

But the soldiers had not noticed his approach. The officer and the new arrivals gathered around a guard who was showing off a broken spear.

"He bit off the point and chewed it up," the guard was explaining.

"Have you been drinking on duty?" the officer demanded.

"Nay, and the others will bear me out. I was stopping a dwarf I had reason to question. He just bit the end off the spear and chewed up the point. I never seen the like."

"Saw it myself, Captain," a second guard spoke up. "That dwarf just bit off that spearhead and chewed it up. He never even spit out the shards."

The officer glared at the two guards, but he had heard the approach of the stranger and turned, his expression harsh, as if he intended to use Kaldre as the target for his frustration.

"It's late to approach a city, traveler," the captain called. The words had been formed in advance of his turning to face the man, but they came out stiffly. An air of decay hung about the stranger like the stuffiness of a garment left too long in an old chest, but the aura of evil emanated from the figure and not his garments. The officer nearly choked with fear.

"I seek only information," Jaerume Kaldre said quietly. "I have traveled far and seek news. My destination is Garnet, and I would know if humans are welcome there or if some trouble has closed their gates."

"They're open to humans as far as I know," the captain said. The fear that created a cold, hard knot in his stomach warned him to be more courteous than usual. "Lytburg does not bar peaceful travelers who arrive after sunset," he said, hoping the stranger would not avail himself of the amenities of the city.

"If that is an invitation, I thank you," Kaldre replied. "But the moon is bright and I can travel miles before I rest." He turned his horse and walked back across the bridge, away from the gate.

The death knight had been careful not to let his anger show. By the conversation he had overheard, he knew his quarry was no longer in Lytburg. Only the merchesti could have chewed up a spear point. If the little fiend left, disguised as a dwarf . . . the kender had disguised it and helped it to leave the city.

He walked casually until he was well away from the bridge, then mounted his horse, spurring it east. Not far away, in a group of abandoned farm buildings, the kobolds waited.

Chapter 11

My Uncle Trapspringer loved to travel. . . .

Shortly after dawn Trap and Ripple saddled the ponies, loaded the pack animal, and were on their way again. The few trees west of the abandoned farm gave way to more open country. The sun was still low in the morning sky when they reached what, on Trap's map, was a line of hills.

When they left the fields behind they discovered that "hills" did not quite describe the terrain they faced. In some distant past it might have been a plateau stretching south from the mountains. Run-off from the heights to the north had dug gullies that had, through the years, become arroyos and small canyons, leaving the upper surface a series of small mesas with steep sides, many of sheer rock. Where there was soil, range grass and small bushes softened the landscape.

Their path was limited to the arroyos that were between eight and twenty feet deep. Often, when the passes were too narrow for two to ride abreast, Trap led the way. When possible he chose a path leading west. The dry watercourses twisted about and they found themselves traveling north, south and even east again. Halmarain, Ripple, and even the gully dwarves made suggestions to correct their course. Their choices were no better than Trap's. After hours of trying to find their way out of the maze, Trap brought the group to a halt.

"Gosh! Where are we? What sort of place is this?" Ripple asked when she, Halmarain, and Trap dismounted for a conference.

"I'd say it was left over from some sort of natural up-heaval," Halmarain said. "Runoff from the mountain storms, but judging by the vegetation, I'd guess they're no longer stream beds."

"It's strange. It's interesting. I think it was made by water that couldn't make up its mind where it was going," Trap said, looking first to the north and then south. "These old gullies seem to run in all directions and I bet they go on forever, so it would be a wonderful place for hide-and-find, if we had anyone interested in play-ing." He eyed the wizard hopefully.

"We may be playing that game without meaning to," Halmarain said. "We could stay lost in here for days."

"Do you think so? That sounds like fun," Trap said.

At the wizard's urging he dismounted and climbed up a steep but negotiable slope. From his vantage point he could see more arroyos to the north, south, and west, all running into each other. To the east was the plain they had crossed. A group of travelers was approaching the maze by a washout half a mile to the north. One, heavily cloaked—which seemed strange in the warmth of the day—rode a horse. The others walked behind him and in the distance they seemed small in comparison to the rider.

Trap climbed down, intending to tell Halmarain he thought they should turn north at the first opportunity and follow the other group of travelers. On the way down, he changed his mind. The small human wizard saw danger everywhere, and she would certainly object. He would relieve her of her fear by not telling her about the travelers.

"Did you find a way out?" Halmarain asked.

"Of course. I know how to get us through," he said, not really lying.

"Then you lead us out of here," she said, taking the leads for the two gully dwarf mounts. Because of the narrow trail, Umpth was carrying the wagon wheel, much to the irritation of his pony.

Trap led the party north at every opportunity and within an hour he found the trail of the other group of travelers. Their trail twisted about too, but he followed along, confident they would sooner or later work their way out of the maze.

He was just rounding a turn in the path when he stopped. Further up the trail, he saw several kobolds walking in a line. Their backs were to the kender and the last was just disappearing when Halmarain rode abreast of Trap.

"What is it?" she asked, her tiny voice pitched even higher because of her worry.

"Kobolds," he told her. "Maybe they know a shorter path. I could ask them . . . I should have thought of it before the last one disappeared."

"Certainly not. They'd give you directions, get ahead of us, and set an ambush. They'd want our mounts and supplies," she warned. "How many did you see?"

"At least ten," Trap replied. "I couldn't tell how many had passed before I saw them, but they seemed to know where they were going, and if we want to find our way out—"

"Ten is too many for us to fight," Halmarain murmured as if to herself.

"But if we were nice to them—"

"No, leave them alone," Halmarain ordered.

Before Trap could object he heard the clump of heavily

booted feet, the rattle of equipment, and the snarling complaints of goblins before he saw them. They were heading northwest, using an arroyo that ran parallel to the one in which the kender and their group hid.

"Goblins on one side, kobolds on the other," Halmarain said. "What do we do now?"

"For a line of deserted hills, this place certainly is busy," Trap said to himself half an hour later. He had rounded a curve in a gully and saw the retreating back of a goblin. Forgetting the wizard's warning, he stepped out, shouting to catch the last goblin's attention.

"Hello!" he called as the last in the line of humanoids stopped and turned to stare at him. "I'm lost. Can you tell me how to get out of this maze?"

The goblins stopped to confer, and he decided they were working out the best directions they could. Then, from an intersecting passage just beyond the goblins, came another shout and the kobolds rushed into sight again. They charged in Trap's direction.

The kender waved and smiled. They wanted to be helpful too, he decided. So much for the little wizard's fears.

The goblins spotted the kobolds and two of the goblins threw spears. One kobold fell and the others attacked the goblins.

"What have you done?" Halmarain rode up and stared at the battle. It was increasing in size as more goblins and kobolds charged out of the narrow gorges.

"I just asked a question," Trap said, disappointed that she didn't seem to understand. "And you're wrong, they're so friendly and want to help so much that they're fighting over who will give us directions."

"I'll decide where we go," Halmarain glared at him and turned her pony around, trotting back the way they had come. At the first intersection she took a westerly path that turned south in less than a hundred yards.

Trap vaulted into the saddle and raced to catch up with the little wizard. It was only luck that their next turn took them into an arroyo that definitely sloped down and to the west. Judging by the sounds in the distance, the goblins and the kobolds would be too busy with each other to chase them. When the sounds of battle faded, Trap reduced the pony's pace to a trot. After an hour of travel they left the last of the maze behind.

According to the map, the low line of hills that were an extension of the Vingaard Mountains, were no more than ten miles wide. It shouldn't have taken them more than six hours to cross the hills if they moved in a straight line. They had entered the maze early that morning, and the sun was just touching the horizon when they finally came in sight of the plain to the west.

They continued until they found a natural swale where the grass was tall and thick. They made camp in the semi-darkness, hobbling the ponies so they could graze. Since they lacked firewood, and could barely find enough thick limbed brush to satisfy Beglug's appetite, they made a cold camp.

"Pony tired," Grod said the next morning. "Me tired."

"We can't stay here," Halmarain said, looking around at the empty countryside. "Those kobolds and goblins may find our trail and we already know they outnumber us."

"By the sounds, they were having a great fight," Trap said wistfully. "They may have killed each other off, but maybe they didn't and they'll start fighting again. I'd be glad to go back and see."

"Yes! That's a good idea. I can go with you," Ripple said eagerly.

"With our luck, they may have joined forces," the little wizard griped.

"Look bad things, find bad things," Umpth told his brother as he shoved the last of his travel bread into his mouth.

"Think bad, find bad," Grod agreed. "Wizard think up bi-i-ig mess."

"I'll have no more gully dwarf philosophy," the little wizard snapped.

"I will," Ripple's voice grated with that particular harshness of kender anger. "If you can bring trouble on by thinking about it, then you can bring fortune on by thinking good thoughts."

"Kender optimism," Halmarain snapped. "Kender foolishness."

"Yes, kender optimism!" Trap said, wondering exactly what optimism meant. It sounded good, so he decided he must have some, since he agreed with his sister.

Halmarain glared at the kender and silently followed Ripple toward the pony carrying packs and bedrolls. The tiny wizard raised her bedroll to the pack frame, but she was too short to hold it in position and tie it. After three tries she slammed the roll to the ground and marched off to stand staring out into the distance. Trap and Ripple had loaded the pack animal and saddled the ponies when the little wizard returned.

"Perhaps you're right," she said reluctantly. "Maybe I do worry overmuch, but Orander is in that awful place, we have that . . . we have Beglug to worry about and all the dangers between here and Palanthus." She glanced at Ripple who did not seemed swayed by her explanation. "I'll decide that we're fortunate, that we'll be safe, and that we won't face any dangers. Will that satisfy you?"

"Great! And you'll feel better too," Trap said. Even if her good thoughts didn't really help, she might be happier and more fun on the journey.

"If we can just order up our good fortune, we should find a peaceful village with an inn before the day's journey is over," Halmarain said. "And a good wood pile to keep that . . . to keep Beglug from eating the furniture."

Beglug seemed to like riding though he was unable to mount without help. Trap picked up a few dried sticks and gave them to the merchesti to snack on. Umpth, the largest of the two gully dwarves, put both hands on the rusting iron rim of the wheel.

"Find good place," he intoned. "Find good food, good dump." He handed the wheel back to Grod and with the kender's help, climbed into the saddle.

Halmarain glared at the dwarves as, with a boost from Ripple, she mounted her own pony.

"We should stay in the foothills," she told Trap as they set out on their second full day's journey. "We'll travel slower, but there's less danger of being seen by anyone who might follow us."

Trap sighed and pulled out the roll of maps that had belonged to the captain of the ship on which they had sailed from Hylo to Solamnia. He reminded himself he must find the captain and return the maps the next time he was near a seaport.

How the ship's master had been so careless as to put them into Trap's pack by mistake, he would never understand. At that moment he was just glad of the error.

He unrolled a particularly pretty one that showed the western section of Solamnia and studied it as Halmarain led the way north. Some careful hand had painted it with different shades of brown for the hills and mountains, green for farm and range land, and blue for the seas and rivers. The locations of many cities, forts, and castles had been drawn in. Beneath some had been written the word "ruins." The map showed no villages, and the nearest point of civilization marked on the map was a fortress with the name of Ironrock.

With a road and fresh ponies they could reach it by nightfall, but traveling through the hills on tired mounts they would be two days reaching the fortress.

"Do you think many people live close to the mountains?" he asked Halmarain. "I hope the rest of the area isn't as deserted as this. We might find some friends—then again they might not be friendly, so many humans aren't—but we're thinking good thoughts so I'll pretend they will be."

"I'd be happy not to see another person or animal larger than a rabbit from here to Palanthus," Halmarain said as she adjusted her hair combs to keep her dark curling hair out of her face. "I'd just like a peaceful, quick journey."

"I like meeting people," Trap said. "Adventurers have so many tales to tell, and dwarves make such good stuff."

"Stuff that would end up in your pouches," Halmarain

retorted, pulling a small spellbook from the bag she kept slung over her shoulder. She began to study, just giving the reins a tug now and then to keep the placid pony moving in the general direction she wanted it to go. Beglug's mount and the pack animal followed hers on long leads tied to her saddle.

Trap sighed and dropped back to ride beside his sister. She was still leading the two gully dwarves. Trap and Ripple wiled away the morning trading old gossip about their friends back home.

"Legup was more fun than this," Trap said as he shifted in the saddle. "We knew all the places, but at least there were people to talk to—"

"And everyone had a story," Ripple broke in to add her part. "I know! Tell us a tale of Uncle Trapspringer. That should be interesting."

"Him dead," Grod said.

"Yes. He never should have stepped into the middle of the fight between the goblins and the kobolds," Trap said as he began his story. "Of course, he didn't know he was going to get killed so we won't really blame him for making a mistake, and after all it was his last one. . . ."

Trap wiled away a couple of hours letting his imagination soar.

"That was a wonderful tale," Ripple said when Trap had finished. She wiped away a tear as she mourned an uncle she had never had. "When we get back to Hylo, everyone will want to hear your tales."

"And before long every kender on Krynn will have an Uncle Trapspringer," Halmarain said. Until she spoke she had given no hint that she was listening.

"Why would every kender want one?" Trap asked, suspicious of the remark.

"They'll need one to keep up with your tales. I don't imagine they'll want to tell stories about *your* uncle when they can claim him for themselves. He has died so many times there will have to be a thousand of him. Before you get through he will have traveled all over this world and to the moons too."

"That's an idea," Trap said, thinking he would really love to tell a tale of someone going to the moons.

"And you'll have to have him eaten by a real dragon," the little wizard said, staring into the distance. For once she sounded enthusiastic. "How many times and ways do you think he could drown?"

"In the sea, and a river, and in a well. . . ." Trap was thinking over the wizard's idea.

"And how many things could he fall from?" Halmarain asked.

"Off a roof, and a cliff, and out of a tree. . . ." Ripple added suggestions. "You're right, every kender will want an Uncle Trapspringer," she agreed.

"You'll need to think up some more tales," Halmarain said to Trap. "Where else could he go? What else could he see and do?"

"I don't know," Trap said and fell silent, thinking about the suggestions the others had made.

"He could see lots of places," Ripple said. "We're seeing some of Krynn, but I don't think it's the best part. How long do you think it will take us to reach Palanthus?"

"One, possibly two weeks," Trap said. "And the journey might still be fun. There could be all sorts of creatures to see on the way and I bet most will be friendly. Then, Palanthus is a large city and there's probably lots to do and see there."

"Palnnus got dumps?" asked Grod. Usually the gully dwarves just talked among themselves, but they liked listening to the others.

"Aghar like Palnnus?" Umpth asked.

"Sure. You'll like it a lot," Trap said. "Lots of dumps and other gully dwarves, and a lot of places that would make a good This Place, and maybe this one won't get knocked flat . . . but then it might, because lots of kender go there. We'll find you a good This Place."

"Maybe new This Place near dump," Grod said, clapping his hands in anticipation.

"Jiggy biggies! Jiggy biggies!" Umpth shouted, mangling the kender's favorite expletive. "Maybe *big* dump,"

Umpth clapped his own hands. With four hands clapping, there were none left for the wheel. It stopped, remained balanced, and started rolling backward.

"*Wheel!*" Umpth shouted, but he was too late to catch it.

Trap looked back and saw the wagon wheel taking off on its own. He turned his pony and galloped after it. Behind him he could hear the dwarves, Ripple, and Halmarain shouting. Beglug wailed because the young merchesti could not understand the trouble.

Trap's mount did its best, but the wheel had gathered momentum on the slope. It changed course when it came to a steep incline that led west, between two high hills. It slowed as it rolled part of the way up the first hill, bounced into a little gully and hurtled off in a different direction. It left the kender behind as he slowed his pony to keep it from losing its footing on the rocky slope.

At the bottom of the slope he urged his mount to a gallop again, but the wheel was out of sight. He raced after it, thinking the chase was at least more fun than riding through the valleys. He had traveled nearly a mile when he saw it again, rolling up a slope, slowing until he thought it might fall over.

It struck something, too small for him to see what, though it could have been a rock. The wheel bounced off course, just enough for it to roll back down the far angle of the slope.

"Gosh! It just keeps going! It *must* be magic," he told the pony. "I don't see how it could stay upright so long otherwise."

The wheel gathered momentum again and continued down the slope, rolled to a stop and fell over in the grass not thirty yards from the end of a village street.

Trap rode his pony forward and stopped by the wheel, letting his mount drop its head to graze while he dismounted and picked up the runaway wheel. His sharp ears had caught the distressed calls of the gully dwarves and the thud of hooves so he knew Ripple and the Aghar were following. Moments after Ripple came into sight, leading the dwarves, Halmarain appeared with the two other ponies following.

The gully dwarves scrambled out of their saddles to check the wheel. By the time the little wizard arrived they were satisfied.

"Wheel find—here," Umpth said, pointing to the village.

"Good Aghar magic, this wheel," Grod replied, helping his brother examine it for damage.

"More better magic than short human," Umpth said. "She no find—here"—he pointed toward the village again—"Aghar magic find."

"That monstrosity did not find this village, it rolled to the lowest point—"

"It did. It rolled here on its own," Ripple said, irritated with the wizard's complaints. "And it did find a village, you can see that for yourself and—"

"Mad she no find," Umpth said to Grod.

"No do herself," Grod nodded as he answered. "Mad she no find."

"I am not jealous of those dirty—"

"Are you here for the celebration?" A strange voice called, interrupting the argument.

They turned to see the strangest creature on all Krynn. It stood as tall as a man, but with a lion's head and a humanoid body covered with feathers.

Chapter 12

The group stared in silence as the strange creature approached. Trap started forward, eager to meet this odd being. Halmarain pulled her axe, though she had no experience in using it. The weight of the weapon nearly pulled the tiny human out of the saddle.

When the creature saw her weapon, he stopped, laughed, raised his hands, and lifted his lion's head off his shoulders. Beneath it they saw a smiling human face.

"Forgive me if I startled you," he said. "This is Wizards' Day in Deepdel. We forget that not all of Krynn knows of our yearly celebration."

"Oh, look! It's a costume!" Ripple said, sliding from her saddle and hurrying forward to see it better.

"Celebration?" Trap asked brightly. "You're having a party? Wow, that's great. Can we come?"

"Of course you can." the strange man replied. "Once a

year—on Wizard's Day—we have a village party. It's in honor of a battle between two wizards that took place here a millennia ago. Oh, where are my manners? My name is Earne Jomann. My father is the mayor.

"Later this afternoon, we will enact the historic battle. We welcome travelers any day of the year, but on this day there is a condition to entering the village. You must wear a costume. Only a few of the pageant players are allowed to be without one because of their parts in the reenactment."

"We thank you, but we must continue our journey," Halmarain said.

"No," Ripple objected. "We want to see the costumes—"

"Kender. . . ." Earne Jomann interrupted, his eyes narrowing. His smile disappeared and he stared at them with suspicion. "You will be seeking the traveler that stopped here earlier? A man heavily cloaked and hooded? He was seeking two kender traveling with a dwarf."

"Seeking *us*? Who was he? Do we have any friends here?" Trap said, wondering who might be searching for them. "He could not have been looking for us, we don't know anyone in Solamnia—until today," he added hopefully.

"No, we are *four* dwarves, not one. He must not have been searching for these kender," Halmarain spoke up quickly, lowering her voice so she sounded like a dwarf.

Earne Jomann seemed to relax. "I'm glad of that; he wasn't the sort of person I'd want as a friend."

"Thank you for your invitation," Halmarain said. "We will join your celebration if you'll give us a little time to prepare for the occasion."

Earne bowed and replaced his lion's head. "Then I will see you soon in the village square," he said, turning away.

As soon as the villager was out of sight the little wizard turned on the kender. She seemed more frightened than angry.

"Who would be seeking you?"

"No one," Trap replied.

"We don't know any humans in Solamnia except you,"

Ripple added. "The only ones we've met since leaving home were on the ship, and how would they know we were traveling with dwarves? Mayhap you were right and the cloaked man really was looking for two other kender."

"We'll stay here the rest of today and tonight if we can find lodging," Halmarain decided. "By then he may be far away. Let's see what we can do about costumes. And for Gilean's sake, straighten Beglug's boots! They're backward again." She glared at the two kender who were exchanging looks with raised eyebrows. She understood their expression as if she had heard their thoughts. "You're right, they could look like part of a costume."

Half an hour later they led the ponies down a path that winded between two large barns and came out into the village square across from an old inn. Earne had been on the lookout for them and called them over to the inn to meet his father. They could tell nothing about the mayor because of the strange outfit he wore. He resembled a large, round, blue ball with a carved wooden mask.

"And you'll have to identify your costumes," Earne said, grinning at the little wizard. For Halmarain, they had cut long blades of grass that covered her clothing and stuck up from her dwarf helmet. She wore a beard of grass. Like the green on her clothing and helmet, it was held in place by a spell.

"I'm a grass elemental," Halmarain said. "My friend here is the creation of an inept wizard"—she pointed to Beglug, who wore his own face without makeup and his boots were backward—"This is a whirly-gig"—she indicated Umpth, who wore the wagon wheel atop his pointed helmet. It too was held in place by one of the wizard's spells—"These two are kender-dwarves." Trap wore Beglug's beard while Ripple had tied the little fiend's wig under her chin.

"And me gully dwarf," Grod proudly announced. They had liberally coated his hauberk, helmet, and face with mud.

"You did an excellent job for travelers who had not

expected to join our celebration," the mayor said. He bobbed up and down until Trap wondered if Braad Jomann would bounce away. "Come leave your mounts in the stables and partake of the day."

A crowd of several hundred humans and dwarves were strolling about, eating, drinking, and dancing. All the revelers wore strange costumes. Most combined the features of animals, birds, fish, and dragonlike shapes. The overall scene resembled the result of some insane and inept wizard's experiments.

At one end of the square a group of musicians performed on a raised wooden platform. The two lute players appeared to be wearing one costume that joined their bodies and near legs into one. Together they formed a two headed creature with four arms, three legs, and a body that was more than five feet wide. Beside them, two human arms reached out from a carved dragon shape, overlaid with painted wooden scales. The hidden musician beat out the rhythm of the music on a drum.

The two kender stood wide eyed, completely forgetting their companions. They wandered around fascinated by the costumes. For the first few minutes they were too busy looking to handle the few loose items available.

Not even their interest in the costumes could long hold down kender nature. They spent a couple of happy hours standing quietly on the fringes of chatting celebrants, their hands busy exploring pouches and pockets. There were so many pockets, and people were moving about so much, even the kender lost track of who owned what when they attempted to replace the many items they'd inspected. The kender's pouches bulged with items accidentally dropped inside and other things they intended to return when they found the owners again.

Trap and Ripple saw Grod, who had found the tables laden with food and was busy stuffing himself. The villagers, well aware of the reputed gully dwarf appetite, were offering him food. They complimented him on getting into the spirit of his costume.

Umpth was near the musician's platform, dancing by

himself, spinning around and around. His dark hair and beard flowed out from under the wagon wheel that was still in place on his helmet.

Then the mayor jumped onto the platform and called everyone to attention and ordered them to take the seats that had been placed around the edge of the square.

The villagers knew what was coming and willingly obeyed. Earne found seats for himself, Trap, and Ripple. Halmarain and Beglug sat by a tall human on the other side of the square. Their feet dangled as they sat on the seats made for humans. The merchesti seemed fascinated with all the creatures and for once he was not trying to eat the furniture.

At the southern side of the square, a juggler kept four apples in the air at one time. The crowd watched him until they heard a sizzle and a low boom at the north-western corner of the square. They jerked their heads around to see billowing black smoke. When it cleared, a black-robed figure stood on the platform.

"Hey! That's great! You have wizards and magic?" Trap asked Earne. "I really like magic."

"So do I," Ripple said, leaning forward to watch.

"No, we don't have any real magic, the smoke is only a dwarf trick, and the wizard is a local weaver in costume," the young man said. "He's playing the part of Canoglid, the black wizard that enslaved our village a thousand years ago."

The story enacted that afternoon was in mime but was easy to understand. The villagers feared the wizard who, using horrible beasts to keep them in order, had enslaved them. Then another wizard—this one in white robes—appeared and brought other creatures to drive the evil ones away.

The black-robed wizard leaped off the platform and his foe in white moved forward to meet him. They threw fireballs at each other and at first Trap agreed with Ripple, magic seemed the only explanation for the small fires that blossomed around them.

Still, his eye was quick. The mock battle brought the

white-robed wizard close to where Trap and Ripple sat. The kender noticed that when the black-robed figure pretended to throw a spell, the other would flinch away as if he had been struck. His movements disguised the fact that he dropped a small object onto the ground and a short-lived blaze erupted from it. One fell without exploding. Trap kept an eye on it.

The mock battle continued until all the evil creatures and the black-robed wizard had been driven away.

"We are saved! Thanks to Paladine, we are saved!" the players in human dress shouted and the onlookers jumped up from the benches and joined in the jubilant shout. The musicians hurried back onto the platform and the music began again.

As the crowd began to mill about, Trap hurried to pick up the little unexploded ball and examined it. Slightly smaller than a chicken egg, it was made of very thin glass and was partitioned. One side held powder and the other a liquid. He slipped it in his pouch, thinking someone might step on it and break it, setting fire to his or her feet.

He decided that he should give it back to the man who played the white-robed wizard. When he went in search of the tall human, all he found was the white robe, discarded on a bench at the end of the square. He fingered the robe, and inside a pocket he found six more unexploded flame balls.

"Gee! That's dangerous! What if someone were to sit on the cloak?" he asked himself, grinning as he pictured one of the revelers setting his pants afire. He put the rest of the balls in his pouches, intending to return them when he found the player that had worn the white robes.

He had just fastened the strap on his pouch when Halmarain appeared from behind a group of dancing villagers. She seemed to be fighting her heavy boots as she hurried toward Trap. Her face was stiff with anger and worry.

"I've lost that . . . I've lost Beglug," she said in a soft voice that was loaded with frustration.

"Let him have some fun. He's probably just looking at

the costumes," Trap said, sure there was no cause for worry. "He seemed to be fascinated by them."

"That wasn't fascination. I had him under a calming spell to keep him quiet," Halmarain whispered. "But I was speaking to another . . . to someone I met and I forgot to renew the spell. We have to locate him before he does something terrible. You start looking. I'll find the others and set them to searching."

Trap sighed. He would be glad to get the little fiend and the wizard to Palanthus so he'd be free to explore. He slipped through the crowd, but as far as he could tell, the merchesti was not among the dancers. Then he heard a barking, snarling dog and a sound that was half whine, half roar. The noises came from behind the inn. The dog snarled again and gave a yelp of pain. Silence greeted the kender as he trotted around the corner and into the rear yard of the inn. Beglug stood backed up against the wall of the inn. He was holding a headless dog and crunching away.

Trap shuddered at the sound of breaking bones, but he could hardly blame the little fiend, who had not been doing any harm by exploring. The dog had been snarling and should have been more friendly. Still, he didn't want any of the villagers to see the merchesti eating the dog.

A few feet from the back of the inn was a small shed. "Bring it in here," he said, gesturing for Beglug to follow him. He managed to get Beglug into the woodshed and had just closed the door when a burly human in the costume of a beast-man came through the rear door of the inn. He carried a plate of meat scraps which he placed on the ground as he glared at Trap.

"What are you doing back here?" he demanded.

"Uh, trying to find a way into the inn," the kender said. "I wanted to arrange lodgings for the night, but the front door was blocked by benches." From the half closed door of the wood shed he could hear the crunch of bones. "Yes, trying to find a way into the inn," Trap repeated, nearly shouting as he tried to cover the sound of the merchesti's grisly feast. "I couldn't find the way in. We're travelers, and we want rooms for the night."

"People usually enter the inn by the front door," the man said, staring at the kender suspiciously.

"I tried. There were so many people and so many benches I couldn't get in," Trap said. "They blocked your door. You shouldn't allow them to do that, they keep your customers away."

He had to draw the man away before Beglug came out of the shed.

"We'll need four rooms," Trap said, just picking a number at random. Anything to keep the man away from the shed.

"If I had four extra rooms, I'd be a fool to let them to a kender who would leave in the morning without paying," the human said. He looked around, eyeing the broken rope tied to a hook near the door. "You're just lucky the dog wasn't back here. He's a mean one; you'd be chewed to pieces."

"I'll pay for the rooms now," Trap said, reaching in his pouch for Orander's magic purse which was nearly bursting with coins. "I don't understand why you would think I wouldn't, but if you want to be sure, I'll pay for the rooms in advance." Trap pulled out the little leather bag which seemed to be heavier than ever. He brought out a handful of steel pieces and skipped away from the shed and into the alley. He hoped the sight of ready money would draw the innkeeper along with him.

"Four rooms," Trap said, pouring the steel pieces from one hand to the other, using the clink of the money to help hide the crunching noises. "We're traveling and we really need our rest, and even if we don't rest much because there's a party going on we still need a place to put our packs."

"Well. . . ." the innkeeper breathed, following along. "I've only got one room left, but it's big. I've some straw pallets, and I'll be wanting two steel pieces for each person using it." The stout human glanced around, still looking for the dog.

"I'll pay for the six of us, twelve steel pieces," Trap said as he led the innkeeper down the alley on the way to the front of the inn. The price was outrageous, but since the purse refilled itself every time he took coins from it, Trap didn't mind.

"And you can include our food in the price," Trap said quickly. He flipped a steel piece into the air and it glittered in the sunlight.

"I guess I can hunt up the dog later," the innkeeper said, greed dripping from his speech.

When they reached the square, Trap spotted Ripple and Halmarain as they searched through the crowd for the merchesti. He winked, nodded, and keeping his hands out of sight of the innkeeper, pointed down the alley he was just leaving. Halmarain frowned. Ripple understood. She was whispering to the little wizard when Trap followed their soon-to-be-host. The stout human stepped over a bench and into the front door of the inn. The kender scrambled along behind him.

Trap secured the room. Halmarain and Ripple had located Beglug, cleaned the dog's blood from his face and clothing, and brought him back to the square. While Halmarain took the little fiend up to their chamber, the kender located the gully dwarves.

An hour later the little wizard sat curled up on the bed in their chamber, her spellbooks stacked beside her. Beglug slept off his dinner on a straw pallet. All their gear lay in the corner of the room and the gully dwarves had washed off the soil of their celebration. They seemed to pick up dirt just walking across the room. Ripple looked around the room, looked out the window, and smiled.

"Oh, look. They're bringing out more food. If we find celebrations like this in every village, the trip to Palanthus will be fun," she said.

"May Gilean preserve me from any more celebrations," the wizard said. "I just want a quiet trip."

"Then if we're only to have one fun time, we should enjoy it," Ripple snapped. "You stay and study your books if you want, but we're going back to the party."

"Stay out of trouble," Halmarain warned. "Remember

the reason for our journey."

"Are humans always so serious about everything?" Ripple asked her brother as they descended the steps from their chamber to the common room of the inn.

"I don't think so," Trap said slowly. "After all, look at the people in the square."

Earne had told them the local farmers, hunters and many adventurers came into Deepdel to enjoy the celebration, and the common room of the inn was crowded.

Neither of the kender had eaten anything since they arrived, so they found seats for themselves and the gully dwarves at the end of a table. At the other end, two hunters and a pair of adventurers were trading tales.

The innkeeper had watched them descend the stairs. They had been at the table for a couple of minutes when a roly-poly woman plumped plates of food and mugs of ale on the table.

When Trap had lured the landlord away from the sounds of Beglug's canine feast, the kender had dickered over the high price of the room. The price had not diminished a steel piece, but the innkeeper had agreed to include their food and drink. The trenchers were well filled; the innkeeper was not stinting them on food. Grod cleaned his plate and looked around for more to eat. Umpth, larger but not quite as greedy as his brother, slurped the last of his ale. The kender were still munching away when a chorus of complaints came from the other end of the table.

"And the scabs robbed us on the way to Ironrock," one of the adventurers was saying. He glared down toward their end of the table. "One of the group was a kender."

Trap and Ripple looked up, both wide-eyed and still chewing their food. They wondered why the adventurers were staring at them. Grod pulled off his helmet, exposing his blond head. He assumed an expression of sorrow.

"That kender dead," he said. "Make a good tale, that."

"If the scoundrel got his just deserts, I'd be glad to hear how," the other adventurer said. He shouted for the innkeeper and gestured for ale all around the table.

"You tell, you make good story," Grod said to Trap.

The kender cast a regretful eye on his still half-filled plate, but more ale would be welcome, and he did love a good story. He considered repeating the one he had told in Lytburg and decided against it. Retold tales were never as much fun as new stories.

He thought quickly, casting his mind about for some interesting subject to use as the center of his fabrication. Outside the windows of the inn he could see the raised platform where the musicians were performing. His eyes rested on the wooden dragon.

He bowed his head, pulled up the image of his dead Uncle Goalong which always brought on tears. He formed the first part of his story, deciding to add a new touch. Before they left Orander's caverns, Halmarain had read them a story in one of the magic books. The beginning had been so solemn, Trap had known immediately that the tale would be important. He worked out the words that would make his tale sound important.

"It is fitting that the tale be told on this day," he said, looking down the table, though he could barely see through the teary blur. He noticed with satisfaction that one drop trickled down his cheek, which made a nice touch.

"Not all the creatures created by the wizard Canoglid entered Deepdel in that terrible time when the white and black wizards fought." He leaned forward and turned his head so he could see the hunters on the same side of the table. They were separated from him by Umpth who sat by his side.

"Sometimes something robs your traps and you don't know what it is—of course sometimes you do, but not always, since you're not there to see, not that you could be there all the time at every trap because you'd have to be ten or twenty of yourself—"

"Kobolds and goblins raid traps," one hunter said. "We know that. Get on with your tale." He had not paid much attention to the kender until asked about his traps. His eyes sharpened and his mouth formed a thin line.

"It's true, they would raid your traps if they had a chance, but there are other, more dangerous creatures in the southern reaches of the Vingaard Mountains," Trap said with a shudder and remembered he was going to make this tale *important*. "Remember, the wizard Canoglid was a servant of Takhisis, Queen of the Dragons."

"You're not telling me a *dragon* has been raiding our traps," the hunter scoffed. "There are no more dragons on Krynn."

"Not real dragons," Trap agreed. "But are there many creatures today that are like the costumes worn by the people of Deepdel? Look into the square, at the size and shape of that wooden carving. Did someone really think it up? Ask yourself if it came from someone's imagination, or if there might be such a creature hidden in the mountains." He bowed his head again. "The Trapspringer who robbed the adventurers could tell you the truth if he were still alive."

"You knew this robber?" the stoutest of the adventurers asked. His face full of suspicion.

"Yes, I fear so. I not only knew him, he was an uncle and we were both the namesakes of a single ancestor," Trap grudgingly admitted. He liked that touch, but the adventurers were getting restless and he wanted to tell his new tale.

First he set the foundation of his story. He told how the dragonlike creature created by the black-robed wizard had chased a hart into the mountains on the day of the fateful battle a thousand years ago. It had not been in Deepdel to be destroyed by the white-robed wizard's creatures.

"Why have we never heard of this monster?" The disbelieving hunter scoffed.

"Because those who see it never live to tell of it," Ripple added to the tale. "Think of the hunters you have known who never came back to trade their furs."

The speaking looks exchanged by the listeners suggested Ripple's remark had made a solid hit. Several that had scoffed lost their sneering expressions.

Trap wove his tale around a group of bandits who had retreated to the mountains to avoid a chase. Bored, the kender outlaw went exploring and had met the small dragon.

Since the creature had speech and was lonely, it always talked to its victims before it killed them. It proposed a game of tales, and if the kender could tell a better story than the dragon, the kender could go away unharmed.

Other patrons of the inn had gathered around the table. The kender wove a tale of how the dragon and the kender agreed on a wager, the dragon promised jewels from its hoard while the kender outlaw produced stolen valuables from his many pouches. But finally the kender had told all his tales.

"So the small dragon, who had developed a tremendous appetite while listening and telling stories of his own—you know how hungry a dragon can get—gobbled up our uncle. Now my journey, my task to find him and bring him back to Hylo, has been for nothing," Trap finished.

By the time the tale was told, the other Trapspringer had become real to Ripple again. She cried at his death. The one fallacy of the tale was caught by the disbelieving hunter.

"If no one has ever seen this dragon, and the kender is dead, how did you hear the story?"

"The half-goblin in the robber band had gone in search of my uncle. He heard the stories. You know what half-goblins are. He sneaked away, leaving my Uncle Trapspringer to his fate." Trap liked that last part—to his fate. That sounded important too.

"There was a half-goblin," the adventurer who had been robbed, nodded thoughtfully. "And they'd not risk themselves to protect their own mothers."

One of the hunters still half doubted Trap's tale. The second had accepted it and followed the kender's story with one if his own. His tale gave credence to Trap's fabrication. The adventurers, not to be left out, related some of their adventures. The sun went down, some hardy villagers kept dancing in the square, but the two kender listened, enthralled. The gully dwarves had slipped away. They wandered about the room, finishing off mugs of ale and meals that had been left on the tables by patrons who gathered around the table where the tales were being told.

Halmarain came seeking the kender, insisting they return to the chambers and their beds. She wanted to make an early start, so they led the two staggering gully dwarves up the stairs.

Chapter 13

. . . and Astinus of Palanthus continued . . .

Draaddis Vulter stood in front of the black globe, where
Takhisis, Queen of Darkness raged.

"He lost them?" she demanded of the wizard. "Kaldre
lost them?"

"According to my messenger, they were all caught up
in the maze of gorges south of the Vingaard Mountains.
Kaldre lead the band of kobolds, as you ordered, but a
group of goblins attacked him. By the time he had driven
off the goblins, the kender and the merchesti had
escaped . . . if they were ever there."

"Are you saying you sent a fool in search of them?"
Takhisis demanded. An illusion of spiders, hundreds of
thousands formed on the walls, the floor, and the furnishings in the wizard's work room.

"My lady can see into all hearts and read all thoughts," Draaddis bowed, knowing he was giving her credit for more than she could really do, yet the flattery might appease her.

"My queen knows I would not willingly send a fool, yet circumstances can form traps for the feet of even the wisest. Who could have foreseen the presence of a band of goblins on their path or that the kender in their silliness would call both groups together and then escape in the ensuing battle? There is another problem as well. The goblins, enraged at being attacked, are following Kaldre and his kobolds. No doubt he will elude them and further trouble."

"Unbelievable! Goblins not withstanding, how could Kaldre and the kobolds have missed the kender and the merchesti?"

"It could only have been bad luck, my queen, since my messenger brought back an image to show they were traveling with a dwarf, Neidar in dress, and two Aghar, who were dressed as Neidar as well."

"What would they want with Aghar, who are even more foolish than kender?" Takhisis asked.

"I have no idea, but as you say, the foolishness of gully dwarves and kender together must deliver them into our hands. I've no doubt that Jaerume Kaldre will find the kender . . . and the little merchesti."

It had been Takhisis, not Draaddis, who had chosen Jaerume Kaldre and insisted that the wizard raise him from the dead and send him after the kender. She had even chosen the kobolds as the death knight's allies. The black-robed wizard just hoped she would remember it. He knew better than to remind her.

"He had better find them," she said, sending out a blast of evil frustration that threatened to crumble the walls of Draaddis' hidden workroom beneath the ruins. She calmed down but glared at the wizard with one perfect eye, enlarged by the globe.

"Are you sure you impressed upon him the urgency of his mission?"

"I tried, my queen. . . ."

"But did you try hard enough?" She paused, her eye blinked several times. "Do you even understand?" She waited but when Draaddis didn't answer she sighed.

"Draaddis, my unwilling but faithful servant, if we have one gate stone, we can get the other. They are mated as the viewing disks are mated."

"Then if we have one, we can get the other," Draaddis mused under his breath.

"Did I not tell you so?"

"If the other still exists," Draaddis spoke up. "You did say, my queen, that the infant merchesti might kill and devour the kender, eating the stone as well. Might the adult parent do the same to Orander and the one he carries?"

"Orander is dead," Takhisis said. "He must be." She realized Draaddis had no idea what she meant.

"Shortly after Orander disappeared," Takhisis continued impatiently, "a portal opened just south of Palanthus. I don't think it was used. This might have been a coincidence. Red-robed wizards are forever traveling between planes and it is not unusual for them to open paths of destruction."

Draaddis bowed his head. He too had walked on other planes, but he did not want to remind his queen of it at the moment. No one prospered from interrupting a god.

"Just so," she nodded, correctly reading his thought. "Still, I divine from the evidence that the red-robed wizard is dead, and that the adult merchesti has the stone and is trying to get into this world to find its young one."

Though his queen often scorned his mortal intelligence, Draaddis was not stupid, far from it. The god herself had expanded his mind, and he saw a flaw in her reasoning. If the gate stones were mated and the adult merchesti on the Plane of Vasmarg had used one of them, the portal would have opened near the kender who had the second stone. The little thieves were still somewhere near the southern tip of the Vingaard Mountain chain, still a long way from Palanthus. His queen's reasoning on that point was faulty, but he dared not tell her so. Instead, he would play the stupid mortal, stay with the subject as long as he dared, and hope she saw her mistake.

"The adult merchesti," Draaddis murmured. "But it couldn't get through the portal when it was open—"

"Do not attempt to appear even more stupid than you are," Takhisis snapped. "Orander opened the portal. He opened it for himself. When he used the stones, he held them no more than three feet apart and the opening formed between them."

"But if the merchesti held one of the gate stones, then the rent in the fabric between worlds would be large enough for the monster to enter our world?" Since necromancy was his primary study, he had given little thought to planes and the subtleties of portals. Like many other wizards he used portals when he needed them, but he knew just enough about them to serve his purpose.

"Is the merchesti intelligent enough to use the stone?" the wizard asked.

"In time," Takhisis replied. "Also, adult merchesti have an innate magic. It sensed the power of the stone, and when it killed Orander, I suspect it took and kept it. Their intelligence is not on the plane with humans, but while their thinking is slow, they are capable of working out problems. And remember, they have been known to open their own portals, though its rare for them to do so."

"How long would it take for the merchesti to learn to use the stone?" Draaddis was as impatient as his queen.

"Years, your lifetime, if we left it totally to the fiend on the plane of Vasmarg," Takhisis replied. "Still, it *will* come after its young. When Orander opened that portal, he set a course of destruction that is inevitable. If we can get the other stone, we can help the monster through to this world in time to help our cause."

"Help it through—bring that monster *here*?"

"Yes!" Takhisis gave a hiss of impatience and two of the jars on the shelves cracked with the power of her mood.

* * * * *

Two hundred feet above the ceiling of the work room, the old lobo wolf awoke from a terrible dream. He leaped to his feet, snarling at the evil that surrounded him. Fully awake, he saw only moonlight through the vines that covered his lair.

He wondered why he had been having such terrible dreams.

Chapter 14

My Uncle Trapspringer, like all kender, was a light sleeper . . .

Trap awoke when he heard an irregular tapping. He sat up on the pallet to see the sun coming through the window. Beglug sat in the corner, holding one of Grod's boots. The young fiend was chewing up the last of the only chair that had been in the room and started eyeing the wood floor. When an ant crawled out between two floor boards, Beglug mashed it with the boot and gave an evil chuckle.

"Little monster," Halmarain said as she climbed down from the bed and went to the corner, searching her pack for her comb.

"Beglug find new game," Grod said. "Can use own boot." The gully dwarf grabbed his boot from the merchesti and put it on. "Lava Belly evil."

"I don't believe it," Ripple snapped.

"If killing and eating the innkeeper's dog isn't evil, I don't know what is," Halmarain spoke up.

"I don't know that," Trap insisted. "The innkeeper said his dog was mean, so Beglug might have killed it because it attacked him. You know he'll eat anything."

"Lava Belly evil," Grod announced, again echoing the little wizard.

"No! He's not!" Trap was growing irritated with the gully dwarf for echoing Halmarain's warnings.

"Maybe not so bad," Umpth said. His real complaint with the little fiend was its occasional desire to munch on his wagon wheel. Otherwise Grod's brother didn't seem to mind Beglug.

The celebration had lasted well into the night. Even though the travelers had turned in at an early hour, they had not slept well because of the noisy party in the square. They packed their belongings and covered Beglug's dark skin with the makeup and adjusted his false wig and beard. The sun was high when they carried their gear down the stairs and entered the common room of the inn. The innkeeper came into the room and glared at the group while they were eating their breakfast.

"Where's the chair that was in your room?" he demanded of Grod, who was closest to the end of the table.

"Lava Belly eat chair," Umpth said, pointing at Beglug. He continued to scoop porridge into his mouth, spilling it on his beard in the process.

"I want to know what happened to the chair in your room," the innkeeper said again, dismissing the truth as a joke.

"I wanted to know too." Halmarain snapped at their host. She squeaked out the comment before remembering to imitate the deep tones of a dwarf. "We paid a lot for that room and we had nothing to sit on except the bed. I didn't bother you with my complaint when you were so busy last night, but now you have time to apologize for the inconvenience to us."

"There were a lot of chairs and benches in the square," Ripple said. "Someone probably took that one out for the celebration and forgot to bring it back, or maybe they didn't . . . maybe they put it in another room, you never know what some people will—"

"Do you want to search our packs to see if we're taking it away with us?" Halmarain asked with a laugh as she interrupted Ripple's chatter. Since the chair had been a large one with a high back and thick arms, it clearly would not have fitted in their bundles, even if they had taken it apart. Their armor was stacked with their belongings. They had decided not to wear it that day. The warm morning promised even hotter weather later in the day.

The innkeeper shook his head and walked away. "Lost a chair and I can't find the dog. I wonder if these celebrations are worth the trouble," he muttered as he disappeared into the back room of the inn.

"We should do something about Beglug's diet," the little wizard said as they gathered their belongings and left the inn, heading for the stable. Halmarain staggered under the load of her armor and the axe at her belt. The others carried the rest of their gear. The square was deserted, not surprising, since the celebration had continued until almost dawn. The little wizard took advantage of the empty street to make the gully dwarves wash at a horse trough.

According to the talk in the inn the night before, a good trail led north from Deepdel to Ironrock. Since their alternative was to travel through goblin infested mountains, they had decided to risk meeting travelers on the road.

"Knowing we have kender with us will probably keep most strangers at a distance," Halmarain said as they rode out of the village.

"Wizard more talk bad," Umpth announced, shaking his head until his dark beard waggled. "No like kender, no like mighty Aglest clan."

"Of course she likes us, she asked us to come with her, didn't she?" Ripple objected. "She'll be sorry when she realizes how she sounds. Just think. If you were as little as she is, you'd be worried about everything too, so don't pay any attention if she complains, though I must say, she really does a lot of—"

"I don't need anyone to apologize for me!" Halmarain snapped.

Trap, leading the way, threw a dark look back over his shoulder. He was forming his objection to the wizard's unjust accusation, but the gully dwarves beat him to it.

"People not like kender?" Umpth asked Grod as he rolled the wagon wheel along beside his pony.

"Like kender more than wizard," Grod said.

"Wizard have bad mood," Umpth said.

"Wizard live in bad mood," Grod agreed.

"I don't need any criticism from filthy gully dwarves," Halmarain snapped.

"Better dirt on body than in head," Ripple announced. She was imitating Aghar speech, but her voice was sharp with irritation. "Personally I prefer gully dwarves to little humans with little minds."

"Do you think large humans have better minds?" Trap asked his sister. "Wonder what giants are like?"

"I hope you find out," Halmarain announced. Her face red with anger. She fell back, allowing the kender and the gully dwarves, their ponies led by Ripple, to go on ahead.

The kender, never angry long or in a bad mood, began to speculate on what they would find in Ironrock.

"The name sounds as if it would be a dwarf town," Ripple suggested. "It will be interesting. Dwarves make wonderful things."

"It's a fortress," Halmarain called to them when she overheard the conversation. "Built back in the time of Huma, I believe."

They had been riding for an hour. The kender keeping up a fruitless, but running speculation on Ironrock that kept pulling the gully dwarves' attention away from the wagon wheel. The third time they dropped it and the entire party stopped while Trap dismounted to get it, he stopped and stood staring from it to a small stand of saplings nearby.

"Well?" Halmarain asked with her customary impatience. "Are we continuing our journey or not?"

"Yes, right—sure we are," Trap led his pony off the rutted road and tied it to a sturdy tree. "But I've got a good idea. Ripple, come help me."

While the little wizard sat on her pony and complained at the delay, Trap explained his idea to his sister. Using their belt knives, they each cut a slender sapling with a fork at the end. They compared them to make sure each was the same length, about seven feet long. Then Trap cut a sturdy one-foot length and they carried the three pieces back to the wheel.

"Now all we need is some rope or leather thongs," Ripple said. She and Trap searched their pouches. She pulled out the bracelet she had picked up when the Lytburg jeweler's display had tilted and looked at it in surprise.

"I thought I gave this back to him."

"Where did these come from?" Trap held up three small glass vials with dark liquid in them.

"They're mine, you thief," Halmarain snapped.

"Well, you shouldn't leave them lying around or I wouldn't have to pick up after you," Trap said, absently returning them to his pouch. He found his ball of strong cord and some thin strips of leather.

The gully dwarves watched anxiously as Ripple held the wheel while Trap slipped the foot long length of wood through the hub. He tied the forked end of the poles to the short axle length.

"Wheel is magic, is not for work," Umpth said.

"Not for work," Grod echoed his bother.

"Why not? You've been working to haul it around ever since we've known you," Trap retorted. "This way you won't keep dropping it."

Working quickly, they notched the blunt ends of the two poles and attached them to Umpth's saddle.

"Now the wheel won't get away from you," Trap said, looking with pride on his invention, a variation on a travois.

"Maybe now we can continue?" Halmarain demanded.

Trap turned, his face crinkled in a frown but he forgot his anger with the little wizard. He laughed at the sight behind her.

"Hey, look! Beglug liked his clothes better than we thought," he laughed.

During the hot morning, the little fiend had apparently decided he was warm enough without clothing. He had used the stop to pull off his trousers and shirt. The pants had disappeared. Only one sleeve of the shirt remained. He was stuffing it in his mouth.

"The monster!" Halmarain looked as if she might kill the merchesti.

"You were supposed to be watching him," Ripple said, laughing along with her brother. "Don't blame him if he has a healthy appetite."

The merchesti was a funny sight in his metal helmet and dwarf beard, naked except for his boots. They had been careful to keep the flesh-colored paste on his hands and face, and he did look strange, since the rest of his body was a deep gray-green.

"How did he get his pants off over his boots?" Ripple asked as she pulled her cloak from her pack and mounted her pony.

"The next time he does something funny when we're not looking, we should watch," Trap said. He took Ripple's cloak and tied it around Beglug's neck. They had to cover his strange gray-green body or leave the road.

"Hey, I like that! We'll watch when we're not looking," Ripple laughed as she led the gully dwarf's ponies on up the road.

They rode on through most of the morning, but the sun in the cloudless, windless sky fulfilled the promise of a hot day. The road seemed nearly straight, but it rose at a constant slope, and the ponies's head's were drooping. Hot dust rose from their passage. When they came to a small copse of woods with deep shade and a running stream, even the little wizard was willing to stop.

They unloaded the animals, gave them a drink from the

stream and tethered them so they could crop the sparse grass and lush underbrush. After the hot dust of the road, the moist air around the little creek smelled fresh and sweet.

Halmarain had slept the least the night before, and she sat leaning against a tree, dozing. Umpth and Grod poked around under the trees, and Beglug munched on a fallen branch held in his right hand, while with his left, he used a second sturdy stick to swat at a squirrel that was well out of reach.

The kender sat by the stream and used the time to redistribute the contents of their pouches, an ongoing chore as well as a favorite pastime.

"Oh, that's nice," Ripple said as Trap examined a cunning sparker, clearly dwarf made. "When did you get it?" she asked, holding out her hand, wanting a closer look.

"I don't know," Trap replied. He handed it to her, but frowned as he tried to remember it. He was certain it had not been in the pouch the day before.

"When, was probably yesterday," Halmarain said sleepily. "And where, was doubtless out of someone's pocket."

"Not true!" Trap said. "I would have remembered it. It's interesting." He pulled several other items from his pouch: a cluster of folded metal rods that opened up to be a roasting rack, a cluster of feathers tied with beaded string, and a small knife with a jeweled handle.

"Someone must have mistaken my pouch for his own," Trap said. "He sure has good stuff. I wish I knew who he was, I know he'd like them back." He also found items he did remember, like the cunning little glass bottle that he had taken from a dwarf's pocket, fingered, and inspected. When he'd tried to return it the dwarf had moved away.

The wizard snorted and closed her eyes as if unwilling to see what else the kender might pull from his pouch.

Ripple was the next one to be surprised. "I didn't think I had so many steel pieces," she said. "No wonder this pouch felt so heavy." She frowned, searched in another pouch and pulled out a small leather drawstring bag.

"Here are mine. Where did these come from?" She held up a hand, heaped with coins.

The conversation brought Halmarain to full wakefulness. She sat up and glared at the kender.

"You've been helping yourself to Orander's purse!" she accused.

"I have not!" Ripple denied heatedly.

"No, she hasn't," Trap held up the wizard's coin bag, red with runes around the sides. "It's so full another piece would cause it to split."

Halmarain came over and took the purse from Trap, first looking in it, then turning it in her hands.

"Orander never mentioned his purse was magic," she said slowly. "I've never heard of any spell that could constantly replenish coins. If there is one I'd think every wizard would be wealthy." Her eyes narrowed as she gazed at Trap. "You *did* pay for our room last night. . . ."

"Of course I did," he said. "The innkeeper wasn't a trusting person, which, I'd think, would be bad for business. I mean how many people want to be accused of sneaking out without paying their bills before they even get a room. I had to pay for it in advance."

"Are you certain?"

Her constant accusations were making Trap angry. She had just handed him back the purse, but he threw it back at her.

"If you don't trust me, you keep it," he snapped.

"Wizard, wizard, warm as a blizzard," Ripple taunted, also angry at Halmarain's doubts.

"Take us she must, but gives us no trust," Trap added, falling into the sibling game of rhyming taunts.

"Complain, complain, that's Halmarain," Ripple capped him.

"That's enough!" Halmarain snapped.

"Fuss and fight, all day all night," Trap said, laughing as if his joke was the funniest thing he had ever heard.

"Argle, bargle, gasp and gargle," Ripple threw herself back on the bed of fallen leaves by the stream, cackling with glee.

"I have heard all I want to hear!" the wizard shouted.

"Moan and shout and flounce about!" Trap rolled into a ball, laughing until tears streamed down his cheeks.

"One more word and you'll end your lives as frogs!" the wizard threatened. "I—"

The gully dwarves' wagon wheel interrupted Halmarain as it came hurtling along the stream bank from the direction of the road. The wheel nearly ran her down. Umpth and Grod followed it.

"Pony come," Umpth said.

"I keep away with magic," Grod said. "Find good magic." He waved a dead squirrel at them. By the flatness of the upper body, the little animal lost its life to a wagon wheel, one attached to a fully loaded cart.

"Beglug!" Ripple said, leaping to her feet, the argument forgotten.

"Repack your pouches, I'll take him into the woods," Halmarain said, dashing away.

The kender stuffed their belongings back in their pouches and retied the fasteners. They gave Umpth the pack that held Beglug's extra clothing and were standing by the stream, watching when six dwarves came in sight and slowed their mounts. They pointed at the woods and the stream. Clearly they also wanted to escape the heat of the road.

Grod stood waving his dead squirrel about as if he were warding off bad luck. The two kender, delighted at the prospect of meeting new people, rushed to the eaves of the copse by the road.

"Hello!" Trap called out. "This is a great place. It's cooler under the trees and the water in the stream is cold. Come and join us."

The two kender stood smiling at the six dwarves, Neidar by the fashion of their armor and clothing. They rode tough little hill ponies.

"A kender," said one of the dwarves. "It could be the one with that outlaw band."

"Oh, we're not outlaws, we're just traveling with a wiz—"

"A wizzy-waddle bunch of ponies, a couple of Aghar and some Neidar," Ripple said quickly, covering her brother's slip of the tongue. "The others are gathering firewood."

"Firewood? In this heat?" the dwarf leader said suspiciously. "Are you sure you're not with that outlaw band?"

"We've heard there is a kender outlaw," Ripple said, but only one kender outlaw and as you see there are two of us."

"Outlaw, him dead," Grod said. "Make good tale, that."

Chapter 15

The six dwarves were adult males, but still young,
Trap decided, since they had no gray in their beards.
They carried heavy axes and crossbows. The ponies
smelled water and strained at the reins. The dwarves
muttered together and one dismounted, carrying his axe
as he stepped into the shadows. His belt bristled with
knives and two large bovine horns rose from his helmet.
His headgear would serve as a deadly weapon if he
butted an enemy with it.

Still half blinded by the sun, he nearly collided with
Grod.

The gully dwarf apparently thought the new arrival
was about to attack him and leaped away and shook his
dead squirrel at the Neidar.

"Make you frog," Grod warned. The gully dwarf's
dodge had taken him into an area where the shade was

speckled with shafts of sunlight. He had removed his helmet because of the heat, and a shaft of light struck his blond head, making it glow. Another shaft illuminated the dead squirrel. With the rest of his body in deep shade, his head and the little carcass seemed to be floating in the air.

The dwarf glared at Grod for a moment and lowered his weapon. "It's an Aghar," he shouted back to his friends. The simple statement carried the implication that no self-respecting band of outlaws would have gully dwarves as members. The rest of the party rode into the shade of the trees and dismounted. The last three dwarves led ponies loaded with boxes and bundles.

"It's cooler here, but there's nothing to do," Trap said, following the dwarves to the stream. He reached for the reins of another pack pony, but the dwarf kept a tight hold on the leather lead. "I couldn't even find a bird's nest, so it will be nice to have someone to talk to. Is this your crossbow?" he asked, reaching for the weapon.

"Keep your thieving hands off that," the dwarf snarled.

Trap stood back, his smile faltering. "I wouldn't hurt it," he said. "I wouldn't take it. You're thinking of that other Trapspringer people keep talking about."

"Well if there's another, so be it, but this one—" the dwarf shook a finger in the kender's face, "—had better keep his hands in his pockets!"

The kender did his best to oblige. Since he had no pockets, he slid his hands into his pouches and fingered the items there. He had to admit some of them were probably more interesting than the possessions of the dwarves, though he would have enjoyed taking an inventory of their belongings.

Halmarain appeared, leading Beglug, who stared at the new arrivals. By his meek manner, the little wizard had put a calming spell on the little fiend to keep him out of trouble. He wore his second set of clothing, boots, beard, wig, and helmet. He gazed at the travelers with a mild interest before curling up at the base of a tree to sleep.

"Good journey to you and a warm dry hall at the end of your wandering," the little wizard said, speaking to the largest of the dwarves. Her greeting was an ancient Neidar tradition, one seldom heard since the Cataclysm.

"A good journey to you, my child," the dwarf replied, bowing. "Tolem Garthwar, at your service. With your permission we will share the shade of this wood and water our beasts."

Tolem's eyes searched the wood, taking in the six travelers. He had first looked toward Beglug, whose beard was streaked with gray. He appeared to be the elder, which should have made him the spokesman for the young female. Tolem ignored the kender and the gully dwarves as if they were unworthy of his time. Halmarain's small size and her delicate features gave her the appearance of a dwarf child, as did her voice. Even though she tried to make it sound deeper, it was still high and delicate, particularly for a dwarf. Tolem's expression demanded an explanation for why Beglug had ignored him.

Halmarain looked in the merchesti's direction and back at Tolem Garthwar. She raised one small finger to her temple and shook her head.

"An old wound," she said. "A blow from a goblin's club addled his brains. I fear my father's father will never be right again," she told him with a sigh. "If I can just get him to our people in the hills below Palanthus, they will help care for him. It's a hard journey, even with these friends to help."

Tolem nodded sympathetically.

"It is a serious matter for one so young to be traveling alone, my lady," he remarked. "We journey south for a time—on an errand of great importance, but. . . ."

"Oh, I'm not alone," Halmarain hastily reminded him in an effort to forestall any offer of help. "The kender and the gully dwarves are loyal friends. They will see me to the end of my journey."

While Halmarain had been dressing the merchesti, the dwarves had watered their animals. They had removed the packs and saddles and tethered their mounts to graze along with the other ponies. Their chores finished, they gathered beneath the deep shade of a large tree and sat on the ground in a semicircle.

Halmarain took the two kender aside, well away from the dwarves. "You touch one thing belonging to those dwarves and you'll end you lives as a pair of rabbits."

Trap scowled. He had expected the dwarves to doze in the heat and had already planned a pleasant afternoon learning about the traveling gear of the strangers. The little wizard read his expression correctly. She took a deep breath and muttered a spell.

The kender found his arms close to his body, and he was unable to move more than the tips of his fingers.

"What did you do?" Ripple was looking down at her own hands, her arms similarly trapped.

"I used a binding spell," the little wizard said. "Do you want to stay that way for the rest of the day, or do you promise not to touch anything that belongs to the dwarves?"

The two kender promised, reluctantly, because when they gave their word they would be bound by it as long as they remembered it, and both knew the little wizard would keep their memories fresh. Halmarain released them but took care to see that Trap and Ripple stayed well away from the dwarves. They sat on the opposite side of the circle, too far for their exploring fingers to reach into packs or pockets.

The dwarves' original dislike of the kender evaporated when Halmarain and Ripple brought out a ham and some day old bread and offered it around. They had brought the food from Deepdel. The dwarves supplied the drink: dwarf mead, strong and heady. When they had filled their stomachs one of them leaned forward, gazing at Grod.

"Did you say you had a tale about a dead outlaw?"

"Trap have tale," Grod answered.

Bored, and with nothing to explore, Trap let his mind wander into another tale of the kender outlaw. Still slightly tiffed at Halmarain's earlier accusations, he wove a red-robed wizard turned renegade into his story. His tale stretched out through the hot afternoon as he made sly digs at Halmarain and received angry glares in return.

Since she was sitting with her back to the tree where Beglug slept, she was not aware that he had awakened. He sat watching the dwarves as they passed earthen jugs around the circle. After several minutes he crept forward. He picked up one of the crocks that a dwarf and placed in the stream to cool and took it back to his tree.

Trap nearly lost the thread of his story as he watched the merchesti down the contents of the jug in one long gurgle. Then Beglug ate the jug.

The kender's story suddenly included a group of stone golems that made loud and crashing noises as he tried to cover the sound of Beglug's crunching. The little fiend was looking around for something else to snack on when Halmarain noticed him. She turned so the dwarves would not see her weaving a spell and in seconds Beglug curled up and went back to sleep.

The gully dwarves wandered around the area, so only Ripple, Halmarain, and the travelers heard how the imaginary Trapspringer met his fate in a ball of fire.

"A good tale, that," Tolem congratulated the kender. "The worst heat of the day has passed, so we'll be on our way."

As the dwarves rose and began to load their ponies, Halmarain and the kender discovered that Beglug was missing. The calming spell had worn away. They found him upstream, poking a stick into the hole of an unoffending mole.

"My calming spells don't seem to be strong enough," Halmarain said as they returned to the stream to saddle their own mounts. "I'll need to work on a stronger one."

By the time they returned, the dwarves had continued their journey. They had taken Halmarain's pony and had left a raw-boned, sickly looking animal in its place.

The little wizard glared at the dispirited animal and

out toward the road. "I should have let you and Ripple steal them blind," she said.

"Stop saying that! We don't steal," Trap objected. "How many times do I have to say it? Just because people are careless with their belongings, or they reach for their own pouches and we happened to be next to them and they put their—"

"I don't want to hear it," Halmarain snapped.

Chapter 16

The afternoon cooled and Halmarain was impatient to continue their journey. Since the kender had totally explored the small copse they had no objections and quickly saddled their ponies. The old pony, left them by the dwarves, seemed relieved to be carrying a lighter load.

The gully dwarves still had not learned to control their own mounts, but they had a talent for making useful items out of any material at hand. Umpth had found a length of rope he insisted had been left behind by the dwarves. He fashioned it into a series of three loops and attached it to the left stirrup of Halmarain's saddle. With a practicality belied by their otherwise childish behavior, he had even tied a short length of rope to the bottom loop. The little wizard used the loops to climb into the saddle. When she mounted she could pull her makeshift ladder up behind her and keep it from snagging on weeds and bushes on the trail.

"I guess Aghar have their uses after all," she admitted after she tested her new method of mounting her pony.

Trap was ready to lead the way and Halmarain kept the leads of Beglug's mount and the pack animal tied to the back of her saddle. Ripple brought up the rear leading Grod's and Umpth's mounts. The Aghar's wagon wheel, again set in it's travois-like frame, rolled along behind Umpth.

The road that ran north between the village of Deepdel and the fortress of Ironrock curved to skirt the foothills. The stand of woods where they had taken shelter from the midday sun gave way to gentle brush-covered slopes that rose to meet the mountain range beyond.

Before they began their journey Trap, Ripple, and Halmarain sat their mounts in a row, taking another look at one of Trap's maps.

"You'd think with all the pains the cartographer took with that *picture*, he would have added some practical detail," the wizard said with a snort. "He didn't even show Deepdel or the road to Ironrock."

"Still, it's a beautiful map," Trap said, defending his ill-gotten possession. He carefully rolled it, tucked it back into a pouch, and was just urging his pony forward when Umpth gave a hoot.

"Dwarves come back," the gully dwarf announced.

Trap looked back over his shoulder to see the dwarves galloping up the road. The kender stood up in his saddle. He was about to wave when Halmarain reached over and slapped his hand down.

"What did you take from them?" she asked, her eyes blazing in anger.

"Nothing!" Trap retorted. "You know that! You put a spell on us until we promised we wouldn't."

"Not soon enough, apparently," she spat out the words as she looked back at the road. "They're riding like they're chasing someone or being chased, and there's no one behind them. Get us out of here before they find us."

"Wizard fuss again," Umpth muttered.

"Not really fussing, she's just tired," Trap said, giving Halmarain the benefit of the doubt. "She'll apologize when she's in a better mood, but I know what you mean, she does get—"

"Enough of that," Halmarain practically growled. "Let's go."

"They've probably discovered they took the wrong pony and they're bringing it back," Ripple suggested.

"Tell another one," Halmarain said. She picked up her own reins, turned, and raced back into the small wood. Behind her, Beglug's mount and the pack animal followed on their leads.

"Trap tell one," Grod said as Ripple followed the wizard. "Him tell good tales."

The kender didn't answer the dwarves. Ripple's attention was on her route, not because of the ponies, but to protect the wagon wheel that bounced along behind Umpth. Since Halmarain had taken the lead, Trap rode beside his sister.

"I didn't get near their packs," he told Ripple with a sigh. "I would have enjoyed seeing what was in them, but I didn't get a chance."

"Neither did I," she replied. "They couldn't be after us. I wish she wouldn't be so suspicious." Ripple threw an angry look at the departing Halmarain.

"They probably want to return the pony," Trap said, agreeing with the suggestion Ripple had made earlier.

"They can't trade it for their animal if Halmarain keeps running away," Ripple said. "And if we don't hurry, we'll lose her."

Trap was forced to agree. The sun, still hot on their backs since Halmarain was leading them east into the hills, was dipping toward the horizon. In minutes the road was left behind and they were working their way between the foothills. Halmarain had been riding furiously, anxious to lose the dwarves. The kender galloped after her, keeping her in sight until she suddenly changed course, traveling south.

"Hurry, she's gone behind that hill," Ripple said.

"She could wait for us," Trap complained. He had not seen the dwarves turn off into the copse. They might have been hurrying up the road for some reason that had nothing to do with the kender and their party. Tolem's group could have lost something on their way south and they could be returning to find it. As far as the kender knew, they had not left anything behind in the copse except a length of rope. The kender had been bored and they had been looking for any diversion. They would have noticed.

Trap fell back as Ripple followed the wizard. He was sure the dwarves were not after them. As his sister led the mounts of the gully dwarves around the base of the hill behind which Halmarain had disappeared, Trap decided to put the wizard's doubts to rest. He dismounted, tied his pony to some high brush to keep it out of the sight, then walked back up to the top of the nearest knoll.

He stood watching, fully expecting to see the dwarves race by the woods and on up the road, but they had disappeared. In minutes he saw them again. They came out of the woods, traveling east. They moved more slowly, watching the ground as they followed the trail left by Trap and his companions.

One of the dwarves looked ahead, spotted the kender on the hillside, and shouted. The rest gave up their inspection of the trail and galloped toward Trap.

"Hello again," he called as they rode up. "I thought you were on the way to Deepdel. Did you come back to return our pony and get yours?"

"Thieving kender!" the leader shouted. "I'll have your head off your shoulders quick enough."

"But why? I don't know why you're so angry, because you were the one that left your pony. We didn't keep your animal on purpose and you took one of ours," Trap said, trying to be patient and understanding. He was getting tired of the accusations made against him, but he was willing to be reasonable.

"And we don't have any of your belongings. Here, I'll show you if you like," Trap said, opening the first of his pouches and reaching inside. He was not adverse to displaying his belongings. They were fun to look at and he would enjoy telling any tales that accompanied them. Perhaps he could even trade for something new and more interesting.

As he reached into the pouch, he felt an object he could not identify and pulled it out. He stood a moment gazing down on a gold ring he could not identify, until he remembered it had come from the wizard's chest beneath Orander's bed. He had intended to put it back, but in their hurry to leave he had forgotten it. To keep it from getting lost, he slipped it on his finger and held up his hand for the dwarves to see.

"This isn't yours, it belongs to a—" Just in time he remembered not to say wizard. "To a friend of mine," he said, taking a step forward, intending to show the dwarves the ring.

The step should have moved him forward approximately two feet. He heard the wind singing in his ears and he found himself standing fifty feet farther down the hillside. He gazed around him, wondering what had happened.

He heard dwarven oaths behind him and turned around. The dwarves were still sitting on their ponies, surrounding an empty space.

"Wow, that was *interesting*," he said.

The nearest dwarf heard the kender, twisted in his saddle, and stared at the Trap, who smiled back.

"Wonder how I did that?"

"There he is!" the dwarf shouted. "He's using some filthy wizard's spell."

"I did not!" Trap objected, and then changed his mind, though he decided not to mention it to the dwarves.

The nearest dwarf turned his mount and galloped toward the kender. Trap was still willing to turn out his pouches and prove he had nothing of theirs, but thinking the dwarf might run him down in his haste, Trap took a step to the side. He found himself another fifty feet away, this time to the north.

"A person should wear a hat when he uses this ring," he said, more to himself than the dwarves. The wind, whistling in his ears, was enough to give him an earache.

The first dwarf was still galloping toward where the kender had been before he took his last step. A second charged Trap's new position.

"What a wonderful game," he said and took another two steps, completely bypassing the four still on the slope. He stopped twenty feet away. Tolem, the leader, started toward him.

"Can't catch me," Trap caroled as he leaped into the air, spinning around. Definitely a mistake, he decided. He continued to spin four feet above the ground as he whipped through the brush. He seemed to be flung in several directions at once.

The dwarves charged in all directions, trying to catch him. He saw their faces, red with rage, and their glaring eyes as he sailed by them.

For a moment Trap seemed to hang in the air right above Tolem who reached up to grab him. Then by some perversity of the ring, he whipped around and dropped to sit on the croup of Tolem's pony, facing backward.

The startled animal reared. Tolem lost the reins as he grabbed at the saddle to keep from falling. Trap slid off the croup, stumbled twice, and found himself more than a hundred feet away, standing at the bottom of the hill.

He lost his balance and sat on the ground, his head still spinning. The dwarves had not spotted him, so he stayed where he was, letting his equilibrium settle while they raced around looking for him. Four of the six had pulled out their axes and were shouting threats and imprecations.

"Find that thief!" Tolem shouted to the other dwarves.

"There they go again, calling me a thief," Trap muttered. He was growing irritated with all the distrust.

"I know! I'll show them!" he announced, speaking at large to the nearest bushes. Ten magic steps took him around the hill and to his tethered pony. He retrieved his hoopak. Then, careful to measure his steps, he came to a stop in the exact middle of the group of angry dwarves.

He appeared so suddenly that the dwarves' surprise slowed their reactions, but Trap was ready. Using the pointed steel end of his hoopak he poked one rider in the rear. The dwarf gave a yell, jumped up in the saddle, and fell off his mount.

The rest waved their axes and charged him.

Confident he could elude his pursuers, he took two long steps and moved six feet.

"Oops," he muttered and ducked behind a bush as the dwarves charged, so intent on him they nearly struck each other with their weapons.

"Excuse me!" he said, ducking down into the under-brush. Keeping his head down, he scampered from bush to bush, narrowly escaping the dwarves. He dashed into a thick, high clump of bushes. Momentarily out of sight, he picked up a stone. Using the sling of his hoopak, he sent it skittering along the ground to the north.

The dwarves charged the sound of clattering rock. Trap crept south and then back toward the small copse of woods, the direction the dwarves would not expect him to go.

Still, they might think of it, and it would be best for them to think he was seeking the safety of the trees. He found a spring with a muddy bank and was careful to leave footprints heading west until he was on firm ground again. Then he turned south and hid under a large, thick bush.

Safe for the moment, he gazed down at the ring, took it off and inspected it closely. He shook it and held it up to his ear. Then he decided magic wouldn't slosh like water in a jug. He put the ring back on his finger and took another cautious step. No magic widened his kender pace. Disappointed, he took the ring off and slipped it back into his pouch.

He hated to think he had used up all the magic. Taking giant steps had been fun. Even spinning around in the air had been interesting. And he had accomplished some-thing important. He had kept the dwarves, now milling about trying to find him, from following Ripple and Halmarain.

But the sun was down, it would soon be dark, and how was he to find his sister and the little wizard?

Trap sat on the ground inside a clump of bushes and thought about the dwarves as well as his friends. The dwarves were still beating the bushes when one found the footprints by the spring.

After a short conference they dashed off toward the woods. The little wizard, Ripple, and the animals they led had been out of sight when the dwarves appeared. Trap had hidden his mount, the dwarves seemed to think that their quarry had returned to the copse and the road.

The kender worked his way through the underbrush until he reached his mount and set out in search of the rest of his party.

"The way they brandished those axes, they certainly weren't friendly anymore," Trap told his pony. "And I'm tired of being called a thief. I didn't take anything from them. Not one even came close enough to me to drop anything in my pouches."

To make certain, he opened them one at a time, fingering and identifying various items. Except for a pretty little stone he had found in the creek, he could not find a single item he had not possessed before he met the dwarves.

He pulled it out and held it close to his face since the sun had set and he could barely see it. He considered it as the pony picked its way through the brush. It was only a rock, smoothed by the stream. He had picked it up before the dwarves arrived. In putting it back into his pouch he found another one. He pulled it out too. By that time the twilight had deepened until he could not see the second stone, but by touch he remembered it. It was not stone at all, but the little gray-green disk of glass he had found on the floor of the wizard Orander's workroom after the attack of the merchesti.

"And I had this one long before I met the dwarves," he said as he put it back in his pouch. Since he could not see the trail in front of the pony, he dismounted and led the animal as he went in search of his sister and his friends.

He wandered for hours trying to find the others. Unable to see their trail, he had decided to stop for the night and continue his search at dawn. He was looking for a likely place to stop for the night when he stumbled on their camp. He startled them as he walked out of the darkness.

"Trap!" Ripple cried out and jumped up from the fire.

"Him dead, make a good tale. . . ." Grod said. At the approach of the pony he had jumped up and waved his dead squirrel in an attempt to ward off anything unfriendly. Umpth stood holding the wagon wheel.

"I'm not so dead!" Trap replied with heat as he led his pony into the shallow cave which was hardly more than a depression in the stony hillside.

Ripple filled her cup with hot tea and cut him a generous slice of ham. She tucked it into a bun of day old bread and he was munching away when Halmarain looked up from the study of her spellbooks.

"You were able to keep the dwarves from following us," she said. She made a statement as if she expected no less from the kender.

"Of course I did!" He accepted the credit as if he had planned the outcome of his adventure "They were certainly mad and I don't understand it at all," Trap said. "They kept calling me a thief, but you know we don't have anything of theirs."

"Of course I do," Halmarain mocked Traps tone.

"Then you might reward him by doing some nice magic," Ripple said, a martial light in her eye.

"Then Trap tell story," Grod said with a grin.

Chapter 17

So no part of history would be lost, Astinus recorded . . .

Draaddis Vulter gave out with a string of curses that turned two confused mice into cats. They dashed into a strange orange cloud that suddenly filled the center of his work room.

Once the kender tucked the rune-trimmed viewing disk into his pouch, Draaddis and Takhisis were blind to their whereabouts. Draaddis decided the little thief had even forgotten he carried it. Still, the black-robed wizard thought it fortunate that the kender had it with him. Sooner or later his desire to handle and inspect his possessions would lead him to pull it out of his pouch. If it had been left on the floor of Orander's laboratory, they would have no way of ever telling where the kender might wander.

It was just bad luck that when the little thief finally

pulled it out, darkness had prevented the wizard from getting a clear idea of the location of the kender.

He stood wondering what he should do. Did he dare tell his queen he had finally seen the kender again but could tell her nothing about them? He would not. He could not. Despite knowing Takhisis could only torment him through his own mind, he still lived in terror of the illusions she could plant in his head.

"There was more to see than you supposed," Takhisis spoke from the orb.

The wizard whirled around, dizzy as fear drained the blood from his head. He saw the humorous glitter in the eye of the goddess as she watched from the black orb. Obviously she knew he had been considering whether or not to tell her he had seen the kender again. Since she did not mention his omission, he would not be the one to bring it up.

"It is my good fortune that you, my queen, have better eyes than mine," the wizard replied.

"The kender was traveling east, toward the mountains," the Queen of Darkness informed him. "They are not far north of where they crossed at the southern end of the Vingaard Mountains when they were traveling west."

"First they go west, across the highlands, then north for a short distance, now east, back into the mountains again?" Draaddis pulled at his ear while he considered the confusing route of the kender. He shrugged away the inconsistency.

"At least we can put Kaldre on their trail again," he told his mistress.

"Yes, send your messenger," Takhisis smiled in anticipation.

"We must have that stone if we are to bring the merchesti into this world," Draaddis agreed.

"It will come, and more," Takhisis smiled wickedly. "Once we have both stones we will open the portal wider and bring more of its kind. They will rampage across the lands and the world of Ansalon will be in a turmoil as great as the time of the Cataclysm."

Takhisis drew back from the orb, her entire face became visible and glowed with an unholy light as she seemed to savor the idea of what was to come. Then her beautiful features sharpened.

"But your death knight must get the gate stone from the kender."

"He will, my queen, he has been given life to serve you. He is ambitious and you have offered to make his dreams a reality—"

"But they will only be a reality if he hurries," Takhisis snarled. The vision of the beautiful woman shimmered and her true self—the five headed dragon—writhed in the globe. The eyes, flat and merciless, glared at the trembling wizard. Then, just as quickly, the image of a human female appeared again.

"Have I not told you, Draaddis, that the infant will grow? The rate of its increase is still slow, but any day now it could reach the stage when its development is rapid and it will turn ravenous, chewing up everything within sight. In their voracious appetites when they grow they have even been known to devour their parents. It looks to the kender! When that hunger begins, the kender will be its first targets. If the little female thief still has the gate stone it will be endangered."

"How—how long will it be before the stage of rapid growth begins?"

"I don't know. Not even the gods know much about the Plane of Vasmarg, and the creature as been removed from its own world, which means it could develop more slowly or even more rapidly."

"I will urge speed upon Jaerume Kaldre," Draaddis replied.

"See that you do. Time does not favor us in any way, Draaddis. Daily the lands of Krynn become more peaceful. The distrust after the wars following the Cataclysm is waning. I do not want to face a unified world when I return to your plane."

Takhisis wore a slightly dissatisfied expression as her face retreated from the globe and reverted to the shape of the five headed dragon.

The last the wizard saw of her was one head, the nostrils smoking, and those flat, implacable, merciless eyes glaring at him before the orb clouded.

At least she had not tortured him, he thought, thankful for small blessings. Still, he would not escape her wrath for long if Jaerume Kaldre did not succeed.

Chapter 18

The next morning my Uncle Trapspringer was glad his sister asked a question that was on his mind as well. . . .

"So now where?" Ripple had asked Halmarain. They were saddling the ponies. The little wizard was trying to pull her pony's head down to put the bridle on it. The animal was restive and kept raising its head.

"Why do you keep trying?" Ripple asked, forgetting her earlier question.

"I'm not helpless, just . . . vertically challenged," the little wizard snapped as she tried to reach the pony's head again.

When they finished saddling their mounts they would be ready to continue their journey. They had made their camp the previous evening in the high foothills. As they began the day's ride, Ripple asked her question again.

"We should try to reach the road again," Halmarain said and then shook her head. "No not the road, we'll ride north through the foothills. We must reach Palanthus."

Ripple sighed and her brother understood. They wouldn't have any opportunity to make any new friends. Ripple's dejected expression soon gave way to limitless kender optimism.

"But maybe we'll see some new creatures," she said. "Trap, remember Studder Rangewide's stories about ogres, nagas, griffons and—"

"—And satyrs, hulderfolk and bakali," Trap added to the list, skipping about with excitement. "If we stay close enough to the mountains, maybe we'll meet some really interesting people!"

"You're scaring me to death!" Halmarain shuddered. "And you'll probably set out to find monsters the minute my back is turned. I'd say let's use the road, but we're being chased by dwarves, and remember, there is still the cloaked man on your trail. He's after you, even though you won't admit it. If Orander is still alive, every day we lose lessens his chances of returning to Ansalon. Every day increases the danger of Beglug's parent breaking through to Krynn." She glanced around at the young fiend who crouched and poked a stick into a ground squirrel's hole. "And he's becoming meaner every day."

Trap sighed. Halmarain insisted on distrusting the little merchesti. As if to prove his prowess, the little fiend froze, his eyes on something in the undergrowth. He slowly drew back the stick he had been using to torment the ground squirrels. With a flick of his wrist he sent the stout little staff sailing and it thunked down on the head of an unwary rabbit.

Chuckling evilly, he scuttled across the camp and came back holding the small stunned animal by one of its hind legs.

Trap had picked up Umpth's saddle when he heard the scream of the rabbit and looked back to see Beglug tormenting it. The merchesti tugged at the rabbit's forelegs, as if he intended to tear them off while the rabbit still lived.

"Stop that!" Trap grabbed his hoopak and dashed across the camp. A sound crack on the little fiend's arm convinced Beglug to drop his captive. The rabbit dashed away into the underbrush, its front legs gave way and it rolled as much as it ran. Beglug bared his teeth at Trap and snarled, but the kender refused to be intimidated.

"You can kill to eat, but you don't hurt things for fun," the kender told the little merchesti.

"You'll never teach him mercy or kindness," Halmarain said.

Beglug rubbed his arm and whined, gazing up at Trap and the little wizard with a pathetic expression.

"And don't let that sad look fool you," Halmarain warned. "He's an evil fiend and will never be anything else."

"He'll learn not to hurt things for fun," Trap said, determined to civilize the little merchesti.

Trap didn't like her distrust of the little merchesti, but even worse, she was scaring Grod. The smaller gully dwarf's eyes widened every time she mentioned evil, and he was beginning to watch Beglug as if he expected the little fiend to bite the arm off one of his friends.

When they began their day's journey, Trap led. He angled north through the foothills. At dawn the sun had risen, promising a bright day, but the clouds began rolling in before they had been traveling for an hour.

Half an hour later, a bolt of lightning struck the side of the mountain. Beglug roared in delight and waved his arms. The little wizard gave a startled scream that set the ponies to sidling.

"We should find a shelter before the ponies bolt," Halmarain suggested.

Trap agreed. He wouldn't mind walking through the mountains, but like all kender he loved riding and would hate to lose his mount. He hurried ahead searching for any type of overhang that would protect them from the approaching storm.

He didn't go far. Traveling along the easiest path, he discovered a shallow cave with a low, narrow entrance.

The rest of the party reached shelter just minutes before the storm broke.

The entrance was so low they had to dismount and pull the heads of their mounts down as they entered.

"Another delay," Halmarain muttered as she followed her mount into the dimness.

Further back in the cave, Grod gave Beglug a few sticks for a snack while Umpth freed the wagon wheel from its makeshift travois.

"Many feet come," Umpth called out, tugging his dark beard in distress.

The two kender and the little wizard turned to see him standing with his ear against the metal rim of the wheel.

"That gully dwarf—" Halmarain started to complain but Trap interrupted.

"Don't pick on him. He was right the last time," the kender reminded the little wizard.

Halmarain's eyes flickered and she nodded. "I suppose that loose rim could pick up and magnify vibrations," she said, providing a logical explanation for what the Aghar considered magic. "We should camouflage the entrance if we can."

Halmarain trotted to the entrance of the cave and peered out. "I don't see anyone yet," she said to Trap. "Can you cut that large bush and prop it up in front of the entrance? I'll keep the ponies quiet."

Trap dashed out into the downpour and reached for his knife, but it was not in his sheath.

"Beans! I lost it," he muttered. He rammed his hand in his pouch, seeking the other knife, the one similar to Orander's.

His finger encountered a ring and it was on his finger before he realized it. Still he had found the knife. To his surprise the knife cut the bush as easily as if the wood was warm cheese. He turned and started back for the mouth of the cave. He took one step and bounced off the face of the low cliff that had been thirty feet away.

The ring had magic again! Unfortunately it would give him problems returning to the cave.

He reluctantly slipped the ring off his finger and dropped it back into his pouch. Four hurried steps took him back to the cave entrance where he rammed the pointed end of the brush into the rain-softened ground. Halmarain had been watching from the shelter, and she gazed at him with speculation.

"What did you do out there?"

"I cut a bush." He thought she had been watching.

She opened her mouth to object when a bolt of lightning struck nearby. They heard the panicked scream of a horse and several frightened voices. She put a finger to her lips for silence.

The tiny human and the kender peered between the leaves of the bush as a mounted rider in a cloak with a cowled hood rode by. He lead a large group of kobolds. A wash of evil menace hung in the air with the rider's passing.

They continued to watch, but none of the travelers gave the brush a second look as they passed. Minutes later another bolt of lightning flashed and distance muted the frightened screams of the kobolds.

Halmarain turned away from the entrance, fear and anger fighting for dominance in her expression.

"Someone wearing a black cloak went to Deepdel looking for kender," she whispered. "That rider fitted the description, and he's on our trail. He has to be after you."

"No! I told you! He couldn't be looking for us," Trap said. "I don't even know who he is."

"I've never seen him, and he's not someone we'd forget," Ripple added with a shiver. "There was such an evil feeling about him."

"True," the little wizard nodded. "You wouldn't forget him, and his isn't a purse you'd be likely to rifle."

"We don't—" Trap started an angry denial, but Halmarain interrupted him.

"I want to know how you took that enormous step," she demanded.

"With this ring," he said, forgetting his anger. He opened his pouch and searched in it with his fingers until he found the little golden object. He was willing, even anxious to show it to the wizard's apprentice and get her opinion.

"I guess it fell into my pouch when we looked through a chest under Orander's bed," he said. He told her about their exploration while she had been studying the wizard's books. He also related his first experience with it, when he had jumped around and confused the dwarves that had called him a thief.

"Wonderful! I wish I could have seen you whizzing about. I don't blame you for tricking them," Ripple said. "It wasn't nice of them to call you names. Even Halmarain knows we could not have taken anything from them. She had pinned our arms to our sides with a spell, though I must say I don't think that was a good thing to do at all. And anyway, we promised we wouldn't, and even then she kept us away from them."

"Apparently I didn't take precautions soon enough," the little wizard muttered.

"You did. We didn't touch anything of theirs. Now, I want to know about the ring," Trap insisted, unwilling to be sidetracked.

"Orander made the ring," Halmarain replied. "But he put an extra spell on it." She gave them a rare smile. "I have to admit not all the thieves in this world are kender. Years ago he had an apprentice with sticky fingers, so he protected his belongings by limiting their powers."

"You mean it works for a while and then quits?" Ripple asked. "Interesting. Not too much fun, though, if it quits in the middle of a step. A person could fall in a creek, or on his face or something."

Trap had been fingering other items in his pouch. If he remembered correctly . . . and he did. He pulled out a second ring.

"I have this one, too," he said, holding it out. "I haven't tried it yet, so I don't know what it does, except it could be the one that makes the big steps, but if it is, then I don't know what that one does," he said. He slipped the second ring on his finger. Nothing seemed to happen so he pulled it off, handed it to Halmarain and took the first one back. When he slipped it on his finger, Halmarain jumped in surprise. Ripple gasped and whirled around.

"Trap!" she shouted.

"I'm right here," the male kender said. He pointed to himself, but he couldn't see the finger that should have been aimed in his direction. "At least I think I'm here. What happened to . . . Wow! Great! Big jiggies! I'm invisible!" He slipped off the ring and became visible again. He inspected it. "Does it have a limiter too?" he asked.

"Probably," Halmarain said. "It will continue to work if you know the word that negates the limiting spell. I don't know it. Many of Orander's belongings have limiters."

"I wonder if this is one of Orander's rings," Ripple said, reaching in her pouch. She pulled out one that exactly resembled the two Trap was holding. "I don't know how I came to have it but it looks like those." She handed it to Halmarain and leaned over to look at the ones her brother held. "I tried it on, but it didn't do anything, so maybe it came from somewhere else."

"No, it has Orander's mark, so it does something," the little wizard said as she gave it back. "I'll let you keep them for now, but take care of them. I think you'd better turn out your pouches and show me what else you took."

"Fine! I'll show you. And are you going to show us what's in your bag?" Ripple asked, her eyes flashing with anger over the insult.

The little wizard frowned, thought better of it and nodded. "Perhaps I'd better. Then, if you find one of my possessions, you'll know it belongs to me and give it back."

"You first," Ripple said. She had less patience with Halmarain's accusations than her brother.

"Very well. I'll show you what's in my bag and I warn you, none of my possessions should ever—" She shook her finger in the faces of the two kender. "—*ever* fall into your pouches."

The ragged little bag Halmarain habitually wore over her shoulder was deceptive. She carefully pulled out a stack of ten spellbooks, each one as large as the bag. A small purse, two outfits of clothing, an extra pair of boots, and a cloak followed.

"How do you get all that in a bag that's so small?" Trap asked.

"Wizard's have their secrets, even apprentices," she said as she continued to dig, her brows rose in surprise and dipped in a frown.

She upended the bag and out came a large pile of steel pieces, a wicked looking knife, and a pair of finely stitched gloves that were too large for her hands. The last item to fall out appeared to be a necklace made of thirty overlapping silver disks, each an inch and a half wide, fastened together with silver links. Each disk had been delicately engraved with pictures and dwarf runes.

She hurriedly pulled her clothing, boots, and spell-books away from the last items to fall from her bag, as if they might be contaminated by contact.

"These things aren't mine!" she insisted.

Chapter 19

Halmarain continued to deny any knowledge of the items, waving a hand to indicate the loose steel pieces, the knife, the gloves, and the necklace. She glared accusingly at the kender. They seemed so delighted with the gloves and the necklace that it soon became plain that they were seeing the items for the first time.

"You didn't put these things in my bag?"

"I'm sure I didn't," Ripple said. "You usually keep such a tight hold on it I don't think I could, and I've never seen these things. These gloves are beautiful. If they won't fit you, I'd really like to have them, if you gave them to me, that is."

"Of course, one steel piece looks like any other," Trap added, "But I'm sure I would remember this necklace. It's interesting—all these drawings on the disks." He picked it up before Halmarain could stop him. "Wonder if these runes and drawings are just ornamental or if they mean something special?"

Ripple scooted across the dirt floor to join her brother and they both inspected the finely worked drawings. The little wizard worried over how it came into her possession.

"I didn't take that necklace," she insisted. "I don't know how it got into my bag! By the Book of Gilean, I sound just like a kender!"

"Someone dropped it into your purse by mistake. We keep telling you that people are so careless with their belongings," Ripple answered absently, most of her attention still on the silver disks.

"They're always forgetting where they leave their stuff," Trap agreed.

"When did it get into my bag?" Halmarain's mind was off on another track. "It wasn't there when we left Deepdel. I repacked everything." Her eyes widened. "The only people we've been near since we left our rooms were the innkeeper and the dwarves. It wouldn't have belonged to the man in Deepdel. It looks as if it could have been dwarf made—*that's* why the dwarves are chasing us."

The kender were more interested in the string of disks than in the wizard's ruminations.

"We need more light." Trap looked suggestively at Halmarain's staff.

"No," the wizard answered, shaking her head and glancing toward the cave's entrance. "I don't know what I felt from that rider in the black cloak, but there was something strange. I don't want to use any magic right now. He might sense it and come back."

"Then I'll get us a light," Trap said, accepting her objections as reasonable. He jumped up and searched for the dwarf sparker that had found it's way into his pouch while he was in Deepdel.

A sparker was no good without wood to burn, so he gave the cave a quick scan. He was hampered by a number of roots hanging down from the ceiling. He touched one. It was dry and would make a good torch. A one handed tug was not sufficient to pull it free, so he tucked the sparker back into his pouch and used both hands. The root was stubborn so he jumped, grabbed it, and swung back and forth.

"I'll help," Ripple said. She gave a short leap and added her weight which was enough to dislodge the root, though not to pull free.

The root dropped three inches, bringing down a foot of earth from the ceiling.

"Oops!"

"What have you done?" Halmarain cried as she jumped to her feet.

"I was just trying to get that root to use as a torch," Trap began an explanation. He was interrupted as mud gushed from the hollow where part of the dry earth ceiling had been a moment before. He skipped to the side.

"It sure is wet up there," he announced. "I guess there must be a stream close by—"

A wail interrupted the kender. They turned to see the young merchesti scrambling to his feet while he wiped a glob of mud from his face. Before either of the kender or Halmarain could move, the kender's surmise was proven correct. A steady stream of water, well laden with mud, poured down from the ceiling.

"Cave fall in," Umpth announced as he stood looking up. A face full of mud was the reward for his wisdom.

"The ponies!" Ripple squealed and dashed for the back of the cave. Halmarain grabbed Beglug's arm and led the little fiend out onto the trail, pushing aside the camouflaging bush as she went. The kender tugged at the reins of the ponies, leading them toward the exit while the two gully dwarves trotted along behind them. A huge hunk of wet soil fell and knocked Grod off his feet. In seconds he was half buried in mud.

"Grod!" Umpth cried, alerting the kender, who dropped the reins of the animals and hurried back.

"Mud fall," Grod gasped, his bright blue eyes wide with fright. Umpth sent the wagon wheel sailing out the entrance to the cave. Then he turned and pulled on one of

Grod's arms. Trap and Ripple hurried back and tugged at the gully dwarf's other arm.

More of the ceiling came down. It oozed around the legs of the kender and Umpth, completely covering Grod.

The kender and the gully dwarf stood knee deep in mud as they tugged at Grod. With a heave they brought his head out of the wet soil. As quickly as they could move, lifting one leg at a time—they couldn't wade through the thick sludge—they moved toward the entrance. They continued to pull at the smaller gully dwarf until he was free.

"Long arms now," Grod moaned as they hauled him out into the open. Behind them the cave fell in completely and the mud rolled out onto the mountain trail completely blocking their intended path.

Umpth retrieved his artifact while the rest stood in the pelting rain that quickly washed away the mud, but the storm frightened the already skittish ponies.

"Kobolds in front of us, dwarves behind us and caves that turn into mud pits," Halmarain muttered as she led her pony back down the trail until they could start across country again. "We'll need a lot of luck if we're to get through these mountains." Her wet curls hung down in her face, and she blew at them before reaching up to push them back.

At first they could only see a few feet through the deluge, but in half an hour the storm passed, leaving as quickly as it had arrived. The sun peeked briefly through the low clouds, giving the slopes a dewy sparkle. Trap walked as he led the way and Ripple joined him. They led their mounts.

"We'll just keep going north," Trap said with a sigh. "I sure hope we stop off at Ironrock, because it might be a nice place to see, even if it does take us a little out of the way . . . but if we're going to be traveling for weeks anyway, then what difference would it make if we took a little longer? I mean, between the gorges we came through and the circling around we've done trying to get away from the dwarves and that person in the black cloak, we're just going around in circles anyway. I bet we've really confused everyone."

"Why shouldn't they be confused?" Ripple asked. "We are, and if they're following us, they should be too. And you're right about going in circles."

Her brother nodded.

Grod and Umpth still had not learned to control their mounts when they rode, but they could lead the animals if given the reins. Halmarain walked behind them, leading her own animal, the pack pony, and Beglug's. Ripple and Trap took turns walking well ahead to find the easiest course.

For the first two hours after leaving the cave they traveled slowly. The hooves of the ponies sank to the hocks in the mud. Every step was accompanied by sucking noises as the animals lifted their feet. As they continued northward they left the mud behind. Trap had removed the young fiend's boots and Beglug scampered about, a stick in his hand as he chased every wild creature unwary enough to show itself.

Before long, Trap found a use for the young merchesti's exuberance. Using the sling of his hoopak, he brought down two rabbits the little fiend flushed out of hiding. Soon he killed a third, which he allowed Beglug to eat.

They came to a small creek, merely a trickle in a bed of mud and stones. Trap spotted the tracks of boots and ponies.

"Gee! People! We're not the only ones traveling through the hills," he told his sister as he paused to study the prints. He frowned at one. Grod came up to stand beside him. The gully dwarf pointed at the indentation in the firmer mud.

"Wizard's pony," he said. "Maybe pony magic. It find her."

"Big jiggers, it *is* Halmarain's first pony," Ripple said with surprise. She pointed to the irregularity in the hoof print that the gully dwarf had noticed. "The one the dwarves took by mistake."

"Is," Umpth said as he drudged across the stream carrying the wheel. The magic artifact of the Aglest clan was unsoiled but the gully dwarf had managed to get mud on his hands, face, beard, and helmet.

"I thought the Neidar were following us," Ripple said with a puzzled frown.

"It's strange," Trap said thoughtfully. "The stranger and the kobolds are following us, but they're up ahead, and the dwarves are supposed to be trailing us but they've passed us too."

"Maybe following is different here," Ripple said.

"How different?" Umpth asked, his dark wrinkles deepening as he tried to work out the solution.

"In Hylo, when you follow someone, you stay behind them." Trap explained. "But here, we're behind everyone who's after us. I'm glad they're not chasing us, we might never catch up."

Chapter 20

Astinus of Palanthus described the scene. . . .

Jaerume Kaldre stilled the horse that fidgeted under him. He waited on the ridge of the mountain spur, hidden from the trail below by a clump of bushes and the limbs of a small tree. Below him, the string of seven ponies led by the kender, the gully dwarves, and the dwarf, wound their way up the mountain trail, slowed in their ascent by the mud of the recent rain.

Luck and the blessing of Takhisis had finally favored him. When the sudden rain ceased, he soon realized he had somehow missed the kender and the little fiend. He had been on their trail, had even seen their tracks. During the rain any prints left by his quarry would have been washed away, but when the rain stopped Kaldre knew the ensuing mud would show the party's trail. Soon after he found himself leading the kobolds along a muddy track free of any prints. The kender and their companions were behind him. He forced the protesting kobolds up the steep sides of the mountain until he spotted the party traveling around the hills just west of the mountains.

His plan for the ambush was hasty, but his motley group of humanoids were in place. All he had to do was wait.

Beside the death knight, Malewik, the kobold leader, fidgeted too. His expressed reason for his impatience was to join the band of kobolds that were waiting to ambush the travelers. Kaldre knew the humanoid's desire to be on his way stemmed from his wish to part company with his undead commander. Far from resenting the kobold's nervousness and fear of him, Kaldre enjoyed it. His ability to instill fear was a heady power.

"Keep your group hidden in the bushes and behind boulders until the travelers are even with you," the death knight cautioned. "Then capture the two kender and the little fiend. They are not to be injured."

"Kill the others," Malewik nodded, wrinkled his nose, and opened his mouth in a silent laugh.

"Kill them or leave them, I don't care," Kaldre said. He was not interested in three dwarves. Gully dwarves were of no use to him, and he had never understood the purpose of the small one that was traveling with them. His orders were to get a stone the girl kender had in a pocket or pouch and to secure the little fiend. The male kender had a magic viewing disk belonging to Draaddis Vulter, and the wizard wanted it back, but the death knight's priorities were plain.

"Kill the kender if you have to, but bring them to me to search," he ordered Malewik. "Do not harm the little fiend or I'll skin you alive." With those last instructions he sent the kobold leader down the hill to join the others.

Kaldre knew he would have to watch the thieving humanoid. Malewik's eyes had brightened when the death knight had ordered him to bring the kender to him to be searched. Kobolds were alert to anything that smacked of value and could be stolen.

"Remember, we're taking what the kender carry and the fiend to the wizard," Kaldre reminded Malewik. "You don't want to fail Draaddis Vulter, do you?"

"Kobolds is not making wizard mad," Malewik said and for once he did not laugh.

Kaldre wanted to ride down the mountainside himself, but the fear that he engendered in the kobolds radiated from him like a cloud and might alert the kender before they reached the ambush. There were drawbacks to his renewed existence, he decided. Still, once the kobolds sprung the trap, he could be on them before they had time to search the kender.

Fear of Jaerume Kaldre would make them capture the kender and the little fiend, but they should then be too interested in killing the dwarves to do more than disarm the prisoners and hold them until the bloody work of destruction was over.

Below him he could see Malewik working his way down to his people. They were crouched behind bushes and boulders on both sides of the trail where a gentle slope gave them easy access to their prey.

Movement off to Kaldre's left caught his attention. He turned his head just in time to see a goblin slip behind a bush. The death knight recognized the hardened leather helmet with the rusting metal plates attached. The humanoid was the leader of the band that had attacked the kobolds in the maze of gullies at the southern tip of the Vingaard Mountains.

The stupid humanoids were still following, wanting revenge for the attack.

Kaldre had lost five of his followers to the goblins before he had routed them, more with fear than with weapons. He had killed three, but they had numbered more than forty. While he watched, four advanced toward the ambush. They were moving cautiously, as if not sure whether to attack or not.

Not, he decided.

He had routed them once, he could do it again. He

turned his horse and moved slowly over the crest of the ridge. Hidden by the growth at the top, he was able to ride out of sight of the trail. Cursing the kender, who had alerted the goblins by shouting up and down the gullies, he gritted his teeth and spurred the horse along the steep slope.

Because of the kender he had to leave the scene of the ambush to drive off the goblins. Because of the kender the kobold might find the gate stone the female carried and damage it in some way before the death knight could get back to them.

A shout might have warned the goblins off, but it might also alert the kender who were said to have sharp ears. Kaldre rode straight at the goblins, hoping they did not cry out. Unfortunately he had not seen all the band. Two had crept closer to his position than he had realized. His eye had been on the leader and he flushed two who were further up the slope and nearer to him, though they had been well hidden until he rode by the bushes where they had taken cover.

They broke and ran, shouting a warning as they went. Neither took more than ten steps before the death knight was on them. His swinging sword decapitated one and hacked through the shoulder of the second, leaving the goblin on the ground, screaming in misery. The rest of the goblins broke away, all except one, smaller than the rest.

A goblin shaman.

Unafraid of the death knight, he threw a spell, a greenish cloud that spread itself as it neared Kaldre. Not sure what the magic of a goblin could do to him, the death knight hauled back on the reins of his mount. The horse skidded and managed to turn away from the greenish cloud, but he slipped and lost his footing on the muddy mountainside.

As Kaldre went down, he saw another, blue white mist leave the hands of the shaman. He was crouched, just getting to his feet and knew he could not escape the second spell. As it closed over him with a cold deeper than death, his arms and legs froze into immobility.

Helpless, held in place by the freezing spell, Kaldre expected the goblins to attack and hack him to pieces, but they backed away, down the mountain. It was then he realized that less than half the goblins had been creeping up the spur.

Where were the rest of them?

Chapter 21

All kender love travel, and my Uncle Trapspringer was no exception. . . .

As they journeyed north, Trap felt the warmth of the sun on his left cheek, while his right was cooled by a late afternoon breeze. Soon they should begin looking for a place to camp for the night. He was looking about for a stream—they should camp near water—when he saw a snake gliding over the grass. The reptile's intended victim was a bright blue bird who tugged at a worm.

"Oh, no you don't," Trap shouted and forgot he was leading his pony. He released the reins and scampered up the gentle incline. He picked up a rock, flipped his hoopak up and set the stone in the pouch. His aim wasn't as good as it should have been, but he did startle the snake.

"Your pony!" Halmarain cried, pointing down the slope. Trap's mount, freed from the restraints of the reins, had left the trail and wandered off down the slope toward a smooth stretch of range grass.

"Hey, where are you going?" Trap shouted at the animal and dashed after it.

The pony saw the kender chasing it and trotted away. It stopped just long enough to grab a bite of grass and chewed as it moved off again.

"Come here," Trap laughed, not at all irritated with the animal. It seemed to be teasing him, playing a game, and he was willing to take part in the fun.

"Will you stop clowning around and catch that pony?" the wizard yelled at him as the rest of the party approached an area of low bushes and boulders.

Trap turned his head to answer. Definitely not a good idea, he decided. While he had been looking back over his shoulder, he had stepped into a shallow swale of loose rock. He lost his footing and fell sprawling. By the time he regained his feet he realized the pony had trotted farther away.

"I won't be long, he's stopped—" Trap forgot what he'd been saying. He had reached a clump of bushes and out of it came a goblin. The kender stared at the humanoid, who seemed as surprised as Trap, for a long, uncertain moment. Trap recovered first.

"Hello. Would you mind helping me catch my pony?" he asked brightly. "Do you live here? Maybe you know where the rocks are. The grass hides them you see, and—"

"Kill kender, eat pony," the goblin interrupted with a snarl and stepped forward with his spiked club raised.

"No. I don't think so. I don't like that idea at all," Trap said, dancing back just as a second goblin appeared from concealment behind a second bush. Then he paused.

"Eat pony? Wow! That would be interesting. What does pony taste like?" He would not want to make a meal of his mount, but the question intrigued him.

It also intrigued the goblins. Their battles were usually against their own kind, kobolds, or humans, and neither of the two had ever found themselves in conversation with their enemies. They exchanged puzzled looks, apparently not knowing whether they should answer, or how.

Their confusion gave Trap just enough time to slip a hand into his pouch and fumble for one of the two rings he carried. When he had slipped one on his finger, he looked down at himself. He was still visible, so he knew he must be wearing the one that let him take giant steps. He took one step backward and nearly fell over the cliff behind him.

"Wow! That was close. Not such a good idea," he told himself as he teetered on the edge and looked down at the drop of thirty feet. Bruises were not interesting at all.

The goblins stared at his sudden removal from the reach of their weapons, but an enemy running away was something they understood. They howled and chased after him. One stumbled on the uneven ground and fell on his face, but the other skidded across the stones seemingly too intent on his prey to fall.

Trap heard a shout from up the mountains and saw more goblins. He heard Halmarain cry out, Beglug wailed, and then came the high pitched scream of a kobold. He saw one of the small humanoids racing for cover.

For a brief second, Trap stood on the edge of the precipice, wondering what was happening. Kobolds and goblins again. Up the slope he saw a goblin stagger into sight with a kobold spear in his chest. A hundred yards away the goblin who had suggested eating his pony was chasing the kender's mount. The animal trotted back toward the trail. The other goblin charged Trap as Ripple screamed his name.

Since he wore the magic ring, Trap knew he was in no danger and had planned to tease the goblin, stepping out of the way. He knew he was being attacked, but he was not at all angry about it. When Ripple called to him, he lost all interest in the game. His sister needed him, and he had no time for his attacker.

Holding his hoopak in front of him like a spear, he stepped forward, using the force of his giant step to drive the sharp, metal-tipped point through the humanoid's belly. The goblin's spear had been pointed at him and Trap had twisted to avoid the point, still it clipped the shoulder of his tunic. When the goblin fell backward, Trap jerked his hoopak free and looked around.

He had decided his first course of action would be to rescue his pony, but if his sister was in trouble, he wanted to get to her. What to do—which way to go? Would he reach Ripple faster if he caught his mount? No, he decided, but he was not going to allow the goblin to eat his pony either.

He reached into his pouch, hoping to find a sharp stone, but the only shapes his fingers found were round, smooth creek stones. He pulled one out and was setting it in the sling of his hoopak when he realized he had one of the glass flame balls from Deepdel.

"Great! Even Better," he told his hoopak. "Do your best," he murmured as he swung the weapon and let fly with the glass ball. He had aimed for the broad back of the goblin, but he had not reckoned on the uneven ground. In its attempt to catch the pony, the goblin had leaped up onto a pile of boulders, and the flame ball caught it on the back of its thighs. The liquid and powder flew when the glass broke, spreading the fire down the back of its legs and onto its buttocks.

The humanoid took two steps before it realized it was on fire. It gave a howl and a leap, hitting the ground hard as it landed in a sitting position. As it rolled on the ground, Trap dashed past on his way to find Ripple.

One of his giant steps took him past the burning goblin. The second brought him into a collision with a humanoid who stepped out of the brush and directly into his path. The force of Trap's magic steps knocked the goblin sideways and off its feet. Its helmet flew off and its head hit a rock with a sickening crunch.

Trap fell between two bushes and landed so hard he was stunned. He lay on his side, wondering what had happened to him. Nothing felt broken, but he was several moments getting his breath. He stood up, still weak and a little dizzy. An interesting feeling, he thought; one of those experiences he would not have missed but one he had no desire to repeat.

Somewhere ahead was his sister and she would not have shouted for him if she had not been in trouble. He staggered, found himself bouncing about all over the mountainside, and fell sprawling again before he remembered he still wore the magic ring. What he needed, he decided, was the other one so he would be invisible.

He sat up, dug in his pouch and found the second ring. When he stood he could not see his own feet. He spotted his hoopak that he had laid on the ground while searching for the ring and picked it up. When he lifted it off the ground, it too became invisible. With the weapon in his hand he raced up the trail.

The first person he saw was Umpth who sat on the ground, one hand on the wheel and the other on his metal helmet.

"Wheel, make hurting stop . . . wheel, make hurting stop . . ."

Trap ran past the gully dwarf, who did not seem to be in any danger. He shouted for Ripple. The sound of his voice brought a goblin from behind a bush, his spear arm back and ready to strike. His small eyes searched for the source of the voice.

Trap slid to a stop and grabbed the spear out of the startled goblin's hand. The humanoid goggled as its weapon disappeared. His mouth was still open when the kender swung the heavy shaft and caught the goblin in the throat. The goblin was just collapsing, the stupid look still on its face when Trap ran by on his way to find Ripple.

A few steps further on he passed a bush that was half burned away. Up ahead he smelled smoke. He rounded a curve in the trail, skidded to a stop, and backed up two steps.

Halmarain was holding her staff in both hands, using it like a club. The end was glowing and where it touched a bush, fire sprouted. As she swung the staff in his direction a kobold stepped in sight behind her.

"Look out!" Trap called out. He had not indicated any direction, but she whirled around and struck the small humanoid on the head and shoulders with her staff. When the kobold ducked, the tip of the staff touched its clothing, and the staff set the kobold's sleeve on fire. The creature gave a squeal of fright and disappeared, the smell of burning cloth and flesh following it.

"Trap, where are you?" she asked, keeping her voice low as she searched the area. Her head moved in little jerks as she watched nervously for attacking enemies.

"Here I am, but where is Ripple?" Trap pulled off the ring and dropped it in his pouch. "I don't see Grod and Beglug either."

"I don't know," Halmarain whispered. "I haven't seen anyone since the goblins and kobolds attacked. You can't see ten feet in this brush. The gully dwarves ran away, I think."

"Umpth didn't," Trap pointed back down the trail. He could still hear the leader of the Aglest clan moaning.

"What's happening?" he demanded. "Who is fighting who and why? Little jiggies! I didn't know we could have so much fun in the hills."

He had just finished speaking when they heard running footsteps and Grod rounded a bend in the trail. He was breathing hard. The tears had left flesh colored tracks down his dirty cheeks. He wiped his nose on his sleeve.

"No catch kobolds," he said; each word came out as a gasp. "Where Umpth?"

"He's back on the trail," Trap said. "Did you see Ripple? And where is Beglug?"

"You were chasing the kobolds?" the little wizard showed her disbelief.

"Go after kobolds," Grod said. He was better able to get his breath. "Kobolds catch Pretty Kender and Lava Belly. Goblins come. Kobolds run away. Take Pretty Kender and Lava Belly." More tears trickled down Grod's dirty cheeks. "Don't want them take Pretty Kender."

"They took Ripple?" Trap pushed past the little human and the gully dwarf and ran up the trail.

"Where are you going?" Halmarain cried, forgetting to keep her voice down.

"To find my sister!" he shouted back.

Trap had begun his quest at a sprint, but he learned not even his anger at the kobolds for taking Ripple could maintain his fast pace. He continued at a fast trot. On the eastern side of the spur he could make better time. He was pleased with his speed. Faster than his feet, his mind ran all sorts of possibilities for daring rescues.

"I'll put on my magic ring of invisibility and. . . ."

He had forgotten the magic rings.

He should find the one that allowed him giant steps and he'd catch up with the kobolds in minutes. He slipped his hand in one of his pouches, as usual found the wrong ring and had to try again. His fingers scrambled blindly in the purse, the ring slipped on his thumb.

"Now," he said, racing along with fifty foot steps. The trail led directly east, right over the top of the hill. He had taken no more than twelve giant steps before he realized the fallacy of his plan. He had been moving too fast to keep an eye on the kobolds' trail.

"They must have angled off in another direction," he said to himself and took two steps toward the top of the ridge that ran along the spur of the hill. The second step took him over a precipice.

Chapter 22

. . . and in the great book, Astinus recorded the anger of the Dark Queen.

"I'll tear his head from his shoulders!" Takhisis raged. "I'll boil the flesh from his body!"

The Dark Queen continued with her threats and even Draaddis trembled at the horrors. He could only catch part of them. Takhisis was so angry she had reverted to her dragon shape and all five heads were raging at one time. The sphere was filled, first with one fire breathing head and then another would take its place, but out of sight of the wizard the continued imprecations and threats interrupted and roared over each other.

"Loosing the kender was bad enough," the Dark Queen shouted. "To lose the kobolds as well? He will pay for his incompetence."

Dixie Lee McKeone

Draaddis stood quietly, not daring to interrupt. He let her rage herself out. Hours passed before she was calm again.

"Where is he? What does your winged rat tell you?" she asked after her tirade was over.

"Jaerume Kaldre is still in the mountains, my queen. The freezing spell the goblin used was powerful. He is still in the foothills, frozen by the spell, but he will soon be on the trail of the kobolds. Bad luck—as well as the goblins—has been his adversary, but he did instill in the little humanoids the need to bring the kender and the merchesti to us."

"Yes, but will they remember their purpose?" Takhisis demanded.

"My messenger tells me the kobolds are traveling east as fast as their strength will allow. Apparently Kaldre convinced them they would suffer not only my wrath, but yours if they did not succeed."

"That is so now. Will they continue until they have reached Pey?" Takhisis was still not convinced.

"Kaldre warned them I have a messenger watching them. Several times the messenger has reported they search the sky looking for him. If they believe he watches, they will continue."

"You said they have the kender girl. That means they must have the gate stone. They did not take the male kender?"

"No, my lady. On that part I am unclear. The messenger gave me a picture of the male kender dashing off to chase a pony just as the others reached the ambush point."

"Does he follow? Will the rest of the party catch up with the kobolds and attempt a rescue? Is there any way to warn the kobolds?"

"I have no way of warning them, my lady, but what can one kender and a small dwarf do? The other two of the party are Aghar, and they will not fight. In the meantime, Kaldre is now out from under the goblin's spell and he is on their trail."

"I would like your news better if you were not so hesitant

in your delivery," the Dark Queen replied. "What news are you withholding?"

"Only the trouble with the merchesti, great one. Every time they approach a stream they have trouble with the creature. Apparently it does not like water."

"The kender had no trouble with it."

"No, but it was riding on a pony and did not have to put its feet in the streams. It has already killed two kobolds and injured two others. I fear that if Kaldre does not catch up soon, the merchesti will destroy our minions."

Takhisis flew into another rage. The five dragon heads appeared again. Within the wizard's workroom the air clouded with thick, sulfurous fumes. Draaddis knew he was suffering from an illusion, but so strong was her power to make him believe that he felt himself choking.

* * * * *

Two hundred feet above, the wolf woke from a nap. He sneezed and choked until he staggered out of his lair and into the surrounding woods. Would he have to find a new home? He wondered as his nostrils cleared and he began his night's hunt.

Dinner that night consisted of a wounded goblin. The wolf ate an arm and a leg and buried the rest of the body so it would season.

He returned to his lair in the ruins, dreading what he would smell. Still, the safe haven drew him back. He approached cautiously, but picked up no hint of the terrible odor that had driven him out.

He curled up on his bed, dozed, sniffed, dozed, sniffed, and repeated the exercise several times before he decided it was safe to sleep again.

* * * * *

Trap stepped over the precipice, but he had not fallen far before a clump of bushes broke his fall and he rolled down a steep slope.

A few scratches from the bushes and a few bruises from rolling down the hill made him uncomfortable, but he was not injured. Since he still wore the ring, he confidently bent his knees and jumped. His feet rose a foot off the ground. He tried again, using all his strength, and jumped two feet.

"I must remember to talk to Orander about this ring," he muttered. "Have I said that before?" He decided he had probably used those very words.

Unable to jump out of the gorge, he put the ring back in his pouch and tried climbing. In the growing darkness he could not see his way and lost his footing. After sliding down the steep slope three times he gave up and found a dry place to sleep. He'd be able to see to climb out in the morning.

"Maybe Orander made a lot of little magic jars, filled them with power and put them all in the ring and I can only use one jarful at a time," he muttered sleepily before he dozed off.

The next morning he stood up, twisted to ease his sore muscles, found the ring again, and jumped. The magic worked! He sailed to the top of the gorge, landed on a rock that tilted with him and he went sprawling again.

"So much for you," he told the ring, taking it off again. "You can wait until I get out of these mountains."

He still had the problem of finding the kobolds' trail, so he trotted along the mountainside, his face to the sun. They had been traveling east when he had lost their tracks.

After traversing a rocky slope he came to another area of thickly clustered high brush. He was trotting through it when he heard a shout.

"Wheel! Come back!"

"Umpth? Oomph!" Trap's second cry sounded like an echo, a combination of being startled and having the wind knocked out of him. The wagon wheel had hurtled out of the bushes, caught the kender's right arm and flipped him head over heels. He hit the ground with a thud, one arm and one leg through the spokes of the wheel. In seconds Umpth and then Grod appeared from behind a large clump of brush.

"Jiggy biggies! Wheel find kender!" Umpth triumphantly shouted.

"I don't believe it!" Halmarain's voice, saturated with irritation, reached Trap as he struggled to extricate himself from his strange captor.

Before he was on his feet the little wizard arrived on the trail of the gully dwarves. Her face was red with exertion and her eyes snapped with anger. She hauled on the reins of her pony. Behind her the entire string of animals appeared. Trap saw Ripple's whippik tied to a bundle on the pack pony.

"I don't believe it!" she snapped as the two gully dwarves grinned at her.

She glared at them and turned on Trap. "You didn't get very far," she said. Her attempt at a smug I-told-you-so was heavily tinged with relief.

"I'm going to talk to Orander about that ring," Trap told her. "He needs to put a second spell on it, so it doesn't carry a person over a cliff." He gave them an account of his bad luck.

"I'm really glad we found you," the wizard admitted, frowning at the gully dwarves. "I can't get these idiots on their ponies."

"Need ride ponies," Grod said, pulling at his red-blond beard in his impatience. "Kobolds run fast. Goblin run fast. Ponies run fast. Wizard run slow."

"As much as I hate to admit it, Grod's right," the small human female agreed.

"Beans! I want to go! I'll help them onto their ponies, but I'm going on ahead," Trap said obstinately. "I'll come back for you when I've found Ripple and Beglug."

"You can go faster on a pony than on foot," Halmarain said.

"Then I'll take mine—"

"No you won't. I bought them, they're all mine and they'll all stay together. To ride, you'll have to stay with us."

"I could use the magic ring—"

"For how long before the limiter takes over or you go off another cliff?"

Trap frowned at the wizard. He didn't have an answer.

"And you need us to help you rescue the merchesti and Ripple," Halmarain added. "I know you want to find your sister, but no more than I want to rescue that little fiend. If we can't send him back, his parent may come to Krynn looking for him."

"Waste time," Grod said. "No more talk."

"Ride pony now." Umpth nodded at his brother.

Trap stopped arguing and helped the gully dwarves mount. Halmarain volunteered to lead all the beasts with the exception of Trap's pony on one string while Trap rode ahead to search for the easiest path through the mountains. He was not to go too far ahead, she warned him.

"But what about finding the trail of the kobolds?" Trap demanded.

"We can find it on the other side of the mountains," the little wizard said. "They're traveling east. Directly east, even though they are taking the roughest paths. They won't be hard to locate on the plain."

"Found trail once," Umpth said.

"Did—did you find any sign. . . ." Trap stopped, not wanting to voice his niggling fears over Ripple.

"Yes, and we know they were both alive this morning." The little wizard nodded. "Where they crossed a stream, we could see the marks where Beglug struggled to keep from stepping into the water. Off to the side were footprints Grod insisted were Ripple's. This was looped over the branch of a bush." She held out a blue feather with two green beads sewn to the quill. Around it was a thin blue leather thong.

"It's Ripple's," Trap crowed with delight. Occasionally she wove feathers into her topknot, and he had often seen her wear that particular decoration.

"If Beglug can fight and she can leave signs for us, they are both alive and uninjured," Halmarain said. "They are being taken east."

"Then let's hurry," Trap said, leading the way again. "And on the way we'll make a plan."

Trap found a low saddle between the mountains. Since they were not seeking a trail, Trap paced Halmarain. He was busy with his plans to rescue the captives.

"Here's what I think we should do," he said. "When we catch up with the kobolds, you, Grod, and Umpth will climb up in a tree where a limb juts out over—"

"How do you know there will be a tree?" the little wizard asked. "And if the gully dwarves can't mount a pony without help, how can you get them up a tree?"

Trap frowned. "Then we'll do this: we'll take a wagon—"

"Where are we going to get the wagon?" Halmarain asked.

"Thorns! Thistles! You don't like anything. Do you want to help rescue Ripple and Beglug or not?" Trap demanded.

"Yes!" the wizard spat out the word. "But you can't make a plan until we find them."

"Lava Belly eat kobolds, maybe," Grod suggested.

"He wouldn't do that," Trap objected, conveniently forgetting the innkeeper's dog in Deepdel.

"Oh, you never know, and it would be a fitting revenge," Halmarain smiled. "They may wish they had never taken him."

"Why take Beglug?" Grod asked. "Kender pretty, but Beglug mean."

"Because . . . ?" Trap's explanation became an echo of Grod's question.

"I don't know, and I don't like it." Halmarain's eyes, already dark with worry, seemed to deepen.

"I certainly don't," Trap announced pugnaciously, as if he resented anyone else's criticism of the capture. Ripple was his sister, and he was the most concerned.

"There's more than kobold meanness behind this," Halmarain said. "That's why we should be careful."

"Man in black cloak," Grod said, nodding.

"Oh. Yes. I'd forgotten about him," Trap said. "Was he with the kobolds?"

"I didn't see him," the little wizard said. She and Trap turned inquiring gazes on the gully dwarves who shrugged their shoulders.

"He was with the kobolds on the mountains," Halmarain said thoughtfully. "And before that in the maze?" Trap nodded in response to her questioning frown. "And they fought with goblins who could have followed them," she continued. "I think we can expect to find him with the kobolds when we catch them."

"Who is he?" Trap asked. "How do you know where they are heading? Do you know him and where he lives?"

"Lives? I doubt he lives; but yes, because of him I think I know where the kobolds are going."

Trap waited, but when the little wizard didn't explain, his natural impatience overrode his usual good temper.

"Well, are you going to tell us?"

"No. I'm not sure I'm right, and if I am you don't want to know," she said, spurring her pony to greater speed. She kept the ponies at a gallop for a few minutes, but when her mount faltered she pulled him up.

"We've been riding these animals too hard," she said. "We should walk them and let them rest after we cross that stream." She pointed a hundred yards ahead.

"Here's Ripple's print and Beglug's," Trap said when he reached the bank of the stream. "And the dwarves are ahead of us again."

"The same ones?" Halmarain asked.

"It must be, because here is your pony's print. They crossed after the kobolds," Trap told her as he studied the ground intently. "Gee, look at this, a snail is crossing too."

"How far ahead?" The little wizard asked.

"You'll pass him by the time you get to the water if you don't step on him."

"Oh, forget it," the wizard snapped. She forded the small stream and descended from the saddle. The gully dwarves dismounted and walked on ahead, rolling the wheel. They had not traveled far when Grod came running back.

"Wheel tell goblins come," he gasped.

"Oh now it's telling the future," Halmarain snapped.

"No tell, fall down!" the blond gully dwarf insisted. "Umpth stop to pick up. Look back and see. They come." Grod pointed back toward the top of the pass between the mountains.

"That doesn't mean the wheel found them," Halmarain argued.

"She no like wheel," Grod muttered, glaring at the little wizard, his blue eyes sparkling with anger.

"She really didn't mean it," Trap soothed the feelings of the gully dwarf. "Remember, she can do magic, but she can't tell if people are coming like the wheel can."

"Oh, I really needed that!" Halmarain snapped. "Still, if they're coming we'd better hide."

Trap was ready to argue, but she forestalled him.

"If we let them pass us by we can be on our way that much faster."

"I know!" Trap pointed to the left where deep shadows lurked beneath a small, dense forest. The others nodded. It seemed the best of a few unsatisfactory choices.

The entire party moved through the high, dense brush, but none of them doubted the goblins could follow their trail. Trap bent occasionally to pick up stones for the sling of his hoopak as he led the way toward the trees.

By common and unspoken consent, they moved quietly. They tried not to frighten the wildlife and any birds that might fly up and give away their position. The fallen leaves of the thick brush near the eaves of the wood muffled the ponies' steps. Fifty yards inside the wood they entered a small, muddy stream. They walked their mounts a hundred yards east before turning back on their trail again. If the goblins did follow their trail, they would fall into an ambush.

Since the morning had passed and the sun had reached its zenith, Trap raided the ponies' saddle bags and handed around a small midday meal. They had all found hiding places when they heard the first voices, some distance away, raised in argument.

Trap was a moment realizing that the sounds came not

from the southwest from where the goblins approached, but from deeper in the woods. To his right, Halmarain peered from behind her bushy shelter and mouthed the word, "Dwarves."

Trap slipped out of his hiding place and hurried through the forest, slipping from tree to tree. Before long he could see into a small clearing where a group of sturdy hill ponies grazed. He recognized the six dwarves who had been chasing them. They appeared to be in council, and in strong disagreement.

The kender slipped away and returned to his defensive position. When Halmarain raised her brows in silent communication he used his hands, running his fingers from his neck in a circle on his chest to indicate the stolen necklace. She sighed as she realized he'd identified the dwarves.

Then he drew back into his own bushy shelter just as the goblins stepped out of the high brush, heading for the eaves of the forest. To his surprise, they were not following the trail of the kender, wizard, and gully dwarves, but strolled along more than sixty yards west of the trail left by the small party.

As they approached the forest they seldom looked at the ground. They weren't following anyone. If they continued on their course they would pass the adventurers, but they would travel through the clearing. The noise of the dwarves' argument would cover the approach of the savage humanoids.

The dwarves and the goblins would have a grand fight, and Trap wanted to see it. He thought of Ripple somewhere to the east and knew he could not long delay, but Halmarain had kept them moving and away from everyone and he was bored. Even though he was worried about his sister, he knew they had to hide until the goblins passed. Since they could not continue on the trail of the kobold for a while, he would just see a little of this battle.

He reached into his pocket and pulled out the two rings. He slipped the first one on his finger and looked at himself. He was still visible. Careful not to move his feet, he pulled off that ring and slipped it into his left pouch.

When the other was on his finger he could not see himself. Good enough. He hurried through the forest until he had a perfect view of the clearing.

Three of the dwarves were still sitting on the ground. Two were stomping up and down, arguing with each other. The sixth was leaning against a tree, pulling off his right boot. He had his back to his companions. His back was to Trap as well. The dwarf turned the boot upside down, shook it as if removing a stone and reached one hand inside, checking it. Then, carefully balancing on one foot, he raised the other, doubling his body as he held the boot, ready to slide his foot into it.

With his back to Trap, his posterior presented a wide soft target no kender with a hoopak and a pouch of stones could resist; particularly not a kender who wore an invisible ring. In a flash, Trap had a stone from his pouch and had sent it zinging across the fifty feet that separated him from the dwarf.

The stone struck the dwarf on the soft part of his right buttock. Startled, he gave a cry and spun as he fell. He lost his hold on his boot and it went flying out in the tall grass. While his companions stared at him, he scrambled to his feet with a roar. When he turned around, Trap realized he had hit the dwarf leader, Tolem.

Trap clapped his hand over his mouth to stifle his laughter. If one stone was that much fun, then more might be even better, he decided.

His first missile forcibly caught the attention of the leader. The second, hitting another dwarf on the knee brought all the dwarves to their feet. The kender choked back a gurgle of laughter as he watched the stolid demihumans running about in a circle.

Magic rings could be fun! Who would be his next target? he wondered, and decided on a stout fellow with faded black clothing and a dark, dusty beard. He flung his third stone, but the dwarf moved out of the way. The small rock struck the leader again, hitting him on the toe of his right foot. Since he had not put on his boot, the rock hurt and he hopped around in a circle. The others scurried for cover.

Trap's fingers were scrabbling in his pouch for another stone when the last dwarf disappeared behind the trunk of a tree. He sighed for the lost opportunity. Before he could give full rein to his disappointment, he heard breaking twigs and the rustle of bushes that alerted him to the arrival of the goblins.

They strode into the clearing, all unaware that six angry dwarves were hiding behind the boles of the nearest trees and undergrowth. Thinking the goblins were the cause of their recent discomfort, the dwarves attacked with shouts and war cries.

Tolem, wearing both boots, dashed out swinging his war axe before he was close enough for a killing blow. He clipped the point of the nearest goblin's spear.

The humanoids were caught by surprise, but always alert when traveling, they recovered quickly. One thrust a spear that the largest dwarf blocked, but the big goblin had put all his force behind the attack and the point penetrated the metal shield. The dwarf and the humanoid danced around each other, trying to separate their defensive and offensive weapons.

The other dwarves were wading in with their axes. The battle was fast and furious when Trap heard more breaking twigs behind him.

"Wheel find kender."

Trap turned to see Umpth and Grod approaching, looking around them as they walked. Apparently they had not connected the sound of the battle with any personal danger. Neither gully dwarf was armed, not that they could have made effective use of their weapons if they had been carrying them.

Trap sighed, turned away from the battle and hurried toward the Aghar. As soon as he was out of sight of the clearing, he removed his ring.

"I guess we had better leave," he told them regretfully and led them back to Halmarain.

"Maybe they'll kill each other off and we'll be free of

them," the little wizard said, though only after she had argued with Trap over his little escapade.

He was shocked by her attitude. "That's not nice! In fact it's mean. I don't blame them for following us," he said. "They want their necklace and I don't see why you won't give it back. I can't believe you want anything bad to happen to them."

"No," the little wizard admitted. "And I really don't want to see them killed, either, I just want to get away from them. I'll return the necklace if I can, only I don't think I'll be able to, and I can't even explain it to you right now, because I'm not sure what I suspect is true . . . No, don't ask me, I'll tell you when I've thought it over."

"It was a great fight," Trap said softly, wishing he could go back and watch.

Chapter 23

The kender, the two gully dwarves, and the wizard rode for several hours after leaving the woods where the dwarves and goblins fought. The night passed without incident, but adventure overtook the group the next morning before they had been on the trail for an hour.

A wide but shallow stream ran across their trail. Since they had not seen any sign of the kobolds for several hours the evening before, and had not found any marks that morning, Trap and Halmarain split up, each taking a gully dwarf with them as they rode up and down the banks. Trap had only been riding downstream for ten minutes when he found confused tracks. He gave a shrill whistle to call Halmarain back.

"They crossed here," Trap pointed out the marks to Grod. "See, there's Ripple's print. She was standing off to the side for some reason. Beglug gave them a hard time.

See how he fought crossing? You can see where he dug in his hooves, and here's blood too, he must have bitten one of the kobolds, and I hope he did," the kender said as he surveyed the muddy bank.

"Lava Belly no like water," Grod said.

"No, not cold water," Trap amended. He reminded the Aghar of the fun the merchesti had in the warm bath in Orander's kitchen. Since Beglug came from a much hotter world, nothing cold pleased him.

Halmarain came trotting up, and they gathered at the spot where the kobold had crossed.

"Wheel get wet," Umpth complained. He had made the same objection at every stream. "Wheel no like water."

"Magic wash away," Grod added.

"Don't be ridiculous," Halmarain snapped. She had been ready to cross, but she pulled up her mount and frowned at the stream.

Trap turned away to hide his grin. The little wizard would rather die than admit she gave Aghar magic any credence, but the hesitation of the gully dwarves had affected her.

"I'll just find out," Trap said.

While the others waited on the western bank, he dismounted and removed his boots. Directly in front of him the bottom of the stream was rocky. A wide slab of rock stretched halfway across, and the rest of the way the smaller rocks had been smoothed by the running water.

"It's fine," he called back.

Umpth dismounted and walked behind his pony. He picked up the wheel, still attached to the travois, and splashed through the stream after his mount.

Halmarain waited until the others had safely crossed before she urged her pony forward. Their trouble came from her hesitation. The pack pony edged up to the stream to get a drink. It was just lowering its head when a huge bullfrog gave a croak and jumped between the pony's rear hooves. Startled, the beast with the packs plunged to the left, just upstream from the rocky ford. The pony took one leap and landed up to its shoulders in mud.

"Quicksand!" Halmarain cried out, pointing to the floundering animal.

Trap had been sitting on the ground, putting on his boots. He jumped up, one foot shod, the other boot in his hand. He threw the boot aside and dashed back into the stream. The two gully dwarves ran after him.

Trap grabbed the lead from the screaming little wizard and pulled, but he only succeeded in pulling off the pony's bridle. Umpth and Grod, less finicky, plunged into the mud, tugging at the heavy straps that held the packs in place. The dwarves gave a couple of tugs, lost their footing at the edge of the quicksand pit, and sunk to their shoulders.

"Deep mud," Umpth said, looking over his shoulder at the kender.

"Deep mud!" Grod gasped just before his head disappeared. One grubby hand appeared out of the goo, just far enough for Trap to get a grip. With Halmarain's help he hauled the smaller gully dwarf out of the quicksand.

"Quick! No hold up pony long," Umpth burbled. He had managed to splay his body on the surface and was not sinking so rapidly.

"Can you use these?" Halmarain splashed through the water, carrying the leads from the ponies as well as the reins from her own mount.

"Great! They'll work if we could get them under the chin straps," Trap said. "Umpth, can you?"

"Good, need puller," Umpth announced with a sputter. His face had dipped into the mire and he had raised his chin. He waved one hand behind him, reaching for the leather straps.

"Here," Halmarain threw the long, heavy leather leads to him. The ends fell just beyond him, the trailing lines across his back.

Umpth fumbled for a moment, muttered something that was lost under the squeals of the terrified pony. The gully dwarf kept making unintelligible remarks as he fumbled again. He crawled halfway across the pony's back, causing the beast to sink deeper in the mire. Trap, keeping a tight hold on the Aghar's legs, was pulled out onto the mud until he too was sinking in the mire.

"Me got you," Grod assured Trap who felt the dwarf's hands take a grip on his legs.

"Wow! Big jiggies! This is interesting," he said, keeping his face up out of the marl. "I don't feel like I'm sinking, but I think I am. I wonder what's at the bottom of all this mud? I bet lots of interesting things have disappeared here, and if we could find them—"

"You don't have time to explore," Halmarain snapped. "If we don't get Umpth and the pony out they'll drown in that mess.

Trap sighed. He would never again travel with a wizard; she wanted to take all the fun out of everything. Still the gully dwarf and the pony didn't appear to want to explore the bottom of the marl pit, so he supposed he should rescue them.

Umpth had almost disappeared before he raised a hand and waved it, signaling he had finished fastening the leads to the pony's girth.

"Halmarain, pull the pony out," Trap said, taking a firmer grip of the gully dwarf's legs. He was being pulled back slowly when he heard a squeak from Halmarain and a splash.

Grod released his hold on Trap long enough to haul the little wizard back to firm ground. Then he started tugging at the kender's legs again.

"Give me those leads," the wizard commanded.

The little wizard had been splashing about behind them. She had caught and brought her mount up close behind them and had thrown the left stirrup over the saddle, ready to tie the leads to the leather saddle girth. By now, they could only see the sinking pony's nose above the surface. In moments Halmarain had taken a strain on the leads and the strain on the others lessened as the wizard walked her mount slowly downstream, away from the quicksand.

Trap, firmly grasping Umpth's legs, was a part of the chain that included Umpth and the pony. He felt as if he were being pulled apart, but he kept his grip. Soon he felt his feet dragging on the stones of the ford, and moments later his knees bumped across the rocks. He drew them up under him while Grod released him and moved forward to help him tug on Umpth.

The kender and Grod found it easier to pull Umpth out of the marl. He still had not released his hold on the pony, but Halmarain's mount slowly pulled the foundered animal up and toward solid ground.

In less than a minute the frightened animal reached firm footing and scrambled out of the mire. The kender and the gully dwarves scuttled out of the way of its thrashing feet.

While the pony stood trembling, Umpth, for once, washed his face in the stream without being instructed. He raised his face, looked around as he blinked the water out of his eyes. His gaze locked on the wizard and he grinned.

"Wizard become Aghar," he said. "Join Aglest clan?"

"Kender too," Grod said.

"Careful," Halmarain snapped as she worked to wash away the clinging mud of the marl pit. "And you can get yourselves cleaned up too."

"Knew she say that," Grod said, but even he wrinkled his nose at the mud.

"And we should wash the pony and probably everything in the packs. . . ." Halmarain said, then paused. "Where are the packs?"

"In mud," Umpth said as he took a casual swipe at his sleeve. "No pull pony *and* packs out."

"He lost our packs?" Halmarain stared in disbelief.

"Gee! They're gone . . . everything. . . . Still, Umpth is right, we couldn't have pulled out the pony and the packs too," Trap said. "Maybe I can go back and get them," he suggested hopefully. "You could tie a lead on me and—"

"No, you won't," Halmarain paled at the idea.

"No! Now no wash packs and clothes," Grod said, as if the loss had become a bonus. "Lost magic," he said, feeling his clothing. "Dead squirrel stink too."

Trap and Halmarain considered Grod's loss a bonus, but the cooking pots had been lost along with the packs. Trap used Grod's helmet to pour water over the pony's hide and scrub the animal down while the others cleaned away the mud from themselves and their clothing. They worked for an hour.

"At least it's sunny and hot," Trap said as he pulled on his boots. "Our clothes will dry in no time, and at least we didn't have to wash Beglug."

Halmarain climbed into her saddle. "We'll need to buy more supplies when we get to Thelgaard. I hope Orander's magic purse is still full."

"Thelgaard," Trap smiled. "Maybe it will be an interesting place."

Chapter 24

Trap was disappointed with Thelgaard. The city walls and most of the buildings were constructed of gray stone. No carving relieved the square buildings. Occasionally shutters flanked the windows, but they were weathered gray wood. The kender peered hopefully down every street, but the plain gray buildings were all the same and quickly became boring.

They had left the ponies in the first boarding stable they found. Because the morning was hot, Halmarain and the gully dwarves had left their armor, weapons, and helmets behind with their mounts.

Since the city offered little of interest, Trap didn't object to Halmarain's haste. She was shopping in a hurried frenzy, and Trap agreed that they should not waste time. They should get back on the trail of the kobolds again—particularly when there seemed to be nothing of interest in the city and the people seemed taciturn.

"Thelgaard shuts its beauty behind its walls," Halmarain told them. "The official buildings and the wealthier homes are decorated with great slabs of marble bought from the dwarves of Garnet."

"I haven't seen any marble," Trap said, wondering if he could slip away from the little wizard and explore.

"And you won't," Halmarain snapped. "We're only here to buy supplies. We can't afford to attract attention."

"Left wheel, still no please wizard," Umpth muttered.

"Her still mad," Grod agreed with a sigh.

The gully dwarves weren't too happy. Before entering the city Halmarain had made them wash again and had cleaned their clothing so they looked like Neidar. In addition she had made them leave the wheel in the stable where they boarded the ponies.

"She's not mad at you," Trap said to the Aghar who walked behind him and the wizard. "She's just—"

"She's just mad," Halmarain interrupted. "Do you realize we've been traveling for days and days and we're only twenty-five miles from where we started? And we're worse off than when we left Lytburg. We've lost the little fiend and the gate stone."

"Grod and Umpth no do," Grod said, pulling his blond beard in confusion.

"No, and wizard no do either," Halmarain sighed, for once slipping into the patios of the Aghar. "That's why I'm mad."

"Did you ever live in Thelgaard?" Trap asked, hoping for a story.

"No, but Orander grew up here. He told me what little I know."

Trap sighed and followed the wizard as they moved from shop to shop. He found a number of fascinating things, but when he reached out to pick up a belt knife with an ornately carved handle, the little wizard grabbed his arm and kept him from touching it.

"You can handle that," she said, pointing to a bag of

flour. "Also Grod can take a few of those apples, this salt, tea, these blankets . . ."

Trap's arms were soon too full of mundane supplies to allow him to finger anything. He suffered the increasing load for an hour before complaining and even then Halmarain was still loading both the kender's and the Aghar's arms with purchases.

"We've just about finished," the little human said as they left one of the shops. "We just have to buy pots and—"

They were standing outside on the street when two human youngsters, about eight years old, came running along the street and bumped into Halmarain, sending her spinning.

"Look out," she snapped as she regained her footing. Her voice was high as a child's, but her tone was that of an irritated adult.

The youngsters spun around and stared at her. Seeing a figure the size of a child with the face of an adult, they paused a moment. Then the smaller of the two, who was much larger than the little wizard, marched up and glared down at her.

"What are you?" he demanded with definite menace.

"Some sort of freak," the other said, reaching down to pick up a rock. He was drawing back his arm, getting ready to throw the stone when Trap stepped forward.

"You're not very nice," he shouted. Among the purchases he carried was a small bag of salt, which was heavy for its size. Since his hoopak was strapped to his back, he slung the bag of salt instead, connecting with the arm of the boy who was ready to throw the rock.

As the boy backed away, Grod ran forward and picked up the bag of salt. In gully dwarf fashion he was not about to allow anything useful to get away.

"Look out, its a dwarf!" the boy who had been menacing the little wizard cried out and ran off down the street. The other followed.

"I'll tell my father, he'll take care of you," the taller boy called as the two boys disappeared around a building.

"We need to get off the street in case he does bring his father back," she said and looked around for an inn. Two doors down, a faded sign board with the likely name of the Traveler's Haven promised food and drink as well as accommodations.

"We'll eat if you three stay out of trouble," the wizard said as she led the way through the door.

Like the rest of the "Gate Quarter," the section of Thelgaard that specialized in goods for transients, the inn catered to travelers with leaner purses. Several tables and stools had new wood rungs and legs, showing they had been recently mended, doubtless after a brawl. Still, the scarred tabletops had been scrubbed clean.

Three men who looked to be laborers were drinking at a table at the far end of the room. They were absorbed in their conversation and paid no attention to the three who entered.

Halmarain led the way to a table in the farthest corner. When a stout young woman arrived with four mugs of ale, the wizard ordered enough meat rolls to satisfy even the Aghars' appetite.

"Why were those boys so mean?" Trap asked when the server left the table to get the meat rolls.

"Children can be cruel," Halmarain said, shrugging off the incident. "Many people believe the gods use deformities to punish the evil, and that they should do so too—a man with a twisted leg, someone who's blind or who can't speak, the dim-witted or those who don't grow. . . ."

"But that's not right," Trap said, frowning.

"No, but that's why it's best for me to appear to be a dwarf on this journey," Halmarain said sadly. "Just be glad you're normal for your race."

The server returned with their meat rolls and they concentrated on the food. Trap had finished eating and was working his way through his second mug of ale when the door opened and a group of five travelers entered.

They were well armed with swords, bows, and several carried axes of strange, wicked styles. Several wore odd pieces of armor and all of them carried packs and bedrolls. They were all humans.

With hard eyes they took in the room before taking a table not far from where Grod placidly munched on the last of the food and Halmarain shifted uneasily. Trap peered at them from over the top of his raised mug. He put it down hastily and smiled at the newcomers. They must have some lively tales, he thought, looking at the scarred armor and the weapons that showed use.

"Hello," he said when one of the adventurers looked his way.

The human's eyes narrowed as he stared at Trap. He nodded and leaned forward, speaking to his companions in a low voice. All the three at the table in the corner could hear was the word "kender." Then all five of the heavily armed men turned to stare at Trap and the one he had greeted gave him a crooked smile.

The delighted kender wriggled on his stool, thinking he had at last met some friendly people.

"You keep your hands to yourself," Halmarain whispered to him.

"A fair day to you," the adventurer said to Halmarain since she had been speaking and was eyeing the newcomers with concern. "Are you travelers?" He nodded to their bundles.

"Yes, on our way to Palanthus," Halmarain replied. "We've a far distance to go, so we're leaving quite soon."

She nudged the kender suggestively, but he ignored the hint. His mind was on what she had said, and he didn't like it.

"But what about Ripple and—"

He paused in mid-sentence and glared at her when she kicked him.

"We'll meet her on the way," the little wizard said, frowning at him. He still wanted to ask what she meant but the traveler who had first greeted him had questions of his own.

"Then you'll doubtless want to travel in peace," the man said. He was large for a human, but younger than the rest, as attested to by his nearly beardless face. "We are here to make sure you can do so."

"You escort travelers?" Again Halmarain spoke before the kender could get in a word. She kept her voice even, but Trap knew she would not like to be accompanied on the road. He wriggled in anticipation, wondering how she would avoid unwelcome company.

One of the other adventurers, a man with wide shoulders, shook his head, a head that looked too small for his frame.

"No, our task is to rid the roads of bandits," he said. "We seek news of a band of cutthroats made up of humans, half-breed goblins and one kender. The only name we know is Harderk, the leader." He eyed Trap. "One of his band is a kender."

"Him dead," Grod spoke up suddenly. "Make a good tale, that."

"I knew that was coming," Halmarain said with resignation.

"If he is, there's one bounty gone," another of the adventurers muttered.

"What happened to him?" The first asked. They looked at Grod for the answer, but he turned to Trap. The kender sighed for the tales he would not hear, still, telling a tale was nearly as good as listening. He searched his mind for a story, The main part of his thoughts was still taken up with his irritation at Halmarain and her assumption that he was a thief.

"He died because a wizard refused to trust him," Trap said and then wondered how he could continue the story.

"I wouldn't trust a wizard," the young adventurer laughed. "But go on, tell us what happened to him."

Trap's head spun with the tales he had already told. He didn't want to repeat himself, and cast his memory back over the dangers they had faced on their journey.

"His trouble began when he was separated from the rest of his band and was just crossing a stream," he said, shifting on his stool. He gave Halmarain a sour look. "He should have known he was in trouble when, coming from the other direction across the ford, was a wizard wearing red robes."

His tale included the bog where they had nearly lost the pony. The lost bundles became the wizard's bag with his spellbooks and the constant accusations that Halmarain heaped on his head.

In the tale, the fictitious Trapspringer was forgiving of the wizard and had sunk into the bog to try and rescue the mage's spellbooks. He died in the attempt. By the time Trap finished his story, tears trickled down his cheeks.

The adventurers sighed in unison. The youngest seemed to be genuinely moved. Trap had told such a moving tale that no one even thought to question the fact that a thief and an outlaw had died to prove he was trustworthy. Those who did not shed tears were affected by the loss of a part of their reward.

"So there's one less outlaw to give us trouble." Halmarain said, rising from her seat. "We should be going while there's daylight to see our trail,"

Grod, who had been wandering around the room drinking ale from any mug that was unattended, came back to the table and she loaded him with bundles. She hustled the kender and the gully dwarf out of the inn, and down the street to the stables. They hurried through the city gates before they could become entangled with anyone else.

The ride from the foothills to Thelgaard had taken part of the day and the rest was used in shopping, their time in the inn and loading the animals, so sunset was not far away when they rode out of the city. They traveled only two miles before they found a likely place to camp. By the time the gully dwarves gathered firewood and the kender unsaddled and tethered the ponies to graze, darkness had caught them.

"Thelgaard has some friendly people, even if the buildings are boring," Trap said as he looked wistfully over his shoulder. In the distance he could see torches on the walls of the city, far enough away so the flames could have been twinkling stars.

"We entered in peace, we did our shopping without trouble and we didn't have to fight to get out of the city,"

Halmarain said quietly. "I will always remember it as a signal occasion. And since we had Orander's magic purse, we didn't have to worry that we'd run out of steel pieces," Halmarain answered.

Trap pulled out the purse and peered inside. They had nearly emptied it, confident it would fill up again, but it was only half full.

"Only it's not working like it did before," he said as he showed it to Halmarain.

"Maybe the magic is wearing out," Halmarain said as she too peered inside the small leather bag. "All good things come to an end," the wizard sighed. "I had hoped it would fill up again in case we tumbled into another mess."

"Hands too full," Grod said. He was sitting just inside the circle of light thrown by the fire while he inspected his new clothing.

"What do you mean—hands too full?" Trap asked.

"No get more steel pieces. Hands too full of bundles," the gully dwarf answered. He turned over his new shirt to look at the back, decided he was sitting on a rock, and shifted, his feet on his new pants.

"Stop grinding your clothes into the dirt," the wizard said in a hollow voice. Clearly her mind was elsewhere. "You mean you've been. . . ." Halmarain stared at the gully dwarf, her eyes wide with disbelief. "You've been . . . and you put your ill-gotten gains in Orander's purse?"

"Got no pockets, no pouches, no wizard's bag," Grod said as he stood. He picked up the already soiled new shirt and pants. "Wizard say no find dumps."

"He's been stealing from everyone we've met!" Halmarain told Trap in an awed voice. "And he's been putting the steel pieces in Orander's purse! You and Ripple found extra coins in your pouches and I found some in my bag. I accused you, but *he's* been doing it!"

"That's what he said," Trap agreed, wondering why the little wizard had to tell him what Grod had said. After all, his ears were as good as any human's.

"No hunt in dumps, no find things," said Umpth who was busy giving himself a good scratch from his head to his feet.

"Aghar find things. Is what Aghar do," Grod said as if they should understand. He wandered off toward the grazing ponies.

"And if he couldn't search dumps anymore, he searched where he could, which happened to be in the purses of the people around him," Trap summarized, more for himself than for the wizard.

Halmarain trotted after Grod. Not to be left out of the most entertaining conversation of their journey, the kender followed.

"Did you take the necklace from the dwarves?" she demanded.

"Think Pretty Kender like it, but no could open pouch," Grod replied, nodding until his red-blond beard bounced energetically. "Go find more magic," he said. "Need dead squirrel—or rat—or snake. Dead snake good magic. Find one, maybe." He wandered off.

Halmarain stopped and stood staring after the gully dwarf, too concerned with what he had done to give any notice of his intentions.

"I put a shutting spell on your pouches to make sure you couldn't take anything that belonged to the dwarves," she said.

"Well! I like that! We told you before we wouldn't take anything from them," Trap said, laughter making him breathless. "All this time you've been watching us, Grod has been handling everything in sight." Trap was growing increasingly angry at the little wizard for her distrust, and he made the most of it.

"Wizard, lizard, chicken gizzard, can't tell who's the thief," he said. "Dash about like a tiny lout, and brings herself to grief."

"You stop that!" Halmarain shouted at him. She bounced on the balls of her feet, her tiny hands clenched in fists. "Say another word and I'll turn you into a . . . a . . ." Bereft of words she raised her right hand and pointed her finger at the kender.

"Halmarain, she can complain, and finds stuff in her sack," Trap sing-songed as he skipped away. She turned to glare at him. "Fuss and shout and jump about, but she still won't give it back."

Trap laughed until he was weak in the knees.

"A wizard's distrust," Trap said, giving Halmarain a knowing look as he wiped away the tears of his mirth. They both knew he was referring to his story in the inn.

"Very well, I owe you both an apology," the little wizard said as she also calmed down. "But the next time we enter a town, the next time we get near anyone, keep an eye on that gully dwarf."

"He must really be skilled with his hands," Trap said. "I had no idea he was slipping steel pieces into that purse, and it was in my pouch."

"And the overload into yours and Ripple's pouches and my bag," the little wizard said. "Did he bring back anything this time? Oh Gilean, I hope not." She pulled her worn bag off her shoulder. "Trap, check your pouches. I don't want anyone else chasing us."

Trap searched all his pouches and pockets. He found nothing he could not remember having before they reached Thelgaard. Halmarain had taken care to keep his arms so full he had not been able to handle anything. She found a small jeweled cup, a mirror, a comb, and a carving of a bear with runes on its back.

"I wonder who will be chasing us for these things," she muttered as she showed them to the kender.

Chapter 25

While in Thelgaard, Trap had suggested they buy ground maize and everyone was looking forward to a kender pudding, which he could make almost as well as his sister. Making it would help him feel closer to her. He missed his sister, and was also becoming as worried as his kender nature would allow.

The first day after Beglug and Ripple had been captured by the kobolds, they had found tracks, but after leaving the mountains they had not been able to discover any sign at all. But they would find them the next day, Trap decided, and was cheered by the decision.

"I'll get out the maize and you can dig out the pots," he told the little wizard when they made camp after their trip to the city.

"Pots!" Halmarain exclaimed, slapping the side of her own head. "I bought everything I could think of, but I forgot pots!"

"No pots? Big jiggers, I can't boil pudding in my hands." Trap complained.

"Obviously!" Halmarain snapped. "I can't boil water for tea either."

Luckily they had bought some dried meat and traveler's bread in Thelgaard. It sated their hunger, but they were disgruntled over their cold meal. After her trouble with the two boys, Halmarain refused to return to Thelgaard, saying they could pick up pots in Solanthus or perhaps they'd find a village on their way east.

The next afternoon Trap killed a couple of rabbits that they roasted over the campfire, but for the next two days they broke camp without a warming cup of tea. Halmarain was in a foul mood.

They began their third morning's journey at dawn and by early afternoon they were approaching Solanthus. Halmarain called a halt and they sat on a hilltop as they looked across the hills at the city. In the distance they could see the strong outer walls, rooftops blanketing the hills, and in the center a tall fortress.

"We can't all enter the city," she said. "I don't want to take Grod in. There are too many people on our trail now." She looked over her shoulder giving Grod an accusing glare.

"Grod no go, no get more steel pieces," Umpth reminded her.

"That's exactly why he won't go," Halmarain announced. "We don't need more trouble."

"He didn't cause the stranger with the kobolds to follow us," Trap reminded the wizard.

"Whether he did or not, we've too many people on our trail," Halmarain said. "I'll ride in to buy some pots. At least we can have a hot meal tonight."

"I'll go for the pots," Trap volunteered.

"Oh no," Halmarain said. "I'm not having any more trouble with . . ." She paused as Trap's expression darkened with anger.

"Umpth and I will go," Trap announced. His voice

turned hard and raspy, anger just under the surface.

For once, neither Halmarain's glare nor her sharp tongue moved the kender. His grandfather had traveled to Solanthus and had talked about the city. At that time the damage from the earthquakes that had come with the Cataclysm was still visible. Their grandfather had been fascinated by the raiding, the sporadic fighting, and the attempts to rebuild.

Within the hour the travelers found a dry gorge that would give them shelter and hide them from other travelers. Halmarain and Grod made camp, though she was impeded by his wandering off, looking for another dead animal to replace his squirrel.

Trap and Umpth left most of their gear behind and rode into Solanthus, using the south gate. Since it opened toward the mountains, they were in the quarter of the city where most of the dwarven population lived.

"Dwarves make good pots," Trap said softly as if he begrudged the admission. He wanted to see some of Solanthus. He knew he shouldn't spend much time in the city.

"We really should visit more than one shop and try to get the best price," he suggested. "After all, we know Orander's purse doesn't make steel pieces, and we didn't bring Grod."

"Look dumps? Find pots?" Umpth suggested.

Trap ignored the suggestion.

When they had seen the city from a distance, they had seen the towers of the central fortress. Solanthus had spread into the hills to the south and some of the streets climbed steeply to the hilltops while others wound around the lower regions. The tower was not visible from their location.

Like most cities on Krynn, several inns were located near the gates. Beyond them were the shops usually frequented by travelers who wanted supplies for their journeys. After having visited Lytburg and Thelgaard, Trap expected to find stabling for their mounts close to the gate. Dwarves seldom rode ponies unless they were traveling long distances so the stables that served that quarter of Solanthus were on a hill close by.

Trap and Umpth rode into the first stable. The dwarf hostler glared at the kender and the gully dwarf and demanded the price of a day's keep in advance.

"Him not like kender," Umpth said as they left the stable and wandered up the hill. Neither expected to find a tinker's shop on the heights; they wanted to look over the southern quarter of the city.

"Look for good dumps," Umpth said. "Maybe find a good This Place."

They turned a corner and had walked two blocks up a steep street when they heard a shout behind them.

"Thieves!" The shout rang up and down the street.

Trap and Umpth paused and turned to look behind them. They saw two dwarves running up the hill. Four others came around the corner of the street the kender had passed.

"Is mad dwarf?" Umpth asked.

"Big Jiggies! It certainly is," Trap recognized the dwarves from whom Grod had taken the necklace. "Maybe we can explain . . . then, maybe not. They don't look like they want to talk."

"They still mad. We go now," Umpth said hopefully. He turned his back on the dwarves who were fast approaching. "Want to see city. Want to see dumps. Want to find new This Place. Not want to see dwarf." He suited action to words and sprinted up the hill.

At first Trap followed, but just before they came to a curve in the street, he paused to look back. The dwarves were still coming, but they had little chance of catching the fleet-footed kender.

When Trap turned to follow Umpth, the gully dwarf had disappeared.

"Beans! Now where did he go?" the kender asked of no one in particular, since the street was deserted except for his pursuers. What appeared to be an alley opened on his right and he dashed along it until he discovered his mistake. The passage that angled off between the two barn-like buildings gave into a stable yard with high retaining walls on two sides. The third and forth sides were windowless building walls with only the alley width opening. Umpth had not come that way.

Trap turned to reverse his course, but he was too late. The dwarves had seen him run down the alley and they were advancing, blocking the entrance.

"Hello, how are you? Nice day. We could talk about this," Trap suggested to the angry dwarves. "I don't know why you are so anxious for our company, but if you want me to tell another tale—"

He was interrupted by the dwarf leader who stepped forward and swung his axe. The kender brought his hoopak up and struck the side of the weapon, deflecting it. He skipped backward up the alley.

"I know why you're angry, but we didn't know we had your necklace until a few days ago," he said. "We'd be glad to give it back—"

"Kender thief, you'll pay for your stealing," Tolem said.

Trap kept backing away until he was in the storage yard and found himself up against the stone wall.

"That wasn't nice," he said. "You shouldn't interrupt a reasonable conversation by swinging weapons, you could get someone hurt, and then you'd be sorry." He skipped away from Tolem, only to face another dwarf with an axe just as large.

He feinted with his hoopak, ducked to avoid the hacking axe, and lunged by the dwarf. Four had been concentrating on him and he was behind them, but two others blocked the entrance to the alley.

From above came the sound of creaking wagon wheels. The dwarves were too intent on the kender to notice. The sound had not meant anything to Trap until he heard Umpth's voice.

"You no go back!" The gully dwarf cried out.

Trap didn't understand what Umpth meant. Trap certainly wanted the dwarves to go back to wherever they came from.

Trap skipped about, further angering the dwarves who were unaccustomed to such nimble quarry. Then the kender found an opening and dashed for the wall. In his efforts to guarantee that no one could get behind him, Trap failed to think things all the way through. Suddenly he realized that he was trapped. The two dwarves who had been guarding the alley to prevent his escape, joined the others. All six dwarves, their axes ready to swing, advanced on Trap.

"This isn't fair," he told them. "You almost make me sorry I saved your lives. You could thank me instead of being so mean."

Tolem stopped in surprise. He stared at the kender for a moment and then took another step forward.

"*You?* Save *our* lives? Bah!"

"I did," the kender insisted. "Who threw rocks at you and made you stop arguing in the forest? Who made you hide and listen for the goblins that would have surprised you? They could have killed you, you know. You should be thanking me, not threatening me."

"I don't believe it," one of the other dwarves said, continuing to advance on Trap.

From directly above Trap's head came the crash of wood striking heavily on the top of the stone wall. A deluge of manure poured down on the dwarves who stood directly in front of him. In the blink of an eye they were almost buried in cow and horse dung. A few pieces struck Trap, but he was partly sheltered by the wagon that sat rocking on the top of the wall.

"Grab cart wheel! Climb!" Umpth called down to him.

Not one to hang about when it was time to leave, Trap grabbed a rear wheel and scrambled up. His weight caused the vehicle to tilt and more manure poured down on the hapless dwarves who were struggling to escape their malodorous confinement. Just as Umpth reached down to give Trap a hand, a dwarf, who had been able to dodge most of the manure, grabbed the opposite rear wheel and started up. His weight was enough to topple the wagon and it slid over the wall.

Trap had just grasped a capstone when the wagon started to slide. He held on, his whole body dangling until Umpth caught him by the arms and pulled him up. In front of the wagon, two sturdy ponies were fighting a loosing battle to keep the weight of the wagon from pulling them into the lower courtyard. Trap whipped out his knife and cut their harnesses. Behind and from below came the crash of the wagon and the shouts of the dwarves.

"Ponies back away from axe, wagon fall over edge," Umpth said as he picked up his weapon.

Trap decided he would ask the gully dwarf to explain later, but at that moment he knew they had to get away, buy their pots, and leave the exploration of Solanthus for another time. Stopping to buy some pots was one thing, messing around with the dwarves when he needed to rescue Ripple was another.

"Wizard make kender wash," Umpth said with a sniff as they trotted around the upper part of the building and back out onto the road. Trap bent forward to brush away the muck, but soon gave it up.

Twenty minutes later they had made their hurried purchases and had left Solanthus behind. They rode down the trail until they found the gorge, but the others were nowhere in sight.

"Where go?" Umpth asked.

"I don't know, but we'll find them," Trap said, angry because Halmarain had demanded that he stay with her, but now she had left them. At least he had found the tracks of the five ponies that she had kept with her.

"Just wait," he groused at Umpth as they followed Halmarain's trail. "When I find her I am going to tell her . . . why is she going south? She said the kobolds were going east."

Trap and Umpth rode through the shallow valleys between the foothills, watching for the tracks of the ponies. The kender had been keeping his eyes on the ground until movement ahead attracted his attention. He looked up to see Halmarain just coming around a hill. She was riding in their direction. When she saw him she spurred up her mount. Behind her, Grod, the pack pony, and the two extra ponies picked up speed.

"No need tracks now," Umpth said, pointing ahead.

"I can see that," Trap answered him. "Just wait until she gets here. I'm going to tell her what I think of her leaving us like that."

When Halmarain approached within speaking distance he opened his mouth to have his say, but she forestalled him.

"I'm glad you came after me," she said with no apology for leaving the meeting place. "Now we can make a plan. I've found them."

"Found who?" Trap forgot his anger. Finding things or people was always more interesting than arguing.

"The kobolds who took Ripple and Beglug!" The little wizard shook her head as if she couldn't believe the question.

"Good! Great! Big jiggers! Did you see Ripple and the merchesti? Where are they?" Trap asked.

Halmarain pointed west. "They're coming—"

"I *knew* there was something strange about following on Krynn," Trap said. "People who follow always get ahead. Tolem and his friends are in Solanthus."

"Forget them," Halmarain said, but before she could say more, Trap took offense.

"I will not forget my sister," he said, reverting suddenly to the original subject under discussion. Halmarain's face reddened and she was puffing herself up for an explosion when she suddenly took control of her emotions.

"No, we won't," she agreed. "You're right about the following. What we didn't consider is that we were riding, so we were going faster. Somehow we passed them."

"Then why did you ride south?" Trap asked.

"Because I hadn't thought we were ahead of them. I was looking for their tracks. I was sure they would have to cross the foothills south of the city. When I didn't find any sign of them, I rode to the top of a hill to look for you and I saw them in the distance. They're coming this way.

"Now, you wanted to make a plan, so let's make one. They're staying in the valleys and don't want to be seen from the city. We have to hurry. They're not more than two miles away."

"I still think we could all climb up in a tree—" Trap voiced his first plan, which was still his favorite, but Halmarain interrupted.

"Look around you," she said. "There are very few trees, and those are up on the hillsides. The kobolds won't pass anywhere near them."

"We could take some large horses and pull down a dam and let the water of a river wash down the valley—"

"Don't be ridiculous! There's no large river or dam near by and even if there was, we'd wash away Ripple and the merchesti. . . ." She stopped, thinking, then brightened suddenly. "A stream! By the marks we saw, Beglug always puts up a struggle when they want him to cross a stream."

"Beglug no like water," Grod said.

"Here's what we'll do . . ."

Halmarain laid out the plan. Trap was disappointed that she used mainly her own ideas, but he had thought of water, and she had given him the best part of the action.

They rode east searching for a watercourse that flowed out of the northern end of the Garnet Mountain range. Half a mile after they crossed the track leading from the south gate of Solanthus toward the mountains, they found what they were looking for. A wide, shallow stream with a muddy bank crossed the path of the kobolds.

Leaving the gully dwarves to hold the ponies, Trap and Halmarain climbed a hill they thought the kobolds would pass and waited. When they were sure of the humanoids' course they scurried and slid back down the slope to join the gully dwarves. When they had tethered the ponies out of sight, they cut four bushes and carried them back to their chosen spot, firmly anchoring them along the path the kobolds would be taking. Luck was with them. The trail would lead the travelers around a rocky outcrop and they would not see the stream until they were within fifty feet of it.

"Now you remember what you are to do?" Halmarain asked Grod as Trap pushed the sharp end of a bush into the soft earth.

"Run," he answered, his eyes big with worry. "Run, run, run." He crouched down behind the bush, knocking it over as he tried to hide in its foliage.

"I wish I was sure of the direction you intend to take," the little wizard said as Trap pushed the end of the bush into the ground again. In minutes they were crouching behind their camouflage. The kender and Grod were hidden on one side of the trail while Umpth and Halmarain were on the other side.

Trap knelt on the ground and waited. For the first two minutes he was full of anticipation, but then he started getting bored. He forced himself to stay physically still, but his mind was active, going over the plan of attack. His agile thoughts skipped through the plan and devised several new ideas.

"Halmarain," he whispered, looking out from behind his bush.

"Stay down," she hissed back.

"Oh, okay, I forgot. Look . . . I just thought of how—"

"Wheel think," Umpth said softly. "Think kobold come."

"Now?" Trap whispered.

"Now."

In moments they heard a twig break, a rock clattered, and a curse in the kobold language came from close by. Trap peeked through the foliage. The first two kobolds were in sight. One was limping, raising his left foot to rub his ankle.

The other spotted the stream, pointed, and they both growled angrily. Trap started to rise, but Grod, who had listened with rapt attention to Halmarain and had obediently repeated everything she had said, put out a hand.

"Wait. Beglug must reach water," Grod cautioned.

Trap dropped back to sit on the ground. He fiddled with the two rings he held, one in each hand, and began to juggle them.

"Beglug come, now time for ring," Grod said, holding out his hand.

"You know what to do?" Trap asked the gully dwarf.

"Me tell two times," Grod said impatiently. Actually he had repeated his instructions ten times. "Run, run, run."

Trap slipped a ring on the gully dwarf's finger and he disappeared.

"Wait, that's not right, *I'm* supposed to be invisible," Trap whispered, reaching out, trying to find the gully dwarf's hand. The kender was unable to locate the gully dwarf, so with a shrug he put the other ring on his own finger.

He hopped to his feet, forgot how far a step could take him and suddenly found himself on the other side of the trail, just beyond Halmarain and Umpth.

"Get down!" the little wizard hissed, but she could have shouted and the kobolds would not have noticed. The lead group of ten were gathered around Beglug. They had three ropes tied to his waist and two humanoids kept a tight hold on each rope. The rest of the band had not come into sight.

Beglug had seen the stream and instantly howled his displeasure. He jerked from side to side, then dug in his hooves, fighting to keep from approaching the water. When the merchesti started to struggle the others also grabbed the ropes. All the kobolds were struggling with the little fiend and they had no time to notice the kender.

"Wait until Ripple comes in sight and then we'll—"

Ripple had appeared around the rocky outcrop and Trap stood up.

"Ripple! We're here to rescue you!" Trap shouted, taking a giant step in her direction.

While the kobolds preferred to speak their own language, they understood at least a smattering of the national tongues of the lands in which they lived. The six kobolds that guarded the kender girl stopped in their tracks. The ten struggling with Beglug faltered as they heard the kender's shout.

"Oh, for Gilean's sake!" Halmarain stood up and glared

at everyone in general. She spoke a word of command and the top of her staff glowed. With her right hand she swung it like a club and slapped it into her left hand. A ball of fire flew from it and landed near two of the kobolds that were struggling with Beglug.

"Trap, wait until you hear my story," Ripple shouted back. She tried to take a step forward, but her hands were tied and she too was being led with a rope around her waist. She struggled.

Trap took a step in her direction, which brought him into a violent collision with the kobold who held her rope. The humanoid went flying, Trap stumbled, and as he tried to balance himself he stepped back, taking a second kobold with him. The kender's giant step carried him, along with the kobold, all the way to the stream where they slammed into two of Beglug's captors.

The force of Trap's magically enhanced steps threw him, the three kobolds, and Beglug into the stream. The merchesti, angered by having simply to cross the stream went mad in the cold water that flowed from the mountains. He rose, grabbed two of the kobolds, and slammed them together, knocking them senseless. The third, caught in the coils of the rope, tried to get away, but Beglug grabbed him and bit his arm. The kobold screamed and kicked. The little fiend dropped him and the kobold splashed through the stream, holding the bloody stump of its arm.

The injured humanoid's screams were almost hidden under Ripple's crow of triumph and the cries of the kobolds who had been guarding her.

Trap saw a large stone suddenly appear in mid air as Grod, wearing the ring of invisibility, threw it and knocked a kobold off its feet. A second attempted to run away and crashed into some invisible barricade. Ripple, though her hands were still bound, was kicking one of the smaller humanoids.

Trap had accidentally taken a small step in the direction of the other kobolds and he landed in the middle of the remaining seven who had been guarding the merchesti.

By that time they had their spears and clubs ready, but they had not expected the kender, who stood in the middle of the stream, to suddenly sail into their midst. Trap bumped into two, knocking them sideways. The sharp, metal tipped point of his hoopak stabbed a third in the shoulder before he swung it to knock another down.

The other four charged him and Trap decided it was the better part of valor to retreat a step. His backward step took him completely across the stream. He was ready to cross the creek again when Halmarain shouted to him to stay where he was. She used her staff to throw another flash of fire and it landed in the midst of the quartet of angry kobolds.

The flames splashed against the legs of two and they danced up and down before throwing themselves in the stream. The other two found themselves facing Beglug who had shaken off the excess water and was ready to attack anything in sight.

The two remaining kobolds were not willing to face the little fiend without their fellows. They shouted to their companions and dashed across the stream. The kobold who had been guarding Ripple broke and ran, dashing up the side of the hill.

"Kobolds go!" the still invisible Grod shouted.

"Trap!" Ripple called, running toward him. Trap took two steps in her direction and passed her by thirty feet. He took off the ring and went running back.

"Wait till I tell you what happened to us," he said, skipping up to join her.

"Save your stories until we get away from here," Halmarain said as she trotted down the hill. "I sent Umpth to stay with the ponies. We had better hurry, some of the kobolds went that way."

Trap had forgotten Beglug, but the young merchesti came trotting up to join the others. He growled low in his throat, more a greeting than a threat.

"Want to ride your pony?" Ripple asked him. "Ride?" She raised her hands as if holding the reins and rocked back and forth as if she were on a pony.

"You won't be able to snack on any more kobolds," Ripple said, "But we'll find you something to eat."

"Lava Belly eat kobolds?" Grod asked.

The two kender and the little wizard looked around, but they could not see Grod. The little fiend whirled, turning a complete circle before he whined his confusion.

"Give me back the ring," Trap instructed Grod.

With Halmarain urging them they hurried around the hill to where Umpth was keeping the ponies calm. They were in the saddles and on their way in minutes.

"Oh, just in time," Halmarain pointed across the hills. In the distance they saw the black-cloaked rider galloping toward a group of five kobolds. The humanoids were shouting and pointing before he brought his horse to a halt.

The six reunited travelers hurried down the side of the hill just in time to keep the black-cloaked figure on the black horse from seeing them.

Chapter 26

"I don't know why they captured us," Ripple was saying to Halmarain. "They were really strange. When one of the kobolds tried to take one of my pouches, the leader beat him. They weren't allowed to touch us for some reason, and they seemed in a terrible hurry. I asked them where we were going, but they wouldn't tell me. They weren't very nice."

Ripple's voice, though she spoke softly, carried a little way up the hill where Trap and Grod lay on their stomachs behind some low brush. They were watching for the man in the cloak.

The first question Halmarain had asked of Ripple when the battle was over was if she still had the gate stone. The little wizard turned pale as the kender girl seemed not to know, but a bit of searching in her pouch produced the small, white, slippery rock.

"Me see," Grod pointed north and Trap looked just in time to see the dark rider appearing at the top of another hill more than a mile away. A few kobolds were strung out behind him in a straggling line, just as they had been when Trap first glimpsed the rider. While the kender and the gully dwarf watched, another two small humanoids joined the group. The black-robed man and the humanoids watched for a couple of minutes and then turned north, toward the city. When they were out of sight, Trap and Grod hurried down the hill.

"They're going toward the city," Trap told his sister and the little wizard. "He's gathering up the kobolds, and they seemed to be following a trail."

"Maybe he's following your tracks into the city," Halmarain said. "That's the most likely place for us to seek shelter. Even if the man in the cloak could go in after us, the guards would never allow the kobolds to enter Solanthus."

"Let's go," Ripple said. "I'd like to see the city."

"But if we did, they'd be watching the gates when we came out and they'd attack before we were a mile away," Halmarain objected. "We need to leave this area now, while they're still searching."

"Are we going west again, around the end of the Vingaard mountains?" Trap asked. "If we are I hope we stop at Deepdel again and they have another party, though I don't think we should allow Beglug to eat . . . has anyone noticed? Beglug is getting bigger. Still, he shouldn't eat any more dogs."

"No," Halmarain said slowly. "No, we'll go east."

"I thought you said the wizard that was a friend of your master's lived in Palanthus."

"They'll be expecting us to travel toward Palanthus," Halmarain said. "We'll never escape them. No, we'll go where they least expect, in the direction they were traveling."

"Great! We've been west. Let's go someplace new. But what about a wizard to help open the portal?" Trap asked.

Ripple was not satisfied. "I don't understand," she complained.

Halmarain sighed. "I'm not sure I do either. There was something strange about your capture. Kobolds don't take prisoners, treat them reasonably well, and transport them long distances unless they are ordered to do so—ordered by someone they have reason to fear."

"Gee! Wow! You mean someone wanted us to visit them?" Ripple asked. "Why didn't they just invite us, we like meeting people. Why, I can't think of anything I like better."

"If I'm right, you would not have wanted to meet your host," Halmarain said softly. "The emanations from the black cloaked man suggest he's undead—a death knight—and that means he was brought back from the dead by a black-robed wizard; their order studies necromancy. I think someone knows you have the gate stone."

"Undead! Big jiggers!" Trap's eyes widened with interest. "He's died and come back to life. I'd sure like to talk to him."

"Make good tale, that." Grod nodded.

"Gee! It would!" Trap said, thinking of his stories of Uncle Trapspringer.

Halmarain glared, appeared to reflect, then sighed. "Who would be more interesting, a death knight or a wizard? Death knights can do magic, but he won't make illusions just to please you."

"Why can't we just talk to him and then see the wizard?" Trap asked, wondering why the little human was always trying to take the fun out of everything.

"Because if you talk to the death knight first, he will probably kill you and you'll never get to see Orander."

"Oh," Trap was dubious, but he had not liked the aura of evil that emanated from the dark rider. "You're sure we'll be able to talk to a wizard? I mean, we could talk to the death knight and he would be so interesting, and we're not. It wouldn't be fair if we didn't get to meet a wizard after we give up the opportunity to talk to someone really interesting."

"I think I know who raised the death knight." Halmarain said. "If I'm right we need the help of someone more powerful than the wizard in Palanthus. The trouble is, I know I could count on help if we go north, and I'm not sure of—the one to the east, though he has the most power."

"Who are these wizards?" Ripple asked. "Why won't you tell us about them?"

Halmarain gazed at the expectant faces of the kender and sighed. "I suppose I'll have to. If I don't I'll never get any peace. I'll tell you what I suspect and why. Perhaps it will help you to understand the danger. When we first saw the death knight, he was leading the kobolds. When they captured you they hurried east, which makes me think he was leading them, but their orders came from someone more powerful than the undead warrior."

"Who?" Trap asked.

"Master Orander often spoke of a black-robed wizard of great power, Draaddis Vulter, who lives east of here and the wizards who serve Takhisis are skilled in necromancy, an art white and red-robed wizards seldom use."

"And they were taking us east," Ripple said.

"If I am right, the death knight is seeking you on orders from Draaddis Vulter. He has great power. We must find a wizard as powerful as Vulter to help us. The only one I know of is Master Chalmis Rosterig. He lives further east than Vulter. Understand, I can only seek the help of the wizards I learned about from my own master. Master Orander used to say Chalmis Rosterig would probably lead the wizard's council one day. He's widely known as one of the most powerful wizards on Krynn, but then so is Draaddis Vulter."

"This Chalmis Rosterig that lives east of here; can he do a lot more magic?" Ripple asked, her eyes sparkling. "Then let's go east."

Their direction decided, they rode through the valleys between the higher foothills at the northern tip of the Garnet mountains. They found an overhang that was sheltered from prying eyes and made camp for the night.

The next morning they awakened to rain and a cold wind. Shortly after dawn the rain stopped but the wind whistling through the valleys was still unseasonably chilly. They hunched in their saddles, nearly as dour as the weather.

"I remember grandfather's stories about Solanthus," Ripple said. "I wish we could go back so I could see the city."

"We could," Trap replied. "Halmarain could put Beglug under a spell and make him behave until she reached this wizard. She really doesn't need us." He glanced back over his shoulder, throwing a dissatisfied look at the little wizard. As usual, she led Beglug's pony and the pack animal on long leads while Ripple led the gully dwarves' mounts.

Because of the rain, they were all huddled in their blankets, worn over their heads and shoulders like cloaks. At first Trap, after his casual glance, thought the little wizard and his sister had somehow confused the mounts they led. Then he realized he had mistaken the huddled figure that was Beglug for one of the dwarves. The merchesti *was* growing.

And Ripple had told him the merchesti was getting meaner every day. Neither she nor Trap could blame him for attacking the kobolds when they beat him, trying to make him walk through the streams of cold water. Still, according to Ripple, once the little fiend had discovered he could kill the kobolds, he had attacked several with no provocation. That was why they had tied several ropes to him, to prevent him from wreaking more havoc.

"And he was sly about it," Ripple said. "It seemed as if he was enjoying it." Both kender shook their heads over the idea.

"No, we can't leave Halmarain," Trap said with a sigh. "Even if she can control Beglug, she still can't saddle a pony. If you want to, you could go back to Solanthus. I'll return as soon as I can."

"If you're staying with the wizard, so will I," she sighed. "We'll go back together later." She gave him a small smile. "Dumping manure on more dwarves would be fun, but not without you."

Trap smiled back. He understood his sister's feelings. They had grown up together and had shared most of their adventures. They had spent most of last evening telling each other tales of what they had done while they had been separated. A chance remark in their conversation reminded Trap that the kobolds weren't the only ones on their trail.

"I'll climb that hill and see if the dwarves are following," he told his sister.

While she led the string of ponies east through the valleys between the hills, Trap rode up a steep slope and dismounted near the top. He climbed to the summit where he could check their back trail. In the distance he could see the road that led south from the gate of Solanthus into the mountains. It was hardly more than a track, used only by hunters and dwarves, but it was not empty. Six small, stocky figures sat on their ponies and appeared to be in an argument. They were waving their arms, pointing in several directions. While he watched, three of them started riding south, two seemed inclined to head east, and one wanted to go west, but after some hesitation they followed the first three.

From Trap's position on the heights he had a good view to the east. The morning rain had left the air crystal clear. He was standing on the last steep slope. Two miles further on the hills gave way to rolling country. For fifteen miles, most of the area ahead appeared to be range land. Further on, they would enter a dark forest if they continued directly east.

"We should travel as fast as we can," Halmarain said when Trap brought her the news about the dwarves and the terrain to the east. "The dwarves will learn their mistake quickly enough. Then they'll be on our trail again."

"Why don't we just give them their necklace?" Ripple asked again. "It isn't right to keep other people's property."

"That from a kender," Halmarain sighed. She reached in her bag and pulled out the string of disks. Ripple called it a necklace, but the little wizard didn't think it had been created to be a piece of jewelry unless it was meant to be an emblem of rank.

"Can I look at it?" Trap had turned in the saddle and eyed the disks wistfully.

"Just don't put it in your pouch by mistake," the little wizard said as she handed it to him.

Trap fingered the disks, enjoying the feel of the metal in his hands. The drawings were intricate, and on many disks he could not tell which were sketches and which were runes. He looked at each disk, flipping it over to see a different drawing on each side. He was so intent on his inspection he had not realized Halmarain had ridden on ahead leading Beglug's mount and the pack pony. Even Ripple had passed him.

"Grod see."

"Gee! Sure! Why didn't we think of you. Yes, you look at it and see what you can make of it," Trap said. "You're a dwarf, maybe you can make sense of it."

"Pretty," Grod said and removed his helmet. He was attempting to put the string of disks around his neck when the kender stopped him.

"No. Stop. It's not for wearing. Look at it and tell me what the drawings mean."

Grod frowned, replaced his helmet and began inspecting the disks. He worked at the task for ten minutes and removed his helmet again.

"Stop that. I told you. I said you couldn't wear it," Trap snapped, impatient with the dwarf. "We need to learn about the drawings."

"Only know one," Grod said, handing the string of disks back to Trap.

"You know one? Show me." The kender gave the necklace back to the gully dwarf. He didn't really believe Grod could understand what he could not, but even Aghars were dwarves of a sort.

Grod listlessly flipped through the disks. "Only see high place like ball," he said, pointing to one of the disks.

"High place like ball. . . ." Trap took a grip on the disk that the gully dwarf showed him. He squinted at it and grinned. "You're right! It's one of the mountains we saw near the southern tip of the Vingaard Range," he said. "Why would they put that picture on a disk?"

He flipped the disk over and inspected the back. Another tiny drawing was of a cliff they had passed when they had rounded a spur of that very mountain. He remembered the striations on the rock, and on the disk some were darker, as if outlining a door.

They had passed close to the entrance of a dwarf mine and had not even known it! Trap urged his pony to a trot and rode up to pace Halmarain.

"I know what one disk means," he told her and showed her the drawing of the mountain on one side and the hidden door on the other. Honesty demanded he give Grod the credit for discovering the secret.

"Of course I would have recognized it right away, but I was working my way through the drawings and I hadn't come to that one."

"I think the rest of the disks are the same, with mountain peaks on one side and entrance details on the other," Trap said. Once he understood the purpose of the disks they were not too difficult to read.

"That's not good news," the wizard said.

"What? Why? I think it's wonderful. We could visit lots of mines and caverns and—"

"That's why its not good news. Dwarves are jealous of their secrets. We can't even give the disks back. Those Neidar would believe we had memorized or copied all the information and could raid their mines if we wanted to. Returning the necklace would not save us. They'll kill us if they can."

While she was speaking they followed a little valley out of the hills. Beyond lay the rolling grassland. Halmarain urged her pony to a trot.

"You said there was a forest ahead. We must reach it before the dwarves find our trail. Our lives and the rest of Krynn may depend on it."

"Gee, riding at full gallop would be fun," Trap said.

"No, I'm wrong," she said, shaking her head decisively

as she reined in her mount. "We shouldn't travel across that open country in daylight. There are too many people on our trail. "Let's find a place to camp, rest until sunset, and cross the plain tonight."

"But—"

"Don't argue with me," the little wizard snapped. "Somewhere ahead is danger greater than you can imagine. If I'm right and Draaddis Vulter *is* behind our troubles, he will have spies everywhere."

Chapter 27

Trap found another sheltered valley and the group slept through the day. Twilight found them threading their way through the hills and they reached open country just before dark.

"A lot of things can see in the dark," Ripple had told Trap while they were saddling the ponies. He had grinned at her and said nothing, because Halmarain had arrived with her bedroll.

But by the middle of the night Trap decided traveling at night was even more boring than plodding along during the day. As far as he could tell, the grassy plain that stretched east from Solanthus to the border of Lemish was completely empty.

From time to time, just to relieve his boredom, Trap reached out to pluck a leaf from a bush as he passed it. He twirled the stems in his fingers, raised them almost to his nose to get a better look and threw them away when he lost interest. As he passed a particularly large clump of shadows, he reached down to pluck another leaf.

"Oops," he said as he felt something that was definitely not foliage. He had plucked a feather.

"Aawk!"

The "bush" came to life and stood up. Beside him stood a frightened 'wari. The huge flightless bird stood six feet tall, three feet of which was taken up by sturdy legs and thick, clawed feet. The heavy body sat like a flattened, feathered ball on legs and above it stretched a long neck and a small head with a wicked-looking beak. Trap raised his head and found himself looking into a whirling, gold and black eye.

"What is it?" Ripple called out.

The bird's alarm had not been nearly as loud as Ripple's shout. She, as usual, was bringing up the last of the line. She knew Trap had disturbed something. Her shout brought the clumps on the hillside into action.

More than a hundred 'waris leapt to their feet, squawking and running in circles.

"What have you done?" Halmarain squealed over the racket. "Get us out of here!" She kicked her pony into a gallop and went charging by Trap.

"They're 'waris," Trap said, undisturbed by the panicked birds. 'Waris were huge and wild, essentially stupid and easily startled. They could be pesky, but they weren't really dangerous.

"We woke them up, but if you'll stop shouting and racing around they'll go back to sleep again." He urged his pony forward to keep up with the little wizard. Behind them he could see Ripple urging her mount to a gallop, trying to catch up with the others. He immediately located her by the long blond curl that bounced up behind her. Grod and Umpth were bouncing in their saddles. Behind Halmarain, Beglug, who had been sleeping in the saddle, woke up, noticed the excitement and started swinging his newest tree branch, trying to hit everything in sight.

"We can get killed in a 'wari stampede," Halmarain shouted back and urged her pony to a full gallop, pulling Beglug's mount and the pack pony along with her.

In the darkness, the huge flightless birds seemed unable to distinguish one of their own from the shadowy forms of the mounted group. More than a dozen 'waris stopped their aimless panicked circling and followed the little wizard.

"Hey, how did you get them to do that?" Trap joined the chase, kicking his pony into a gallop. He had not traveled a hundred yards before he too had an escort of the huge birds. So many crowded around him, he could only cling to the saddle and hope his mount kept to its feet. The thudding of the birds' big, horny feet over-rode the sound of the galloping hooves.

Smaller birds flew up out of the grass and bushes and circled overhead as the stampede of 'waris, carrying the group along with them, charged across the plain.

Trap kept a tight grip on the saddle as he allowed his pony to find its own way in the stampede. He stood up in the saddle to look around, thinking this ride was the most fun he'd had on the entire trip. Rising above a fast moving mass of 'wari bodies, the slender necks of the 'waris moved back and forth, each bird setting it's own special rhythm.

He twisted to see a more solid shape among the birds behind him. He waved and Ripple waved back. She was also standing up, looking around. Ahead he could not see Halmarain. Behind her the birds occasionally parted as they avoided the swing of Beglug's tree branch.

Trap's pony splashed through two small streams the kender could not see. In the distance he could see the shadowy eaves of the forest of Lemish. The dark line of the forest became blacker as they approached it.

Halmarain, at the front of the stampede, gave a scream. Trap, who had nearly lost his balance at the last stream and was sitting in his saddle, stood up in the stirrups again. He could barely make out the little wizard. Pacing her, and not twenty feet away, was a creature he could not quite identify. Clearly it was a tall humanoid, but it could not be one of the larger goblin kin because it was keeping pace with—even outrunning—the 'waris.

"She would have to be in front," he groused to himself and his surrounding companions.

Trap stretched to see what sort of creature was outrunning the large birds, but he could only make out indistinct shapes in the darkness. They were bearing off to the right, trying to get away from the birds, he decided, but the 'waris were having none of it. They followed the strange creatures. Halmarain, leading the pack pony and Beglug's mount, was being carried along with them. The stampede topped a rise, and at the bottom of the low hill, the kender could see the glow of a campfire.

"More people," he told his galloping mount. "Maybe this trip will turn out to be fun after all." He could see nothing but indistinct shapes as the campers scuttled around their fire.

"And if we don't stop there, it should still be fun, riding through the forest with all these birds," he told his mount.

The huge flightless birds charged straight down the slope toward the camp. They gawped and squawked as they became aware of the fire and Trap expected the entire stampede to veer north or south. Wild animals and birds usually fled any flame.

The 'waris were clearly aware of the fire. The ones in the center of the stampede were veering to the right and left. In their fear and stupidity, the birds on the outside of the group were pressing in, seeking comfort from their companions.

Halmarain and her escort of strange humanoids were left to gallop directly for the campsite. A few seconds later, Trap, still in the center of the stampede, was swept down the hill and nearly into the camp. The 'waris around him followed the others, splitting to the right and left.

Just beyond the fire were the eaves of the forest. The large birds, creatures of the plains and open fields, wanted nothing to do with the shadowy wood. They charged around the camp, running in both directions. The kender was nearly knocked out of the saddle as four birds on his right jostled to move to his left.

The 'waris circled the fire in both directions, still too panicked to stop running, but also afraid of the fire. Trap heard shouts and saw the heads of a band of more than a dozen goblins appear in the tall grass. The humanoids jumped to their feet and raced for the dubious safety of the campsite.

As Trap galloped closer to the edge of the camp, he heard the clang of weapons, Halmarain's screams, and angry shrieks from Beglug. The strange shapes that had paced Halmarain also ran into the light of the fire. From the tales he had heard since childhood, Trap recognized a group of wemics, centaur-like creatures who had humanoid torsos joined to lion-type bodies.

The six wemics seemed to have joined forces with the goblins who had dashed into the camp from the other side. Meanwhile several kobolds and goblins were fighting the wemics, the kobolds and wemics were fighting the goblins, and off to the side, two goblins were fighting each other.

"Golly! How do they know when to switch sides?" Trap asked his pony as he tried to figure out who he should attack.

Just within the circle of light, and trying to avoid the panicked 'waris, a seventh adult wemic was circling with two young ones at her side. Closer to the fire and still mounted, Halmarain had pulled her axe, which she still wore as part of her disguise. She used the flat side of the blade to slap at a hapless kobold who came within her range as he tried to escape the spear of a wemic. Beglug, frightened and angry, howled and swung his tree branch at everything within reach.

Beglug, striking wildly at a wemic, tangled the small branches of his weapon in the flowing mane of the lion-humanoid and jerked to free his weapon. When he yanked it back, he struck his own mount on the rump and the pony sidled and bucked. The little merchesti kept his seat, but his wildly swinging limb struck a goblin. The humanoid raised his spear to retaliate.

Trap had set a stone in the pouch of his hoopak and was swinging it over his head as he watched for an optimum target. He let the stone fly and caught the goblin on the side of its flat nose. The humanoid roared and spun like a top, its spear knocking down one of its companions.

"What's happening?" Ripple, who had reached the scene of the fight shouted over the din of the stampeding 'waris and the shouts, roars, and screams of the fighting mass. She stood up in her saddle, her whippik in her hand, a short kender arrow fitted to the loop.

"This looks like fun! Which side are we on?" she called as she sought a target.

"Everyone's fighting everybody." Trap said, enjoying the excitement. "Why don't you throw something at Halmarain?"

He pulled out another stone as he watched the battle. One goblin was trading spear thrusts with a wemic, while the others were battling the kobolds. Halmarain, still leading the pack pony and Beglug's mount, had been shunted to the other side of the campfire. She had lost her axe and gripped the saddle with her left hand. She used the butt end of her wizard's staff to beat off a kobold. Beglug howled with glee and swung his tree limb. The leaves had long since fallen off and two kobolds backed away from the still flexible branches that stung like willow switches.

Behind Ripple, one of the confused and still circling 'waris collided with Umpth's mount. The pony leaped forward, almost into the fire. As the animal tried to pull away from the confines of his lead, he dashed across the path of Ripple's and Trap's mounts. The wagon wheel, still in its travois, knocked a kobold into two of its fellows.

A group of kobolds decided the gully dwarves would be easy prey. Unused to fighting, Umpth and Grod ignored the axes in their saddle scabbards and pulled off their helmets. Holding their headgear by the straps, they deflected weapons and struck their attackers with a rain of blows.

Across the campfire, a wemic seemed intent on hacking the little wizard with her own axe. Ripple sent an arrow into his rump just as Trap struck him on the jaw with a stone slung from his hoopak. The wemic roared and backed away from the wizard.

The roar seemed to echo across the plain and the kender realized that the 'waris had finally sorted themselves out and were charging off to the north.

A lighter roar came from Trap's left and he felt the small claws of a young wemic. It had reared and clawed at his left leg. He raised his hoopak, intending to spear his attacker with the sharp, steel-shod point and realized he had been struck by a child.

"Stop! Behave! That's not nice," he warned, but seeing it was ready to claw him again, he had to drive it off. He flipped the hoopak and struck it sharply on the nose with the forked end of his weapon. It howled and backed away to be grabbed by the female who was trying to keep the young ones out of danger. She pulled the child away and was growling at the kender when she raised her eyes and gave a wail of distress.

Trap looked in the direction of her staring eyes and saw what had frightened her. A dark figure in a black cloak was wading through the goblins, hacking with a sword. The kobolds and the wemics were giving way in front of him.

He wore a heavy, black, cowled cloak. When the robed figure turned his head toward the kender, Trap could see a red glow from his eyes.

Chapter 28

Trap shivered at the aura of evil emanating from the tall robed figure, but he never considered backing away. His fingers were already digging around in his pouch, seeking another stone for his hoopak. He was sufficiently awed so that his gaze was transfixed. Almost automatically he fitted the projectile into the leather pouch of his hoopak and swung the weapon over his head.

Beneath the cowl, he saw the almost skeletal face twist into an evil grin as if a stone slung by the kender was nothing to fear. He made no effort to duck the stone that whipped from Trap's hoopak, and when it struck him on the side of his head he ignored it. In one lightning-swift move he stepped around the campfire, reached past Umpth, nearly knocking him out of the saddle, and grabbed Ripple by the arm. With super strength he dragged the kender girl from the saddle.

The cowled figure had moved so rapidly Trap and the gully dwarves were caught completely off guard. Umpth gave a roar and struck out at the stranger with his helmet, but the gully dwarf barely touched the death knight. The undead warrior had turned his back and strode away, dragging Ripple with him.

His next object seemed to be Beglug. In another swift movement he strode toward the merchesti. Beglug gave a howl of terror and struck at the tall figure with his tree branch.

Trap urged his pony forward, but his mount was affected by the aura of evil and fear. It bucked and the kender left the saddle at the arc of the pony's leap. He flew through the air and attempted to land on Ripple's empty saddle, but his foot slipped and he fell on the opposite side of the frightened animal.

Blocked by three panicked ponies, he gave up trying to scramble between them and reached for another stone, the only thing he could think of at the moment.

Trap spun the hoopak over his head and sent the missile flying. He knew immediately that his aim had been off. He had aimed for the back of the man's neck but the evil influence had deflected his aim. The stone dipped low, narrowly missed a scuttling kobold and struck the death knight in the middle of the back.

But Trap had not thrown a stone as he intended. He had accidentally grabbed one of the flame balls he had picked up in Deepdel. The impact, when the glass struck, was strong enough to break the thin glass globe and fire raced up and down the back of the black robe.

The garment, incredibly old and dry, ignited in a flash. The death knight freed Ripple and she tumbled on the ground as he fumbled with the ties that held the garment in place. He turned, staring at Trap as if he could not believe what had happened. Beneath his hood the death knight's red, glowing eyes widened in fear as he struggled unsuccessfully to rid himself of the burning garment. In less than two seconds, his entire body was aflame. He staggered about, a pillar of fire, and from him came a wail that seemed to originate from some incredible and terrifying distance. He bumped into a goblin whose leather vest sprouted flames. The goblin screamed and rolled on the ground.

More fearful than the danger of being burned was the evil emanating from the dying figure. Goblins, kobolds, and wemics all cried out in fear and dashed in all directions. Halmarain's pony reared and charged off into the darkness, taking the little wizard, Beglug, and the pack pony toward the dark forest of Lemish.

"We'd better follow her," Ripple warned as she ran for her mount and jumped into the saddle.

By the time Trap reached his pony and vaulted into the saddle she was right behind him, leading the two gully dwarves. Ahead, they could hear Beglug still complaining. They passed the running kobolds, then the stumbling goblins, and finally caught up with Halmarain. They had outrun the others who were fleeing the aborted battle at the campsite, but Trap took the lead.

Their mounts stumbled. Trap's pony nearly fell as the animals stepped on tree roots in the darkness, so the kender was forced to slow their pace. They traveled for an hour before they stopped. At the little wizard's insistence, they unloaded the tired animals in silence.

The kender quickly grew bored.

"If we don't light a fire they won't find us," Ripple told Halmarain. "The kobolds and the goblins, if they came this way, have passed us by now."

"Everything that's supposed to be chasing us always goes on ahead," Trap grumbled.

"I hope you're right," Halmarain said. She cleared her throat. "I must give you credit, Trap. Killing the death knight was a very brave act, one worthy of any famous warrior. Not even your Uncle Trapspringer could have accomplished such a deed."

"I—uh—I did, didn't I?" Trap didn't want to admit he had thrown the flame ball by accident.

"You removed a terrible danger to Beglug, and to the world. I could have done it—if I had not been too scared to think about it," she fairly admitted. "If anything were to happen to Beglug, we'd never get Orander back or prevent his mother from entering our world to search for him."

"Was good to fight kobolds?" Umpth asked.

"Golly, yes, they were fighting us," Trap replied.

"Good. Gave good hits with helmet," Grod said with a sigh. He sounded relieved, as if he needed approval for his actions. He spread his bedroll and plopped it down. He sprawled half on, half off it, his right knee scrubbing the dirt as he worked his way into a comfortable position.

"Wheel knock kobold down," Umpth added his bit. "Aghar magic good."

"Here we go with the wheel again," Halmarain groused.

"Me need magic too," Grod muttered. "Lose dead squirrel—not find another." He sat up and looked at Halmarain hopefully. "You make dead frog, maybe?"

"No, I will not!" The little wizard glared at him before turning back to the kender. "What started the 'wari stampede?"

"That was an accident," Trap replied. "I wanted to pull a leaf to see what sort of bushes we were passing."

"Only it wasn't a bush," Ripple, as quick witted as her brother, gave a chuckle.

"You pulled out a 'wari's feather?" the little wizard demanded. "*You* started that stampede?"

"Gee! I didn't know it was a bird," Trap explained.

"I didn't either, I thought the clumps were bushes," Ripple defended Trap. "And they didn't start stampeding until you and I started shouting and you whipped your pony into a gallop."

"I don't know much about 'waris, but I've heard noise frightens them," Trap added, partly in defense of his own actions and partly because it was a fact he could impart.

"Well, it's done now," Halmarain said grudgingly, which meant she didn't like being partly responsible. "But that fight—what was that about?"

"I don't know," Trap said after a moment's thought. "I think there would have been one anyway. Those goblins were so close to the camp, I bet they were sneaking up on the kobolds."

"The wemics were probably camping on the plain," Ripple said. "We might have met them if the 'waris had not stampeded. I'm almost sorry they did now, I would have liked to talk to a wemic—if they talk, but the stampede was fun."

"That was fun?" The little wizard sounded as if she could not believe her ears.

"Kender fun no Aghar fun," Umpth muttered. He had decided to take Halmarain's advice and lie down.

"Kender got no smarts," Grod added his mite.

"Well, one thing is certain," Halmarain sighed. "That creature in the black cloak won't be following us again. You did get rid of him, whoever he was, and probably his kobolds too."

"Was he the one following us?" Ripple asked.

"I recognized that feeling of evil," Trap said. "Now I wish I hadn't been so quick to throw the flame ball. I would have liked to know why he was after us."

"I don't think you want to know," Halmarain said as she wrapped herself in her blanket.

"Thorns and thistles. We didn't get to talk to him, and we didn't get to really meet the wemics," Ripple complained as she found her own bedroll. "I'm beginning to think we'll never get to do anything that's fun."

"We did enjoy the stampede," Trap said.

"Maybe we can go back and find the 'waris again," Ripple suggested.

"You lie down and go to sleep or I'll put a spell on you," the little wizard warned them.

"The 'waris are probably too tired to run anymore tonight anyway," Trap said philosophically. He had spread out his bedroll and had stretched out on it before he thought of a question he had wanted to ask. He sat up again.

"Halmarain, you were hitting that kobold with the butt of your staff. I thought magic was supposed to come out of the top end."

"And why didn't you use any of your spells?" Ripple asked.

"Magic should be kept for when it's needed," she answered in a superior tone.

"I like that," Ripple muttered. "He had me by the arm and had pulled me off my pony. I thought it was needed."

A long silence followed Ripple's complaint.

"If you must know, I was too scared to remember any of my spells," Halmarain admitted. "I had memorized my magic missile spell and could have thrown a flame ball. I could have set that creature alight too." She gave a long, gusty sigh. "I was just too scared to think about it, so it's a good thing Trap used one of the flame balls."

Trap smiled in the darkness and lay back on his bedroll again. He had not even thought of using a flame ball. He had plucked it out of his pouch thinking he held a stone. No one had asked him if he meant to set the evil human on fire. If the little wizard wanted to think he did it on purpose, he would let her.

Suddenly Halmarain jumped up. "This is not my bedroll!" she shouted, unmindful of her earlier caution. "By the smell it belongs to one of the gully dwarves."

"Then make them trade with you," Ripple said in a sleepy voice.

"Umpth? Grod?" the little wizard called, but the Aghar were asleep, and when they slept it wasn't easy to wake them up.

Trap grinned and drifted off to sleep, leaving Halmarain to solve her own problem. He knew she'd never wake the gully dwarves, but her frustration might make the rest of the night more exciting. When he went to sleep she was still complaining.

Chapter 29

. . . and in the musty library in Palanthus, the words flowed from the pen of Astinus . . .

"Impossible!" Takhisis glared through the orb at Draaddis Vulter. The walls of his underground laboratory seemed to writhe with the anger of the Dark Queen. The black-robed wizard bowed, hoping to deflect the anger of his god.

"If you want to question the messenger yourself, I'll bring it to the globe," he said. "When it returned its memory was of a confused fight and the death by fire of Jaerume Kaldre. If I have somehow erred in creating the messenger, I am not able to discover how, but with your wisdom and power, you could show me how I went astray."

"Your flattery does not impress me," Takhisis snarled. "Bring the messenger to the orb."

Draaddis placed a high stool a foot from the black globe and crossed the room. The winged rat, busy with a crust of bread, was not aware of the wizard until Draaddis picked it up by the tail. He carried it, squeaking and struggling, back to the stool.

The wretched creature shrank from the glare of the evil god, shrieking in terror as she probed its memory. Freed after five minutes of her probing, it launched itself off the stool and flew to the far corner of the chamber where it huddled behind a large earthen pot, gibbering in terror.

"Impossible!" Takhisis repeated. "How could a kender destroy Kaldre? How would he know Kaldre's only vulnerability was fire?"

"Perhaps he did not know, my lady queen. Kender are strange creatures. They're seldom logical by our standards." Draaddis sought a way to soothe her anger, which could rapidly turn on him. "You feel the messenger's news is the truth?"

"The creature is only a rat with wings. It would not have the ability to lie. It must speak the truth about what it sees unless you put a falsehood in it's mind. . . ."

Draaddis shrank away from the globe, though he knew no distance would protect him.

"Cease your fear, even you know you would not benefit from bringing me such ill news."

"No, my queen, nor would I ever want less than the success of all your aims."

"You will insure that success," Takhisis replied. "You will get the kender, the gate stone, and the merchesti yourself, and when waves of merchesti roam Krynn, you will have your reward."

"*Waves* of—" Draaddis was surprised into blurting out his ignorance. Once he had shown his queen his confusion, he decided he might as well explain it. "I knew we planned on trying to bring the parent of the infant fiend to Krynn—"

"Not only that particular fiend, but as many as can come through," Takhisis hissed. The one perfect eye seen through the black crystal globe paralyzed him. "The lands and races of Ansalon are still divided. The distrust after the Cataclysm is still rampant, but every day they fight less, they draw closer together. I must enter Krynn while they are still at odds. Half a score of merchesti could create just the diversion I need."

"How—" Draaddis bit back his question. Takhisis was clipping her words, a sign she was impatient to get on with her plans. He did not want to irritate her further.

But the Queen of Dragons and Darkness understood his mind. She gave another hiss that broke another bottle, and then forcibly calmed her emotions.

"We will be able to use the kender's gate stone in conjunction with the one on the other plane. If we succeed in the first effort, then what is to prevent two people from standing far enough apart to create an opening large enough to bring in more merchesti?"

"Your mind, my queen, is both wise and subtle. I stand in awe of it."

"You have no time to stand, in awe or otherwise," she replied. "I felt the power of the stones. I felt the tremor of the fabric between planes and after some thought, I understand how they work. It is possible for even the little apprentice to have opened the portal, though she might have been sucked through as well. Fortunately they left her in Lytburg."

"Yes, fortunately," Draaddis agreed.

"We'll still get the little thieves and that fiend. Then we can open the portal. Once we have the adult merchesti on this side, you and those you command will lead it on a chase to find its young one."

The Dark Queen's face lit with a terrible smile.

"In its trail will be a wake of destruction such as Krynn has never known."

"And then you can enter this world," Draaddis whispered, trembling in anticipation and dread.

"At which time you and I will travel about the world, opening more portals into Vasmarg, bringing in more merchesti. While they are about their business of destruction in hopes of finding their way home again, we will be building our armies."

"Ostensibly to fight the merchesti?" Draaddis asked.

Takhisis laughed again, this time with delight.

"A brilliant and subtle idea, Draaddis. You are growing in wisdom. We will draw our armies from the very people who would fight against us, and by the time they discover their true leader, they will be mine!" Takhisis' smile of triumph died.

"Draaddis, there is something else I want."

"Yes, my queen?"

"I want those kender alive. You will keep them prisoners in your underground chambers. When I return to Krynn, they will deserve my special attention."

"I will do as you ask, my queen," Draaddis replied with a shudder. He had seen the malice in the goddess's eyes and while he usually felt no sympathy for any creature but himself, he knew the kender would face a horror even he had never known.

*   *   *   *   *

Sladge Grafont, bugbear leader of a motley band of eight bugbears and four hobgoblins, scratched his stomach and grinned. He stood on a steep hillside, staring down at the small campfire in the narrow valley. He had been searching for days, but now he had finally found his quarry. Too canny to charge in until he was sure of his course, he would watch the six around the campfire for a few minutes more.

In the two years he had been leading the band, they had not lost a single battle, but none had been as important as this one. Death would be his reward if he failed in his mission.

"Be finding travelers?" Brudge, his second-in-command asked Sladge.

"Think so, think so," Sladge answered. "Wizard say travelers be six, and six strangers be camping."

Sladge did not like to think about the wizard that had suddenly appeared in his camp three or four—maybe even five—days before. Sladge had trouble keeping days straight. Draaddis Vulter had promised a reward of good, dwarf-made weapons if they found the strangers he was seeking, but he threatened punishment if they didn't do as he asked.

Shivering at the memory, Sladge reminded himself how the human mage had made a dark shape appear. The black creature, like a dismembered part of a moonless night, had not had a head or feet, or any weapon that the humanoids could see, but it took Mishag. It just enveloped him and he was gone. The wizard had then ordered Sladge to locate and ambush a group traveling east. If he didn't capture them, the black thing would come for him and the rest of his band.

Sladge scratched again as he stood staring down at the camp. How to attack was his problem. He knew how to attack if he came upon a group unexpectedly. He'd just kill everyone and take anything of value . . . but this battle would be different.

The wizard had told him he could destroy and rob the three dwarves, one a Neidar and the other two Aghar. The two kender and the strange little creature that traveled with them were to be taken alive.

He must also keep his band from searching and robbing the kender, though how he was to do that, he was unsure. They had seen the wizard, they had heard his threats, but would they remember when their blood was hot for killing and pillaging? He did not want to be fed to the black thing because some of his people forgot they must follow the wizard's rules.

"Be going now?" Brudge asked.

"Want to be moving too quick, no think," the leader chided his companion.

"Can be using atl-atl," Brudge suggested, brandishing his short spear and the throwing stick.

"Brains be leaking out," Sladge grumbled. Brudge was always too impatient. Sladge also wondered if he was a little bit of a coward. His second-in-command always wanted to attack from a distance. He didn't care for hand-to-hand fighting.

"Wizard say can kill all but kender and thing with hoofs. How tell from here which be hoof-feeted?" Sladge asked. His wisest course was to do exactly as the wizard asked, which meant keeping all his people under strict control. For that, he needed a careful plan.

Brudge scratched his own belly, his head, and his pointed left ear. He looked around, seeking an answer.

"Can kill dwarves," he growled, low in his throat, his bloodlust already rising. He was still fingering his throwing weapon. Brudge was too smart to endanger himself unnecessarily. That was why he was second-in-command.

"But do something, else sleep ends plans," Brudge said, pointing to the rest of the band. They were sitting on the side of the hill, slumped against the boles of the trees while their leaders made their plans. "Take earth shake to be waking them."

Sladge knew his companion was right. They had been searching for the travelers for days with very little rest. At the moment they were running on push time, he called it, understanding but not knowing any other way to describe the nervous energy that came from pushing the body past ordinary limits. Still, he knew they had to use that energy or lose it to fatigue.

"Creep quiet down hill," Sladge instructed. "Be close, must see which is hoof-feeted before kill the rest." He waited for Brudge to pass the word to the others and then led the way. His sneak attack might have succeeded if his own fatigue had not caused him to step on a lose rock. He slid twenty feet, snapping twigs off bushes and causing a small rock slide.

Chapter 30

*My Uncle Trapspringer did admit that his journey with the
little wizard, the gully dwarves, and the merchesti was interesting. . . .*

"Wheel say somebody comes!"

The gully dwarf's warning brought Trap out of a deep
sleep straight to his feet. Ripple was just as quick, her
whippik in her hand.

Umpth slept with his ear against the rusty rim of the
wheel, and as usual, he was the first to give the alarm.

"What—what is it?" Halmarain asked, looking around.
She had been on guard for the last few hours of the night,
but she sat in a huddle, her head nodding as she napped.

"Wheel say somebody comes," Umpth repeated.

Halmarain glared at the gully dwarf and rose, looking
around.

"Who is it?" she asked. "And where is Trap?"

"He put on Orander's ring of invisibility," Ripple said, scrounging in her pouch with her left hand while she held her whippik in the other.

Meanwhile Trap, unseen by the others, had walked away from the fire. At first he heard nothing, then from high on the hillside to the north, he caught the hiss of a whispered sibilant. He slipped away from camp and up the hill. In the darkness he passed the humanoids, and would have missed them completely, but the bugbear bringing up the end of the line stubbed his toe on a rock and staggered into a tree, snapping a branch.

"Oh-ho!" Trap murmured. "Sneak up on us, will you?" He hurried down the slope until he was pacing the last humanoid. He took a grip on the metal-shod end of his hoopak and thrust the forked end between the knees of the bugbear. The humanoid gave a howl and tumbled down the hill, bowling over four hobgoblins and three more bugbears. In an effort to stop themselves from falling, they grabbed at each other.

The would-be ambushers rolled down the hill taking the steepest path, which was a dry watercourse. They rolled over rocks and boulders as they went. As the watercourse angled, they tumbled down the southern side of the small hill's spur, downstream from the camp.

Trap dashed after them, fascinated by the combination of legs, arms, and weapons sticking out of the ball of tangled bugbears and hobgoblins. He discovered he was too interested when he tripped over a tree root and went flying over a steep incline. He landed on the huddle of tangled bodies.

The reaching hand of a bugbear grabbed the back of his vest and the kender found himself rolling with the rest. Most of his attention was taken up with his own progress, but he did hear the clang of a metal helmet. It sounded as if some head had struck a rock.

Being part of a ball was a new experience, but when the tangle rolled over, he found himself on the bottom. The bangs, bruises, and the weight of the large humanoids were uncomfortable and not fun at all. Luckily when the tumble reached the bottom of the incline, the kender was near the top. The bugbear released his hold on the kender's vest and he quickly rolled away. Others were struggling to their feet, though one bugbear and two hobgoblins lay where they had stopped. One of the larger humanoids had a badly dented helmet.

The others were half stunned and staggered about. They had reached the bottom of the incline, only three paces from the creek, but around a bend in the stream and were out of sight of the camp. Stunned and seemingly unaware of where they were, they were no immediate threat to the adventurers. Trap, bruised and battered but not really injured, shook himself and staggered toward the four bugbears who had not been caught in the fall. They too were off course, searching for their stray companions.

The ring's spell of invisibility still held, so he had no fear of getting close to them. First he walked in the footsteps of the last in line, then stepped up between the last two. They were whispering to each other, talking right over his head.

Trap decided it was fun, being able to sneak up on people without their knowing he was there. It would be more fun if he understood their speech, but even if he couldn't he liked being where he was. He was looking up at the huge creature beside him when he slid on a stone and nearly lost his balance. His right arm shot out as he flailed to keep from falling and the sharp, steel tipped point of his hoopak jabbed one of the first two in the back.

The big humanoid turned and snarled at the bugbear who followed him. He was answered in a tone of surprise and denial. Trap grinned, walked quietly for a few steps, and poked the bugbear in the buttocks. The big goblin-kin snarled again, but he didn't turn around. The third time, Trap jabbed harder and then skipped out of the way as his victim turned on his companion.

The enraged bugbear howled in rage and knocked his companion down. The surprised follower barked out a string of oaths and kicked at the first. Their angry shouts echoed through the hills. The two others, angry that their surprise attack had failed, turned on the two fighters and clouted them with the butts of their spears.

The kender skipped on ahead and reached the camp. Ripple had been busy. She and Grod had thrown the saddles on the ponies. She had tightened the saddle girths on three while Halmarain and Umpth kept watch.

"I've slowed them, but they're coming," Trap whispered to Ripple, who jumped and skittered away from the disembodied voice. Still, she was not one to squeak and squeal.

"You're wearing one of Orander's rings," she said. "I wish I knew what to do with mine."

"Put it on and see what happens," he suggested as he took a quick look over his shoulder. Since the attackers weren't yet in sight, he tightened two of the cinches while Ripple finished with the sixth. Trap looked around for the little fiend. If they could get him into his saddle, they might have a chance to flee the humanoids.

"I don't see Beglug," he said, peering into the shadows.

"Where is he?" Halmarain demanded.

The little fiend had disappeared.

* * * * *

"Beglug gone?" Umpth asked, looking around, his dirty face twisted with concern.

"Maybe the wheel can find him," Halmarain snapped. Then her voice softened. "It's my fault. I couldn't saddle the ponies; I should have been watching him."

"You were watching for an attack," Ripple said, always ready with sympathy and understanding.

"No one can do everything," Trap said. "We'll just have to find him, but in the meantime, we'll have to stay here. Maybe he'll come back."

"Go find Beglug now," Umpth said, his ear to the metal rim of the wheel. "Big feet come."

"The bugbears," Trap said, taking a good grip on his

hoopak. He reached in his pouch where he kept his slinging stones. He wanted one of the flame balls he had
picked up in Deepdel. They should have been easy to
find, he reasoned, since he had wrapped them in his extra
shirt, but the round stones from the river had worked
their way to the bottom of the pouch and in the darkness
he could not tell one from the other.

Since they could not run away and leave the little
merchesti behind, they led the ponies up the western side
of the hill behind them and stood their ground on the
forested slope just above the campfire. Three large trees
separated them from the clear area around the campsite.
No one made a decision or gave an order, it just seemed
the thing to do.

On the opposite slope they heard snarls and muttered
orders as the group of humanoids regrouped for their
attack. A howl and a growled order suggested the leader
was having trouble with his troops.

Grod announced his intention to find Beglug and disappeared up the hillside. Umpth, his expression full of
fear, dashed back and forth from the campsite to the
ponies, bringing the packs and the bedding they had not
had time to load onto the pack pony. No one warned him
that in his desire to gather up their possessions, he was
pointing the way to where the others hid. By the time he
finished his trotting, the ponies were loaded. If they could
locate the other gully dwarf and the little fiend, they
could escape.

"Go find Beglug?" Umpth suggested in a frightened
voice. He threw a timid glance over his shoulder. "All go
find Beglug."

"We can't be running around in the woods in the dark,"
Halmarain said. "Our only chance is to stay together,
though I can't think what we can do against bugbears."
Her voice trembled, but she stood ready.

"See if you can remember a spell," Ripple suggested to
Halmarain. "Maybe if you decide on one before they
attack, you can use your magic."

"I'm trying," the little wizard whispered and muttered

under her breath. She squeaked slightly as they saw movement under the trees on the other side of the stream. The dozen large humanoids stepped out into the moonlight across the stream from the campfire. They had not seen the four travelers beneath the shadows of the trees on the hillside, nor the ponies tethered further up the slope.

"Now it wears out," Trap muttered in disgust as he discovered he was visible again. "If we ever see Orander again, I'm going to speak to him about his magic." He took off the ring and stored it back in his pouch, feeling for the second one.

"I wish this ring had some magic," Ripple said, holding up her hand for him to see she was wearing the ring she had taken from Orander's chest. "I wish it would make me twice as large as a bugbear and then they'd see something—*oops!*"

Branches snapped as Ripple shot up to nearly fifteen feet in height.

"Wow! Big jiggies! How did you do that?" her brother asked, stepping quickly away from the enlarging feet of his sister. "Can you make me big too?"

"I don't know how I did it," she said as she stepped away from the confining tree limbs. As she pushed one aside, they heard a squall of fear. Ripple looked up, reached out and plucked Beglug out of the tree. When she lowered him to the ground, he looked around with sleepy eyes and yawned widely.

"If Grod were here we could. . . ." Trap had intended to say "leave," but there was no point. Their talk, the noise of Ripple's growth, and Beglug's howl of fright had drawn the bugbears. They had not seen Ripple, since she was still hidden from them by the leaves of the tall trees.

The largest of the bugbears charged toward the trees, but after three steps he stopped, roared at the others, and let them pass him by. He followed close behind, whacking two bugbears whose pace had slowed. They splashed through the stream, passed the dying campfire, and started up the slope.

Ripple pushed past the concealing trees and stepped into the open to meet the first two attackers. The humanoids skidded to a stop and stared up at her. Both were bugbears, seven feet tall and used to thinking of themselves as the largest and most fierce creatures in the world. They stood staring, their low foreheads wrinkled in confusion, their tall, pointed ears twitching.

"Hello," Ripple said as she reached out and grabbed the nearest by the arm and slung him back on his companions.

"I'm glad you came to visit," she caught the second's spear which he pointed at her as he tried to back away. His own grip on his weapon jerked him forward.

"Let's play a game."

She caught him up by the shoulder and slammed him into three others, knocking all four back into the stream.

Trap had found the second of the two rings he had taken from Orander's treasure chest. He slipped it on his finger, drew a stone from his pouch and fitted it into the sling of his hoopak. He caught sight of the largest bugbear who had slipped out from behind the rest of the retreating group. The humanoid used the night shadows to slip around behind Ripple.

"This should stop you," he murmured as he whirled his hoopak. Unfortunately, while his attention was on the sling and twirling it over his head, he forgot about the ring. He took a step forward to put more force behind his throw. His unlucky step carried him well away from the trees and he slammed up against a bugbear who was just coming out of the shadows on the far side of the stream.

The stone went wild and struck Ripple on the back of her left calf. She jerked her leg back and kicked the bugbear who was sneaking up on her from behind. He gave a howl as he sailed through the air, slammed into the trunk of a tree, and slid to the ground.

Trap, slightly stunned by his collision with the bugbear, shook his head, glanced at the ring on his finger, and crowed with delight.

"That was fun!"

He stared at one of the bugbears who had regained his

feet after being bowled over by Ripple. The male kender took a step in the bugbear's direction and slammed into him. The big humanoid went flying back into the stream.

"One more time," Trap said, his ears ringing from the impact. He took a step toward another bugbear, but his aim was slightly off and the bugbear, suddenly noticing Ripple was turning her attention toward him, backed away. Trap found himself on the hillside, beneath the shadows of the trees, and he had found a target. He had collided with Grod. Luckily, the gully dwarf had been near the end of the giant step.

Grod picked himself up. "No find Beglug," he said. "Was coming back." The last sounded as if it could be an accusation, as if Trap had not needed to be so abrupt in approaching him.

"We found Beglug and Umpth's looking after him," Trap told Grod. "You go help him."

The kender turned, ready for another giant step, but most of the bugbears and hobgoblins—those still able to stand—were retreating across the creek. Ripple was scourging them with her whippik, which, since she had been holding it when she made her wish, had grown with her.

The stunned leader had regained consciousness again. He had found his short spear and his spear-throwing stick, which the humanoids called an atl-atl. He was taking aim on Ripple's retreating back when Trap whipped out a stone and sent it flying toward the bugbear. This time he had found an exploding fire globe, and it crashed into the back of the humanoid leader. The bugbear felt the fire through his leather vest and ran howling toward the stream.

Most of the bugbears and hobgoblins had lost their larger weapons. Some had been dropped in the tumble down the hill. Others had been knocked from their hands when Ripple had thrown one attacker into a group of the others. Two had axes, and one a short spear, but their reach could not match that of the giant kender girl. She delivered a rain of stinging blows with the leather loop of the huge whippik.

Downstream from Ripple, the leader of the attackers splashed out of the water, the back of his vest still steaming. He skulked into the woods.

The leaderless humanoids howled in pain and snarled threats as they scuttled across the small clearing and into the trees. Ripple was ready to follow when Halmarain shouted for her to come back.

Trap took a giant step through the trees to join the others as Ripple easily overstepped the stream and came back into the trees, pushing limbs aside as if they were tall weeds.

"We've got everyone together, let's leave before your spell wears off," the little wizard said.

"Until it does, Ripple can't ride," Trap reminded Halmarain.

"But I can wish myself—"

"No!" Halmarain interrupted. "I don't know how many wishes you can expect from the ring, but it won't be many. Don't waste them."

Ripple lifted Beglug into his saddle with one hand while the others mounted. Trap led his sister's pony as well as those of the gully dwarves. Halmarain followed him with Beglug's mount and the pack pony as usual. Ripple walked behind them, watching their back trail for any sign of the bugbears.

Just before they reached the edge of the forest, Ripple shrank suddenly to her original size.

"I'm glad," Halmarain said. "We don't need a giant following us on the open plain. You would have been seen for miles."

Once they were out of the forest, Trap angled southeast where a swale prevented them from being seen from a distance. They continued within its protection until after dawn. Then they angled northeast to bypass another spur of mountains.

Late that afternoon they stopped, again choosing low ground. Halmarain lit a fire and Ripple cooked two rabbits Trap had killed with stones from his hoopak. While the tired ponies grazed and Halmarain watched the fire,

Trap and Ripple walked up the slope to find a good place to keep watch.

"Stay low," Halmarain called to them.

"As if we didn't ride over this ridge less than an hour ago," Trap complained.

They stayed low when they reached the top of the slope, looking around without much interest. They had seen enough grassland to last them for a while.

"What's that?" Ripple crouched as she pointed out movement to the northeast.

"It looks like the dwarves who have been following us," Trap said. "And would you believe it, they are ahead of us again!"

Chapter 31

"What sort of creatures live in ruins?" Trap asked. He turned in the saddle, looking back over his shoulder at Halmarain, and waited for an answer.

"Things you don't want to know anything about," she said, but the interested gleam in the kender's eye caused her to amend her answer. "Things *I* don't want to know anything about. Things that might endanger Beglug."

"Something else we don't get to see," Trap mumbled, turning back to watch the trail ahead of them. He turned in the saddle again, his eyebrows down, his voice harsh in the way of angry kender.

"We haven't had much fun on this whole trip," he said. "When we find this new wizard, I want to see some magic, and if I don't. . . ." He let the threat lie, not sure what he would do.

"And so will Ripple," he warned.

Trap felt used and abused. They were just passing the ruins of Pey in the distance and he wanted to explore.

The little wizard had heard of Pey, knew it's location and knew that they were close. Since they had seen the dwarves on the horizon, she had insisted they travel by night except through the area near the ruins. For some reason she refused to explain to the kender, she seemed to be terrified of getting close to Pey.

They were riding through the night again.

Trap could see only one advantage to night travel; Beglug slept in the saddle and didn't torment the pack pony. The little merchesti was becoming meaner every day. Just before they broke camp he had used his newest tree limb to swat Umpth, chasing the gully dwarf around the camp.

The two kender and Grod caught the infant fiend and took his switch away, but the merchesti's squeals and squalls of frustration were so loud he could be heard for miles.

"Give it back to him," Halmarain had said with a sigh. She had used all her calming spells on him, but her magic had less and less effect on him as he grew. She was studying to relearn the spells. Before long they'd only give them a brief respite from his caterwauling.

"Why don't you just turn him into a frog or something until we reach the wizard?" Ripple asked. "We could put him in a sack and he'd be easier to manage." Since the kender girl loved the ponies, and Beglug tormented them at every opportunity, she had developed an active dislike of the merchesti.

"Because I don't know how," Halmarain muttered. "If I did, we would have had a lot less trouble on the journey."

"No can make frog?" Grod demanded.

Trap stared at the little wizard for a moment and then started to laugh. He laughed until he couldn't stand up and so he sat on the ground. Ripple stared at him in confusion, but she soon started to giggle, infected by his mood.

"What's the matter with you two?" Halmarain demanded.

"Along comes a wizard and sits on a log," Trap gasped.

Ripple instantly caught on. "And threatens to turn us all into frogs," she added.

Grod laughed and started to clap.

"I don't need any of that," Halmarain shouted.

"She huffs and she puffs and fills us with fear," Trap giggled.

"But her spells and her threats never appear," Ripple capped him, with a sly look at the tiny wizard.

"Grod make one!" the gully dwarf shouted at the kender, jumping up and down with excitement. When he had their attention, he puffed himself up with a huge indrawn breath and clasped his hands behind his back.

"No more have to wash!" he said and waited expectantly.

"By golly and gosh," Trap obligingly did the capping.

"Are you finished?" Halmarain asked quietly. She had just lost her major weapon against the dirt on the gully dwarves.

Since he still did not know their destination, Trap had begun the next leg of their journey on an angle that would take them past the last mountains in the next chain, approximately twenty five miles to the east.

"No, we should go directly east from Pey," the little wizard told him when she realized they were on a northeasterly course. We want to reach the mountains about ten miles south of Castle Kurst. Then the dwarf necklace will come in handy."

"You mean we're nearly there?" Trap could hardly believe it. "We'll find this new wizard and see some magic?" The kender referred to the magic-user at the end of the trail as the "new" one since finding him was their newest goal.

"I don't promise you anything," Halmarain said quietly. "Remember, I don't know Chalmis Rosterig. All I'm sure of is that he is a wizard of great power."

"Hey! Great! Now we know his name and we'll soon be there."

Having a name seemed to make the wizard more real.

Trap urged his pony forward, anxious to reach their destination. The wizard's chambers would be full of all sorts of things to see and touch, and he might be able to talk Chalmis Rosterig into showing them some fun magic.

They rode through the night and dawn found them in the middle of the hill country between the ruins of Pey and the westernmost spur of the Khalkist Mountains. They made camp and slept through most of the day, but during the late afternoon they were awakened by the scream of one of the ponies. As usual, Trap woke rising, his hoopak in his hand. His first thought was that the dwarves or the kobolds might be attacking. He was stunned and disgusted to see Beglug squatting on the ground, just out of reach of Halmarain's mount. It was on the ground, its legs thrashing. Even as the kender stared, the kicks weakened and the animal died. The little merchesti had bitten out its throat.

"Oh! No! No, no." Ripple rushed forward, stopped a few feet away and sobbed. The kender girl loved the ponies and begrudged no work in rubbing them down, combing their manes and tails and brushing their hides.

"Beglug! Bad! Bad!" Trap yelled at the little creature, still too shocked to say more.

Halmarain rushed over, muttered a spell, and the evil glow in the merchesti's eyes died out. He hummed his calm little sounds and stood. When Halmarain told him to, he wandered back to the fire to curl up and sleep again.

"I told you that monster was evil," the little wizard said, staring at her dead pony.

"No good make Lava Belly sleep," Umpth said, staring at the dead animal. "Him eat pony now, no bad two days maybe."

"He will not eat that animal!" Halmarain snapped. "The last thing we need is for him to develop a taste for our mounts."

"No make good magic," Grod said as he too stared at the carcass. "Too heavy. No can carry."

They cooked a quick meal, loaded the surviving

animals, and broke camp. Halmarain rode the pack animal and they divided the supplies between them, loading a few on the backs of her mount, and those ridden by the Aghar and the kender.

At dawn of the second day, they found a deep gully where they would not be seen and made camp. Not two miles ahead was the foot of the first mountain in the range.

"When we finish eating can we go visit the wizard?" Ripple asked. She was as happy as her brother to have the boring trip behind them.

"That would be nice," the little wizard agreed with a despondent sigh.

"Gee! You sound sad. I thought you'd be happy to be here," Trap said, surprised that she seemed disappointed.

"We still have to search miles of mountains for a hidden entrance to an abandoned dwarf city—one abandoned a thousand years ago," Halmarain said. "That will be the hardest part of our journey."

"Hard? No, it'll be fun. I like looking for things," Ripple said. "How do we recognize it when we find it?"

"I don't know."

The kender stared at Halmarain. Even the gully dwarves paused, forgetting to eat as they gazed at the wizard.

"Wizard no smart," Umpth said.

"Done said that," Grod agreed.

"Just shut up!" Halmarain jumped up and stomped away from the campsite, her tiny feet making poofs of dust in the dry bed of the gully.

"She's tired," Ripple said. "When a person is very tired, everything seems harder than it really is. But I don't see the difficulty. We won't have any trouble finding the entrance."

"How do that?" Umpth asked.

"You're dwarves—not Hylar, Neidar, Daewar, and certainly not Daergar, but dwarves. You should be able to find the entrance to this dwarf city."

"The Aghar don't live underground," Trap reminded

her. "They don't know anything about mines and caverns."

"Aglest Clan use wheel," Umpth announced. "Wheel know everything."

"Know more than human wizard," Grod said, turning so it was apparent he was speaking to Umpth.

"Can find village," Umpth agreed. He scuttled around to sit facing Grod and held up one finger, then a second. "Wheel know someone comes, two times." He held up two more fingers, became confused. He stared at the three fingers, confused because one limiting trait of their race was their inability to count above two. He solved his problem by tucking one finger under his grubby thumb.

"Wheel find Trap," Grod said, holding up a finger.

Halmarain's fit of temper had not taken her far from camp and as she returned she heard the last of the conversation.

"That's enough!" Halmarain shouted at the dwarves, remembered loud noises could attract unwanted attention, then spoke more softly. "If that wheel is so powerful, I'll let it find the entrance to the dwarf caverns."

"Does this place have a name?" Trap asked.

"Digondamaar, it means 'the golden halls' in the Neidar tongue."

"Neidar?" Trap looked up.

"Really? That's interesting. Tell us about it," Ripple suggested. "Perhaps knowing more could help us locate the entrance."

"This city isn't Hylar. The Neidar started the mines and the city more than a thousand years ago. For some reason they abandoned it," Halmarain said, then paused to sigh before continuing. "How much they built, how deep they delved, and why they left are secrets known only to the dwarves. Chalmis Rosterig lives in the underground chambers near one of the entrances—the west entrance, according to rumor. That's all I know."

"That's really not much," Trap said with a hint of censure. "And you didn't make much a tale of it. Still, it's a start. You stay in camp with Beglug and rest. We'll go searching for the entrance. If two kender and two gully dwarves can't find the entrance, it isn't there."

Halmarain appeared undecided. She glanced around the camp, which was well hidden in the gully, and then at the little fiend, who had curled up in the early morning sunshine and was asleep.

"I know. I'll get you some water from the stream and you can have some more tea," Ripple said quickly. "You can sit and relax and let us explor—*search*."

"Take care, you don't know what sort of creatures you might find in those mountains," Halmarain said.

Trap considered the wizard's warning and checked his pouches to see if he had any more stones for his hoopak pouch. His exploring fingers discovered something he could not identify by feel and he drew it out.

"I had forgotten about this," he said, inspecting the small, gray-green glass disk. He moved it to another pouch to make sure he didn't make a mistake and use it as a slinging stone.

* * * * *

Astinus of Palanthus is rumored to serve the god Zivilyn or perhaps Gilean, the god of knowledge. No one has ever known the truth. Nevertheless, he shook his head as he described the satisfaction in the Dark Queen's voice. . . .

"At last!" Takhisis said, her words a sigh of relief. Then she gave a snort of disgust. "They're in some gully, and I can't see the surrounding area.

"Look at those striations of red and gray," Draaddis Vulter pointed. "There's only one place on Krynn where that geological anomaly occurs. They're east of here . . . in the hill country. They passed right by us!"

"At least that stupid kender hasn't lost the viewing disk."

As they watched, the kender slipped the viewing disk back into his pouch and a small dark cloud hovered over its mate that lay on the mirror in Draaddis' laboratory.

"I will have them, Draaddis." The Dark Queen's voice was full of menace. "You will not employ any more fools. No death knights, no goblins, no bugbears, no kobolds . . . and if you value your life, no more mistakes."

The chamber seemed to fill with an evil vapor again. From it came the grasping arms on which long-fingered hands reached out with even longer claws. Draaddis felt the ripping of his skin, the flesh being torn from his face and limbs. No matter that the wizard knew his torture was illusion, the pain in his mind was real. He screamed and fell, begging his senses for the oblivion of unconsciousness or death. Since the wounds were mere illusions, he received neither.

Dimly, between his own screams, he could hear the little winged rat shrieking. It staggered out from behind a stack of books and flapped it's wings pathetically, as if it had lost the ability to fly.

When the illusion faded, and the pain with it, the rat continued to whimper. Draaddis was minutes getting his breath, calming his senses, and regaining his feet.

"Do you understand, Vulter? I will have the kender; I will have that stone."

"I shall begin my search at once," Draaddis bowed to his queen. He did not tell her that the hills between Pey and the westernmost range of the Khalkist Mountains were riddled with deep gullies, all looking just alike.

* * * * *

Two hundred feet above the laboratory the old wolf had leaped from his bed of leaves and streaked out into the night. He kept his left hind leg raised, because some creature with claws had reached from a cloud and had torn his flesh.

He raced around the ruins and as he turned the corner, he passed two squirrels who were squabbling over a place to bury some early ripening nuts. Bowled over, the squirrels rolled in the high grass as the wolf went by.

He ran for half a mile before he realized he had begun

to use the injured leg. He slowed to a trot and then a walk and stopped. The place seemed safe and he wanted to clean the wound before it began to hurt again. He inspected his fur and found no mark.

What was happening to him?

Chapter 32

My Uncle Trapspringer once told me that sometimes the hardest part to unlocking a lock or springing a trap was in locating it. He also told me he learned that particular lesson on his first journey. . . .

"Finding Neidar mine hard," Umpth said. "Tired." He plopped down on the ground, sending the dust flying.

"Bugs and worms! You're as bad as Halmarain. We won't have any trouble," Trap said. "We just have to find the right place."

They had left Halmarain in camp and been searching for nearly the entire day. The dwarves were tired and so were the kender, but the latter were thoroughly enjoying their escape from the little wizard's fears and gripes.

"Hey! Big jiggers! I forgot! I know what we should do," Trap said as he pulled the dwarf necklace from his pouch.

He had purloined it from Halmarain's bag. It was the first time he had deliberately taken anything from her, but he thought they might need it. Just before they left camp he remembered there had been tiny drawings around the rim of the disks and many of them were of mountains. If they represented the terrain above the dwarf mines he might find a match. That had been his intention when he took the necklace. Shortly after leaving camp he had become absorbed in the surroundings and had forgotten all about the disks and his need for them.

While Umpth sat on the dusty ground, Grod had announced his intention to search for another dead animal to use for Aghar magic and walked up the mountainside a short distance. He occasionally splashed in a tiny brook before he dropped to sit under a tree.

"Cool here," he called to his brother.

The kender knew the gully dwarves would not be traveling further until they rested, so brother and sister found a boulder and sat close together. Trap took one side of the necklace and Ripple the other, looking for sketches of mountaintops and comparing them with the scene in front of them. They were working their way steadily around the string of disks when Trap looked up, back at the disk he held, and crowed.

"Look! See the double peak?" He pointed first to the mountain and then to the disk. "And right beyond it is that tall rock formation."

"Yes. That's the right disk," Ripple said, but I don't see the mountains in front of it." They stood and looked around, trying to decide from which angle the tiny sketch had been drawn.

Grod had apparently had enough rest; when the kender started walking about, he came down the hill to join them. Each time they had inspected the string of carved disks the smaller gully dwarf had expressed an un-Aghar interest, but this time he ignored it. He walked over to his brother who still sat in the dust.

"Tired, tired, hungry," he said. "Go camp. Sleep."

"Eat, then sleep," Umpth said, getting the priorities in

the correct order. He scrambled to his feet.

"No! Not yet, we still have some daylight left," Ripple objected, but this time the gully dwarves were not amenable to persuasion.

"Go now," Umpth said, and kept walking east.

"Stop! Wait! We've found the disk. . . ." Trap had started to object and gave up. He understood how they felt. They had ridden all night and had spent the day wandering in the mountains. He was tired too, but he resented the defection of the dwarves, but even he was too tired to argue very much.

"Thorns and thistles. A plague on gully dwarves. We can't let them go alone," Ripple said. "They'll get lost in all those gullies."

The sun was dipping below the mountains to the west when they reached the camp in the arroyo. They found Halmarain quarreling about carrying water for the stew only to have Beglug pour it out on the ground where he was busily playing with the softened clay. He had plastered himself with the quickly hardening mixture.

"At least he didn't try to eat any more ponies," the little wizard said with a sigh.

"Or the stew," Ripple said appreciatively. During their ride the night before, Trap had been lucky enough to kill three rabbits. One had satisfied Beglug's growing appetite for meat. The other two were simmering in a savory stew.

The gully dwarves were trying to help themselves when Halmarain slapped Umpth's hands with her wooden spoon. She hurriedly dished out two large helpings before the Aghar reached in the pot with their dirty hands.

She filled bowls for the kender and they all sat in a circle as they ate. After a good sleep, the little wizard was more hopeful and more cheerful than she had been that morning. She said nothing when the two kender told her about finding a mountain peak that corresponded with the drawing on one of the disks, but her eyes brightened.

Even the kender were too hungry to talk much during their meal. The gully dwarves gobbled down their first helping and finished off another while the kender were still on their first bowl.

"Sleep now," Umpth announced in a tone that brooked no argument. He picked up his bedroll and stumped over to a level area.

"Sleep good," Grod agreed, following his brother. "Door no go 'way. Dwarves no go 'way too."

"What? What door? What dwarves?" Trap put his half filled bowl aside and jumped to his feet, following Grod. "What dwarves? Where were they?"

"Hey, don't glare at me. I didn't see any dwarves," Ripple said when Halmarain turned a questioning eye on her.

"See from hill," Grod said as he curled up in his blanket and closed his eyes.

"From what hill?" Halmarain demanded, but the gully dwarf, with the single-minded pragmatism of his race was already drifting off to sleep. While the two kender and the tiny human traded looks, his greasy long mustache fluttered with his first snore.

"Wretched creatures," Halmarain glared at him before walking back to the campfire. "Do you think he did see the dwarves?"

"Yes," Trap said slowly. "Umpth and Grod don't lie."

"No," the little wizard replied. "They don't have the imagination for it."

Trap didn't agree. He thought the gully dwarves showed a lot of imagination and a good deal of shrewdness, but to say so to Halmarain would only cause an argument, and he had other concerns. If Grod said he had seen the dwarves, he had seen them.

"You think the dwarves are the ones who were following us," he said, gazing at the apprentice wizard. "Maybe they're not."

"Of course they are," Halmarain snapped. "They have to be."

"Why?" Ripple demanded. Like her brother she failed to see the little wizard's reasoning.

"We took the necklace—"

"*We* didn't take it," Trap objected.

"*Grod* took it, but they don't know that," Halmarain sounded exasperated. "To them that string of disks, which appears to be a map of the entrances and traps in their mines is a priceless thing. They'd never believe the gully dwarf just wanted it to give it to Ripple as an ornament."

"So they followed us to get it back, but that still doesn't explain why they're waiting at our destination," Ripple said.

"Yes, it does," the little wizard insisted. "As soon as we got it, we started east as if we made the decision on our destination according to what we found on the necklace. They probably knew nothing about the capture of you and Beglug. Their mines are always in the mountains, particularly in the Garnet Range. When we left Solanthus, they went south towards the Garnet Mountains."

"Oh, I see! They thought we were heading for one of the hidden mines in that range," Ripple said with a gurgle of delighted laughter as she suddenly understood Halmarain's reasoning. "But since we continued east instead. . . ."

"They decided we were heading for Digondamaar," Halmarain continued. "It's probably the only abandoned dwarf delving on our route, or at least the nearest one." She gave a smile of wicked delight. "And since they're waiting for us, they've pointed out the entrance, only how do we get past them?"

Trap yawned, suddenly feeling his fatigue. Ripple found the unplanned suggestion irresistible, and she too yawned.

"You must be exhausted," the little wizard said, for once sympathetic. "Get a few hours' sleep. We'll move into the mountains just before dawn. Then we can think of a plan."

Night shadowed the hills and gullies when Grod awoke. He sat up, stretched, gave himself a good scratch and yawned until his jaws and ears popped. How long had he been asleep, he wondered, and why had he awakened while it was still dark?

Then he knew. He had been sleeping in fits and starts, waking for days. The two kender and even Grod's brother, the wise leader of the Aglest clan, paid little attention to the warnings of the little wizard, but Grod believed her. The merchesti was evil. Even though he wanted to keep an eye on Lava Belly, he had been asleep when the fiend killed one of the ponies. Grod was determined to keep Beglug from killing any more.

The smallest of the Aghar cared nothing for the animals, and would as soon walk as ride, but Pretty Kender would cry again, and he didn't want her to be unhappy.

He looked around the camp, dimly lit by the dying campfire and suddenly he understood the reason he had awakened so suddenly. The little wizard was supposed to be on watch, but she was sitting with her back to a boulder, sleeping soundly. She made little wheezes like whispers when she slept.

And over on the other side of the camp, Lava Belly was creeping toward Pretty Kender. His eyes were shining red like they did when he was ready to attack something.

"Wizard!" Grod gulped, so terrified on Ripple's behalf that his voice was hardly more than a croak. He launched himself in Beglug's direction, charging across the camp, butting the fiend with his head and they both went over in a heap.

Beglug was the first to gain his feet. He growled deeply, softly, his voice low, throaty, full of menace. He extended his claws and bent his knees, ready to pounce on the still rolling gully dwarf.

Grod, realizing his danger, was attempting to flee when behind him he heard the little wizard chanting. Her spell took effect after the merchesti launched himself at Grod, and even as he landed by the gully dwarf his eyes had lost their bloodlust.

"Beglug, go back to sleep," Halmarain snapped as she trotted over. "Did he hurt you?" she asked Grod in the gentlest voice she had yet used when addressing the Aghar.

"Him no hurt me. Go hurt Pretty Kender," he told the wizard.

"It's a good thing you woke up, you saved her life," Halmarain said.

"Me tell me wake. Lava Belly evil. Do bad things," Grod insisted, glowing with the idea that he had saved the kender girl's life. "Find big wizard soon. Beglug go his This Place. No hurt ponies and Pretty Kender," he suggested, speaking more at one time than he usually did in a week. Still, it puzzled him that the wizard was giving him such a hard, speculating look as if she could see into his brain.

"You're a lot smarter than you pretend, aren't you?" she said, making her remark a question that he did not know how to answer. Then a pelter of raindrops drove Halmarain's question from his mind.

"Wake the others. We should get out of this gully," she warned as she scurried around to gather up their belongings. "If the rain is heavy this ditch might flood."

Trap did not need Grod's help to wake up. The cold rain, falling on his face brought him to full consciousness. Ripple, Umpth, and Beglug were already struggling in their blankets. The merchesti whined and shivered.

Halmarain repeated her warning about flash floods and in a short time they had saddled the ponies and slung the packs across the saddles. Beglug and Umpth complained about being awakened in the night but they followed the two kender who led their mounts. They crossed the stream at the foot of the gully and traveled up the little watercourse. By the time the worst of the storm hit they had found another depression that led into the mountains and used it until it began to fill with water.

"That way," Ripple shouted to her brother. She had remembered a small, blind valley they had discovered that morning. They could not subject the ponies to the fear of the darkness and the echoes of a mine, and the valley seemed the perfect place to leave them.

The entrance was narrow, and could be easily blocked with cut brush. It was a perfect place to leave the ponies. Near the entrance, the hillside was dotted with large thorn bushes, some of which they cut. It made an excellent fence.

"Now, would be the best time to approach the dwarf camp," Halmarain said, gazing at Grod. "Do you remember the way?"

"Dark," the dwarf objected. "No see where go."

"I can," Trap said. "I know where he was when he spotted the dwarves."

"Why go now?" Umpth complained. "Dark, cold, wet."

"And the dwarves will be huddled in their blankets around the fire," Halmarain answered him. "They won't be expecting us."

"No believe we so dumb," Grod muttered as he fumbled with his bedroll and pulled out his blanket to use for a cloak. Over it he draped the waterproof ground sheet. He followed Trap, huddled inside his blanket as he trudged along, dragging the ends in the mud of the hard summer rain. Umpth had followed his brother's example, and Beglug had whined until he was similarly protected. Umpth had a problem as he tried to hold his blanket and roll the wheel at the same time.

"I'm beginning to think they've got more sense than I gave them credit for having," Halmarain said after they had been walking for an hour. She was soaked to the skin and shivering.

"Wizard learn," Grod said in a smug voice that angered the little human. She clamped her jaws shut and tramped silently behind the two kender.

Trap grinned. Halmarain could not have used her blanket and ground sheet even if she had wanted to. In the darkness they had overlooked her bedroll and left it in the gully. She wasn't too happy about it, but believing they would soon reach the wizard, she had not complained too loudly.

Chapter 33

A single candle illuminated the historical tome as Astinus inscribed. . . .

Down in the foothills, on the ten foot promontory that jutted up above the intersection of the gully and the stream, a rabbit, taking advantage of the higher, dryer ground, was startled as a dark shape suddenly appeared within five feet of him.

The rabbit dashed away, too frightened to notice the shape was one made by a human in a long black robe and cowled hood. Even if the creature had recognized clothing he would not have understood the runes that trimmed the robe, or that he was looking at a wizard.

Draaddis Vulter staggered with fatigue. He had been searching for the kender and the merchesti without pause for two days.

Draaddis had mentally traced the party on its travels. Since they crossed the southern Vingaard Mountains after turning east, they had skirted around the northern ends of the Garnet Mountains and around the north end of the little range that stopped only a few miles from Pey.

When he had left his laboratory Draaddis had tele-ported into the mountains where he knew another band of goblins made their home. Takhisis said he was not to depend on humanoids again and he would not, but he needed them to search. The foothills and the deep gullies hid the travelers, and depending on their direction of travel they could have been anywhere within an area that covered nearly three hundred square miles.

He had sent most of his goblins northwest, beyond the Castle Kurst, thinking the kender and their party would continue to avoid mountain travel if they could.

Most of the goblins were out of reach when he discovered a set of pony tracks traveling due east from Pey. He followed them but to his disgust, he found a group of six dwarves at the end of the trail and had to start again. Just before the rain started he discovered a second set of tracks that had disappeared into the gully at his feet. The runoff from the surrounding hills had half filled the little arroyo.

Several charred pieces of wood had been washed against a small outcrop of rock and gave evidence of an abandoned campsite. Had they left it by choice or had the torrent of water, now washing down the gully, carried the campers and their gear away?

Draaddis spoke a word of command and a tiny ball of light appeared just above the rushing torrent. He sent it downstream until he saw a deeper shadow, and hurried down the bank. The light bobbed above a blanket that had been caught on a thorn bush at the stream's edge.

His quarry had been caught in a flash flood, he decided, and hurried downstream, along the bank of the rushing water. He wondered how far he would have to follow the watercourse before he found the bodies of two kender and the merchesti.

*My Uncle Trapspringer has a saying: As much as he likes
meeting people, sometimes, some people can make life hard.
This was the trouble with those pesky dwarves—not that I have
anything against dwarves, you understand. . . .*

"If we find the dwarves, we still can't drive them away
from the entrance," Halmarain said. She was tired of the
rain, of slipping and sliding on the sloping ground at the
feet of the mountains, and her earlier cheerfulness had
washed away with the storm. "We don't know the
dwarves are camped in front of the entrance," she continued. "Maybe they just picked that place because they
were tired too."

"Can't, don't, won't, because," Trap chanted, irritated
with Halmarain's negativity. "We can find out," Trap said.
"I can use my invisibility ring—"

"*Orander's* invisibility ring," Halmarain reminded him.

". . . *Orander's* invisibility ring to slip around them and
look for the entrance," the kender finished. "If it's not
there we can start a new search."

Halmarain nodded. "Just remember, the spell won't
last too long. You don't want them to catch you."

The lashing rain continued. They found it slow going as
they climbed the side of the mountain to stand under the
tree where Grod had been sitting. In a spirit of helpful-
ness, he pointed north, then south, then to be sure he was
right, east and west. In the distance, the others spotted the
faint glow of a fire.

"How do they keep it going in the rain?" Ripple asked.
The black clouds were dumping a deluge on them, yet the
dwarf fire seemed unbothered by it.

"Great! Fire that can burn in the rain. I'd like something
like that. Is it magic? Do dwarves have magic too?" Trap
asked, his eyes alight with hope.

"None that I know of, but then dwarves have not been
my study," Halmarain replied. "Except the Aghar, of
course," she said after a hard look from Grod.

Trap thought she had finally accepted the idea of the gully dwarves' magic wheel until he saw her dip her head and smile.

While the others waited under the tree, which gave them a little shelter from the rain, Trap hurried down the slope, slipping and sliding. At the bottom of the valley that separated the two mountains he found a rushing stream, but luckily for him, a large tree had fallen across it, and he used the thick bole to cross the worst of the current.

The climb up the other slope was more difficult, because of the torrent of water washing down the steep slope, but at last he was within fifty feet of the dwarves' camp. The six Neidar were sitting beneath a tent-like structure that was nothing more than a canvas roof on hastily erected poles, but it did keep the rain, which was falling straight down, from drowning their fire. They appeared to be partially dry as they sat on the saddles they had removed from their mounts. Not far away and partly sheltered by an overhang of the cliffs, their ponies stood hobbled and sleeping.

Trap frowned. If this had been one of his tales, the dwarves would have been talking and he would have learned all he needed to know. Instead they stared into the fire, and he would have to search out the entrance for himself.

The kender pulled out a ring, slipped it on his finger and checked himself. He was still visible. Wrong ring, he decided. He held the first in his left hand while he searched his pouches with his right. Aha! With the second ring on his finger he had disappeared, even from his own sight.

Since the dwarves seemed unwilling to talk about anything of interest, he circled around the camp and took a close look at the cliff wall. Beyond the fire he found a strange formation. Where the base of the stone cliff curved, a thin, almost crust-like wall jutted out from the cliff like a curtain. A narrow opening, one that would not be noticed unless the searcher pressed right against the cliff, allowed access into a chamber about twelve feet long and six feet wide. In spots the outer wall was wafer thin, and the faint light from the dwarves' fire penetrated it. Trap looked around.

He had found the entrance to the abandoned city of Digondamaar, he decided. He could see the cracks where the cliff wall was unnaturally smooth and even. They outlined a door five feet high and four feet wide. Behind him the irregularities in the curtain wall were made by nature. The rest of the cliff side was rough as well, except for the curtain wall. The big secret was a failure.

He slipped out of the small antechamber, hurried along the base of the cliff until he would be lost in the darkness, and pulled off the ring. Back under the tree on the other side of the valley, he told the others what he had seen.

"Then all we have to do is hold off the dwarves while we open the door by means unknown to any of us." Halmarain said in a voice that made the task seem impossible. The rain had drowned her enthusiasm.

"I've been thinking about that," Trap said. "Where is that knife that cuts so well?" He scrounged around in his pouches, but it was Ripple, digging in her own bags, that discovered it.

"You must have put it in my pouch by mistake," she said, handing it over.

"Pretty Kender need pretty knife," Grod said.

"You mean you've been stealing from them too?" Halmarain looked up, surprised. The idea of anyone taking a kender's belongings seemed to astonish her.

"Have you? Trap eyed the gully dwarf with awe rather than anger. "We'd better check our pouches and sort out our belongings again," Trap told Ripple as he tucked the knife in his belt.

They made their plans and slogged their way across the valley. By traveling in the storm and the darkness they could get quite near to the dwarves' camp without being seen. When they were as close as they dared go, Trap put on the ring of invisibility again and slipped around the dwarves who, by that time, had rolled themselves in their blankets and were snoring loudly. Trap crept along the base of the cliff until he reached their mounts. Then with Orander's knife he cut the leather straps that kept the ponies hobbled.

When the last animal was free, he made a noise like a frightened whinny and slapped the animals on the rump. They went charging along the foot of the cliff, passing close to the sleeping dwarves.

The first dwarf to hear them gave a shout, bringing the rest to their feet. All six went chasing after their mounts. As soon as they were away from the fire, Trap ran over to stand in its light, took off the ring, and signaled the others to hurry. Within minutes they were all within the dry shelter of the stone curtain wall. Trap pulled Halmarain over to the outline of the door while Ripple watched for the return of the dwarves.

"It's here." He stood in front of the smooth section and sketched a door with his out-flung arms, showing Halmarain the outline. "It's strange they would hide the antechamber so well and make the area of the door so obvious," he said.

"I'll try an opening spell," the little wizard said, pushing back her sleeves as if getting ready for a difficult chore.

"And don't forget your other spells," Ripple spoke from the shadowy entrance to the outer chamber. "Two of the dwarves have caught their ponies. They'll soon be coming back."

"Quiet, don't break my concentration," Halmarain said. She muttered an incantation that sounded like gibberish.

"Well? Nothing happened," Trap said, pointing out the obvious.

Halmarain frowned. "I didn't think my spell would be strong enough to open the door, but there should have been a glimmer—the seams around the door should have glowed for a moment—something should have happened. I'll try a finding spell."

They watched the wall, but the little wizard's spell brought no result.

"Wheel try door?" Umpth asked. He stood stroking the rusty and now muddy metal rim expectantly.

"Fine, you try," Halmarain sounded exasperated. She put her small hands on her hips and glared at the gully dwarf. "Go ahead, see what you can do."

"The dwarves are coming back," Ripple warned.

"If I had enough light to see, maybe I could find a lock," Trap suggested.

"You'll have to wait until daylight. The dwarves will see a light through the curtain wall," Halmarain said. "If we're very quiet no one will know we're here."

She was wrong.

Chapter 34

In his great history, Astinus recorded. . . .

Draaddis Vulter's foot slipped as he whirled around. He had been walking south, along the wet clay bank above the rushing stream. He had been expecting to find the drowned bodies of the kender and the merchesti when he sensed the message that reached him from the northeast.

He was surprised, surprised because he had for some hours entirely forgotten his messenger, the winged rat. Because he had forgotten it, forgotten to reinforce his commands to it, the little creature had allowed the wind to blow it into the mountains. It had taken shelter from the storm on the leeward side of an outcrop.

He had felt but ignored its dim mind as it watched Draaddis's goblins farther away. The humanoids were, like the rat, trying to shelter from the storm. The winged rat, its thoughts of the chilly storm air and hunger, passed along its recognition of the goblins. Though most of its thoughts centered on its discomfort.

Its panic squealed in Draaddis's mind as it flashed him an image of two kender who passed along a trail and came within two feet of the rat's dark shelter. The kender were rapidly followed by the gully dwarves, the merchesti, and bringing up the rear was the smallest of the dwarves. Until the rat sent Draaddis the clear image of Halmarain's face, he had not realized that the tiny wizard was with the party—probably leading it.

His mind backed up, reconsidering his conclusion. He had to be wrong, he decided. He had seen the little apprentice in Orander's laboratory. He had seen the kender on the trail, along with the merchesti, two gully dwarves, and another smaller dwarf, a youngster who had no beard. . . .

The apprentice had been traveling in disguise. He had seen the dwarf clothing and dismissed her without a second look. He had made a serious error in not recognizing her; the dragon queen would not be pleased, though she had not seen through the disguise either.

The apprentice had led them to the western arm of the Khalkist Mountains, close to the dwarf mines. They had traveled east for a reason, and their destination had to be . . . *Chalmis Rosterig!*

He was opening his mouth to use a teleport spell when he realized he had no memory of it. Relearning his spell and teleporting would be faster than physically walking the distance in the storm.

He pulled out his book, found a rock which, though wet, was not covered with mud. Draaddis sat, pulling up a fold of his cloak to protect the spellbook and his little magic light from the weather.

He mouthed the words, driving them into his memory. He had to reach Digondamaar before the apprentice and the kender reached the white wizard.

* * * * *

As much as I like telling this tale, it's been a long one, and my throat is so very, very dry . . . thank you, innkeeper, that's much better, and you do serve excellent ale.

Now, where was I? They were just leaving Solanthus . . . I told that part? Did I tell you about the 'wari stampede? I liked that. You wouldn't like to hear it again, would you?

Now I remember . . . they had chased off the dwarves' ponies and had reached the secret entrance to Digondamaar. . . .

"Two dwarves are coming back," warned Ripple, who had been watching the dwarves as they tried to recapture their mounts. "Three have caught their ponies and are chasing the others—"

A terrific flash of lightning threw the mountainside into high relief, and for a split second the light penetrated the thinnest sections of the stone curtain wall.

"What's this?" Trap had been searching along the cliff wall, trying to find a way to open the secret door. In the high relief of the lightning flash, he thought he saw a rock he had not noticed before. When the light died he tried to find it but was unsuccessful.

"Wow! That lightning startled the dwarf ponies and one threw his rider," Ripple said. "It scared the rest and they're all galloping down the mountain."

"Are any of the dwarves looking this way?" Halmarain asked.

"No, they're too busy slipping and sliding."

The little wizard raised her staff, spoke a word of command, flipped her staff, and from the top came a little ball of light that sailed over to Trap and settled itself over his head.

"You brag about being able to find traps and locks, find this one," she said, her expression a challenge.

"Gee, that's not fair! No one can see in the dark—though, Ripple, didn't Makeway Northgo once have some sort of magic glass that. . . ." Trap turned from the wall, his question about a distant relative uppermost in his mind.

"Are you going to look for that rock?" Halmarain demanded.

"Oh. Sure! I forgot." Trap resumed his search. He had just begun to look about him when Ripple came running over.

"They've caught the ponies and are starting back up the slope," she warned.

Halmarain spoke another command word and the little ball of light zipped back to disappear into the top of her staff.

"We'll have to wait until the sun rises," she said. "Everyone be as quiet as possible. She laid a calming spell on Beglug, who wrapped himself in his blanket and lay down to sleep. The two gully dwarves sat. They leaned against the curtain wall with every evidence of comfort.

The wait was harder on the kender who were bored in less than a minute. Trap heard sounds that could have been slight scuffling and realized his sister was scrounging in her pouches to find something to occupy her time. That seemed like a good idea, so he began to finger his own possessions. He pulled out one of the smooth stones and stood tossing it from one hand to the other for what seemed like hours until he heard the dwarves arriving back at their camp.

"Someone cut the hobbles," one dwarf was saying. "There are goblins or kobolds around somewhere." The dwarves were speaking in their own tongue. He said something else, but while the kender spoke a little dwarvish, Trap could not understand the rest.

"I'll make a torch and take a look," another said. "*Ai-i!* Those thorns hurt—"

The dwarf didn't finish his sentence because his cry of pain had startled Trap who dropped what he had thought was a rock.

He had been playing with one of the glass flame balls he had picked up in Deepdel and when it hit the stone floor of the antechamber it broke. It exploded almost between Ripple's feet and she gave a cry as she jumped back.

"Of all the stupid—" Halmarain bit back her complaint. If the dwarves hadn't heard Ripple, she had certainly given away their location.

"He's not stupid! Stop fussing and remember your magic," Ripple, who had skipped away from the dying fire, warned the little wizard. In an instant she had grabbed her whippik and stood ready to drive off the first of the dwarves.

The gully dwarves had awakened, recognized the fighting stances of their companions, and backed away to stand against the far wall.

"Halmarain, don't forget, you have some magic you might use," Ripple said. "We'd really like to see you do some."

"What am I supposed to do?" Halmarain demanded. "I don't want to kill them so do I mend their clothing or clean their dishes?"

Even if the dwarves had not seen the flash of fire, they had certainly heard Ripple's cry and the talk that followed. From inside the antechamber, Trap heard the rattle of weapons and saw the moving light that approached the entrance.

Since the secret of their arrival had been discovered, Halmarain called the little light from the staff and sent it sailing just outside the entrance, where it illuminated the Neidar but left the defenders in the shadows.

When Tolem, the first dwarf, approached the entrance, Trap let fly with a real stone. He made sure of what he was shooting by picking one up off the floor. His aim had been the middle of the dwarf's breastplate and the force of the rock sent the Neidar staggering back into his friends.

"Sorry, I didn't mean to hurt you," Trap called out. "If you'll just calm down, we can explain and I don't think you'll be angry anymore. You notice I didn't try to kill you."

"That was your mistake," the dwarf roared back. He came charging into the antechamber, his axe held over his shoulder as if he would hack Trap in half as soon as he reached him.

"You need to learn to listen," Trap said as he skipped aside to avoid the dwarf. Tolem, unable to see the rough, rock-strewn floor of the antechamber, stepped on a stone and nearly fell. As he staggered he turned to the left. He was facing Ripple when he regained his balance.

"No hurt Pretty Kender!" Umpth cried out. He had been cowering against the far wall, but seeing the axe ready to descend on his friend gave him courage. He had one hand on the rim of the wheel. In a move too swift for anticipation, he grasped the rim and threw it, sending it sailing toward the dwarf.

The hub caught on the horn of Tolem's helmet and spun. The weight of the spinning wheel threw the dwarf off balance. He staggered back toward his companions that had charged into the chamber behind him. Four went down in a heap.

"Him make good whirly-gig," Grod said, dancing in excitement and fear.

"Aghar magic more big than Neidar," Umpth said with satisfaction. He hurried over to help Trap to his feet.

Ripple knelt on the floor. She had less patience than her brother and had given up any idea of explaining the theft to the dwarves. She set her whippik in a crack in the floor, picked up a stone, and used the loop on the end of her weapon as an improvised sling.

The rock pelted one of the dwarves that had scrambled out of the pile of arms and legs. She struck him a strong blow on the shoulder and he was knocked into the last of his companions.

The last two dwarves were behaving strangely. They had charged into the shelter of the antechamber but they seemed less interested in the small group of adventurers than something outside.

Ripple's whippik was not really designed to sling rocks and her second one sailed over the dwarf's head. It flew out into the darkness and struck with a thud. The cry of pain and the curse that followed the strike was definitely humanoid.

"There's someone else out there," Trap said, almost forgetting the dwarves as he stood on tiptoe in an attempt to see.

"Goblins," one of the dwarves nearest the entrance replied. He seemed to have forgotten his anger at the adventurers in the face of a more dangerous enemy.

"How many?" Tolem, the dwarf leader, asked his companion. He had freed his helmet of the wagon wheel and was ready to charge Trap again. He clearly begrudged having to turn his attention to a more dangerous enemy.

"Looks like a score or more and some bugbears with them, I can't tell how many."

"Goblins? Bugbears? Golly, we sure are running into a lot of people all of a sudden," Trap danced in excitement. "Together we should be able to drive off twenty goblins."

"There's no together . . ." the largest dwarf snarled, but Tolem, interrupted him, proving why he was the leader.

"Our fight with the kender can wait," he said. "Let's handle our common enemy first." He glared at the group at the far end of the antechamber. "One of you is a magic-user, can you direct that light out there and find out how many we have to fight?"

Halmarain sighed for the loss of her secret and eased past the dwarves to the entrance. She guided the light and they saw nine bugbears as well as the twenty goblins in the distance.

"You'll never hold them off," she said to Tolem. "Tell us how to get into Digondamaar. It's our only chance."

The goblins were sneaking up toward the entrance, but the dwarves, each with a crossbow, now had targets. Tolem caught one goblin in the throat, one died with a short quarrel in his eye and another fled with his companions, limping from a wound in his right leg. Once out of range of the dwarves' missiles they stopped and huddled together, apparently discussing strategy.

"*You* took the map," the dwarf snarled as the goblins retreated. "Or the kender, more likely."

"If you mean that string of disks," Halmarain said, "That was one of the Aghar, and he didn't know what he had. He just wanted something pretty to give the kender girl."

"And you didn't study and memorize it?" Tolem demanded.

"If we had, we'd know how to get inside," the little wizard snapped.

"No need necklace," Grod spoke up. "Dwarf lead. Dwarf camp by door of dwarf This Place."

"We could have used the disks," Trap said, unwilling to admit there was any secret he could not ferret out. He dug in his pouch and handed the string of disks to the dwarf. "But we didn't have time with all the traveling and the following and everything that happened. Now I suppose you'll want it back and I'll never get to study all the drawings."

Halmarain drew the little light back into the shelter to aid the dwarf in his search for the opening.

"You know I'll want it back," Tolem snarled. "And we'd better get inside fast. Those bugbears can knock down these thin sections of this curtain wall with one blow."

"At least it's getting bright enough so you can see what you're doing," Trap said as he watched the dwarf flip through the disks, looking for the one that told the secret of Digondamaar.

"Of course, if I had light enough, I could probably have opened the door myself," he sniffed. Even as a small child he had showed promise with traps; it was the reason he had been given his name. It seemed unjust that he had so little chance to use his talents on his first adventure.

By the time Tolem had found the disk he had no time to study it. The goblins and bugbears were advancing up the mountainside to the foot of the cliff. Since the entrance was narrow and its configuration too eccentric to allow more than two dwarves to see out at one time, the goblins had little fear of a truly concentrated attack from within.

Halmarain doused the light, though the humanoids had obviously seen it glowing through the wafer-thin rock. The bugbears hammered against the curtain wall with their spears, but with no light to indicate the thin sections, they missed the more vulnerable areas.

The dwarves used their crossbows. Two at a time they stepped out of the entrance to shoot and darted back in again to give others with ready bows a chance, the kender stood by, dancing with impatience, wanting to get into the fight. Halmarain held the arm of the little fiend and stayed as far away from the entrance as possible. She did not have to urge the gully dwarves, who would much rather hide than fight.

The bugbears continued to hammer against the stone curtain wall.

The little wizard squealed as from behind her came the sound of sliding stone and a door opened, not where the cut lines indicated, but at the far end, where the roughest of the stone seemed to have been left untouched.

"Who invades my privacy?" the voice boomed.

The gigantic sound came from a human who stood only slightly taller than the dwarves. He was surrounded with light which showed him to have a bright pink complexion, at least partially accounted for by the anger that snapped in his bright blue eyes. His beard and hair were snow white and long. He kept it out of his way by dividing both hair and beard on each side of his head and plaiting it in two long braids that hung to his knees.

He wore a dirty white robe trimmed with runes.

He was only a moment understanding that the dozen beings sheltering in the antechamber were being attacked by humanoids on the outside.

"Inside," he ordered. Pointing to the door behind him, he muttered an incantation.

Trap felt as if he were being whisked along in a strong wind. He looked down at his feet, which were moving rapidly across the floor, but they acted according to a will other than his own.

In front of him, Halmarain, the gully dwarves, and Beglug were traveling just as rapidly. Trap couldn't stop himself but he could turn his head and look over his shoulder. Ripple, right behind him, and the dwarves further back, were moving at the same speed. The dwarves were staring down at their feet with eyes wide.

Chapter 35

As Trap was whisked through the hidden door and into the outlying passage of Digondamaar, he smiled up at the wizard.

"Hello, my name is Trapspringer Fargo," he held out his hand but he was moving too fast for the wizard to take it. "I appreciate being saved from the goblins, but did you have to move us so fast? I would have liked to take a look at the secret door." He had to turn his head to look back at the wizard. Behind him the last of the dwarves rushed through the doorway. The grinding began again as the door closed.

The involuntary movement of his feet stopped and he nearly fell over. Ahead of him Halmarain and the gully dwarves staggered. Beglug danced sideways on his tiny hoofed feet and fell against the wall, scraping his hand. He whined and licked at the abrasion.

The kender could see the others in the light that emanated from the wizard. He seemed to be enveloped in a glow that lit the entire passage.

He strode past the dwarves, who were alternately looking at the walls of the passage and giving wary attention to their glowing and magical host. The wizard was more interesting than the walls, the kender thought. The floor, ceiling and walls were as smooth and even as if they had been cut with a knife, but one spot looked just like any other. The name of the delving in the dwarvish tongue meant golden halls, but there was no evidence of gold.

Chalmis Rosterig attempted to pass Ripple. She stepped into his path, and like her brother, she held out her hand.

"I'm Ripple Fargo, and I'm pleased to meet you," she thrust her hand into his, so he could not ignore her. "Are all wizards so small?" she asked him, oblivious to the frown her remark brought out. "If it's a requirement for the art, maybe I could become a wizard. I'd love to study books and learn spells and do magic. Can you make fireworks?"

"Kender!" The word burst out of Chalmis in an explosion of sound. "That's all I need—kender."

"Oh yes, we can be really helpful if you give us a chance," Trap agreed, pacing the rapid steps of the wizard on the right while Ripple walked on his left. "We tried to help Orander, but he went through a portal and we weren't able to do much, but if you'll bring him back—though he may not want to return if he likes it over there—and that would be a shame, because Halmarain said he would do magic for us. Is that pendant magic? It certainly is beautiful. Can I touch it?" He reached toward the jewel that hung from a chain and laid on the wizard's chest.

Chalmis pushed the kender's hand away as he turned to look back over his shoulder.

"Come along!" he shouted at the dwarves. "If not you'll be left in the dark. You don't want to meet what crawls through these tunnels when the lights are out."

While the dwarves hurried to catch up, Halmarain caught Beglug's arm and rushed him down the passage just ahead of the white wizard. Umpth and Grod, Umpth still rolling the wheel, trotted along just behind Halmarain and the little fiend.

Behind them they could hear a faint thudding as the humanoids apparently tried to open the secret door. Ahead they could see torchlight. The glow that surrounded the wizard died away as they reached a chamber that was lit with torches set in wall sconces.

"Wow, this is more like it," Trap said as he looked around. In the light of the torches he could see what appeared to be golden drawings on the wall. Even to his limited knowledge of metal working, it was apparent that refined gold had been used to fill grooves in the stone. The drawings were hardly more than sketches, yet finely detailed. Several colors of gold had been used, and in the light of the torches, the tints of green, red and yellow gave a hint of color to the drawings.

The chamber had obviously been created as a dining hall. More than fifty tables and benches, also of stone, sat in long rows. Several had been broken; the slabs that had been seats and tabletops leaned askew, but most were still intact.

When they were all in the room, Chalmis stopped and glared at them, his glance lingering longest on Beglug.

"Why have you come here, bringing those foul creatures in your wake and disturbing my solitude?" The wizard thundered. He pointed his finger back in the direction they had come when he spoke of foul creatures, obviously meaning the goblins. The gully dwarves, who still clutched their blankets around their shoulders, thought it safest to take shelter behind the kender. Beglug snarled and swiped at the wizard with a clawed hand.

Chalmis Rosterig pointed a finger at the merchesti and muttered under his breath. Beglug was frozen on the spot.

"Now answer my question!" Chalmis ordered.

The wizard's question brought out a deluge of explanations and excuses, questions and comments. Everyone seemed to be pointing at Trap as Halmarain rattled off a full account of Orander's attempt to travel between planes and the result of the kender's drastic intervention. The dwarves had not accepted the idea that a mere gully dwarf could have picked their pockets. They were loudly blaming the kender for the theft of the Map of Secret Lore, as they called the necklace.

Trap himself was explaining that he neither stole the necklace nor intentionally interrupted Orander's spell, and he certainly wanted Orander to return from the other world so he could discuss with him the problems with the magic rings. Ripple was renewing her request to study magic, and in the meantime, could Chalmis please do some fireworks? She really wanted to see some. The gully dwarves, their fright temporary, were discussing all these people interrupting each other, which the kender had told them was rude and inconsiderate.

"Enough!" Chalmis boomed.

"My, you have a loud voice," Trap said. "Can you teach me how to roar? It would be great. I could sneak up behind people very quietly—I wouldn't want to roar all the time, of course, but—"

"I'll turn you into a frog, and that will stop your chatter," Chalmis warned.

"Will you really?" Ripple taunted, suddenly angry. "That's what Halmarain said, but she couldn't do it."

"But Master Chalmis can, so you'd better watch your manners," the little wizard warned.

"One thing at a time," Chalmis spoke in a lower tone. "If I'm going to have any peace, who took the lore map from the dwarves? Give it back."

"They got," Grod said.

"Then your problem is solved so we don't need to hear anymore about it," the white wizard told the dwarves. "Now what is this about the merchesti, Orander, and the plane of Vasmarg? And know, little red-robe, I have no truck with those outside my order."

Halmarain answered with a humility that surprised the kender.

"I understand, Master Chalmis, but we are in dire need and beg your assistance—not only for ourselves and Orander—our entire world could be affected."

She went through the story again, this time putting less emphasis on the fault of the kender and more on the danger of Beglug's parent entering the world, or of Beglug growing up on Krynn. She was clearly bent on rescuing Orander if he were still alive. She raised imploring eyes to the master wizard.

"And I believe others know of Beglug and the gate stone the kender carries."

She described Jaerume Kaldre and told Master Chalmis she thought he was one of the undead.

Chalmis Rosterig listened with steadily lowering brows. The last bit of information seemed to affect the white wizard more profoundly than the rest.

Halmarain went on to describe the kidnapping of Ripple and Beglug. "Since the kobolds were careful not to injure them, but traveled as fast as they could in this direction, I suspect they were under instructions to take them to Pey." She paused expectantly.

"To Draaddis Vulter," Chalmis announced on cue, his face darkening in anger. "He came to mind when you mentioned the undead. I wish I could believe the Dark Queen was not behind this, but that would be too much to hope for."

"I didn't know any of that," Trap spoke up. "You didn't tell us. That wasn't fair. The trip would have been much more interesting if we had known that Takhisis was after us. Do you think she might come here? I'd love to see a dragon."

"Why do you think I've been fighting to get to Master Chalmis?" the tiny female rounded on the kender "Did you think I fussed and fought through the entire journey because I enjoyed it?"

"Did," Grod nodded decisively.

"Did too," Umpth was quick to second his brother.

"Oh, shut up!" Halmarain glared at the Aghar and turned back to the white-robed wizard. "I've brought

Master Orander's books written by the great Master Alchviem. I can open and read them, but I'm not powerful enough to use them."

"Pretty Kender bring cook pot," Grod added.

"Still, we have only one gate stone," Master Chalmis said. "But if Orander still has the other we might have a chance. . . ." He tugged at his long white braids. "Let's take a look. If Takhisis has her minions on your trail, we don't have much time."

"Eat now?" Grod asked.

Master Chalmis frowned at the gully dwarf and then looked over the rest of the assembled group. He pointed across the large chamber toward another door.

"You'll find the scullery through there. Take the gully dwarves and leave us in peace." he said, and then turned his attention back to Halmarain. "Bring the merchesti and books back to my laboratory." He led the way through another door.

"Pretty Kender make maize pudding?" Grod asked as he followed Ripple. Behind them the six Neidar stumped along, but the Aghar's suggestion caught their attention.

"I've heard that kender women make the best maize pudding," one said, begrudging the compliment, but obviously looking forward to the treat.

"And Ripple's is famous," Trap told the large dwarf. Now that the dwarves had their necklace back, he didn't see any reason why they couldn't all be friends.

In the scullery they found a pot of water already hot, and while Ripple tested it to be sure it was just water and not some potion, the dwarves searched and found some ground maize as well as the other ingredients she asked for.

In minutes the maize was in the pot.

While the kender girl stirred, the rest stood around, watching the kettle hopefully. Before long they heard a droning from the other chamber. The dwarves proved they were from one of the highly musical societies by covering their ears to block out the noise.

"They're singing again, and if there's one thing a wizard can *not* do, its sing," Trap said with a frown. "I'd better go and teach them how to—" He started for the door when Tolem caught his arm.

"You stay right here! If I understood the little wizard aright," he said with a frown, "It was your wanting to help them that caused this mess."

Two of the dwarves moved to block the door to the scullery and a third, the largest, joined Tolem.

"I'm still not sure you didn't steal the lore map," he said, glowering at the kender. "You stay where we can keep an eye on you."

"I wanted to see some magic," Trap complained.

"Best what they do remains unseen," Tolem replied with a dark glance over his shoulder. "It doesn't do to go messing with wizards."

"I'm not sure you're right," Ripple said as she tapped the large wooden spoon on the side of the pot to knock off the thick mixture. "They are really off key. I don't see how they can do anything—"

Suddenly the strange off key droning of the wizards was drowned under a low booming that echoed down the passage. The booms were soon followed by the sound of cracking stone in the distance and almost immediately by the shouts and roars of goblins.

"They broke in," Tolem said, grabbing his crossbow and drawing his axe.

"How could they when the wizard sealed the door?" one of the dwarves asked as he followed Tolem from the scullery.

Ripple swung the pot off the fire and grabbed her whippik that she had laid on a stool.

"I didn't know he did," she said. "I never get to see any magic."

By now the six dwarves, the kender, and the Aghar had trotted down the passage and were back in the dining cavern where they had parted from the two wizards and Beglug.

"If he really sealed it the goblins couldn't get in," Trap objected, expressing his opinion as well.

"Look out!" one of the dwarves shouted and fell flat on

the floor. Over his head sailed a fireball. It had come down the passage from the front entrance.

"I don't think it was broken by humanoids," Tolem said. "It took another wizard, and he's on the way!"

"Now we'll really see some magic," Ripple said, her eyes sparking.

"And it may be the last thing you see," Tolem replied.

Chapter 36

A second fireball sailed out of the passage and into the chamber. Again the Neidar, Aghar, and kender ducked behind the tilted stone slabs of the broken tables.

"Zow! That was a great shot! Wonder how hard it is to send something down a passage?" Trap asked. He was not seeking an answer from the dwarves. He picked up a small, jagged rock, set his hoopak against the stone column that had once been the leg of a table, and drew back the pouch. The missile went sailing and disappeared into the darkness of the passage.

The reaction was an entirely human curse, the voice full of pain, surprise, and outrage.

"You hit the wizard!" Tolem said, giving Trap a look filled with respect. The dwarf fitted a quarrel to his crossbow and shot down the dark passage. A goblin screamed.

"There must be a lot of them bunched together," Ripple

said. "We'll hit something every time." She set her whip-pik and nocked a small arrow into the loop. Her arrow and five dwarf quarrels entered the dark hole of the passage at once. They heard cries of pain and howls but no one would know which had found a target. Volley after volley of dwarf quarrels, Ripple's small arrows, and Trap's stones went sailing down the passage and by the sound, each one found some target, but they did not hear another cry from the wizard.

"He probably sent his minions on ahead of him," Tolem said. They all knew wizards relied on their arts, not on weapons. It was reasonable to assume that the magic-user was either shielded by his arts or his companions.

The last volley brought no cries of pain. They heard nothing, no footsteps, no shuffling, no rattle of weapons. The complete silence was as eerie as the idea of enemies in the darkness.

"Go get white robe," Umpth suggested. "Him fight black wizard."

"No," the tallest of the dwarves, who was closest to the gully dwarves, grabbed Umpth's arm. "Leave him alone right now."

"Yes, leave him be," Tolem said. "I don't hold with magic, but that creature with you is some sort of fiend. If I understood their talk, they're trying to send it back to its own world?" He was asking the question of Ripple.

"That's what they want to do. That and get Orander, the red-robed wizard, back. Halmarain promised us he would give us some magic, but I don't know if he will. Wizards all seem to be as grumpy as dwarves—oh, I didn't mean . . . well, now that you've got your necklace back. . . ."

Trap had only half listened to the gully dwarf's suggestion and part of the conversation that followed. He was finding the silence and the inactivity boring in the extreme. He had been looking forward to a fight. What had happened?

Had they killed all the humanoids? He didn't believe it. Even if every quarrel and each one of Ripple's arrows had been a fatal shot—which was highly unlikely—they had not sent enough missiles down the passage to account for all the humanoids. Since the last volley had not found targets, either the enemy had retreated or found a way to keep from being struck. While the dwarves asked questions and Ripple tried to explain, he edged away from the others. He crept closer to the dark mouth of the passage.

To keep from being a target, he dropped flat on his stomach and crept up to the wall to see if he could see anything of interest. Keeping his head close to the floor, he eased forward and peered around the corner, and looked straight into the pig eyes of a metal-helmeted goblin.

The humanoid yipped in alarm and drew back. Trap jerked his head back and in an instant was on his feet, dashing for shelter.

"They're crawling down the passage, they're already at the door," he called to the others. He raced for a broken table with a tilted top, looking for shelter and stones for his hoopak.

"Let them have a low volley," Tolem shouted to the other dwarves. They sent six more quarrels down the passage and could be satisfied with the howls that returned.

A low-voiced command from farther down the dark passage reached them and suddenly more than twenty humanoids rushed into the chamber. Some were still in a half crouch.

Ripple and the six dwarves were ready with their missiles. They could see their targets and four bugbears fell dead before they had taken three strides into the lighted hall. The others leaped over their dead companions and were on the dwarves and kender before the crossbows could be loaded and cocked again.

Trap, off to the side, picked up a large, jagged piece of rock and fitted it into to the pouch of his hoopak. He swung the weapon twice around his head before he let fly, and caught a goblin in the back of the neck, crushing its spine. He knelt behind the broken table and felt for another stone, his eyes on the battle in front of him.

He found nothing, but he still had stones in his pouch,

he remembered. When he dug in the bottom of the bag at his waist, he felt a ring. It slipped onto his finger and he was lost from his own sight again.

He paused momentarily. Should he keep it on? Why not? The six dwarves and four companions were still far outnumbered, and they faced a wizard as well.

Did he have any more flame balls? He wondered. He reached into his pouch again, but he faced the same trouble he had before. He could not distinguish a flame ball from a smooth stone without seeing it. The small missiles he was carrying would do no more than irritate the huge bugbears, so he opted to skip around the table and attack with his hoopak.

He picked a likely target, a bugbear that seemed to be after the two cowering gully dwarves. Then he changed his mind. Tolem was holding off two goblins with mighty swings of his heavy axe, but behind him a third humanoid was dancing on the balls of his feet, working in position to attack from behind. The goblin found his opening and rushed forward, his spear ready. The kender, out of position to deliver a fatal blow, thrust his hoopak between the goblin's legs and tripped him up.

The humanoid's stone-headed spear went flying out of his hand just as Tolem stepped aside to avoid a thrust from the goblin in front of him. The goblin that the dwarf faced took the accidental spear thrust in the center of the chest.

Trap was bumped from behind and turned to see a goblin staring at something he had felt but could not see. Trap speared him with the sharp, metal-tipped point of his hoopak.

Two other goblins had seen their companion mysteriously fall and then die by some unseen agency. They backed away and shouted to the wizard that they were facing magic.

Trap ignored them as he looked around for his sister. He was just in time to see her backing away from a bugbear that was twice her height. As the large creature stalked her with a raised, stone headed club, she caught the butt of the iron wood whippik in her left hand and the leather loop in her right. In a lightning move she skipped to the side, jumped onto a stone bench, and then the table it flanked. She let the leather thong go and flailed the bugbear across the face. He screamed and dropped his club as he put his hands over his eyes.

Not to be outdone, Trap raised his hoopak and whacked another bugbear across the face. He missed the eyes but connected with the creature's snout-like nose, breaking and shoving it back into his skull, a fatal blow.

"Trap?" Ripple asked. She had seen the bugbear fall without any visible force. "Are you wearing a ring?" Ripple asked, her glances darting as she looked for her brother and any close enemies at the same time. "Isn't this fun? I was beginning to think we'd never do anything interesting."

She ducked a thrown spear and when it bounced off the wall she picked it up. Grabbing the butt end, she swung it around her head let go, sending it whirling into the melee.

Three of the dwarves were surrounded by goblins, but they were holding their own and even driving the creatures back toward the passage when the wizard stepped into view. He cocked his head as if listening to something beyond the battle.

His eyes burned in anger and he muttered an incantation. When he finished, an icy storm swept down onto the defenders and attackers alike. Icy pellets struck the humanoids and demi-humans as if they had each been shot from a sling. The force of the magic storm drove them back toward the far door of the chamber. Behind the wall of stinging ice the black-robed wizard passed unchallenged.

Even though he was still invisible, Trap backed away with the others, trying to stay out of range of the stinging hail.

The gully dwarves, who had stayed at the back of the gold trimmed hall were the first to reach the passage, the dwarves and kender backing along in their wake. They were followed by the goblins. The larger bugbears had to stoop to pass under the lower ceiling. A tacit truce existed as humanoid and demi-human alike tried to escape the storm.

The pelting ice followed them down a long corridor. The torches on the walls were extinguished one by one as the storm reached them. They retreated in light and behind them the darkness flowed before the storm.

Everyone followed the course set by the Aghar, so Trap was not surprised when he backed through a doorway and found himself in Chalmis Rosterig's laboratory. A brief look showed him it was only slightly different from Orander's, with shelves of books and scrolls, bubbling liquids and strange objects in glass jars.

At the far end of the chamber, Halmarain stood holding the gate stone in one hand, and Beglug's arm with the other. She was singing a note that sounded vaguely familiar to Trap. She could not seem to get off one discordant note and Trap would have liked to help her with her tone. Chalmis stood by her, intoning a spell that seemed to affect her voice, since it was deeper and louder than usual.

The ice storm had stopped just inside the door, and was sweeping around, curving so the dwarves, kender, and humanoids were all trapped against the left wall.

The kender saw Chalmis start as Draaddis Vulter appeared in the doorway. Chalmis bent over Halmarain. He moved his lips in speech, but the howling of the humanoids, the threats and shouts of the dwarves, and the rattle of ice on the floor kept Trap from hearing the white-robed wizard's voice. Then Chalmis straightened and muttered, his hand raised. The ice storm disappeared, and Trap discovered he was no longer invisible.

The white-robed wizard continued his chanting and a glow rose around the tiny human female who stood with the gate stone in one hand and held Beglug's arm with the other. She kept up the discordant note.

Freed from the fear of the ice pellets, the humanoids attacked the dwarves and the kender again. The dwarves' axes hacked at the spears and clubs. Trap was hard pressed to slip away from a goblin that was intent on pinning him to the stone wall with a stone-tipped spear.

Ripple was holding her own against a bugbear twice her height. While backing down the passage she had pulled a small barbed steel ball from her pouch, removed the protective covering and had attached it to her whippik. Her mini-morningstar could hold off creatures much larger than herself.

In the doorway of Chalmis' workroom, Draaddis Vulter cursed as his ice storm was dispelled. He began another chant. The ear-splitting reports of cracking stone filled the chamber and reverberated off the walls. Directly in front of the black-robed wizard, the floor moved and up heaved a stone creature with four legs, six arms, and no head. The stone golem ignored the battle between the dwarves and kender and the humanoids and charged the white-robed wizard.

Chalmis was already chanting, from the floor came another roar of breaking rock. A series of tentacles, also of flexible stone, grabbed at Draaddis's crawling golem and lifted it off its feet. The four-legged creature slammed down to the floor with a force that shook everyone in the chamber.

Ripple fell and was nearly speared by a goblin. Umpth, equally off balance, had tried to support himself with the wheel. It slipped out of his hands, bounced up, and caught the goblin on the side of its head. The half-stunned goblin rose to its feet, glared at the gully dwarves, and shook its head to clear its already slow wits.

Seeing the humanoid's attention turned toward them, Umpth grabbed the wheel and stepped back, holding his artifact in front of him as if it were a shield. Grod, similarly threatened, seemed to suddenly remember that he carried an axe and pulled it from it's sheath. He attempted to raise it over his head, but he lost his grip and it struck the wall behind him. As the steel blade ricocheted off the wall, it caught the goblin a stunning blow with the handle.

That was enough battle for the gully dwarves. Umpth grabbed the wheel, Grod picked up his sodden blanket, and they raced around the stone monsters who were still battling in the center of the chamber. Three of the tentacles had broken off and disappeared back into the floor. Two of the six arms and one leg of the first monster were also broken and had disappeared.

Trap jumped to the side just as a bugbear rushed him. The huge humanoid brought its heavy, iron-tipped club down with a blow that would have crushed the kender's skull if it had connected. The kender's dodge caught the bugbear unprepared. His heavy weapon continued down and struck the floor with a blow that jarred the beast's entire arm. While he was still vibrating from the shock, Trap flipped his hoopak around and threw his entire weight against the weapon as he drove it into the bugbear's chest.

Though intent on his own battle, he was vaguely aware of Beglug, who stood by Halmarain. The little fiend seemed to be waking up, beginning to recognize the fight going on around him. Suddenly he charged the tentacles of the stone golem created by Chalmis and bit off an arm. The remainder of the writhing tentacle threw him sideways where his claws ripped out the throat of a goblin who was backing away from a dwarf's swinging axe. His eyes glowing with the light of battle, Beglug charged toward Ripple.

Trap was, at the moment, backing away from a bugbear's long spear while he waited for an opportunity to move in and used his much shorter reach. He nodded in satisfaction as he saw the merchesti heading in his sister's direction. If Beglug joined with her, they could protect each other and inflict considerable damage on their enemies. At least that was what he thought. He realized his error when he heard Ripple's voice.

"Beglug, what are you doing?"

Beglug was swatting at her, his claws extended.

Trap had never run away from an enemy, but at that moment he was more interested in what was happening with his sister and Beglug than the bugbear. He glanced around, noticed he was perilously close to the remaining tentacles of the stone golem and ducked under one, falling and rolling as he used their threat to dodge the bugbear. The humanoid, too intent on his intended victim to take proper precautions, lunged forward and was grabbed by a stone arm.

Trap rose to his feet and dodged right between a dwarf and a goblin as he tried to reach Ripple. He was prevented from going to her side by a new influx of the enemy that had been late arriving in Chalmis Rosterig's laboratory.

Another score of goblins and bugbears swarmed in, causing Trap and the six dwarves to retreat until their backs were to the wall. The gully dwarves raced between the backs of the goblins and stone golems, seeking a safe corner, but ended up coming face-to-face with Draaddis Vulter. The wizard raised a threatening hand.

Trap had only a moment to see Ripple, on the other side of the chamber, backing away from the maddened merch-esti. She was attempting to hold him off, but the little fiend was clearly trying to kill the kender girl. She had dropped her whippik, which was useless in trying to defend herself from the little fiend. She used a fallen bugbear's spear, careful not to give Beglug the opportunity to bite it.

Trap could see she was trying not to harm the creature, she was just protecting herself from it. What she had not noticed was that she was backing straight into Halmarain, who seemed so deep into her spell-casting that she was unaware of anything else.

Trap, still just holding his own against two goblins could not go to her.

"Grod, help Ripple!" he shouted, but the gully dwarf, spinning to locate the kender in the melee, spotted another figure. Draaddis Vulter was raising his hand to throw another spell at the white-robed wizard.

"No like ice!" Grod said and slung his blanket at the wizard. The heavy, wet covering fell over the wizard's face and head and caused the human to stagger. As Draaddis Vulter tried to keep his balance his feet carried him backward a few steps. With the blanket over his head he staggered too close to Ripple for the gully dwarves' peace.

"Leave Pretty Kender alone!" Umpth shouted and used his most powerful weapon. He threw the wheel. It struck Draaddis in the middle of his back and stumbled toward Halmarain.

At just that moment the little wizard raised her eyes and saw the blanket-shrouded figure hurtling toward her. The tone she had been holding rose in terror.

A glow rose from the gate stone and formed half an arc in the air. Suddenly a void formed right beside her. A searing hot wind blew into the chamber and extinguished all the light.

Chapter 37

In the darkness Trap heard a roar he recognized. A human voice cried out in surprise and alarm. A hot wind blew through the chamber, and he jumped back as he felt the touch of a giant clawed hand. It passed him by and a bugbear gave a scream of terror. Two other howls of fear and pain followed as the kender pressed himself against the wall.

Beglug suddenly gave a gurgling, delighted cry. After Beglug's outburst, several seconds of quiet followed when all they could hear was the sound of the hot wind blowing in the passage. Then the wind stopped. Moments later the dark chamber was dimly illuminated by the light from three wizard's staves. The smallest light, Halmarain's, was barely an inch off the floor. She lay sprawled on her stomach, hardly daring to raise her head.

The second belonged to Chalmis, and the third to a

red-robed wizard who had disappeared weeks before. He looked thin and tired.

Trap recognized Orander, noticed the wizard's weakened condition, and hurried forward to pick up an overturned stool that lay next to a broken table. He placed the stool so the wizard could rest.

"You're Orander, and we've been searching for you. Well, not really for you, but for a wizard that could help get you back because Halmarain said you would give us some magic if we helped, and even if she does say it was my fault you went through the wrong door, I do think—"

"Master Orander!" Halmarain rose to a sitting position and stared up at her teacher with tears streaming down her face. "You're alive! I didn't dare hope," she sobbed. "We tried to get to you before—"

"Time must not be the same over there," Chalmis said to the new arrival, ignoring the outbursts of his visitors.

"If it had been I would not have survived," Orander said weakly when he learned he had been absent from Krynn for weeks. "Since I had one of the stones, I could follow Halmarain's progress, though the distance wasn't the same either, I suppose. I was constantly followed by the merchesti. What it wanted, I do not know. . . ." He frowned as he watched his student. "Girl, what's the matter?"

Halmarain had been twisting as if to work out a cramp, and massaging her shoulder.

"It's nothing now that you're back," she said. "In the darkness someone knocked me down and stepped on me. Draaddis Vulter! He was staggering toward me when the portal opened."

"He went through to Vasmarg," Trap said, awed. He looked around. The black-robed wizard had disappeared along with the battling stone golems. The surviving humanoids were backing away toward the entrance to the wizard's workroom. They fled with the dwarves urging them on.

The two gully dwarves eyed the chatting wizards and walked over to Ripple.

"Eat now?" Grod asked as if the battle between the

dwarves, kender, and goblins, the test of magic between wizards, and the opening of a portal to another plane had only been an interruption of more important matters.

Halmarain turned to gaze at the two gully dwarves and took a reluctant leave of her master. She suggested they finish preparing a meal, sure her mentor could use the nourishment.

By the time Ripple and Halmarain were ready to ladle out the pudding, the six Neidar were back, their axes bloody, but they reported they had chased the few remaining bugbears down the side of the mountain. None of the smaller goblins had survived.

By noon of the next day, the wizards were deep in conversation again, examining the gate stones and discussing them. The dwarves had set out to explore the deep caverns of Digondamaar. The kender had fingered everything in sight and no one, not even Trap and Ripple, realized their pouches were heavier than when they entered the dwarf caverns.

They had just finished exploring all the chambers Chalmis had lit when the two gully dwarves joined them.

"Red wizards 'porting back their This Place," Grod informed them. Even if he didn't get the word right he understood Orander and Halmarain would be traveling by magic. "We go find good us This Place now? Kender help?"

"We did promise them," Ripple reminded her brother. "I'd bet they would like Solanthus, and I didn't get to see it at all."

Bored since they had fingered everything in sight, the two kender and two gully dwarves took their leave late in the afternoon and strolled down the mountainside to find the ponies.

"Master Orander and Master Chalmis are nice wizards," Ripple said, pulling out the ring she had taken from Orander's chest. The red-robed wizard had been so grateful for the kender's help that he had given them the rings. Orander had been too weak to do more than make the gift. Chalmis had reinforced the magic in the rings.

"Master Chalmis added to the magic in mine too," Trap

said, reaching into his pouch to pull them out. His eyebrows rose in surprise as out came the string of disks that made up the dwarf lore map.

"I thought we gave those back to the Neidar," Ripple said.

"Pretty for Pretty Kender," Grod said as he stumped along. He reached out to touch Ripple's shining blond curl that hung down her back and bounced as she walked.

"Grod, you mustn't take other people's things," Trap chided him. "But having it is great! Think of what we can do. Big jiggies, we can visit all sorts of dwarves that never come to visit us. They make wonderful stuff, though some are as cross as Halmarain, but they'd probably enjoy meeting someone new after staying underground so long."

"That would be fun," Ripple smiled at her brother. "And we'll return it the next time we come this way, you know how dwarves are about people taking their things."

"Trapspringer that steal, him dead," Umpth spoke up.

Grod nodded. "Make good tale, that. Kender tell tale?" He glazed at Trap with such a hopeful look, Ripple urged her brother to give them a story.

"My poor Uncle Trapspringer," Trap said, his usual way of starting a story. "I don't think he would have fought that strange creature if he had known it was a stone golem . . ."

* * * * *

Astinus of Palanthus allowed himself a small smile as he wrote. . . .

Deep below the ruins of Pey, a black silk cloth, lavishly decorated in golden runes, covered the black orb. Within her realm the Dark Queen raged. She was aware of Draaddis's passage to the Plane of Vasmarg. She had lost her servant, and with the globe covered, she had no power to see into the world of Krynn.

* * * * *

Two hundred feet above the orb, the wolf woke and stretched. He had slept well. No dreams had tortured his sleep. He didn't know what had caused those terrible nightmares—it might have been someone he ate.

. . . and that's the tale of my Uncle Trapspringer.